GD

About the Authors

Carol Marinelli recently filled in a form asking for her job title. Thrilled to be able to put down her answer, she put writer. Then it asked what Carol did for relaxation and she put down the truth – writing. The third question asked for her hobbies. Well, not wanting to look obsessed she crossed the fingers on her hand and answered swimming but, given that the chlorine in the pool does terrible things to her highlights – I'm sure you can guess the real answer.

With a background of working in medical laboratories and a love of the romance genre it's no surprise that **Sue Mackay** writes medical romance stories. She wrote her first story at age eigh——— hasn't stopped since. She lives in N——————orough Sounds where————————————cling, walking and l—————————he also loves cooki—————————ptuous meals that in—————

Fiona———————Australian midwife who lives in the country and loves to dream. Writing Medical Romance gives Fiona the scope to write about all the wonderful aspects of romance, adventure, medicine and the midwifery she feels so passionate about. When not writing, Fiona's ether at home on the farm with her husband or off to meet new people, see new places and have wonderful adventures. Drop in and say hi at Fiona's website www.fionamcarthurauthor.com

Midwives on Call

Midwives on Call:
A Forever
Family

CAROL MARINELLI

SUE MACKAY

FIONA MCARTHUR

MILLS & BOON

First Published in Great Britain 2020
By Mills & Boon, an imprint of HarperCollins*Publishers*
1 London Bridge Street, London, SE1 9GF

MIDWIVES ON CALL: A FOREVER FAMILY © 2020
Harlequin Books S.A.

Hers For One Night Only? © 2012 Carol Marinelli
The Midwife's Son © 2014 Sue MacKay
Gold Coast Angels: Two Tiny Heartbeats © 2013 Harlequin Books S.A.

Special thanks and acknowledgement are given to Fiona McArthur
for her contribution to the *Gold Coast Angels* series.

ISBN: 978-0-263-28111-8

0420

Printed and bound in Spain
by CPI, Barcelona

Leabharlanna Dhún Laoghaire - Ráth an Dúin

HERS FOR ONE
NIGHT ONLY?

CAROL MARINELLI

For all my readers who are doing it tough – I hope you can find a little time to spoil yourself.

Loads of love

Carol x

CHAPTER ONE

'YOU'RE far too available.' Bridgette didn't really know how to respond when her friend Jasmine's sympathy finally ran out. After all, she knew that Jasmine was right. 'It's me and Vince's leaving do and you won't come out *in case* your sister needs a babysitter.'

'You know it's not as simple as that,' Bridgette said.

'But it *is* as simple as that.' Jasmine was determined to stand firm this time. Her boyfriend, Vince, was a paediatric intern at the large Melbourne hospital where Bridgette had, until recently, worked, and he was heading off for a year to do relief work overseas. At what felt like the last minute the rather dizzy Jasmine had decided to join him for three months, and after a lot of paperwork and frantic applications, finally tonight there was a gathering to see them both off. 'You've put everything on hold for Courtney, you've given up a job you love so you can do agency and be more flexible— you've done everything you can to support her and look at where it's got you.'

Jasmine knew that she was being harsh, but she wanted Bridgette to cry, damn it, wanted her friend to

admit the truth—that living like this was agony, that
something had to give. But Bridgette refused to cry,
insisting instead that she was coping—that she didn't
mind doing agency work, that she loved looking after
Courtney's son, Harry. 'Come out, then,' Jasmine chal-
lenged. 'If everything's as fine as you say, you deserve
a night out—you haven't had one in ages. I want you
there—we all want to see you. Everyone will be there…'

'What if…?' Bridgette stopped herself from saying
it. She was exhausted from going over the what-ifs.

'Stop hiding behind Harry,' Jasmine said.

'I'm not.'

'Yes, you are. I know you've been hurt, but you need
to put it behind you.'

And it stung, but, then, the truth often did and, yes,
Bridgette conceded, maybe she was using Harry as a bit
of an excuse so as not to get out there. 'Okay!' Bridgette
took a deep breath and nodded. 'You're on.'

'You're coming?' Jasmine grinned.

'Looks like it.'

So instead of sitting at home, Bridgette sat in the
hairdresser's and had some dark foils added to her
mousey-brown hair. They made her skin look paler and
her sludgy-grey eyes just a bit darker, it seemed, and
with Jasmine's endless encouragement she had a wax
and her nails done too and, for good measure, crammed
in a little shopping.

Bridgette's bedroom was in chaos, not that Jasmine
cared a bit, as they fought over mirror space and added

another layer of mascara. It was a hot, humid night and already Bridgette was sweating. Her face would be shining by the time she got there at this rate, so she climbed over two laundry baskets to open her bedroom window and then attempted to find her shoes. 'I must tidy up in here.' Bridgette searched for her high-heeled sandals. Her bedroom had once been tidy—but when Harry had been born Courtney had moved in and Bridgette's two-bedroom flat had never quite recovered from housing three—actually, four at times if you counted Paul. Her love life hadn't recovered either!

Bridgette found her sandals and leant against the wall as she put them on. She surveyed the large boxes of shelves she had bought online that would hopefully help her organise things. 'I want to get these shelves put up. Dad said he'd come around and find the studs in the wall, whatever they are...'

Jasmine bit her tongue—Maurice had been saying that for months. The last thing Bridgette needed tonight was to have her parents criticised but, honestly, two more unhelpful, inflexible people you could not meet. Maurice and Betty Joyce just closed their eyes to the chaos their youngest daughter created and left it all for Bridgette to sort out.

'How do you feel?' Jasmine asked as, dressed in a guilty purchase, make-up done and high heels on, Bridgette surveyed herself in the mirror.

'Twenty-six.' Bridgette grinned at her own reflection, liking, for once, what she saw. Gone was the exhausted woman from earlier—instead she literally glowed and not with sweat either. No, it was the sheer silver dress she had bought that did the most amazing things to her rather curvy figure, and the heavenly new blusher that had wiped away the last remnants of fatigue in just a few glittery, peachy strokes.

'And single,' Jasmine nudged.

'Staying single,' Bridgette said. 'The last thing I want is a relationship.'

'Doesn't have to be a relationship,' Jasmine replied, but gave in with a small laugh. 'It does with you, though.' She looked at her friend. 'Paul was a complete bastard, you know.'

'I know.' She did not want to talk about it.

'Better to find out now than later.'

'I know that,' Bridgette snapped. She *so* did not want to talk about it—she didn't even want to think about it tonight—but thankfully Jasmine had other things on her mind.

'Ooh, I wonder if Dominic will be there. He's sex on legs, that guy…' Even though she was blissfully happy with Vince, Jasmine still raved about the paediatric locum registrar, Dominic Mansfield.

'You're just about to fly off to Africa with your boyfriend.' Bridgette grinned. 'Should you be noticing such things?'

'I can still look.' Jasmine sighed. 'Honestly, you can't help looking when Dominic's around—he's gorgeous. He just doesn't belong in our hospital. He should be on some glamorous soap or something… Anyway, I was thinking of him more for you.'

'Liar. From what you've told me about Dominic, he's not the *relationship* kind.'

'Well, he must have been at some point—he was engaged before he came to Melbourne. Mind you, he wouldn't do for you at all. He hardly speaks. He's quite arrogant really,' Jasmine mused. 'Anyway, enough about all that. Look at you.' She smiled at her friend in the mirror. 'Gorgeous, single, no commitments… You're allowed to have fun, you know.'

Except Bridgette did have commitments, even if no one could really understand them. It was those commitments that had her double-check that she had her phone in her bag. She didn't feel completely single—more she felt like a single mum with her child away on an access visit. Courtney and Harry had lived with her for a year and it had ended badly, and though she spoke little to Courtney now, she was an extremely regular babysitter.

She missed him tonight.

But, she reminded herself, he wasn't hers to miss.

Still, it was nice to be out and to catch up with everyone. They all put in some money for drinks, but unfortunately it was Jasmine who chose the wine and it was certainly a case of quantity over quality. Bridgette took a sip—she was far from a wine snob, but it really was awful and she sat on one drink all night.

'When are you coming back to us?' was the cry from her ex-colleagues.

'I'm not sure,' Bridgette responded. 'Soon, I hope.'

Yes, it was a good night; it just wasn't the same as it once had been.

She wasn't one of them any more.

She had no idea who they were talking about when they moaned about someone called Rita—how she took over in a birth, how much her voice grated. There had been a big drama last week apparently, which they were now discussing, of which Bridgette knew nothing. Slipping her phone out of her bag, she checked it, relieved to see that there were no calls, but even though she wasn't needed, even though she had nowhere else to be right now, the night was over for her.

She wasn't a midwife any more, or at best she was an occasional one—she went wherever the agency sent her. Bridgette was about to say goodbye to Jasmine, to make a discreet exit, when she was thwarted by some late arrivals, whom Jasmine marched her over to, insisting that she say hello.

'This is Rita, the new unit manager.' Jasmine introduced the two women. 'And, Rita, this is Bridgette Joyce. She used to work with us. We're trying to persuade her to come back. And this is…' He really needed no introduction, because Bridgette looked over and fell into very black eyes. The man stood apart from the rest and looked a bit out of place in the rather tacky bar, and, yes, he was as completely stunning as Jasmine had described. His black hair was worn just a little bit long and swept backwards to reveal a face that was exquisite. He was tall, slim and wearing black trousers and a fitted white shirt. He was, quite simply, divine. 'This is Dominic,' Jasmine introduced, 'our locum paediatrician.'

He didn't look like a paediatrician—oh, she knew she shouldn't label people so, but as he nodded and said hello he didn't look in the least like a man who was used to dealing with children. Jasmine was right—he should be on a soap, playing the part of a pretend doctor, or... She imagined him more a surgeon, a cosmetic surgeon perhaps, at some exclusive private practice.

'Can I get anyone a drink?' He was very smooth and polite, and there was no hint of an accent, but with such dark looks she wondered if his forebears were Italian perhaps, maybe Greek. He must have caught her staring, and when he saw that she didn't have a glass, he spoke directly to her. 'Bridgette, can I get you anything?'

'Not for me, thanks, I'm—' She was just about to say that she was leaving when Jasmine interrupted her.

'You don't need to buy a drink, Dominic. We've got loads.' Jasmine toddled over to their loud table and poured him a glass of vinegary wine and one for Bridgette too, and then handed them over. 'Come on.' Jasmine pushed, determined her friend would unwind. 'Drink up, Bridgette.'

He was terribly polite because he accepted it graciously and took a sip of the drink and managed not to wince. But as Bridgette took a tiny sip, she did catch his eye, and there was a hint of a shared smile, if it could even be called that.

'It's good that you could make it, Dominic.' Vince

came over. He had just today finished his paediatric rotation, and Bridgette had worked with him on Maternity for a while before she'd left. 'I know that it hasn't been a great day.'

She watched as Dominic gave a brief nod, gave practically nothing back to that line of conversation—instead, he changed the subject. 'So,' he asked, 'when do you fly?'

'Monday night,' Vince said, and spoke a little about the project he was joining.

'Well,' said Dominic, 'all the best with it.'

He really didn't waste words, did he? Bridgette thought as Jasmine polished her cupid's bow and happily took Vince's hand and wandered off, leaving Bridgette alone with him and trying not to show just how awkward she felt.

'Careful,' she said as his glass moved to his lips. 'Remember how bad it tastes.'

She was rewarded with the glimpse of a smile.

'Do you want me to get you something else?'

Yikes, she hadn't been fishing for drinks. 'No, no...' Bridgette shook her head. 'Jasmine would be offended. I'm fine. I was just...' Joking, she didn't add, trying to make conversation. Gorgeous he might be to look at but he really didn't say very much. 'You're at the hospital, then?' Bridgette asked.

'Just as a fill-in,' Dominic said. 'I've got a consultant's position starting in a couple of weeks in Sydney.' He named a rather impressive hospital and that just about summed him up, Bridgette decided—rather impressive and very, very temporary.

'Your family is there?'

'That's right,' he said, but didn't elaborate. 'You work on Maternity?' Dominic frowned, because he couldn't place her.

'I used to,' Bridgette explained. 'I left six months ago. I've been doing agency...'

'Why?'

It was a very direct question, one she wasn't quite expecting, one she wasn't really sure how to answer.

'The hours are more flexible,' she said, 'the money's better...' And it was the truth, but only a shred of it, because she missed her old job very badly. She'd just been accepted as a clinical nurse specialist when she'd left. She adored everything about midwifery, and now she went wherever the agency sent her. As she was qualified as a general nurse, she could find herself in nursing homes, on spinal units, sometimes in psych. She just worked and got on with it, but she missed doing what she loved the most.

He really didn't need to hear it, so back on went the smile she'd been wearing all night. 'And it means that I get to go out on a Saturday night.' The moment she said them, she wanted those words back, wished she could retrieve them. She knew that she sounded like some sort of party girl, especially with what came next.

'I can see it has benefits,' Dominic said, and she swore he glanced down at the hand that was holding the glass, and for a dizzy moment she realised she was being appraised. 'If you have a young family.'

'Er, no.' Oh, help, she *was* being appraised. He was looking at her, the same way she might look at shoes in a window and tick off her mental list of preferences—too flat, too high, nice colour, shame about the bow. Wrong girl, she wanted to say to him, I'm lace-up-shoe boring.

'You don't have children?'

'No,' she said, and something twisted inside, because if she told him about Harry she would surely burst into tears. She could just imagine Dominic's gorgeous face sort of sliding into horrified boredom if the newly foiled, for once groomed woman beside him told him she felt as if her guts were being torn, that right now, right this very minute, she was having great difficulty not pulling out her phone to check if there had been a text or a call from Courtney. Right now she wanted to drive past where her sister was living with her friend Louise and make sure that there wasn't a wild party raging. She scrambled for something to say, anything to say, and of course she again said the wrong thing.

'Sorry that you had a bad day.' She watched his jaw tighten a fraction, knew, given his job, that it was a stupid thing to say, especially when her words tumbled out in a bright and breezy voice. But the false smile she had plastered on all night seemed to be infusing her brain somehow, she was so incredibly out of practice with anything remotely social.

He gave her the same brief nod that he had given Vince, then a very brief smile and very smoothly excused himself.

'Told you!' Jasmine was over in a flash the minute he was gone. 'Oh, my God, you were talking for ages.'

'For two minutes.'

'That's ages for him!' Jasmine breathed. 'He hardly says a word to anyone.'

'Jasmine!' She rolled her eyes at her friend. 'You can stop this very moment.' Bridgette let out a small gurgle of laughter. 'I think I've just been assessed as to my suitability for a one-nighter. Honestly, he's shameless… He asked if I had children and everything. Maybe he's worried I've got stretch marks and a baggy vagina.'

It was midwife-speak, and as she made Jasmine laugh, she laughed herself. The two women really laughed for the first time in a long, long time, and it was so good for Bridgette to be with her friend before she jetted off, because Jasmine had helped her through this difficult time. She didn't want to be a misery at her friends' leaving do, so she kept up the conversation a little. They giggled about lithe, toned bodies and the temptresses who would surely writhe on his white rug in his undoubtedly immaculate city apartment. It *was* a white rug, they decided, laughing, for a man like Dominic was surely far too tasteful for animal prints. And he'd make you a cocktail on arrival, for this was the first-class lounge of one-night stands, and on and on they went… Yes, it was so good to laugh.

* * *

Dominic could hear her laughter as he spoke with a colleague, as again he was offered yet more supposed consolation for a 'bad day'. He wished that people would just say nothing, wished he could simply forget.

It had been a… He searched for the expletive to best describe his day, chose it, but knew if he voiced it he might just be asked to leave, which wouldn't be so bad, but, no, he took a mouthful of vinegar and grimaced as it met the acid in his stomach.

He hated his job.

Was great at it.

Hated it.

Loved it.

Did it.

He played ping-pong in his mind with a ball that broke with every hit.

He wanted that hard ball tonight, one that bounced back on every smash, one that didn't crumple if you hammered it.

He wanted to be the doctor who offered better answers.

Today he had seen the dominos falling, had scrambled to stop them, had done everything to reset them, but still they'd fallen—click, click, click—racing faster than he could halt them till he'd known absolutely what was coming and had loathed that he'd been the only one who could see it.

'Where there's life there's hope' had been offered several times.

Actually, no, he wanted to say as he'd stared at another batch of blood results and read off the poisons that had filled this tiny body.

'There is hope, though...' the parents had begged, and he had refused to flinch at the frantic eyes that had scanned his face as he'd delivered news.

He loved hope, he craved hope and had searched so hard for it today, but he also knew when hope was gone, said it before others would. Unlike others, he faced the inevitable—because it was either cardiac massage and all lights blazing, or a cuddle without the tubes at the end.

Yes, it came down to that.

Yes, it had been a XXXX of a day.

He had sat with the parents till ten p.m. and then entered a bar that was too bright, stood with company that was too loud and tasted wine that could dissolve an olive, and hated that he missed her. How could you miss a woman you didn't even like? He hated that she'd ring tonight and that he might be tempted to go back. That in two weeks' time he'd see her. Shouldn't he be over Arabella by now? Maybe it was just because he had had a 'bad day'. Not that he and Arabella had ever really spoken about work—oh, they'd discussed their career paths of course, but never the day-to-day details. They'd never talked about days such as this, Dominic mused.

Then he had seen her—Bridgette. In a silver dress and with a very wide smile, with gorgeous nails and polished hair, she had drawn his eye. Yet on inspection there was more behind that polished façade than he cared to explore, more than he needed tonight.

He *had* been checking for a wedding ring.

What no one understood was that he preferred to find one.

Married women were less complicated, knew the rules from the start, for they had so much more to lose than he did.

Bridgette was complicated.

He'd read her, because he read women well. He could see the hurt behind those grey eyes, could see the effort that went into her bright smile. She was complicated and he didn't need it. But, on the way down to her ring finger, he'd noticed very pale skin and a tapestry of freckles, and he'd wondered where the freckles stopped, had wondered far too many things.

He didn't need an ounce of emotion tonight, not one more piece, which was why he had excused himself and walked away. But perhaps he'd left gut instinct in his car tonight, the radar warning that had told him to keep his distance dimmed a fraction as he looked over to where she stood, laughing with her friend.

'Hey, Dominic…' He heard a low, seductive voice and turned to the pretty blonde who stood before him, a nurse who worked in Theatre and one whose husband seemed to be perpetually away. 'So brilliant to see you tonight.' He looked into eyes that were blue and glittered with open invitation, saw the ring on her finger and the spray tan on her arm on the way down. 'I just finished a late shift. Wasn't sure I'd make it.'

'Are you on tomorrow?' someone asked.

'No,' she answered. 'And I've got the weekend to my-self. Geoff's away.' Her eyes flicked to his and Dominic met her gaze, went to take another sip of his drink and then, remembering how it tasted, changed his mind, and he changed his mind about something else too—he couldn't stomach the taste of fake tan tonight.

Then he heard Bridgette laughing, looked over and ignored his inner radar, managed to convince himself that he had read her wrong.

He knew now what Bridgette's middle name was.

Escape.

'People are talking about going for something to eat…' Vince came over and snaked his arm around Jasmine, and they shared a kiss as Bridgette stood, pretending not to feel awkward—actually, not so awkward now that she and Jasmine had had such a laugh. She wasn't going out to dinner, or to a club, but at least she and Jasmine had had some fun—but then the waitress came over and handed her a glass.

'For me?' Bridgette frowned.

'He said to be discreet.' The waitress nodded her head in Dominic's direction. 'I'll get rid of your other glass.'

Double yikes!

She glanced over to black eyes that were waiting to meet hers.

Wrong girl, she wanted to semaphore back—so very, very wrong for you, Dominic, she wanted to signal. It took me weeks to have sex with Paul, I mean weeks, and you're only here for two. And I don't think I'm very good at it anyway. At least he hinted at that when we broke up. But Bridgette didn't have any flags handy and wouldn't know what to do if she had them anyway, so she couldn't spell it out; she only had her eyes and they held his.

She lifted the glass of temptation he offered and the wine slipped onto her tongue and down her throat. It tasted delicious—cold and expensive and not at all what she was used to.

She felt her cheeks burn as she dragged her eyes from him and back to her friend and tried to focus on what Jasmine was saying—something about Mexican, and a night that would never end. She sipped her champagne that was far too nice, far too moreish, and Bridgette knew she had to get out of there. 'Not for me,' she said to Jasmine, feeling the scald of his eyes on her shoulder as she spoke. 'Honestly, Jasmine…' She didn't need to make excuses with her friend.

'I know.' Jasmine smiled. 'It really is great that you came out.'

It had been. Bridgette was relieved that she'd made it this far for her friend and also rather relieved to escape from the very suave Dominic—he was so out of her league and she also knew they were flirting. Dominic had the completely wrong impression of her— he thought she worked agency for the money and flexibility, so that she could choose her shifts at whim and party hard on a Saturday night.

If only he knew the truth.

Still, he was terribly nice.

Not nice, she corrected. Not *nice* nice, more toe-curlingly sexy and a dangerous nice. Still, no one was leaving. Instead he had made his way over, the music seemed to thud low in her stomach and for a bizarre moment as he joined them she thought he was about to lean over and kiss her.

Just like that, in front of everyone.

And just like that, in front of everyone, she had the ridiculous feeling that she'd comply.

It was safer to leave, to thank him for the drink, to say she wasn't hungry, to hitch up her bag and get the hell out of there, to ignore the dangerous dance in her mind.

'I'll see you on Monday,' she said to Jasmine.

'You can help me pack!'

The group sort of moved out of the bar as she did and walked towards the Mexican restaurant. There had been a burst of summer rain but it hadn't cleared the air. Instead it was muggy, the damp night air clinging to her cheeks, to her legs and arms as her eyes scanned the street for a taxi.

'Are you sure you don't want something to eat?' Dominic asked.

And she should say no—she really should walk away now, Bridgette told herself. She didn't even like Mexican food, but he was gorgeous and it had been ages since there had been even a hint of a flirt. And she was twenty-six and maybe just a bit flattered that someone as sophisticated as he was was paying her attention. Her wounded ego could certainly use the massage and she'd just checked her phone and things seemed fine, so Bridgette took a deep breath and forced back that smile.

'Sounds great.'

'Good,' he replied, except she was confused, because he then said goodbye to Vince and Jasmine as Bridgette stood on the pavement, blinking as the group all bundled into a restaurant and just the two of them remained. Then he turned and smiled. 'Let's get something to eat, then.'

'I thought…' She didn't finish her sentence, because he aimed his keys at a car, a very nice car, which lit up in response, and she glanced at her phone again and there wasn't a single message.

Her chariot awaited.

She climbed in the car and sank into the leather and held her breath as Dominic walked around to the driver's side.

She didn't do things like this.

Ever.

But there was a part of her that didn't want to say goodnight.

A part of her that didn't want to go back to an empty flat and worry about Harry.

They drove though the city; he blasted on the air-conditioner and it was bliss to feel the cool air on her cheeks. They drove in silence until his phone rang and she glanced to the dashboard where it sat in its little charger and the name 'Arabella' flashed up on his screen. Instead of making an excuse, he turned for a brief second and rolled his eyes. 'Here we go.'

'Sorry?'

'The maudlin Saturday night phone call,' Dominic said, grinding the gears. 'How much she misses me, how she didn't mean it like that...'

The phone went black.

'Your ex?'

'Yep.' He glanced over to her. 'You can answer it if she rings again.' He flashed her a smile, a devilish smile that had her stomach flip. 'Tell her we're in bed—that might just silence her.'

'Er, no!' She grinned. 'I don't do things like that.'

On both counts.

'Were you serious?' she asked, because she couldn't really imagine him serious about anyone. Mind you, Jasmine had said they'd been engaged.

'Engaged,' he said. 'For a whole four weeks.'

And he pulled his foot back from the accelerator because he realised he was driving too fast, but he hated the phone calls, hated that sometimes he was tempted to answer, to slip back into life as he once had known it.

And end up like his parents, Dominic reminded himself.

He'd lived through their hellish divorce as a teenager, had seen their perfect life crumble, and had no intention of emulating it. With Arabella he had taken his time. They had been together for two years and he thought he had chosen well—gorgeous, career-minded and she didn't want children. In fact, it had turned out, she didn't want anything that was less than perfect.

'You're driving too fast.' Her voice broke into his thoughts. 'I don't make a very good passenger.' She smiled. 'I think I'm a bit of a control freak.'

He slowed down, the car swishing through the damp city streets, and then they turned into the Arts Centre car park. Walking through it, she could hear her heels ringing on the cement, and even though it was her town, it was Dominic who knew where he was going—it had been ages since she had been in the heart of the city. She didn't feel out of place in her silver dress. The theatres were spilling out and there were people everywhere dressed to the nines and heading for a late dinner.

She found herself by a river—looking out on it from behind glass. She was at a table, with candles and silver and huge purple menus and a man she was quite sure she couldn't handle. He'd been joking in the car about telling his ex they were in bed, she knew it, but not really—she knew that too.

'What do you want to eat?'

Bridgette wasn't that hungry—she felt a little bit sick, in fact—but she looked through the menu and tried to make up her mind.

'I…' She didn't have the energy to sit through a meal. Really, she ought to tell him now, that the night would not be ending as he was undoubtedly expecting. 'I'm not very hungry…'

'We can get dessert and coffee if you want.'

'I wouldn't mind the cheese platter.'

'Start at the end.' He gave her a smile and placed the order—water for him and cognac for her, he suggested, and, heaven help her, the waiter asked if she wanted it warmed.

'Dominic...' She took a deep breath as their platter arrived, a gorgeous platter of rich cheeses and fruits. 'I think—'

'I think we just ought to enjoy,' he interrupted.

'No.' Bridgette gulped. 'I mean...' She watched as he smeared cheese on a cracker and offered it to her.

'I don't like blue cheese.'

'Then you haven't had a good one.'

He wasn't wrong there!

He took a bite instead and her hand shook as she reached for the knife, tasted something she was quite sure she didn't like and found out it was, in fact, amazing.

'Told you.'

'You did.' She looked at the platter, at the grapes and dates, like some lush oil painting, and she knew the dance that was being played and the flirting and the seduction that was to come, and it terrified her. 'I don't think I should be here...' She scrabbled in her bag, would pay the bill, knew that she must end this.

'Bridgette.' He wasn't a bastard—he really wasn't. Yes, he'd been playing the field since his engagement had ended, and, yes, he had every intention of continuing to do so, but he only played with those who were happy with the rules, and he knew now for sure that she wasn't. 'It's cheese.'

She lifted troubled eyes to his.

'No, it isn't—it's the ride home after.'

He liked her. He hadn't wanted emotion tonight, and yet she made him smile as a tear washed away the last of her foundation and he could see freckles on her nose. 'Bridgette, it's cheese and conversation.' He took her hand, and she started to tell him he didn't want just cheese and conversation, oh, no, she knew it very well. She told him she wasn't the girl in the silver dress who partied and he held her hand as she babbled about zebra-print rugs, no white ones, and cocktails. 'Bridgette.' He was incredibly close to adoring her, to leaning over and kissing her right now. 'It's cheese and conversation and then I'll take you home.' He looked at her mouth and he was honest. 'Maybe just one kiss goodnight.'

Oh, but she wanted her kiss.

Just one.

'That leads nowhere,' she said.

'That leads nowhere,' he assured her.

'We're not suited,' she said, and was incredibly grateful that he nodded.

'We're completely incompatible,' Dominic agreed.

'And I'm sorry if I've misled you…'

'You didn't.' He was very magnanimous, smearing more cheese and this time handing it to her, no, wait, feeding her, and it wasn't so much seductive as nice. 'I *let* myself be misled,' he said, and he handed her her cognac. 'I knew from the start you were nice.' He gave her a smile. 'And you are, Bridgette.'

'So are you.'

'Oh, no,' he assured her. 'I'm not.'

CHAPTER TWO

IT FELT so good to feel so good and it was as if they both knew that they didn't have long. It was terribly hard to explain it, but now that there wasn't sex on the menu, now they'd cleared that out of the way, they could relax and just be.

For a little while.

She took a sip of cognac and it burnt all the way down, a delicious burn.

'Nice?' Dominic asked.

'Too nice,' she admitted.

And he hadn't wanted conversation, or emotion, but he was laughing, talking, sharing, and that XXXX of a day melted away with her smile.

So they worked the menu backwards and ordered dessert, chocolate soufflé for Bridgette and watermelon and mint sorbet for him. As he sampled his dish, Bridgette wanted a taste—not a spoonful, more a taste of his cool, watermelon-and-mint-flavoured tongue—and she flushed a little as he offered her the spoon. 'Want some?' Dominic said.

She shook her head, asked instead about his work,

and he told her a bit about his plans for his career, and she told him about the lack of plans for hers.

'You love midwifery, though?' Dominic checked.

'I am hoping to go back to it.' Bridgette nodded. 'It's just been a bit of a complicated year...' She didn't elaborate and she was glad that he didn't push. Yes, she loved midwifery, she answered, loved babies.

'You want your own?' He asked the same question that everyone did when they heard her job.

'One day maybe...' Bridgette gave a vague shrug. Had he asked a couple of years ago she'd have told him that she wanted millions, couldn't wait to have babies of her own. Only now she simply couldn't see it. She couldn't imagine a place or a time where it might happen, couldn't imagine really trusting a man again. She didn't tell him that of course—that wasn't what tonight was about. Instead she gave a vague nod. 'I think so. You?' she asked, and he admitted that he shuddered at the very thought.

'You're a paediatrician.' Bridgette laughed.

'Doesn't mean I have to want my own. Anyway,' he added, 'I know what can go wrong.' He shook his head and was very definite. 'Nope, not for me.' He told her that he had a brother, Chris, when Bridgette said she had a sister, Courtney. Neither mentioned Arabella or Paul, and Bridgette certainly didn't mention Harry.

Tonight it was just about them.

And then they ordered coffee and talked some more.

And then another coffee.

And the waiters yawned, and Dominic and Bridgette

looked around the restaurant and realised it was just the two of them left.

And it was over too soon, Bridgette thought as he paid the bill and they left. It was as if they were trying to cram so much into one night; almost as if it was understood that this really should deserve longer. It was like a plane trip alongside a wonderful companion: you knew you would be friends, more than friends perhaps, if you had more time, but you were both heading off to different lives. He to further his career and then back to his life in Sydney,

She to, no doubt, more of the same.

Except they had these few hours together and neither wanted them to end.

They walked along the river and to the bridge, leant over it and looked into the water, and still they spoke, about silly things, about music and videos and movies they had watched or that they thought the other really should see. He was nothing like the man she had assumed he was when they had been introduced in the bar—he was insightful and funny and amazing company. In fact, nothing at all like the remote, aloof man that Jasmine had described.

And she was nothing like he'd expected either when they had been introduced. Dominic was very careful about the women he dated in Melbourne; he had no interest in settling down, not even for a few weeks. Occasionally he got it wrong, and it would end in tears a few days later. Not his of course—it was always the women who wanted more than he was prepared to give, and Dominic had decided he was never giving that part of himself again. But there was a strange regret in the air as he drove her home—a rare regret for Dominic—because here was a woman he actually wouldn't mind getting to know a little more, one who might get him over those last stubborn, lingering remnants of Arabella.

He'd been joking about Bridgette answering the phone.

Sort of.

Actually, it wasn't such a bad idea. He couldn't face going back to Sydney while there was still weakness, didn't want to slip back into the picture-perfect life that had been prescribed to him since birth.

And it was strange because had they met at the start of his stay here, he was sure, quite sure, time would have moved more slowly. Now, though, it seemed that the beach road that led to her home, a road he was quite positive usually took a good fifteen minutes, seemed to be almost over in eight minutes and still they were talking, still they were laughing, as the car gobbled up their time.

'You should watch it.' She was talking about something on the internet, something she had found incredibly funny. 'Tonight when you get in.' She glanced at the clock on the dashboard and saw that it was almost two. 'I mean, this morning.'

'You watch it too.' He grinned. 'We can watch simultaneously...' His fingers tightened on the wheel and he ordered his mind not to voice the sudden direction it had taken—thankfully those thoughts went unsaid and unheard.

'I can't get on the internet,' Bridgette grumbled, trying desperately not to think similar thoughts. 'I've got a virus.' She swung her face to him. 'My computer, I mean, not…' What was wrong with her mouth? Bridgette thought as she turned her burning face to look out of the window. Why did everything lead to sex with him? 'Anyway,' she said, 'you should watch it.'

There was a roundabout coming up, the last roundabout, Bridgette knew, before her home, and it felt like her last chance at crazy, their last chance. And, yes, it was two a.m., but it could have been two p.m.; it was just a day that was running out and they wanted to chase it. She stole a look over at his delectable profile and to the olive hands that gripped the steering-wheel—it would be like leaving the cinema in the middle of the best movie ever without a hope of finding out the end. And she wanted more detail, wanted to know how it felt to be made love to by a man like him. She'd been truthful when she'd spoken to Jasmine—a relationship was the very last thing that she wanted now. Maybe this way had merit… '*We* should watch it.'

'Your computer's not working,' he pointed out.

'Yours is.' The flick of the indicator signalling right was about half the speed of her heart.

'Bridgette…' He wasn't a bastard—he was incredibly, incredibly nice, because they went three times round the roundabout as he made very sure.

'I don't want you to regret...' He was completely honest. 'I leave in two weeks.'

'I won't regret it.' She'd firmly decided that she wouldn't. 'After much consideration I have decided I would very much regret it if I didn't.' She gave him a smile. 'I want my night.'

She did. And he was lovely, because he did not gun the car home. It was so much nicer than she would ever be able to properly remember, but she knew for many nights she would try.

She wanted to be able to hold on to the moment when he turned and told her that he couldn't wait till they got all the way back to the city for the one kiss they had previously agreed to. She wanted to remember how they stopped at a lookout, gazed out at the bay, leant against his bonnet and watched the glittering view, and it felt as if time was suspended. She wanted to bottle it somehow, because she wasn't angry with Courtney at that moment, or worried for Harry. For the first time in ages she had a tiny glimpse of calm, of peace, a moment where she felt all was well.

Well, not calm, but it was a different sort of stress from the one she was used to as he moved his face to hers. Very nicely he kissed her, even if she was terribly nervous. He let her be nervous as he kissed her— till the pleats in her mind unfurled. It was a kiss that had been building all night, a kiss she had wanted since their introduction, and his mouth told her he had wanted the same.

'I was going to stay for one drink…' His mouth was at her ear, his body pressed into hers.

'I was just leaving,' she admitted as his face came back to view.

'And now look at us.'

So nice was that kiss that he did it again.

'You smell fantastic.' She was glad, to be honest, to have only him on her mind. He smelt as expensive as he looked and he tasted divine. She would never take this dress to the dry cleaner's, she thought as his scent wrapped around them, and his mouth was at her neck and under her hair. He was dragging in the last breaths of the perfume she had squirted on before going out and soaking in the scent of the salon's rich shampoo and the warm fragrance of woman.

'So do you,' he said.

'You taste fantastic,' Bridgette said. She was the one going back for more now.

'You too.'

And he liked the weight of responsibility that cloaked him as he pressed her against the bonnet and his hands inched down to a silver hem. He could feel her soft thighs and wanted to lift her dress, but he wanted to know if her legs too were freckled, so he ended the kiss. He wanted more for her than that, more for himself than that.

Just tonight, Dominic assured himself as she did the same.

'What?' He caught her looking at him as they headed for his home, and grinned.

'Nothing.' She smiled back.

'Go on, say what you're thinking.'

'Okay.' So she did. 'You don't look like a paediatrician.'

'What is a paediatrician supposed to look like?'

'I don't know,' Bridgette admitted. 'Okay, you don't *seem* like a paediatrician.' She couldn't really explain it, but he laughed.

They laughed.

And when she told him that she imagined him more a cosmetic surgeon, with some exclusive private practice, his laugh turned wry. 'You're mistaking me for my father.'

'I don't think so,' Bridgette said.

And he pulled her towards him, because it was easier than thinking, easier than admitting he wasn't so sure of her verdict, that lately he seemed to be turning more and more into his father, the man he respected least.

It was three o'clock and she felt as if they were both trying to escape morning.

There wasn't a frantic kiss through the front door—instead the energy that swirled was more patient.

It was a gorgeous energy that waited as he made her coffee and she went to the bathroom and he had the computer on when she returned. They did actually watch it together.

'I showed this to Jasmine—' there were tears rolling down her face, but from laughter '—and she didn't think it was funny.'

And he was laughing too, more than he ever had. He

hadn't had a night like this in ages—in fact, he couldn't recall one ever.

Okay, she would try to remember the details, how he didn't cringe when she pretended his desk was a piano; instead he sang.

It was the most complicated thing to explain—that she could sing to him, that, worse, he could take the mug that was the microphone and do the same to her!

'We should be ashamed of ourselves.' She admired their reflection in the computer as they took a photo.

'Very ashamed,' he agreed.

She thought he was like this, Dominic realised, that this was how his usual one-night stands went. Didn't she understand that this was as rare for him as it was for her? He hadn't been like this even with Arabella.

He didn't just want anyone tonight; he wanted her.

It was an acute want that tired now of being patient and so too did hers. As their mouths met on time and together, he kissed her to the back of the sofa. It felt so seamless, so right, because not for a second did Bridgette think, Now he's going to kiss me. One moment they were laughing and the next they were kissing. It was a transition that was as simple as that.

It was his mouth and his taste and the slide of his tongue.

It was her mouth and a kiss that didn't taste of plastic, that tasted of her tongue, and he kissed her and she curled into it. She loved the feel of his mouth and the roam of his hands and the way her body was craving his—it was a kiss that was potent, everything a kiss could be, distilled into one delicious dose.

He took off her dress, because he wanted to see *her*, not the woman in silver, and his eyes roamed. They roamed as he took off her bra and he answered his earlier question because her freckles stopped only where her bikini would be. There were two unfreckled triangles that wanted his mouth, but he talked to her as well and what she didn't know was how rare that was.

He left control behind and was out of his mind.

He wanted her in France, he told her as he licked her nipple.

Topless and naked on the beach beside him, and new freckles on her breasts. She closed her eyes and she could smell the sun oil, could feel the heat from the sun that shone in France and the coolness of his tongue on sunburnt nipples. He pressed her into the couch and she pressed back to him.

She was lying down and could feel him hard against her and she didn't think twice, just slid his zipper down.

She could hear her own moan as she held him and he lifted his head.

'We're not going to make it to the bedroom, are we?'

'Not a hope,' she admitted.

Was this what it was like?

To be free.

To be irresponsible.

More, please, she wanted to sob, because she wanted to live on the edge for ever, never wanted this night to end.

She wanted this man who took off his trousers and

kept condoms in his wallet, and it didn't offend her—
she already knew what he was like, after all.

'Bastard.' She grinned.

And he knew her too.

'Sorry,' he said. In their own language he apologised
for the cad that he was and told her that he wasn't being
one tonight.

This was different.

So different that he sat her up.

Sank to his knees on the edge of the sofa.

And pulled her bottom towards him.

'Let's get rid of these.' He was shameless. He dis-
pensed with anything awkward, just slid her panties
down, and she did remember staring up at the ceiling as
his tongue slid up a pale, freckled thigh that didn't taste
of fake tan and then he dived right in. As he licked and
teased and tasted she would remember for ever thinking, Is this me?

And she was grateful for his experience, for his skill,
for the mastery of his tongue, because it was a whole
new world and tonight she got to step into it.

'Relax,' he said, when she forgot to for a moment.

So she did, just closed her eyes and gave in to it.

'Where's the rug?' she asked as he slid her to the
floor.

'No rug,' he said.

He maybe should get one, was her last semi-coherent
thought, because the carpet burnt in her back as he moved
inside her, a lovely burn, and then it was his turn to sam-

ple the carpet for he toppled her over, still deep inside her, and she was on top.

Don't look down.

It wasn't even a semi-coherent thought; it was more a familiar warning that echoed in her head.

Don't look down—but she did, she looked down from the tightrope that recently she'd been walking.

She glimpsed black eyes that were open as she closed hers and came, and he watched her expression, felt her abandon, and then his eyes closed as he came too. Yes, feeling those last bucks deep inside her she looked down and it didn't daunt her, didn't terrify. It exhilarated her as greedily he pulled her head down and kissed her.

'It's morning,' he said as they moved to the bedroom, the first sunlight starting.

Better still as she closed her eyes to the new day, there was no regret.

CHAPTER THREE

IT WAS like waking up to an adult Christmas.

The perfect morning, Bridgette thought as she stretched out in the wrinkled bed.

She must have slept through the alarm on her phone and he must have got up, for there was the smell of coffee in the air. If she thought there might be a little bit of embarrassment, that they both might be feeling a touch awkward this morning, she was wrong.

'Morning.' Dominic was delighted by her company, which was rare for him. He had the best job in the world to deal with situations such as this—in fact, since in Melbourne, he had a permanent alarm call set for eight a.m. at weekends. He would answer the phone to the recorded message, talk for a brief moment, and then hang up and apologise to the woman in his bed. He would explain that something had come up at work and that he had no choice but to go in.

It was a back-up plan that he often used, but he didn't want to use it today. Today he'd woken up before his alarm call and had headed out to the kitchen, made two coffees and remembered from last night that she took sugar. He thought about breakfast in bed and perhaps another walk to the river, to share it in daylight this time. Sunday stretched out before him like a long, luxurious yawn, a gorgeous pause in his busy schedule.

'What time is it?' Bridgette yawned too.

'Almost eight.' He climbed back into bed and he was delicious. 'I was thinking...' He looked down at where she lay. 'Do you want to go out somewhere nice for breakfast?'

'In a silver dress?' Bridgette grinned. 'And high heels?'

'Okay,' he said. 'Then I guess we've no option but to spend the day in bed.' She reached for her coffee and, as she always did when Harry wasn't with her, she reached for her phone to check for messages. Then she saw that it wasn't turned on and a knot of dread tightened in her stomach as she pressed the button.

'Is everything okay?'

'Sure.' Only it wasn't. She hadn't charged her phone yesterday; with Jasmine arriving and going out she hadn't thought to plug it in. Her phone could have been off for hours—anything could have happened and she wouldn't even know. She took a sip of her coffee and tried to calm herself down. Told herself she was being ridiculous, that she had to stop worrying herself sick, but it wasn't quite so easy and after a moment she turned and forced a smile. 'As much as I'd love to spend the day in bed, I really am going to have to get home.'

'Everything okay?' He checked again, because he could sense the change in her. One moment ago she'd

been yawning and stretching; now she was as jumpy
as a cat.

'Of course,' Bridgette said. 'I've just got a lot on...'

She saw the flash of confusion in his eyes and it
could have irritated her—in fact, she wanted it to irri-
tate her. After all, why shouldn't she have a busy day
planned? Why should he just assume that she'd want a
day with him? But that didn't work, because somehow
last night had not been as casual as she was now making it out to be. It needed to be, Bridgette reminded herself as she turned away from his black eyes—she felt
far safer with their one-night rule, far safer not trusting
him. 'I'll get a taxi,' she said as she climbed out of bed
and found her crumpled dress and then realised she'd
have to go through the apartment to locate her underwear.

'Don't be ridiculous—I'll drive you home,' Dominic
said, and he lay there as she padded out. He could hear
her as she pulled on her panties and bra, and he tried not
to think about last night and the wonderful time they'd
had. Not just the sex, but before that, lying on the sofa
watching clips on the computer, or the car ride home.

It wasn't usually him getting sentimental. Normally
it was entirely the other way round.

'You really don't have to give me a lift.' She stood
at the door, dressed now and holding her shoes in her
hand, last night's mascara smudged beneath her eyes,
her hair wild and curly, and he wanted her back in his
bed. 'It's no problem to get a taxi.'

'I'll get my keys.'

And she averted her eyes as he climbed out of the bed, as he did the same walk as her and located his clothes all crumpled on the floor. She wished the balloon would pop and he'd look awful all messed and unshaven. She could smell them in the room and the computer was still on and their photo was there on the screen and *how* they'd been smiling.

'Bridgette…' He so wasn't used to this. 'You haven't even had your coffee.'

'I really do need to get back.'

'Sure.'

And talking was incredibly awkward, especially at the roundabout.

She wanted the indicator on, wanted him to turn the car around and take them back to bed, and, yes, she could maybe tell him about Harry.

About Courtney.

About the whole sorry mess.

End the dream badly.

After all, he was only here for two weeks, and even if he hadn't been, she could hardly expect someone as glamorous and gorgeous as him to understand.

She didn't want him to understand, she didn't want him to know, so instead she blew out a breath and let the sat nav lead him to her door.

'Good luck in Sydney.' She really was terrible at this one-night thing.

'Bridgette.' He had broken so many rules for her and he did it again. 'I know that you're busy today, but maybe…'

'Hey!' She forced a smile, dragged it up from her guts and slathered it on her face and turned to him. 'We're not suited, remember?'

'Completely incompatible.' He forced a smile too.

He gave her a kiss but could sense her distraction.

She climbed out of the car and she didn't say goodbye because she couldn't bear to, didn't turn around because she knew she'd head back to his arms, to his car, to escape.

But she couldn't escape the niggle in her stomach that told her things were less than fine and it niggled louder as she made a half-hearted attempt at cleaning her room. By midday her answer came.

'Can you have Harry tonight?'

'I can't,' Bridgette said. 'I'm on an early shift in the morning...' Then she closed her eyes. She had reported her sister a couple of months ago to social services and finally voiced her concerns. Oh, there was nothing specific, but she could not simply stand by and do nothing. Since she'd asked Courtney to leave her flat, things had become increasingly chaotic and in the end she'd felt she had no choice but to speak out. Not to Jasmine or her friends—she didn't want to burden them. Instead she had spoken to people who might help. Her concerns had been taken seriously, and anger had ripped through her family that she could do such a thing. Sour grapes, Courtney had called it, because of what had happened between her and Paul. And then Courtney had admitted that, yes, she did like to party, she was only eighteen, after all, but never when Harry was around. She always made sure that Harry was taken care of.

By Bridgette.

And as she stood holding the phone, Bridgette didn't want to find out what might happen if she didn't say yes.

'I'll ring the agency,' Bridgette said. 'See if I can change to a late shift.'

Even if it was awkward talking to her sister when she dropped him off, Bridgette really was delighted to see Harry. At eighteen months he grew more gorgeous each day. His long blond curls fell in ringlets now and he had huge grey eyes like his aunt's.

Courtney had been a late baby for Maurice and Betty. Bridgette delivered babies to many so-called older women, but it was as if her parents had been old for ever—and they had struggled with the wilful Courtney from day one. It had been Bridgette who had practically brought her up, dealing with the angst and the crises that always seemed to surround Courtney, as her parents happily tuned out and carried on with their routines.

It had been Bridgette who had told them that their sixteen-year-old daughter was pregnant, Bridgette who had held Courtney's hand in the delivery room, Bridgette who had breathed with hope when Courtney, besotted with her new baby, had told Harry that she'd always be there for him.

'And I'll always be there for you,' Bridgette had said to her sister.

And Courtney was taking full advantage of that.

By seven, when Harry had had supper and been bathed, dressed in mint-green pyjamas, one of the many pairs Bridgette kept for him, and she had patted him off to sleep, she heard a car pulling up outside. She heard an expensive engine turning off, and then the sound of shoes on the steps outside her ground-floor flat, and she knew that it was him, even before she peeked through the blinds.

There was a loud ring of the bell and the noise made Harry cry.

And as Dominic stood on the step, there was his answer as to why she'd had to dash off that morning.

He waited a suitable moment, and Bridgette waited a moment too, rubbing Harry's back, telling him to go back to sleep, ignoring the bell. They were both quietly relieved when she didn't answer the door.

Still, last night had meant many things to Bridgette— and it wasn't all about the suave locum. Seeing her old colleagues, hearing about the midwifery unit, she'd realised just how much she was missing her old life. She knew somehow she had to get it back.

It was a curious thing that helped.

When Harry woke up at eleven and refused to go back to sleep, she held him as she checked her work sheet for the week. She was hoping that Courtney would be back tomorrow in time for her to get to her late shift when an e-mail pinged into her inbox.

No subject. No message. Just an attachment.

She had no idea how Dominic had got her e-mail

address, no idea at all, but she didn't dwell on it, just opened the attachment.

It didn't upset her to see it. In fact, it made her smile. She had no regrets for that night and the photo of them together proved it. The photo, not just of him but of herself smiling and happy, did more than sustain her—it inspired her.

'Harry Joyce,' she said to the serious face of her nephew. 'Your aunty Bridgette needs to get a life.'

And she *would* get one, Bridgette decided, carefully deleting Dominic's e-mail address so she didn't succumb, like Arabella, in the middle of the night. The photo, though, became her new screensaver.

CHAPTER FOUR

'HE'LL be fine.'

It was six-thirty a.m. on Monday morning and Bridgette's guilt didn't lift as she handed a very sleepy Harry over to Mary, whom she had been introduced to last week. 'It seems mean, waking him so early,' Bridgette said.

'Well, you start work early.' Mary had the same lovely Irish brogue as Bridgette's granny had had and was very motherly and practical. 'Is his mum picking him up?'

'No, it's just me for the next few days,' Bridgette explained. 'She's got laryngitis, so I'm looking after Harry for a while.'

'Now, I know you'll want to see him during your breaks and things, but I really would suggest that for the first week or two, you don't pop down. He will think you're there to take him home and will just get upset.' She gave Bridgette a nice smile. 'Which will upset you and you'll not get your work done for worrying. Maybe ring down if you want to know how he is, and of course if there are any problems and we need you, I'll be the first to let you know.' Holding Harry, Mary walked Bridgette to the door and gave her a little squeeze on the shoulder. 'You're doing grand.'

Oh, she wanted Mary to take her back to some mystical kitchen to sit at the table and drink tea for hours, for Mary to feed her advice about toddlers and tell her that everything was okay, was going to be okay, that Harry was fine.

Would be fine.

It felt strange to be back in her regular uniform, walking towards Maternity. Strange, but nice. It had been a busy month. She was so glad for that photo— their one night together had caused something of an awakening for Bridgette, had shown her just how much she was missing and had been the motivation to really sort her life out as best she could. She had been to the social-work department at the hospital she had once worked in and taken some much-needed advice. They suggested daycare and allocated Harry a place. At first Courtney had resisted. After all, she had said, she didn't work, but Bridgette stood firm—relieved that there would be more people looking out for Harry. She was especially glad that she had held her ground when the day before she started her new job, Courtney had come down with a severe throat infection and asked if Bridgette could step in for a few days.

Bridgette's interview with Rita had been long and rather difficult. Rita wasn't at all keen to make exceptions. She would do her best to give Bridgette early shifts but, no, she couldn't guarantee that was all she would get, and certainly, Rita said, she wanted all her staff to do regular stints on nights.

It all seemed a little impossible, but somehow Bridgette knew she had to make it work and get through things one day at a time—and today would be a good day, Bridgette decided as she entered the familiar unit, the smell and sound of babies in the air. This was where she belonged. She made herself a coffee to take into the long handover. Bridgette was hoping to be put into Labour and Delivery—she really wanted to immerse herself in a birth on her first day back.

'You're nice and early.' Rita was sitting at the computer, all busy and efficient and preparing for the day. 'Actually, that helps. It's been a very busy night, a busy weekend apparently. I've got a nurse who has to leave at seven. She's looking after a rather difficult case—would you mind taking handover from her and getting started?'

'Of course.' Bridgette was delighted. It often happened this way, and it would be lovely to get stuck into a labour on her first day back. She took a gulp of her coffee and tipped the rest down the sink, rinsed her cup and then headed off towards Labour and Delivery.

'No, it's room three where I want you to take over—twenty-four weeks with pre-eclampsia. They're having trouble getting her blood pressure back down.'

Okay, so she wasn't going to witness a birth this morning, but still, it was nice to be back using her midwifery brain. 'Hi, there, Heather.' She smiled at the familiar face. The room was quite crowded. Dr Hudson, the obstetrician, was there with the anaesthetist, and the anxious father was holding his wife's hand. The woman's face was flushed and she looked very drowsy. Thankfully, she was probably oblivious to all the activity going on.

'It's so good to see you.' Heather motioned to head to the door and they stepped just a little outside. 'I've got to get away at seven.'

'Is that why it's good to see me?' Bridgette smiled.

'No, it's just good to see you back, good to have someone on the ball taking over as well. I'm worried about this one. Her name is Carla. She came up from Emergency yesterday evening.' Heather gave Bridgette a detailed rundown, showing her all the drugs that had been used overnight in an attempt to bring Carla's blood pressure down. 'We thought we had it under control at four a.m., but at six it spiked again.' Bridgette grimaced when she saw the figures. 'Obviously, they were hoping for a few more days at the very least. She's supposed to be having a more detailed scan this morning. They were estimating twenty-four weeks and three days.' That was very early. Every day spent in the womb at this stage was precious and vital and would increase the baby's chance of survival.

The parents wanted active treatment and the mother had been given steroids yesterday to mature the baby's lungs in case of premature delivery, but even so, to deliver at this stage would be dire indeed. 'She's just been given an epidural,' Heather explained, 'and they're fiddling with her medications through that as well. They're doing everything they can to get her blood pressure down.' It just didn't seem to be working, though. The only true cure for pre-eclampsia was delivery. Carla's vital signs meant that her life was in danger. She was at risk of a stroke or seizures and a whole host of complications if she didn't stabilise soon—even death. 'They were just talking about transferring her over to Intensive Care, but I think Dr Hudson now wants to go ahead and deliver. The paediatrician was just in…he's warned them what to expect, but at that stage we were still hoping for a couple more days, even to get her to twenty-five weeks.'

It wasn't going to happen.

'I hate leaving her…'

'I know,' Bridgette said.

'Dillan starts at a new school today.' Bridgette knew Heather's son had had trouble with bullying and it sounded as if today was a whole new start for him too. 'Or I wouldn't dash off.'

'You need to get home.'

The monitors were beeping and Heather and Bridgette walked back in.

'Carla…' Heather roused the dozing woman. 'This is Bridgette. She's going to be taking care of you today, and I'll be back to take care of you tonight.'

The alarms were really going off now. The appalling numbers that the monitors were showing meant the difficult decision would have to be made. Bridgette knew that Heather was torn. She'd been with Carla all night and at any moment now Carla was going to be rushed over to Theatre for an emergency Caesarean. 'Go,' Bridgette mouthed, because if Heather didn't leave soon, she would surely end up staying, and Dillan needed his mum today.

'Let Theatre know we're coming over,' Dr Hudson said to Bridgette, 'and we need the crash team from NICU. I'll tell the parents.'

Bridgette dashed out and informed Rita, the smooth wheels of the emergency routine snapping into place. Five minutes to seven on a Monday was not the best time. Staff were leaving, staff were starting, the weekend team was exhausted, the corridors busy as they moved the bed over to the maternity theatres.

'Okay.' Bridgette smiled at the terrified father, whom Dr Hudson had agreed could be present for the birth. 'Here's where you get changed.' She gave him some scrubs, a hat and some covers for his shoes. 'I'm going to go and get changed too and then I'll come back for you and take you in.'

Really, her presence at this birth was somewhat supernumerary. For a normal Caesarean section she would be receiving the baby; however, the NICU team was arriving and setting up, preparing their equipment for this very tiny baby, so Bridgette concentrated on the parents. Frank, the husband, wanted to film the birth, and Bridgette helped him to work out where to stand so that he wouldn't get in the way. She understood his need to document every minute of this little baby's life.

'It's all happening so fast...' Carla, though groggy,

was clearly terrified, because now that the decision had been made, things were moving along with haste.

'We're just making sure we've got everything ready for your baby,' Bridgette explained as Dr Hudson came in. The anaesthetist had topped up the epidural and the operation would soon be starting.

'We're just waiting on...' Kelly, one of NICU team called out, when asked if they were ready, and then her voice trailed off. 'No problem. Dr Mansfield is here.'

Bridgette looked up and straight into those familiar black eyes, eyes that she stared at each day on her computer, except they didn't smile back at her now. She tore her gaze away from him and back to her patient. She completely halted her thoughts, gave all her attention to her patient, because the operation had started, the incision made at seven-eighteen, and just a few moments later a tiny baby was delivered.

'She's beautiful,' Bridgette told Carla. 'She's moving.' She was, her red, spindly limbs flailing with indignation at her premature entry to the world.

'She's not crying,' Jenny said.

'She is.' There was a very feeble cry and her face was grimacing. Frank was standing back, filming their tiny daughter. Bridgette watched the activity and for the first time she took a proper look at Dominic.

He needed to shave, his face was grim with concentration and he looked exhausted. Bridgette remembered Rita saying that it had been a very busy weekend, and this emergency had come right at the tail end of his on-call shift.

'Can I see her?' Carla asked, but already the team was moving the baby and she was whisked past. Carla got only a very brief glimpse.

'They're taking her into another area,' Bridgette explained, as the team moved away, 'and then she'll be taken up to the NICU.'

'Can I go with her?' Frank asked. 'Can I watch? I won't get in the way. I just want to see what they're doing.'

'I'll go and find out.'

Bridgette walked into the resuscitation area, where the baby would be stabilised as much as possible before being moved to NICU. Even though she had seen premature babies, now and for evermore the sight of something so small and so fragile and so completely tiny took her breath away. Bridgette loved big, fat babies, little scrawny ones too, but a scrap like this made her heart flutter in silent panic.

'She's a little fighter.' Kelly came over. 'We're going to move her up in a couple of minutes.'

'Dad wants to know if he can come and watch. He's promised not to get in the way. He just wants to see what's happening.'

'Not yet,' Dominic called over. 'I'll talk to him as soon as I can.'

'Tell him to stay with his wife for now,' Kelly suggested. 'I'll come and fetch him when Dominic is ready to talk to him.'

Kelly was as good as her word, and by the time Carla had been moved to Recovery, Kelly appeared, holding some new photos of their tiny daughter, which she handed to Mum and explained a little of what was going on. 'The doctors are still with her, but Dominic said if I bring Frank up he'll try to come out to speak with him. He'll come down and talk to you a bit later.'

It was a busy morning. Carla spent a long time in Recovery before being transferred back to the maternity unit, but even there she still required very close observation as her vital signs would take a while to stabilise after the birth. Carla was still very sick and of course wanted more information about her baby, whom they'd named Francesca. Frank had seen her very briefly and was now back with his wife and clearly a little impatient about the lack of news.

'Mary from daycare is on the phone for you.' Nandita, the ward clerk, popped a head around the door and handed Bridgette the phone.

'Nothing to worry about at all' came Mary's reassuring voice as Bridgette stepped out into the corridor. 'I'm just about to head off for lunch and I thought I'd let you know how well he's gone today. He's found a stack of bricks, which amused him for most of the morning.'

'Thanks so much for letting me know.'

'He's heading for an afternoon nap now. Anyway, you can get on with your day without fretting about him.' Bridgette felt a wave of guilt when she realised she hadn't even had time to worry about Harry and how he was doing on his first day at crèche and a wave of sadness too when she found out that, no, neither had Courtney rung to find out.

'Hi, Carla.' She gave the phone to Nandita, and as she walked back into her patient's room she heard Dominic's voice. If he had looked tired that morning then he looked exhausted now. 'Hi, Frank.' He shook the other man's hand. 'Sorry that it's taken so long to come and speak with you. I've been very busy with your daughter and another child who was delivered yesterday. I wanted to take the time to have a proper talk with you both.' He sat down next to the bed. 'Carla, you'll remember I spoke with you yesterday.' He didn't bog them down with too much detail. Apparently yesterday he had explained the risks of such a premature delivery and he didn't terrify them all over again. He told them their daughter's condition was extremely serious, but there was some good news. 'She seems a little further on than first estimated. I'd put her well into twenty-five weeks, which, though it's just a few days' difference, actually increases the survival rates quite dramatically. She's got size on her side too,' Dominic explained. 'Even though she's tiny, she is a little bit bigger than we would expect at twenty-five weeks, and she's had the benefit of the steroids we gave yesterday. She's a vigorous little thing, and she's doing absolutely as well as can be expected.'

'When can I see her?' Carla asked.

'I spoke to Dr Hudson before I came down, and as much as we know you want to see your daughter, you're not well enough at the moment.'

'What if…?' Poor Carla didn't even want to voice it, so Dominic did.

'If her condition deteriorates, we'll sort something out and do our best to get you up there.' He glanced over at Bridgette and so too did Carla.

'Of course we will,' she said.

'But right now the best you can do for your baby is to rest and get well yourself.' He answered a few more questions and then turned to Frank. 'You should be able to see her for a little while now. I've told them to expect you.'

'I'll get Nandita to walk you up,' Bridgette offered.

'Lunch?' Rita suggested as Bridgette walked over to speak with Nandita. 'Emma will take over from you.'

It was a late lunch, and as Bridgette hadn't had a coffee break, it was a sheer relief to slip off her shoes and just relax for a few moments. Well, at least it was until Dominic came in and sat on the couch opposite and unwrapped a roll. He gave her a brief nod but did not make any attempt at conversation, instead choosing to read a newspaper. It was Bridgette who tried to tackle the uncomfortable silence.

'I thought you were in Sydney.'

'It didn't work out.' He carried on reading the paper for a moment and then finally elaborated a touch. 'The professor I would be working under was taken ill and has gone on long-term sick leave—I didn't really care for his replacement, so I'm just waiting till something I want comes up, or the professor returns. I'm here for a few more weeks.'

He sounded very austere, such a contrast to the easy conversations they had once shared. He didn't say anything else, didn't even read his paper, just sat and ate his roll.

Couldn't he have done that on NICU or on the paed ward? Bridgette thought, stirring her yoghurt. If he was going to sit there all silent and brooding, couldn't he do it somewhere else? Surely it was already awkward enough?

For Dominic, in that moment, it wasn't awkward, not in the least. He was too busy concentrating on not closing his eyes. Fatigue seeped through him. He'd had maybe six hours' sleep the entire weekend and he just wanted to go home and crash. Thank goodness for Rita, who had noticed his pallor and given him a spare cold patient lunch and suggested that he take five minutes before he saw the baby he had come down to examine, as well as speaking with Frank and Carla. Rebecca, his intern, came in. Bridgette recognised her from that morning, and then a couple of other colleagues too, which should have broken the tension, but instead Dominic ignored everyone and made no attempt to join in with the chitchat.

And later, he didn't look up when she had no choice but to sit and join him at the nurses' station to write up her notes before going home.

He told, rather than asked, Rebecca to take some further bloods on a baby born over the weekend, and then when one of the midwives asked if he'd mind taking a look at some drug orders, holding out the prescription chart to him, he didn't take it. Rather rudely, Bridgette thought, he didn't even look up.

'Is it a patient of mine?'

'No, it's a new delivery.'

He just carried on writing his own notes. 'Then you need to ring the doctor on call.'

The midwife rolled her eyes and left them to it, and the silence simmered uncomfortably between them, or at least it was uncomfortable for Bridgette.

'I'm sorry this is awkward.' She tried to broach it, to go ahead and say what was surely on both their minds, to somehow ease the tension, because the Dominic she had seen today was nothing like the man she had met, and she certainly didn't want to cause any problems at work. 'Had I known you were still working here, I wouldn't have...' Her voice trailed off—it seemed rather stupid to say that she'd never have taken the job, that she wouldn't have come back to the unit she loved. But had she known he would be here for a little while more, there might have been a delay in her return—with Jasmine being away she was completely out of the loop as to what was going on at work.

'Awkward?' Dominic frowned as he carried on writing. 'Why would it be awkward?' And then he shook his head. 'Are you referring to...?' He looked over and waited till her skin was burning, till there was no question that, yes, she was referring to that night. 'Bridgette, it was months ago.' She swallowed, because it was actually just a few weeks; she'd counted them. 'We shared one night together.' How easily he dismissed it, relegated it, reduced it to a long-ago event that had meant nothing—something so trivial that it didn't even merit a moment's reflection. Except she was quite sure that wasn't true.

'Thanks for the e-mail,' she said, to prove it had been more than that, that he had come back to her door, had later that night sent her a photo, yet he frowned as if trying to place it and then he had the nerve to give a wry laugh.

'Oh, that!'

'You got my e-mail address?'

'On some stupid group one from Vince and…' He gave a shrug, clearly couldn't remember Jasmine's name. 'Just clearing out my inbox, Bridgette.' She felt like a stalker, some mad, obsessed woman, and he clearly must be thinking the same. 'It was one night—hardly something to base your career path on. Don't give it another thought. There really is no problem.'

'Good.'

'And as for awkward, it's not in the least. This is how I am at work.' And then he corrected himself. 'This is how I am—ask anyone.' He gave a very thin smile. 'I'm not exactly known for small talk. It has nothing to do with what took place. It really is forgotten.'

And over the next few days he proved his point. She saw that Dr Dominic Mansfield *was* cool and distant with everyone. He was mainly polite, sometimes dismissive, and just never particularly friendly. There was an autonomous air to him that wasn't, Bridgette realised, solely reserved for her. Not that she should mind—nothing had shifted her heart. She was still way too raw to contemplate a relationship. And the pa-

tients, or rather their parents, didn't seem to mind the
directness of his words in the least. In fact, as Bridgette
wheeled Carla up later in the week for a visit with her
newborn, Carla admitted it was Dr Mansfield's opinion
she sought the most about her daughter.

'I don't want a doctor who tries to spare my feelings,'
Carla said as they waited for the lift. 'He tells it like it
is, which Frank and I appreciate.

'Mind you...' she smiled as Bridgette wheeled her
in '...he's not exactly chatty. Gorgeous to look at he
may be, but you wouldn't want to be stuck in a lift with
him.' Whether she agreed or not, Bridgette smiled back,
pleased to see her patient's humour returning, along
with colour to her cheeks. It really had been a hellish
ride for Carla. It had been four days until she had been
well enough to see her baby, and there was still, for
Francesca, a long road ahead.

'Carla.' Dominic gave a nod to the patient as
Bridgette wheeled her over.

'Is everything okay?' Carla asked, anxious to see
him standing by Francesca's incubator.

'She's had a good morning, by all reports,' Dominic
said. 'I'm just checking in.'

He gave Bridgette the briefest nod of acknowledgement then moved on to the next incubator. He wasn't,
she now realised, being rude or dismissive towards her.
It was the way Dominic was to everyone.

It hurt more than she had time to allocate to it. Her
days were so busy, and more and more Courtney was
asking her to have Harry. It was hard trying to achieve

some sort of routine and work full-time with a toddler—
a toddler who worryingly didn't toddle very much, one
who seemed far happier to sit with his building blocks,
happier in his own world than hers. But sometimes at
night, when all she should do was close her eyes and get
some much-needed sleep, it was then that Bridgette's
mind wandered. It was on those occasions that she realised not so much what she'd lost but more what she'd
been privy to that night.

A side to Dominic that was rare indeed.

CHAPTER FIVE

'HARRY!' Bridgette gave him a wide smile but Harry didn't look up. He was engrossed with the pile of bricks in front of him. 'How has he been today?' Bridgette asked.

'Busy building!' Mary answered. 'He loves his bricks.'

Bridgette saw her own fingers clench around the pen as she signed Harry out for the day, saw the white of her knuckles as her brain tightened just a fraction, wondering if Mary's comment was friendly chatter or a more professional observation. She was being paranoid, Bridgette told herself, seeing problems where there were surely none, but as she picked up Harry she wished, and not for the first time, that Harry was just a little bit more pleased to see her, a little more receptive.

There couldn't be something wrong with him. It wasn't just for selfish reasons that she panicked at the thought—it was Courtney's reaction that troubled Bridgette, or rather Courtney's lack of reaction towards her son. Her sister wasn't exactly coping now, let alone if her son had special needs.

Special needs.

It was the first time that she had actually said it, even if only in her mind, and instantly she shoved it aside because there was just so much to deal with at the moment. She had so many things to contend with, without adding the unthinkable to the pile. But she had to approach it.

'How do you think he's doing?' she asked Mary.

'Grand.' She beamed. 'Mind, he does have a bit of a temper—' she tickled him under the chin '—if one of the other littlies knocks over his bricks.'

'What about his talking?' Bridgette looked at Mary, who just smiled at Harry.

'He's not much of a talker,' Mary said, 'but, then, he's just been here a couple of weeks and is still settling in so maybe he's a bit shy. If you're concerned, though…' Mary was lovely, but she told Bridgette what she already knew, that maybe his mum should take him to his GP if she was worried that he wasn't reaching his milestones.

'How is Mum?' Mary asked, because, despite Courtney collecting him a couple of times, it mainly fell to Bridgette.

'She's okay,' Bridgette answered. 'Though I'll be bringing Harry in for the next couple of days. She's got some job interviews lined up in Bendigo and is staying there with friends for a few nights.'

'Bendigo!' Mary's eyebrows rose. 'That's a good few hours away.'

'Well, it's early days,' Bridgette said, 'but it's good that she's looking for work.'

Bridgette had mixed feelings. Yes, she wanted her sister to get a job and to make a fresh start, but the thought of her, or rather Harry, so far away had Bridgette in a spin. She was doing her best not to dwell on it as she left the crèche.

'Excuse me!' She heard the irritation in the man's voice as she, a woman who wasn't looking where she was going, collided with him as she walked out of the daycare centre. And then Dominic looked down, saw who he was talking to, saw who she was holding, and she was quite sure that he frowned as he gazed into Harry's eyes. Eyes that were exactly the same sludgy grey as hers, and though he quickly moved his features to impassive and gave her a very brief nod, she could feel the tension. They walked down a long corridor, Bridgette several steps behind him. As he headed out through the ambulance bay and turned left, it was clear they were both heading for the car park.

She should have managed to avoid him, given that she now walked incredibly slowly, but one of the security guards halted him and they spoke for a moment. No matter how Bridgette dawdled, no matter how hard she tried not to catch up, the security guard gave him a cheery farewell at the very second Bridgette walked past and, like it or not, for a moment or two there was no choice but to fall in step alongside him.

'Is that why you had to dash off?'

It was the first time he acknowledged he even *recalled* the details of that night, that morning, the slice of time when things had felt more than right.

'I should have explained...' She really didn't know what to say, what could she say. 'I didn't know how...' She still didn't. Should she plead, 'I'm his aunt. He's not my responsibility'? Harry was, he was solid in her arms—and whether Harry understood her words or not, he certainly did not need to be present as she defended her reasons for not telling this man of his existence. Instead she walked to her car that, unlike his, which lit up like a Christmas tree the second he approached, needed keys. Bridgette had to scrabble in her bag for them, with Harry, who was becoming increasingly heavy, but she was too nervous to put him down in the middle of a car park. He was, she realised, just too precious to let go.

As Dominic's sleek silver car slid past her, she deliberately did not look up, did not want to remember the night he'd driven her to heaven then returned her home again.

She was very close to crying, and that Harry did not need, but finally she found her keys and unlocked the car, opening the windows to let it cool down before she put Harry in.

'Here we go.' The car still felt like a sauna but she strapped Harry in, climbed into the seat and looked in the rear-vision mirror at his wispy curls and serious grey eyes. She gave him a very nice smile. 'You're ruining my love life, Harry!'

CHAPTER SIX

'Wow!' Bridgette walked into the delivery room, where Maria was pacing. 'I turn my back for five minutes…' She smiled at Maria, who had progressed rapidly in the past half hour.

'I was worried you wouldn't make it back,' Maria said.

'I'm sorry I had to dash off.' Harry had been a touch grizzly this morning when she'd dropped him off and had, half an hour ago, thrown the most spectacular temper tantrum, bad enough for Mary to call her on the ward and for Bridgette to take an early coffee break.

'I know what it's like,' Maria said. 'I've got three of my own.'

'Four soon,' Bridgette said, and Maria smiled.

'I can't wait to meet her.'

'Neither can I,' Bridgette admitted. It was, so far, turning out to be a gorgeous labour—especially as it was one that could have been labelled 'difficult' because the testing and scans had revealed that Maria and Tony's baby had Trisomy 21. The diagnosis, Maria had told Bridgette, had caused intense upset between both families—Spanish passion combined with pointless accusations and blame had caused a lot of tension and heartache indeed. Maria and Tony, however, once they had got over the initial shock, had researched as much as they could, and had even met with a local support group who ran a regular playgroup.

'It took away a lot of the fear,' Maria had explained, when Bridgette admitted her. 'Seeing other Down's syndrome babies and toddlers and their parents coping so well. We're so looking forward to having our baby. I just wish our families would stop with the grief.'

So upset was Maria with the response of her family that she hadn't even wanted them to know that she had gone into labour, but with three other small children to care for she'd had no choice but to tell them. And now two anxious families were sitting in the maternity waiting room. Still, Maria was doing beautifully and was helped so much by her husband's unwavering support. He rubbed her back where she indicated, stopped talking when she simply raised a hand. They had their own private language and were working to deliver their daughter as a team.

'How are things?' Rita popped her head around the door. 'The family just asked for an update.'

'It's all going well,' Bridgette said.

'Tell them it will be born when it's good and ready,' Maria snapped, and then breathed through another contraction. She was suddenly savage. 'You'd think they were preparing for a funeral more than a birth!' She let out an expletive or three in Spanish and Tony grimaced, then she told him *exactly* what she thought of Abuela.

'Grandmother,' Tony translated with a smile when Bridgette winked at him. 'My mother.' He rolled his eyes. 'She does a lot for us, but she can be a bit too much at times, though she means well.' He rubbed his wife's back as Maria said a little more of what she thought about her mother-in-law. 'Maria always does this when…' And Bridgette smiled, knew as Tony did, what was coming. Maria leant against the bed, her face changing to a familiar grimace.

'I want to push.'

'That's good,' Bridgette cheered.

'Come on, Tony,' she said and they both helped Maria up onto the bed. 'I'm just going to let Dr Hudson know—'

'No need.' Dr Hudson came in.

'How's she doing?' Rita popped her head around the door again and Bridgette gritted her teeth, while trying not to let Maria see.

'Can we get the paediatrician down?' The obstetrician's tone was a little brusque and Bridgette saw the flare of panic in Maria's eyes.

'It's fine, Maria,' Bridgette reassured her as Rita went to make the call. 'The fact Dr Hudson wants the paediatrician to come down means that you're getting close now and it won't be long till your baby's born.'

'The paediatrician is on his way,' Rita called over the intercom. 'I'll come in and give you a hand in a moment.'

Bridgette watched as Maria's eyes closed; as she dipped into her own private world and just tried to block the gathering crowd out. She had wanted the birth to be as low-key and as relaxed as possible, and had three other births with which to compare, but because of the possible health complications, more staff would be present with this one. Though potentially necessary, it just compounded things for Maria.

'Have you got everything ready?' Rita bustled into the room. 'Dominic is just a couple of minutes away.'

Bridgette felt incredibly confident with Dominic. He was an amazing doctor and very astute. However, for Maria, perhaps it was not the best combination of staff. Dr Hudson believed in planning for every eventuality—*every* eventuality—and Rita was one of those high-energy people who somehow didn't soothe. Now Dominic, a rather aloof paediatrician, was being added to the mix, except... 'Dominic Mansfield?' Tony looked over at Bridgette. 'Is that the paediatrician who's coming?' When Bridgette nodded, Tony hugged his wife. 'That's good news, Maria.'

'Bridgette?' Rita was checking and double-checking everything Bridgette had already done. 'Have you got the—?'

'Shut up!' roared Maria, just as Dominic came into the room.

For once Bridgette was grateful for his silence. He gave Tony a nod as Maria quietly laboured. Dominic took off his jacket and headed to the sink to wash his hands and then tied on a plastic apron.

'Big breath, Maria,' Bridgette said gently. 'Come on, another one…' The birth was imminent. 'And then push until Dr Hudson tells you to stop.' Maria was very good at this. There was grim concentration on her face as she bore down and Bridgette held her leg, relaying Dr Hudson's gruff instructions but in more encouraging tones. 'Don't push now. Just breathe. The head's out.'

The baby didn't even require another push. She slithered out into Dr Hudson's hands, where Rita was waiting to cut the cord and whisk the baby off for examination.

'Up onto Mum's stomach,' Dominic said. 'Tony can cut the cord.' Bridgette silently cheered as his calm, authoritative voice slowed the haste.

'Do you want the baby moved over for examination?' Rita checked when, again, she didn't need to. It had been a very beautiful birth, and Bridgette was especially thrilled that Dominic seemed in no rush to whisk the baby off and examine her—instead, he just quietly observed.

The little girl was small and Bridgette placed a towel over her, rubbing her to stimulate her, but she felt very calm with Dominic's stoic presence so close.

As the baby took her first breaths, Dominic called Tony over and the cord was cut—and Bridgette felt a blink of tears because the birth Maria had wanted so badly for her baby was happening.

'I can examine her here,' Dominic said, when Rita checked again if he wanted the baby moved over. And he did. He checked the little baby's muscle tone and her palate and listened to her heart for a long time. He told Maria he would perform a more comprehensive examination in a little while. 'But for now I'll let you enjoy her.'

There really was a lot to enjoy. She peered up at her mum, her almond-shaped eyes huge and gorgeous; she was very alert, and even though she let out a few little cries, she was easily comforted by Maria.

'Do you want me to let your family know?' Rita asked, and Bridgette's jaw tightened. She could understand the conversation that had been held at Jasmine's leaving do now. Rita really did try and take over.

'They'll want to come in,' Maria said. 'I just don't want…' She held her baby closely. 'I want it to be a celebration, the same as it was with my others.'

'It will be,' Dominic said. 'They just haven't met her yet.'

'She wants to feed,' Maria said, as her daughter frantically searched for her breast.

'Let her.'

'You said they'd scan her first,' Maria said, because, though detailed prenatal scans had not shown anything, the nature of the syndrome meant the little girl was at risk of a heart defect and would need to be checked by a paediatric cardiologist soon after birth, but Dominic was clearly happy with his findings.

'She's looking great,' he said, quietly observing, and the baby did latch on, but Bridgette helped with the positioning.

It was one of those births that confirmed her vocation—there was no greater gift than watching a new life come into the world, and today's so-called difficult birth had been made especially wonderful by the calm presence of Dominic. Again he had surprised her. He wasn't particularly effusive or gushing, he was so much *more* than that, and he was everything this little family needed today.

Dominic stayed and wrote up his notes while the little girl fed and Bridgette watched for any signs that the baby was having trouble sucking and swallowing but she was doing very well. 'Dominic said that breast feeding might be more difficult than with the others...' Maria looked down at her daughter, who was tiring, so Bridgette suggested she take her off now.

'She's doing an awful lot right,' Bridgette said, checking the babe and then filling in her own notes. 'She's cried, pooed, wee'd and fed.'

Dominic came over. 'You remember I said that I'd take her up to NICU for a little while after she was born,' he said. 'I want that scan done. Everything looks good,' he reassured the parents, 'but I just want her thoroughly checked. Hopefully she'll be back down with you soon.'

Maria nodded and then took a deep breath. 'Can you bring in my family first?' Her eyes went to her husband's. 'If they start, I want you to...'

'We'll be here,' Bridgette said. 'You won't have to say a thing. I'm very good at bringing up excuses as to why people have to leave. If you start getting upset, or you've just had enough, you just have to let me know.'

They worked out a little code, and she gave Tony a smile as he walked out. Dominic, she noted, instead of heading out to the desk, was sitting on a couch in the corner of the room, finishing his notes—a quiet, unobtrusive presence that was welcome.

Maria and Tony set the tone, but Bridgette's heart did go out to the family. They were trying to be brave, to not be upset, but there was so much tension, so many questions as they all peered at the newest member of the clan. Then Maria's three-year-old, Roman, climbed up on the bed and gazed at his sister, kissing her on the forehead, and the old *abuela* laughed.

Dominic came over and checked the baby briefly again, more for the family's benefit, or rather Maria's, Bridgette rightly guessed, because the questions they had been asking Maria were aimed at him now.

'She's doing very, very well,' he said, and answered more of their questions and told them that, yes, the pre-natal diagnosis was correct. Yes, shortly there would be further testing, but for now she was doing perfectly. And then Bridgette blinked as he chatted with the *abuela* in what appeared to be fluid Spanish for a moment. *'Sí, ella es perfecta...'*

'We're going to move her up now.' Kelly from NICU had come down just as all the cameras came out.

'Photo with *el medico*,' the *abuela* said.

'We really ought to get moving.' Dominic was reluctant, but then obliged, and it struck Bridgette that though of course he held babies in the course of examining them, he wasn't the type to steal a cuddle.

He held the new infant and gave a smile for the camera and then he looked down at her.

'She's gorgeous, isn't she?' Maria said.

'Oh, I don't do the cute-baby thing,' Dominic answered, 'but, yes, I think I have to agree in this case. You have a very cute baby. Has she got a name?'

'Esperanza,' Maria said.

'Hope!' Dominic smiled.

He popped her back in her cot and at the last minute Tony asked if he might be able to stay with the baby during her tests. When Dominic agreed, the family all followed Dominic, Kelly and the porters in a little procession down the hall.

'He's lovely, isn't he?' Maria said. 'Dominic, I mean. He sort of tells you like it is.'

'He's very good,' Bridgette said, and gave Maria a wink. 'Speaks Spanish too.'

'Abuela was very impressed.' Maria grinned. 'Dominic's mother is Spanish apparently.' She had to find out about him from a patient! 'He's been great. We went to him when we got the amnio back and he told us what to expect. Well, I guess he'd know as his brother has Down's.' She must have seen Bridgette's eyes widen. 'Sorry, maybe I shouldn't have said—it was just that Tony was crying and so was I and it seemed like a disaster when we first found out, but Dominic was terribly patient. He told us what we were feeling was completely normal. We saw him again a couple of weeks ago and we were embarrassed about the scene we'd made, but he said not to give it another thought. It was all very normal, that his mother had been the same.'

They knew nothing about each other, Bridgette realised.

Which had been the point, she remembered.

She really was lousy at one-night stands.

Still, she didn't have time to dwell on it. L and D was busy and she was soon looking after another birth, a first-time mum called Jessica, who was very nervous, as well as keeping an eye on Maria.

Esperanza was gone for about an hour, and her heart test was clear, which was brilliant news, and by the time she was back, Bridgette had just transferred Maria to the ward. Having checked on her next patient, Bridgette was more than ready for lunch.

'What's all this?' Bridgette tried not to care that Dominic was sitting in the staffroom. After all, if he didn't care, why should she? Anyway, Rita was there too and there were other distractions this lunchtime. Instead of plain biscuits the table was heaving with fruit platters, small filled rolls and a spread of cheese.

'Leftovers from the obstetricians' meeting.' Rita gave a wry smile. 'I rescued some for the workers. Enjoy.'

Bridgette selected a roll and a few slivers of fruit. She glanced at the cheese—even though that would usually be her first option, even if it seemed stupid, with Dominic there she chose to give it a miss.

'How's Harry?' Rita asked.

'Better,' Bridgette answered. 'He was just having a

bit of a tantrum. He's not in the best of moods today. I'm sorry I had to dash off.'

As annoying and inflexible as she could be, Rita could, Bridgette conceded, also be very nice. 'No problem. It's to be expected in the first weeks at daycare. He'll soon get used to it. The real question is, how is his aunt doing?'

'Trying to get used to it too,' Bridgette admitted. 'But we're getting there.'

Unfortunately Rita's break was soon over and word couldn't yet have got around about the spread on in the staffroom because only Dominic and Bridgette remained. Well, she wasn't going to give up a single minute of the precious break by going back early. Her feet were killing her and she was hungry too, and Jessica, her new patient, was progressing steadily. If Dominic wasn't feeling awkward then why on earth should she be? And if she wanted cheese, why not?

Bridgette stood and refilled her plate with some Cheddar and Brie and a few crackers and went to sit back down, selecting a magazine to read as she did so.

'I thought you liked blue cheese.'

'Maybe.' Bridgette refused to look up, just carried on reading the magazine. She was not going to jump to make conversation just because he suddenly deigned to do so.

'How's Maria?'

'Marvellous.' She refused to be chatty, just because he suddenly was.

'The baby I saw you with yesterday...' Still she did

not fill in the spaces. 'He's your nephew?' When still he was met with silence, Dominic pushed a little further. 'Why didn't you just say so?'

'I don't really see that it's relevant,' Bridgette answered, still reading her magazine. 'Had our one-night stand been two years ago and you'd seen me walking out of daycare carrying a mini-Dominic, then, yes, perhaps I'd have had some explaining to do. But I don't.' She smirked with mild pleasure at her choice of words and looked up. She was rather surprised to see that he was smiling—not the Dr Mansfield smile that she had seen occasionally since her return to work but the Dominic smile she had once been privy to.

'I'm sorry about yesterday. I just jumped to conclusions. I saw you with—' he paused for a brief second '—Harry, and I thought that was the reason...' He really felt awkward, Bridgette realised. Despite insisting how easy this was, Dominic seemed to be struggling.

'The reason?' She frowned, because he'd done this to her too, made her blush as she'd revealed that she thought about that night—but Dominic didn't blush in the same way Bridgette had.

'The reason that you went home that morning.'

'Oh, I needed a reason, did I?' She went back to her magazine.

What was it with this woman? She had made it very clear that morning that she didn't want more than their one night. Normally it would have come as a relief to Dominic, an unusual relief because he was not the one working out how to end things.

'Excuse me.' Her phone buzzed in her pocket and Bridgette pulled it out, taking a deep breath before answering.

'Hi, Mum.'

Why did he have to be here when she took this call? Hopefully he'd choose now to leave, but instead he just sat there.

'I might need a hand a little bit later,' she said to her mother. She'd left a message for her parents earlier in the day, when she'd realised that Harry might not last out the day in crèche and also she wanted to stay longer for Jessica. 'There's a chance that I won't be able to get away for work on time and it would really help if you could pick up Harry at four for me.' She closed her eyes as her mother gave the inevitable reply. 'Yes, I know the crèche doesn't close till six, but he's a bit grizzly today and I don't want to push things—it's been a long day for him.'

Bridgette looked down and realised she was clicking her pen on and off as her mother reeled out her excuses. She could hear the irritation creeping into her own voice as she responded. 'I know Dad's got the dentist but can't he go on his own?' She listened to the train of excuses, to how they would love to help, but how nervous Dad got at the dentist, and if he did need anything done when they got there... 'You mean he's just having a check-up?' Now Bridgette couldn't keep the exasperation from her voice. She really wanted to be there for Jessica and didn't want to be nervously keeping one eye on the clock in case the crèche rang.

With a pang that she didn't want to examine, her heart ached for the long day Harry was having. She wanted some back-up, and despite her parents' constant reassurances that they would help, she never seemed to ask at the right time.

'Don't worry about it' Bridgette settled for, and managed a goodbye and then clicked off the phone. Then she couldn't help it—she shot out a little of the frustration that her parents so easily provoked. 'Why can't he go to the dentist by himself?' Bridgette asked as Dominic simply grinned at her exasperation. 'They go shopping together, they do the housework together… I mean, are they joined at the hip? Honestly, they don't do anything by themselves.'

'Breathe.' Dominic grinned and she did as the doctor recommended, but it didn't help and she stamped her feet for a moment and let out a brief 'Aagggh!'

'Better?' Dominic asked.

'A bit.'

Actually, she did feel a bit better. It was nice to have a little moan, to complain, to let some of her exasperation out. Her parents had always been the same—everything revolved around dinner, everything in the house was geared towards six p.m. They were so inflexible, right down to the brand of toothpaste they used, and that was fine, that was how it was, that was how they were, but right now Bridgette needed more hands and their four seemed to make a poor two.

'Have you got no one else who can help?' Dominic asked.

'I miss Jasmine for things like this,' Bridgette admitted. It was nice that they were finally talking but of course now that they were, Rita buzzed and told her Jessica was in transition and it was time for her to go back.

'You might be out by four,' he said, and she shook her head, because Jessica was a first-time mum.

'I doubt it.'

Dominic's phone was ringing as she left, and when he saw that it was his father, he chose not to answer it. Stupid, really, because his father would just ring again in an hour, Dominic thought, and every hour after that, till he could tick it off his to-do list.

He finally took the call at three.

'Hi.'

Dominic rolled his eyes as his father wished him a happy birthday. 'Thanks.' Dominic was being honest when he said that he couldn't talk for long, because he was summoned urgently and headed down to Theatre when paged for a child who was having an allergic reaction in Recovery. There was that theatre nurse, her blue eyes waiting, when he and the anaesthetist had finished discussing the child's care.

'Long shift?' Dominic asked when she yawned, because on certain occasions he did make conversation.

And today was a certain occasion.

It was, after all, his birthday.

'It's been busy.' She nodded.

'Back again in the morning?'

'Yes…though I shouldn't moan. My husband's away so I can just go home and sleep.'

He was always away, Dominic thought.

'What does he do?' He broke one of their rules and he watched her cheeks go pink. There were colleagues around, and they were seemingly just chatting, so of course she had to answer.

'He drives a coach,' Blue Eyes said. 'Overnight, Melbourne to Sydney.'

He gave a nod and walked off, felt a bit sick in the guts really, which wasn't like him, but he thought of the poor bloke driving up and down the freeway as Dominic bonked his wife. No questions asked, no real conversation.

Maybe he was growing up, Dominic thought. He hadn't been with anyone in weeks, not since Bridgette, in fact, though he rapidly shoved that thought out of his mind.

Well, why wouldn't he be growing up? It was his birthday, after all.

And birthdays were supposed to be enjoyed.

Never doubt the power of a woman in labour—Bridgette should really have known better. Jessica was amazing, focused and gritty, and the birth was wonderful, so wonderful that she was still high on adrenaline as she sped down the corridor to daycare.

'Bridgette.' He was walking towards her and this time he nodded *and* said her name—progress indeed!

'Dominic.' She grinned and nodded back at him,

ready to keep walking, except he stopped in front
of her.

'I was wondering,' Dominic said. 'Would you like
to come out tonight? You're right, this is awkward, and
I'd really like to clear the air.'

This she hadn't been expecting. 'The air is already
clear, Dominic.' Except it wasn't, so Bridgette was a
little more honest. 'You were right. Harry is the reason
that I didn't want you to come in that first night. My
computer didn't have a virus.' She gave a guilty grin.
'Well, it wasn't Harry exactly, more the cot and the
stroller and the rather blatant clues that were littered
around my flat at the time.' And with Bridgette, he
did ask questions, and got some answers. 'I look after
my nephew a lot. My sister's really young.' He didn't
look away, his eyes never left her face, and she rather
wished that they would. 'So!' She gave him a smile as
his pager went off and Dominic glanced down at it and
then switched it off. 'That's a little bit what my life is
like when Harry's with my sister—I'm permanently on
call.' Yes, the air had been cleared, and now they could
both move on; she truly wasn't expecting what came
next.

'Bridgette, would you like to come out tonight?'

She turned around slowly and he looked the same
as he had before—completely unreadable. She didn't
want a charity dinner, didn't want him taking her out
because he'd already asked her. To make things easier
for them both she gave him a small smile, shook her
head and politely declined. 'That's really nice of you,

thanks, but I have to say no—it's hard to get a baby-sitter.' There, she'd given him the out. It was over and done with, and she awaited his polite smile back—it didn't come. Instead he looked at his watch.

'How long does a dental check-up take?' He even smiled. 'Can you try?' He pulled out a card and wrote his mobile-phone number on it and handed it to her. Maybe he read her too well because instead of saying that he would wait to hear if she could make arrangements, he lobbed the ball firmly back into her court. 'I'll pick you up at seven, unless I hear otherwise. Ring me if you can't get a babysitter.'

It was utterly and completely unexpected. She had thought he would run a mile—she'd given him an out, after all.

She wanted him to take it.

Bridgette really did. She just wasn't ready to get back out there and certainly not with Dominic. Still, maybe tonight he would just tell her how impossible it all was; maybe she would receive a long lecture on how they found each other attractive and all that, but how unsuitable they were—yet, remembering just how good they had been, it was very hard to say no.

'Hi, Mum.' It was the second time that day she'd asked her mum for help. 'Is there any chance you and Dad could babysit tonight?'

'You mean have our grandson over?' Betty laughed. 'We'd love to.' As Bridgette blinked in surprise, as she paused just a fraction, her mother filled the gap. 'Though we do have a couple of friends coming over tonight. Old friends of your dad's—remember Eric and Lorna?' Bridgette felt her jaw tense. Her parents insisted they were accommodating, but it was always on their terms—when it suited them. 'Could we maybe do it tomorrow?'

'I've got an invitation to go out tonight, Mum. I'd really like to go.'

'But we've got people over tonight. Tomorrow we can come over to you and stay. It might be easier on Harry.' Yes, it might be easier on Harry, but it certainly wouldn't be easier on her—or Dominic. He was already taking a leap of faith in asking her out. Though he wasn't asking her out, she reminded herself—he simply wanted to clear the air. Still, no doubt he was used to having the door opened by a groomed, glossy beauty who invited him in for a drink as she applied a final layer of lip gloss—somehow she couldn't imagine inflicting her mother and father and Harry on the guy.

'Mum, I haven't had a night out in weeks.' She hadn't, not since that night with Dominic. 'I'm sorry for the short notice. If you can have Harry, that would be great. If not…' If not, then it simply wasn't meant to be, Bridgette decided. If she couldn't get away for one single night without planning it days in advance, she might just as well text Dominic now with the whole truth.

It would be quite a relief to, actually, but after a moment's silence came her mother's rather martyred response. 'Well, make sure you bring a decent change of clothes for him. I want Harry looking smart. I've got

Eric and Lorna coming over,' she repeated. 'Have you had his hair cut yet?' Bridgette looked at the mop of blond curls that danced in the afternoon sun as Harry built his bricks and wondered why her mother assumed that Harry's hair was Bridgette's responsibility. His mop of unruly hair was a slight bone of contention between them—Courtney would never think to get a haircut for her son and though at first it had irritated Bridgette, more and more his wild curls suited him. Bridgette was now reluctant to get them cut—she certainly wasn't going to rush out and get a haircut just to appease her parents' guests and, anyway, there wasn't time. 'No, Courtney hasn't had his hair cut, but he's looking beautiful and I've got a gorgeous outfit for him.'

And with Harry dropped off and the quickest bath in history taken, the flat had to be hastily tidied, not that she had any intention of Dominic coming in. She'd be ready and dressed at the door, Bridgette decided, so she had about sixteen minutes to work out a not-so-gorgeous outfit for herself.

There was a grey shift dress at the back of her wardrobe and she had to find her ballet pumps but first she had a quick whiz with hair tongs and her magical blusher.

'Please be late,' she begged as she remembered her screensaver was of them. Her computer was in the spare bedroom, but in case of earthquake and it was the room they ended up in, she had to change it.

'Please be late,' she said again as she stashed dishes

in the cupboard beneath the sink and shovelled piles of building bricks into the corner.

'Please be late,' she said as she opened her bedroom door to get her pumps and was distracted by the shelves she'd been meaning to build and the million-thread-count sheets she'd bought in a sale and had been saving for when the room was painted.

But the bedroom was too untidy to even contemplate bringing him in and, no, her prayers weren't answered.

Bang on seven, she heard the doorbell.

CHAPTER SEVEN

'READY!' Bridgette beamed as she opened the front door and stepped out, because there was no way he was coming in.

'Shoes?' Dominic helpfully suggested just after she closed the door.

'Oh. Yes.' Which meant she had to rummage in her bag for her keys as he stood there. 'They must be in here.'

'Can't the babysitter let you in?'

'He's at my parents',' she said as she rummaged.

'Have you locked yourself out?'

'No, no,' Bridgette said cheerfully. 'I do this all the time—here they are.' She produced them with a 'ta ra!' and she let herself in, which of course meant that she had to let him in too—well, she couldn't really leave him on the doorstep.

'Go through,' she said, because she didn't even want him to get a glimpse of the chaos in the bedroom. 'I'll just be a moment.' Except he didn't go through. He stood in the hallway as she slipped through the smallest crack in the door and then scrambled to find her shoes. She must get more organised. Bridgette knew that, dreamt of the day when she finally had some sort of routine. She'd had a loose one once, before Harry was born, but now the whole flat seemed to have gone to pot.

There they were, under the bed. She grabbed her pumps and sort of limbo-danced around the door so that he wouldn't see inside. 'Sorry about that,' she said. 'Just been a bit of a mad rush.'

'Look, if you're too tired to go out for dinner…'

She gave him a strange look. 'I'm starving,' Bridgette said. 'How could anyone be too tired to eat dinner?'

'I meant…'

'So we're not going out dancing, then,' she teased. 'You're not going to teach me the flamenco.' She was leaning against the wall and putting on her ballet pumps, hardly a provocative move, except it was to him.

'Impressed with my Spanish, were you?'

'No Flamenco Medico?' She pouted and raised her arm and gave a stamp of her foot. Dominic stood there, his black eyes watching and sudden tension in his throat.

'Any chance of a drink?'

'Sure!' She beamed and headed to the kitchen and opened the fridge. 'I've got…' She stared at a jug of cordial, kicked herself for not grabbing some beer or wine, or olives and vermouth to make cocktails, she frantically thought.

'I meant water.'

'Oh, I think I've got some somewhere.' She grinned

and turned on the tap. 'Oh, yes, here it is.' Was that a reluctant smile on the edge of his lips? 'Here you go.' She
handed him the glass as his phone rang, and because
of his job he had no choice but to check it. Bridgette's
smile was a wry one as 'Arabella' flashed up on the
screen.

'She's hitting the bottle early tonight.'

He laughed. 'It's my birthday.'

'Oh!' It was all she could think of to say and then her
brain sort of slid back into functioning. 'Happy birthday,' she said. 'I've got candles but no cake.'

Then the phone rang again and they stood there.

And she was annoyed at his ex, annoyed that he was
standing there in her kitchen, and her eyes told him so.
'You really did break her heart, didn't you?'

'Long story,' he said. He didn't want to talk about it,
hadn't ever spoken about it, and really he'd rather not
now.

'Short version?'

'Come on,' he said, 'the table's booked.'

'You know what?' Bridgette said. 'I'm not very hungry.'

'You just said you were starving.'

'Not enough to sit through five hundred phone calls
from your ex.'

'Okay, okay.' He offered a major concession. 'I'll
turn it off.'

'No,' she said. 'I'm not doing it any more, putting
up with crap.' She was talking about Paul, but she was
talking about him too, or rather she was talking about

herself—she would not put herself through it again. 'Even if you turn it off, I'll know she's ringing. What's that saying? If a tree falls in a forest, does it make a noise?'

'What?' He was irritated, annoyed, but certainly not with her. 'I've said I'll turn it off, Bridgette. She doesn't usually ring—I never thought when I asked you to come out that it was my birthday. I don't get sentimental, I don't sit remembering last year, blah blah blah.'

'Blah blah blah…' Bridgette said, her voice rising, irritated and annoyed, and certainly it was with him. 'That's all she was, blah blah blah.' The night was over before it had even started. She really should have left it at one night with him. 'What is it with men?' She stormed past him, completely ready to show him the door, and it was almost a shout that halted her.

'She didn't want my brother and his friends at our engagement party.'

They both stood, in a sort of stunned silence, he for saying it, she that he had.

'He's got Down's,' Dominic said, and she was glad that she knew already. 'He lives in sheltered housing. When I'm there I go over every week and sometimes she came with me. She was great…or I thought she was, then when we were planning the engagement, my dad suggested it might be better if Chris didn't come, Chris and his friends, that we have a separate party for them, and she agreed. "It might be a bit awkward."' He put on a very plummy voice. '"You know, for the other guests. You know how he loves to dance."'

And Bridgette stood there and didn't know what to say.

'I couldn't get past it,' Dominic said, and he'd never discussed this with another person, but now that he'd started, it was as if he couldn't stop. Months of seething anger and hurt for his brother all tumbling out. 'My dad wanted nothing to do with him when he was born, he has nothing to do with him now, and it turned out Arabella didn't want him around either—well, not in the way I thought she would.'

'I'm sorry.' It was all she could say and she could hear the bitterness in his response.

'She keeps saying sorry too—that she didn't mean it and if we can just go back of course he can come to our party. She claims that she said what she did because she was just trying to get on with my dad, except I heard it and I know that it was meant.' He shook his head. 'You think you know someone...'

And when the phone rang again she decided that she did know what to say, after all.

'Give it to me,' she said, and she answered it and gave him a wink and a smile as she spoke. 'Sorry, Dominic's in bed...' She looked at him, saw him groan out a laugh as she answered Arabella's question. 'So what if it's early? I never said that he was asleep.' And she put down the phone but didn't turn it off. Instead she put her hand to her mouth and started kissing it, making breathy noises. Then she jumped up onto the bench, her bottom knocking over a glass.

'Dominic!' she shrieked.

'Bridgette!' He was folded over laughing as he turned off the phone. 'You're wicked.'

'I can be,' she said.

And he looked at her sitting on the bench all dishevelled and sexy, and thought of the noises she had made and what she had done, and just how far they had come since that night. Her words were like a red rag to a bull—he sort of charged her, right there in the kitchen.

Ferocious was his kiss as he pushed her further up the bench, and frantic was her response as she dragged herself back.

His hands were everywhere, but she was just as bad—tearing at his shirt till the buttons tore, pulling out his belt, and she was delighted that they weren't going to make it to the bedroom again, delighted by her own condom-carrying medico. Except Dominic had other ideas.

'Bed.' He pulled her from the bench. 'This time bed.'

'No.' She pulled at his zipper. 'No, no, no.'

'Yes.' He didn't want the floor again. He was leading her to her room, dragging her more like as she dug her heels in.

'You can't go in there!'

'Why?' He grinned, except he'd already pushed the door open. 'Have you got more babies stashed away that you haven't told…?' He just stopped. She doubted anyone as glamorous as he had seen a really messy bedroom, like a *really* messy one. He looked at the chaos and then at the beauty that had somehow emerged out of it.

'I told you not to go in there!' She thought she'd killed the moment. Honestly, she really thought she had, but something else shifted, something even more breathtaking than before.

'In here now, young lady.' His voice was stern as he pointed, and she licked her lips, she could hardly breathe for the excitement, as she headed to her bedroom. 'You can hardly see the bed,' he scolded as he led her to it. 'I've a good mind...'

Yes, they *were* bad. He did put her over his knee, but she nearly fell off laughing and they wanted each other too much to play games. It was the quickest sex ever, the best sex ever.

Again.

Again, she thought as he speared into her. They were still half-dressed, just mutual in want. She'd wanted him so badly again and now he was inside her.

It was bliss to have him back, to be back, to scream out as he shuddered into her.

Bliss for it already to have been the perfect night and it was only seven-thirty p.m.

To be honest, as she looked over he seemed a bit taken back by what had happened.

'Bridgette...' Please don't say sorry, she thought. 'I had no intention...' He looked at her stricken face. 'I mean...I had a table booked and everything.'

'You're not sorry, then?'

'Sorry?' He looked over to her. 'I couldn't be less sorry, just...' He might even be blushing. 'I did want to talk, to take you out. We could still go...'

'If you can sew on your own buttons!' Bridgette looked at his shirt. 'But first you'd have to find a needle. And thread,' she added after a moment's thought.

They settled for pizza. Bridgette undressed and slid into bed, and there would be time for talking later, for now they filled the gap and her roaring hunger with kissing until the pizza was delivered, and then he undressed and got into bed too.

And they did have that grown-up conversation. It sort of meandered around other conversations, but the new rules were spoken by both of them. It was difficult and awkward at times too, but so much easier naked in bed and eating than at some gorgeous restaurant with others around. They spoke about nothing at first and then about work.

'I don't get close.' Dominic shook his head. 'I'm good at my job. I don't need to be like some politician and hold and cuddle babies to be a good doctor.'

'Never?' she checked.

'Never,' Dominic said. 'Oh, I held little Esperanza, but that was more for the parents, for the *abuela*, but...' He *did* try to explain it. 'I said she was cute and, yes, she is, but they're not going to get a touchy-feely doctor if they are on my list.' He said it and he meant it. 'I can't do that. I know all that might happen—I can't get involved and then in a few weeks have to tell them that the news isn't good.' He was possibly the most honest person she had met. 'I'll give each patient and their parent or parents one hundred per cent of my medical mind. You don't have to be involved to have compassion.' It was too easy to be honest with her, but sometimes the truth hurt. 'I couldn't do it, Bridgette. I couldn't do this job if I got too close—so I stay back. It's why I don't want kids of my own.' He gave her a nudge. 'That's why I don't get involved with anyone who has kids.'

'I don't have kids.' Bridgette said. 'And I think it wasn't just the long-term viability of our future you were thinking about that night…' She nudged him and he grinned, though she didn't repeat midwife-speak to him; instead she spoke the truth. 'Here for a good time, not a long time…and not have the night interrupted with crying babies.'

'Something like that.'

'Didn't Arabella want kids?'

'God, no,' Dominic said.

The conversation sort of meandered around, but it led to the same thing.

They both knew it.

'I will be moving back to Sydney.' He was honest. 'It's not just work. It's family and friends.' And she nodded and took a lovely bite of cheesy dough and then without chewing took another. She couldn't blame him for wanting to be with them. She took another bite and he told her about his brother, that he'd been thirteen when Chris was born. 'To be honest, I was embarrassed—I was a right idiot then. So was my dad,' he said. 'They broke up when he was three. I was doing my final year school exams and all stressed and self-absorbed and Chris would just come in and want to talk and play—drove me crazy.

'He didn't care that I had my chemistry, couldn't give a stuff about everything that was so important to me—except clothes. Even now he likes to look good, does his hair.' Dominic grinned. 'Loves to dance!' He rolled his eyes. 'Loves women...'

'Must be your brother!' Bridgette smiled—a real one.

'When I was doing my exams I'd be totally self-centred, angry, stressed. "What's wrong, Dom?" he'd ask. And I'd tell him and he'd just look at me and then go and get me a drink or bring me something to eat, or try to make me laugh because he didn't get it. You know, I stopped being embarrassed and used to feel sorry for him. My dad didn't have anything to do with him, but then I realised Chris was the one who was happy and feeling sorry for me!'

'We've got it all back to front, you know,' Bridgette admitted.

'He's great. And you're right...' He saw her frown. 'I'm not like a paediatrician. I was like my dad growing up—just me, me, me. Without Chris I would have been a sports doctor on the tennis circuit or something—I would,' he said, and she was quite sure he was right, because he had that edge, that drive, that could take him anywhere. 'I'd certainly have had a smaller nose.'

'What?' She frowned and he grinned. 'My father thought I needed a small procedure. I was to have it in the summer break between school and university. He had it all planned out.' He gave a dark laugh. 'The night before the operation I rang him and told him to go jump.'

'Do you talk now?'

'Of course.' He looked over. 'About nothing, though. He never asks about Chris, never goes in and sees him on his birthday or Christmas, or goes out with him.' He gave her a grin. 'I can still feel him looking at my nose when he speaks to me.'

'He'd be wanting to liposuction litres out of me!' Bridgette laughed and he did too.

Dominic lay and stared up at the ceiling, thought about today—because even if he did his best not to get close to his patients, today he hadn't felt nothing as he'd stood and had that photo taken. He'd been angry—yes, he might have smiled for the camera, but inside a black anger had churned, an anger towards his father.

He'd walked up to NICU and Tony had walked alongside him, had stood with his baby for every test, had beamed so brightly when the good news was confirmed that her heart was fine.

'I'll come back to Maternity with you in case Maria has any questions,' Dominic had said, even though he hadn't had to. He had stood and watched when Tony told his wife the good news and wondered what he'd have been like had he had Tony as a father. He didn't want to think about his father now.

'How long have you been looking after Harry?' he asked instead.

Bridgette gave a tense shrug. 'It's very on and off,' she said.

'You said she was a lot younger…'

'Eighteen,' Bridgette said. He'd been so open and honest, yet she just couldn't bring herself to be so with him. 'I really would rather not talk about it tonight.'

'Fair enough,' Dominic said.

So they ate pizza instead and made love and hoped that things might look a little less complicated in the morning.

They didn't.

'Do you want to go out tonight?' he asked, taking a gulp of the tea she'd made because Bridgette had run out of coffee. 'Or come over?'

'I'd love to, but I truly can't,' she said, because she *couldn't*. 'I've got to pick Harry up.'

'When does his mum get back?'

'Tomorrow,' Bridgette said. 'I think.'

'You think.' Some things he could not ignore. 'Bridgette, you seem to be taking on an awful lot.'

'Well, she's my sister,' Bridgette said, 'and she's looking for flats and daycare. It's better that she has a few days to sort it out herself rather than dragging Harry around with her.'

'Fair enough.'

And he didn't run for the hills.

Instead he gave her a very nice kiss, and then reached in for another, a kiss that was so nice it made her want to cry.

'Have breakfast,' she said to his kiss, trying to think what was in the fridge.

And he was about to say no, that he had to go to work in an hour and all that.

Except he said yes.

He thought of the frothy latte he'd normally be sipping right now.

Instead he watched Bridgette's bottom wiggle as she made pancakes because she didn't have bread.

Watched as she shook some icing sugar over them.

How could you not have bread? she screamed inside.

Or bacon, or fresh tomatoes. She had thrown on her nursing apron—it had two straps with buttons and big pockets in the front. She had ten of them and they were brilliant for cooking—so the fat didn't splat—but she was naked beneath.

'We should be sitting at a table outside a café—' she smiled as he watched her '—or at the window, watching the barista froth our lovely coffees.'

She must have read his mind.

As she brought over two plates of pancakes, where Bridgette was concerned, he crossed the line. 'How long ago did you break up with Paul?'

'Excuse me?' She gave him a very odd look as she came over with breakfast. 'I don't remember discussing him with you.'

'You didn't.' He gave a half-shrug. 'You really don't discuss yourself with me at all, so I've had to resort to other means.' He saw the purse of her lips. 'I didn't just happen across it—I asked Vince for your e-mail address. Guys do talk.' He saw her raise her eyebrows.

'He said there had been a messy break-up, that was all he knew.'

'Well, it wasn't very messy for me.' Bridgette shrugged. 'It might have been a bit messy for him because he suddenly had to find somewhere to live.' She shook her head. She wasn't going there with him. 'It's a long story...'

'Short version,' Dominic said.

'We were together two years,' Bridgette said. 'Great for one of them, great till my sister got depressed and moved in and suddenly there was a baby with colic and...' She gave a tight shrug. 'You get the picture. Anyway, by the time Harry turned one we were over.' She had given the short version, but she did ponder just a little. 'He felt the place had been invaded, that I was never able to go out.' She looked over at him. 'Funny, I'd have understood if it had been his flat.' She gave Dominic a smile but it didn't reach her eyes. He could see the hurt deep in them and knew better than to push.

'I'll see you at work on Monday,' she said as she saw him to the door.

'I'm still here for a while,' Dominic said.

'And then you won't be...'

'It doesn't mean we can't have a nice time.' If it sounded selfish, it wasn't entirely. He wanted to take her out, wanted to know her some more, wanted to spoil her perhaps.

'Like a holiday romance?' Bridgette asked.

'Hardly. I'm working sixty-plus hours a week,' he said to soften his offering, because, yes, a brief romance was the most he could ever commit to. But she hadn't said it with sarcasm. Instead she smiled, because a holiday romance sounded more doable. She certainly wasn't about to let go of her heart and definitely not to a man like him. A holiday romance maybe she could handle.

'I won't always be able to come out... I mean...' Bridgette warned.

'Let's just see.' He kissed the tip of her nose. 'Who knows, maybe your sister will get that job, after all, and move up to Bendigo.'

And you should be very careful what you wish for, Dominic soon realised, because a few days later Courtney did.

CHAPTER EIGHT

AT FIRST it was great. Out had come the silver dress, and he *had* taught her the flamenco—not that he knew how, but they'd had fun working it out.

In fact, with Courtney and Harry away, it had been Dominic who had found himself the one with scheduling problems.

'I'll get back to you within the hour.' There was a small curse of frustration as Dominic put down the phone and pulled out his laptop.

'Problem?' Bridgette asked.

'Mark Evans wants me to cover him till eleven a.m. I'm supposed to be picking up Chris from the airport then.' He pulled the airline page up. Chris had been missing his brother, and with Dominic unable to get away for a while, a compromise had been reached and Chris was coming down to Melbourne for the night. 'I'd say no to Mark except he's done me a lot of favours. I'll see if I can change his flight.'

'You could just ask me,' Bridgette said, unable to see the problem. 'Surely if Chris can fly on his own, he won't mind being met by a friend of his brother's.'

'You sure?'

'It's no big deal.'

To Dominic it was a big deal. Arabella would, he realised, have simply had Chris change his flight, which
was maybe a bit unfair on her, because Arabella would
have been at work too. Bridgette was, after all, not starting till later. 'What if the flight's delayed? It doesn't
leave you much time to get to your shift as it is…'

'Then I'll ring work and explain that I'm delayed.
What?' She misread his curious expression. 'You don't
think I'd just leave him stranded?'

Chris's flight wasn't delayed. In fact, it landed a full
ten minutes early and he had hand luggage only, which
left plenty of time for a drink and something to eat at
an airport café before she started her late shift. He told
her all about his first time flying alone and then they
drove back to Dominic's, getting there just as he arrived. There was no denying that the two brothers were
pleased to see each other. 'Come over tonight if you
want,' Dominic said, 'after your shift. We're just seeing an early movie so we could go out for something
to eat if you like?'

'I'll give it a miss, thanks,' Bridgette said. 'I don't
want to spoil your party and anyway I'm on an early
shift tomorrow.' And he was always defensive around
his brother yet not once did he think it was a snub.
He knew Bridgette better than that—well, the part of
Bridgette that she let him know. And he knew that she
wouldn't even try to win points by hanging around to
prove she was nothing like Arabella.

She *was* nothing like Arabella.

'See you, Chris.' She gave him a wave. 'Have a great night.'

'See you, Bridgette,' he said. 'Thanks for the cake.

'We went to a café,' Chris explained, when she had gone. 'Is that your girlfriend?'

'She's a friend,' Dominic said.

'Your girlfriend.' Chris grinned.

'Yeah, maybe,' Dominic admitted, 'but it's not as simple as that.' It wasn't and it was too hard to explain to himself let alone Chris.

There was a reason why holidays rarely lasted more than a few weeks—because any longer than that, you can't pretend there are no problems. You can't keep the real world on hold. Perhaps selfishly Dominic had wanted Courtney to leave, wanted to get to know a bit better the woman he had enjoyed dating, but once Chris had gone home, he realised that it wasn't the same Bridgette when Harry wasn't around. Over the next few days she couldn't get hold of Courtney and they were back to the morning after he'd met her—Bridgette constantly checking her phone. There was an anxiety to her that wasn't right.

He wanted the woman he'd found.

But Bridgette had that bright smile on, the one he had seen when they'd first met. She gave it to him the next Friday afternoon at work as she dropped off a new mum for a cuddle with her baby and he gave her his brief work nod back. Then she stopped by the incubator, as she often did, to speak with Carla.

'How are you?' she asked.

'Good today!' Carla smiled. 'Though it all depends on how Francesca is as to how I'm feeling at any moment, but today's been a good day. Do you want a peek?' There were drapes over the incubator and when she peeled them back Bridgette was thrilled by the change in the baby. She was still tiny, but her face was visible now, with far fewer tubes. It had been a precarious journey, it still was, but Francesca was still there, fighting.

'She gave us a fright last week,' Carla said. 'They thought she might need surgery on the Friday, but she settled over the weekend. Every day's a blessing still. I'm getting to hold her now—it's fantastic. Frank and I are fighting to take turns for a cuddle.'

It was lovely to see Francesca doing so well, but Bridgette's mind was on other things as she walked back to the ward, and she didn't hear Dominic till he was at her side.

'Hi.' He fell into step beside her. Not exactly chatty, he never was at work, but today neither was she. 'How's your shift?'

'Long,' she admitted. 'Everything's really quiet— I'm waiting for a baby boom.' She smiled when she saw Mary walking towards them.

'We're missing that little man of yours,' Mary said. 'How is he doing?'

'He's fine,' Bridgette said, expecting Dominic to walk on when she stopped to talk to Mary, but instead he stood there with them. 'I am sorry to have given you such short notice.'

'Hardly your fault.' Mary gave her a smile. 'You'd be missing him too?'

Bridgette gave a nod. 'A bit,' she admitted, 'but they should be home soon for a visit.'

'That's good.' Mary bustled off and Bridgette stood, suddenly awkward.

'Have you heard from her?'

Bridgette shook her head. 'I tried to ring but couldn't get through—I think she's out of credit for her phone. Right.' She gave a tight smile. 'I'm going to head for home.'

'I should be finished soon,' Dominic said. 'And then I'm back here tomorrow for the weekend.' He gave her a wry grin. 'Some holiday romance.'

'We can go out tonight,' Bridgette offered. 'Or sleep.'

'Nope,' Dominic said, 'we can go out and then…' He gave her that nice private smile. 'Why don't you head over to mine?' he asked, because there were cafés a stone's throw away, unlike Bridgette's flat.

'Sure,' Bridgette said, because she couldn't face pizza again and the flat still hadn't been tidied. The cot was down, but stood taking up half the wall in her spare bedroom, which made it an obstacle course to get to the computer.

Next weekend she was off for four days and she *was* going to sort it.

* * *

Bridgette let herself into his flat, and wondered how someone who worked his ridiculous hours managed to keep the place so tidy. Yes, he'd told her he had some-one who came in once a week, and she knew he did, but it wasn't just the cleaner, Bridgette knew. He was a tidy person, an ordered person.

Knew what he wanted, where his life was going.

She had a little snoop, to verify her findings. Yes, the dishes were done and stacked in the dishwasher; the lid was on the toothpaste and it was back in its little glass. She peered into the bedroom—okay, it wasn't exactly hospital corners, but the cover had been pulled back up. She wandered back to his lounge and over to his desk.

There was a pile of mail waiting for him, one a very thick envelope, from that exclusive hospital where he wanted to work, but it was too much to think about and she had a shower instead. Then she pulled on a black skirt with a pale grey top, because an awful lot of her clothes seemed to live here now. The outfit would look okay with ballet pumps or high heels—wherever the night might lead.

It was a holiday romance, Bridgette kept telling herself to make sense of it, and summer was coming to an end. The clock would change soon and in a cou-ple of weeks it would be dark by now. She felt as if she were chasing the last fingers of the sun, just knew things were changing. Oh, she'd been blasé with Mary, didn't want to tell anyone what was in the bottom of her heart, that things were building, that at any moment now the phone would ring and it would all have gone to pot.

'Sorry about that...' He came in through the door much later than expected and gave her a very haphazard kiss as he looked at his watch and picked up his mail. He didn't want her to ask what the hold-up had been, didn't want her to know the scare little Francesca had given him just a short while before. He had twelve hours off before a weekend on call and he needed every moment of it, but first... 'I've got to take a phone call.'

'No problem.'

'Hey,' Dominic said when his phone rang promptly at seven-thirty. 'How are you?'

'Good,' Chris said, and got straight to the point. 'When are you coming back to Sydney?' Chris was growing impatient. 'It's been ages since you were here.'

And Dominic took a deep breath and told him the news he hadn't really had time to think about, let alone share with Bridgette. 'I got a phone call today, an—' he didn't want to say too much at this early stage '—I'm coming home for a few days next weekend. We'll go out then.'

'It's been ages.'

'I know,' Dominic said, and he knew how much his brother missed him, but he tried to talk him around, to move the conversation to other things. 'What are you doing tonight?'

'A party,' Chris said, and normally he'd have given him details as to who was going, the music that would be played, what they were eating, but instead he had a question. 'Bridgette *is* your girlfriend, isn't she?'

And normally Dominic would have laughed, would have made Chris laugh with an answer like 'One of them', but instead he hesitated. 'Yes.'

And usually they would have chatted for a bit—until Chris's Friday night kicked off and he was called out to come and join the party, but instead Chris was far from happy and told Dominic that he had to go and then asked another question.

'When are you properly coming back?'

'I've told you—I'm coming back soon for a few days,' Dominic said.

It wasn't, from Chris's gruff farewell, a very good answer.

'Right.' He came out of his room and saw that Bridgette was writing a note. 'Finally… Let's go and get something to eat. I've still got the sound of babies crying ringing in my ears.'

'Actually—' she turned '—my sister just called.' Back on went that smile. 'Things didn't work out in Bendigo and she's back. She's a bit upset and she's asked if I can have Harry tonight. I called and asked my parents, but they're out.'

'Oh.' He tried to be logical. After all, apart from one time in the corridor he'd never even seen Harry, and if her sister was upset, well, she needed to go. And even if more children was the last thing he needed tonight, she really had helped out with Chris and, yes, he did want to see her. 'We can take him out with us.'

'It's nearly eight o'clock,' Bridgette said, though when Harry was with her sister his bedtime was erratic at best.

'It's the Spaniard in me,' Dominic said.

Courtney, Dominic thought as he sat in the passenger seat while Bridgette collected Harry, didn't look that upset. But he said nothing as Bridgette drove. They'd gone out in her car because of baby seats and things, but they drove along to the area near his house and parked. It was cool but still light as they walked. She felt more than a little awkward. Walking along, pushing a stroller on a Friday night with Dominic felt terribly strange.

They sat out in a nice pavement café. They were spoiled for choice, but settled for Spanish and ate tapas. It was a lovely evening, but it was cool, even for summer. For Bridgette it was made extra bearable by one of Dominic's black turtlenecks and a big gas heater blazing above them. It was nice to sit outside and Harry seemed content, especially as Bridgette fed him *crema catalana*. Dominic had suggested it, a sort of cold custard with a caramel top, and Harry was loving his first Spanish dessert, but the mood wasn't as relaxed as it usually was. Dominic was lovely to Harry, there was no question about that, but Bridgette knew this wasn't quite the night he'd had planned.

'So, what's Courtney upset about?' He finally broached the subject

'I didn't really ask.'

'Does she do this a lot?'

Bridgette shot him a glance. 'It's one night, Dominic. I'm sorry for the invasion.' She was brittle in her defence and he assumed she was comparing him with Paul. She changed the subject. 'Have you been to Spain?'

'We used to go there in the summer holidays,' Dominic said. 'Well, their winter,' he clarified, because in Australia summer meant Christmas time. 'My father had a lot of social things on at that time, you know, what with work, so Chris and I would stay with Abuela.'

'And your mum?' Bridgette asked.

Dominic gave her an old-fashioned look, then a wry grin. 'Nope, she stayed here, looking stunning next to Dad. And I spent a year there when I finished school. I still want to go back, maybe work there for a couple of years at some point. It's an amazing place.'

And there were two conversations going on, as she ate thick black olives and fried baby squid, and he dipped bread in the most delicious lime hummus, and Harry, full up on the custard, fell asleep.

'I'd better get him back.'

They walked back along the beach road, a crowded beach full of Friday night fun, except Dominic was pensive. He was trying to remember the world before Chris had come along and Bridgette was for once quiet too.

She drove him back to his place. Harry was still asleep, and she didn't want to wake him up by coming in. Dominic had to be at work tomorrow, so there was no way really he could stay at hers.

And they kissed in the car, but it was different this time.

'Not your usual Friday night,' she said. 'Home by ten, alone!'

He didn't argue—she was, after all, speaking the truth.

CHAPTER NINE

RATHER than change things, the situation brought what was already coming to a head.

Dominic didn't know how best to broach what was on his mind.

He was used to straight talking, but on this Tuesday morning, lying in bed with Bridgette warm and asleep beside him, he didn't know where to start. He'd been putting this discussion off for a couple of days now, which wasn't at all like him.

'Hey, Bridgette.' He turned and rolled into her, felt her sleepy body start to wake, and he was incredibly tempted to forget what had been on his mind a few seconds ago and to concentrate instead on what was on his mind now. 'When do you finish?'

'Mmm...?' She didn't want questions, didn't want to think about anything other than the delicious feel of Dominic behind her. She could feel his mouth nuzzling the back of her neck and she wanted to just sink into the sensations he so readily provided, to let him make love to her, but automatically she reached for the phone that was on her bedside drawer, checked there were no messages she had missed and frowned at how early it was—it wasn't even six a.m.

'It's not even six,' she grumbled, because they hadn't got to bed till one—an evening spent watching movies and eating chocolate, laughing and making love, because neither wanted to talk properly.

'I know that you're off next weekend, but when do you actually finish?'

'I've got a long weekend starting Thursday at three p.m. precisely.' She wriggled at the pleasurable thought. 'I'm not back till Wednesday when I start nights. Why?'

'Just thinking.'

Though he didn't want to think at the moment, it could surely wait for now, Dominic decided, because his hands were at her breasts, and how he loved them, and her stomach and her round bottom. She was the first woman he loved waking up with.

It was a strange admission for him, but he usually loathed chatter in the morning. Arabella had driven him mad then too.

'Do you want coffee?' Arabella would ask every morning.

It was just the most pointless question.

Okay, maybe not for a one-nighter, but two years on, had she really needed to start each day with the same?

He looked at Bridgette's back, at the millions of freckles, and she was the one woman who could make him smile even in her sleep. 'Do you want coffee?' he said to a dozing Bridgette.

'What do you think?' she mumbled, and then…

'What's so funny?' she asked as he laughed and his mouth met her neck.

'Nothing.'

'So what are you lying there thinking about?'

'Nothing.'

'Dominic?'

He hesitated for an interminable second, his lips hovering over her neck and his hand still on her breast. 'I've been invited for an informal interview.' He was back at her neck and kissing it deeply. 'Very informal. It's just a look around…'

'In Sydney?'

Her eyes that had been closed opened then. She'd sort of known this was coming. He'd always said he wanted to work there; they'd been seeing each other just a few short weeks and there had been that envelope she'd peeked at.

'Yep—there's a position coming up, but not till next year. It's all very tentative at this stage—they just want me to come and have a look around, a few introductions…'

'That's good.'

And that wasn't the hard bit.

They both knew it and they lay there in silence.

Like an injury that didn't hurt unless you applied pressure, they'd danced around this issue from day one, avoided it, but they couldn't keep doing that for ever.

'Come with me,' he said. 'We could have a nice weekend. You could use the break before you start nights.'

She didn't want to think about it.

Didn't want to think about him going to Sydney, and there was still something else to discuss. Bridgette knew that, and Dominic knew it too.

There was a conversation to be had but it was easier to turn around, to press her lips into his. 'Bridgette...' Dominic pulled back. 'It would be great.' He gave her a smile. 'I won't inflict my family on you.'

'What?' She tried to smile back. 'You'll put me in some fancy hotel?'

'We'll be staying at my flat,' Dominic said—and there it was, the fact that he owned a flat in Sydney but he was only renting here. He had a cleaner there, coming in weekly to take care of things while he was temporarily away. 'Bridgette, you've known from the start that was where I was going.'

'I know that.'

'It's only an hour's flight away.'

She nodded, because his words made sense, perfect sense—it was just a teeny flight, after all—but her life wasn't geared to hopping on planes.

'Look,' Dominic said, 'let's just have a weekend away. Let's not think about things for a while. I'll book flights. The interview will be a morning at most. I'll see Chris...'

And so badly she wanted to say yes, to say what the hell, and hop onto a plane, to swim in the ocean, shop and see the sights, to stay in the home of the man she adored, but... 'I can't.'

'You've got days off,' Dominic pointed out.

'I really need to sort out my flat.' She did. 'I've been putting it off for ages.'

'I know,' Dominic said. 'Look, why don't I come round a couple of nights in the week and help with those shelves?'

'You!' She actually laughed. 'Will you bring your drill?' She saw his tongue roll in his cheek. 'Bring your stud finder…' she said, and dug him in the ribs. He would be as hopeless as her, Dominic realised. After all, his dad had never been one for DIY—he wouldn't know how to change a washer. But it wasn't the shelves that were the real problem. Yes, it would be so much easier to talk about stud finders, to laugh and to roll into each other as they wanted to, but instead he asked her again.

'If I can't do it—' he had visions of her being knocked unconscious in the night by his handiwork '—then I will get someone in and those shelves will be put up on your return,' he said. 'But it really would be nice to go away.'

'I can't,' she said, because she simply could not bear to be so far away from Harry. Courtney's silence was worrying her and it couldn't be ignored; also, she couldn't bear to get any closer to Dominic. To open up her heart again—especially to a man who would soon be moving away.

'Look, I have to go back this weekend.'

'Go, then!' Bridgette said. 'I'm not stopping you. I'm just saying that I can't come.'

'You could!' he said. He could see the dominos all

lined up, so many times he'd halted them from falling, and he was halting them now, because when talking didn't work he tried to kiss sense into her. She could feel her breasts flatten against his chest and the heady male scent of him surrounding her, and she kissed him back ferociously. It was as close as they had come to a row: they were going to have a row in a moment and she truly didn't want one, knew that neither did he. This way was easier, this way was better, this simply had to happen, because somehow they both knew it was the last time.

He kissed her face and her ears, he pushed her knees apart and they were well past condoms now. He slid into her tight warmth, went to the only place she would come with him and she did. They both did.

It was a regretful orgasm, if there was such a thing, because it meant it was over. It meant they had to climb back out of the place where things were so simple.

'I think a weekend away would be great.' He tried again. He'd heard the first click of the dominos falling and still he was trying to halt them. 'I think we need to get away. Look, if you don't want to go to Sydney...' He didn't want to let down Chris, didn't want to reschedule the interview, but he didn't want things to end here. He wanted to give them a chance. 'We could drive. There's a few places I want to see along the coast...'

'I can't this weekend,' she said. 'I told you, I've got the flat to sort out. Courtney's still upset...'

'Well, when can you?' And he let them fall. 'I want to get away on my days off.' He really did—it had been a helluva weekend at work. He wanted to be as far away from the hospital as possible this next weekend, didn't want to be remotely available, because he knew that if they called, he'd go in. What was he thinking, driving to the coast when he had an interview, letting down Chris? For what? So that they could stay in and wait for her sister to ring?

'Look, I know you help out your sister...' He simply did not understand her. In so many things they were open, there were so many things they discussed, but really he knew so little about her. There was still a streak of hurt in her eyes, still a wall of silence around her. 'But surely you can have a weekend off.'

'Maybe I don't want one,' Bridgette said. 'Maybe I don't want to go up to Sydney and to see the life you'll soon be heading back to.'

'Bridgette...' He was trying to prolong things, not end them. 'I don't get you.'

'You're not supposed to, that's not what we're about.' It wasn't, she told herself. It was supposed to be just a few short weeks—a break, a romance, that was all. It was better over with now. 'Just go to Sydney,' Bridgette said. 'That's what you want, that's where you've always been heading. Don't try and blame us ending on Harry.'

'I'm not blaming Harry,' Dominic said, and he wasn't. 'I'll admit I was a bit fed up with his aunt on Friday.'

'Sorry to mess up your night.' She so wasn't going to do this again. 'God, you're just like—'

'Don't say it, Bridgette,' Dominic warned, 'because

I am nothing like him.' He'd heard a bit about her ex and wasn't about to be compared to Paul. 'I'll tell you one of the differences between him and me. I'd have had this sorted from the start. Your sister's using you, Bridgette.' He looked at her, all tousled and angry, and truly didn't know what this was about.

'Do you think I don't know that?'

'So why do you let her?' He gave an impatient shake of his head. 'Do you know, I think you hide behind Harry. He's your excuse not to go out, not to get away.' Bridgette was right, Sydney *was* where he'd always intended to be—that was his hospital of choice and he wasn't about to have his career dictated to by Courtney.

'I'm going for the interview. I'm flying out on Thursday night. I'll text you the flight times. We'll be back Sunday night.'

'Don't book a ticket for me,' Bridgette said. 'Because I can't go.'

'Yes, you can. And, yes, I am booking for you,' Dominic said. 'So you've plenty time to change your mind.'

He did book the tickets.

But he knew she wouldn't come.

CHAPTER TEN

'SORRY to call you down from NICU.' Rebecca, the accident and emergency registrar, looked up from the notes she was writing. It was four a.m. on Tuesday morning. It had been a long day for Dominic and a very long night on call. After the interviews in Sydney and long walks on the beach with Chris, his head felt as if it was exploding, not that Rebecca could have guessed it. He was his usual practical self. 'I'm trying to stall Mum by saying we're waiting for an X-ray.'

'No problem. What do we know so far?'

'Well, the story is actually quite consistent—Mum heard a bang and found him on the floor. He'd climbed out if his cot, which fits the injury. She said that he was crying by the time she went in to him. It was her reaction that was strange—complete panic, called an ambulance. She was hysterical when she arrived but she's calmed down.'

'Are there any other injuries you can see?'

'A couple of small bruises, an ear infection, he's a bit grubby and there's a bit of nappy rash,' Rebecca said, 'but he is a toddler, after all. Anyway, I'm just not happy and I thought you should take a look.' She handed him the patient card and as Dominic noted the name, as his stomach seemed to twist in on itself, a young woman called from the cubicle.

'How much longer are we going to be waiting here?' She peered out and all Dominic could think was that if he had not recognised the name, it would never have entered his head that this woman was Bridgette's sister. She had straggly dyed blond hair and was much skinnier. Her features were sharper than Bridgette's and even if she wasn't shouting, she was such an angry young thing, so hostile in her actions, so on the edge, that she was, Dominic recognised in an instant, about to explode any moment. 'How much longer till he gets his X-ray or CT or whatever?'

'There's another doctor here to take a look at Harry,' Helga, the charge nurse, calmly answered. 'He'll be in with you shortly—it won't be long.'

'Well, can someone watch him while I get a coffee at least?' Courtney snapped. 'Why can't I take it in the cubicle?'

'You can't take a hot drink—' Helga started, but Dominic interrupted.

'Courtney, why don't you go and get a coffee? Someone will sit with your son while you take a little break.

'Is that okay?' He checked with Helga and she sent in a student nurse, but Rebecca was too sharp not to notice that he had known the name of the patient's mother. 'You know her?' She grimaced as Courtney flounced out, because this sort of thing was always supremely awkward.

'I know his aunt.' Dominic was sparse with his reply but Helga filled in for him.

'Bridgette. She's a midwife on Maternity. She's on her way. I called her a little while ago—Courtney was in a right panic when she arrived and she asked us to.'

'Okay.' Dominic tried not to think about Bridgette taking that phone call—he had to deal with this without emotion, had to step out and look at the bigger picture. 'I'm going to step aside.' He came to the only decision he could in such a situation. 'I'm going to ring Greg Andrews and ask him to take over the patient, but first I need to take a look at Harry and make sure that there's nothing medically urgent that needs to be dealt with.' His colleague might take a while. He did not engage in further small talk; he did not need to explain his involvement in the case. After all, he was stepping aside. Dominic walked into the cubicle where Harry lay resting in a cot with a student nurse by his side. Rebecca came in with him.

'Good morning, Harry.' He took off his jacket and hung it on the peg and proceeded to wash his hands and then made his way over to the young patient. He looked down into dark grey eyes that stared back at him and they reminded him of Bridgette's. He could see the hurt behind them and Dominic did not try to win a smile. 'I expect you're feeling pretty miserable? Well, I'm just going to take a look at you.' Gently he examined the toddler, looking in his ears for any signs of bleeding, and Harry let him, hardly even blinking as he shone the ophthalmoscope into the back of each eye, not even crying or flinching as Dominic gently examined the tender bruise. Through it all Harry didn't say a word. 'Has he spoken since he came here?' Dominic asked

'Not much—he's asked for a drink.' The curtains opened then and Helga walked in. Behind her was Bridgette, her face as white as chalk, but she smiled to Harry.

'Hey.' She stroked his little cheek. 'I hear you've been in the wars.' She spoke ever so gently to him, but her eyes were everywhere, lifting the blanket and checking him carefully, even undoing his nappy, and he saw her jaw tighten at the rash.

'How is he?'

'He just gave everyone a fright!' Helga said, but Bridgette's eyes went to Dominic's.

'Could I have a quick word, Bridgette?'

He stepped outside the cubicle and she joined him.

'He's filthy,' Bridgette said. She could feel tears rising up, felt as if she was choking, so angry was she with her sister. 'And he didn't have any rash when I saw him on Friday. I bought loads of cream that she took—'

'Bridgette,' he interrupted, 'I'm handing Harry's care over to a colleague. You will need to tell him all this. It's not appropriate that I'm involved. You understand that?' She gave a brief nod but her attention was diverted by the arrival of her sister, and he watched as Bridgette strode off and practically marched Courtney out towards the waiting room.

'I'll go.' Helga was more than used to confrontations such as this and called to the nurses' station over her shoulder as she followed the two sisters out. 'Just let Security know we might need them.'

And this was what Courtney had reduced her to, Bridgette thought, standing outside the hospital early in the morning, with security guards hovering. But Bridgette was too angry to keep quiet.

'He climbed out of his cot!' Courtney was immediately on the defensive the moment they were outside. 'I didn't know that he climbed. You should have told me.' Maybe it was a good idea that security guards were present because hearing Courtney try to blame her for this had Bridgette's blood boiling.

'He's never once climbed out of the cot when I've had him,' Bridgette answered hotly. 'Mind you, he was probably trying to get out and change his own nappy or make himself a drink, or give himself a wash. You lazy, selfish…' She stopped herself then because if she said any more, it would be way too much. She paused and Helga stepped in, took Courtney inside, and Bridgette stood there hugging her arms around herself tightly, mortified when Dominic came out.

'This has nothing to do with you,' Bridgette said, still angry. 'You've stepped aside.'

'You know I had to.'

She did know that.

'Is this why you couldn't get away?' Dominic asked, and she didn't answer, because a simple yes would have been a lie. 'Bridgette?'

'I don't want to talk about it.'

'You never do,' he pointed out, but now really wasn't the time. 'I know that it doesn't seem like it now,' Dominic said, 'but Harry being admitted might be the best thing that could have happened. Things might get sorted now.'

As an ambulance pulled up she gave a nod, even if she didn't believe it.

'Bridgette, I was actually going to come over and see you today,' Dominic said, and she knew what was coming. 'I didn't want you to hear it from anyone else—I've just given notice. I'm leaving on Saturday.' He chose not to tell her just how impossible the decision had been, but in the end it had surely been the right one—he wanted simple, straightforward, and Bridgette was anything but. He'd opened up to her more than he had with anyone, and yet he realised that, still, despite his question, he knew very little about her and even now she said nothing. 'Anyway, I thought I should tell you myself.'

'Sure.'

'I'd better get up to…' His voice stopped, his stomach tightened, as the ambulance door opened and he met Tony's frantic eyes.

CHAPTER ELEVEN

DOMINIC checked himself, because it should make no difference that it wasn't Esperanza on the stretcher. Instead it was Roman, their three-year-old, and he needed Dominic's help and concentration just as much as his little sister would have. 'Dr Mansfield's here...' Tony was talking reassuringly to his son, who was struggling hard to breathe as they moved him straight into the critical area. 'The doctor who looked after Esperanza. That's good news.'

'He did this last year...' Tony said as Dominic examined him, and Tony explained about his severe asthma. 'He does it a lot, but last year he ended up in Intensive Care.'

'Okay.' Dominic listened to his chest and knew that Roman would probably have to head to Intensive Care again this morning.

Roman took up all of Dominic's morning, but by lunchtime, when he'd spoken to the family and the frantic *abuela*, things were a little calmer.

'While he's still needing hourly nebulisers it's safer that he is here,' Dominic explained, but then it was easier to speak in Spanish, so that Abuela understood. He told them things were steadily improving and would continue to do so.

Tony rang Maria, who was of course frantic, and Dominic spoke to her too.

'You get a taxi home,' Tony said to Abuela, 'and Maria can come in between feeds.'

Writing up his drug sheets, Dominic listened for a moment as they worked out a vague plan of action, heard that Tony would ring his boss and take today off.

'You think he might go to the ward tomorrow?'

'Or this evening.' Dominic nodded.

'I'll stay with him tonight and if you can come in in the morning to be with Roman I can go to work tomorrow,' Tony said to his mother. She rattled the start of twenty questions at him, but Tony broke in.

'We'll deal with that if it happens.'

Dominic headed down to the children's ward. Bridgette wasn't around and neither was Courtney. An extra layer had been added to Harry's cot, in case he was, in fact, a climber, and it stood like a tall cage in the middle of the nursery. He walked in and took off his jacket, washed his hands and then turned round and looked straight into the waiting grey eyes of Harry, who wasn't his patient, he reminded himself.

Harry's head injury wasn't at all serious, but he had been moved up to the children's ward mid-morning. Bridgette knew it was more of a social admission. Maybe she had done rather too good a job of reassuring her parents that it wasn't serious when she rang them, because they didn't dash in. After all, her father had to have a filling that afternoon, so they said they would come in the evening and, with a weary sigh, her mother agreed, yes, they would stop by Bridgette's flat and bring a change of clothes, pyjamas and toiletries.

Bridgette took the opportunity to voice a few of her concerns about his speech delay with the doctor and he gave her a sort of blink when she spoke about Harry's fixation with bricks and that he didn't talk much.

'Has he had his hearing checked?'

'Er, no.'

'He's had a few ear infections, though,' Dr Andrews said, peering through his examination notes. 'We'll get his hearing tested and then he might need an ENT out-patient appointment.'

Later they were interviewed by a social worker, but by dinnertime Courtney had had enough. 'I'm exhausted,' she said. 'I was up all night with him. I think I'll go home and get some sleep.'

'We can put a bed up beside his cot,' a nurse offered.

'I'd never sleep with all the noise,' Courtney said, gave Harry a brief kiss and then she was gone, safe in the knowledge that Bridgette would stay the night. Dominic was on the ward when Bridgette's parents arrived, talking with the charge nurse. She saw him glance up when her mother asked to be shown where Harry was.

'Here, Mum,' Bridgette said as they made their way

over, all nervous smiles, slightly incredulous that their grandson was actually here.

'Here's the bits you wanted,' her mum said, handing over a bag.

Bridgette peered into the bag and flinched. 'Did you deliberately choose the ugliest pyjamas I own?' She grinned. 'I'd forgotten that I even had these!' They were orange flannelette, emblazoned with yellow flowers, and had been sent by her granny about five years ago.

'You're lucky I could find anything in *that* room!' Betty said. 'I could barely see the bed.'

Yes, she really must get organised, Bridgette re-membered. Somehow she had not got around to it last weekend. She had either been worrying about Harry or mooching over Dominic. Well, Dominic was gone or going and Harry would be sorted, so she would get organised soon.

'So what is he in for?' Maurice asked. 'He looks fine.'

He certainly looked a whole lot better. He'd had a bath and hair wash and had a ton of cream on his bot-tom. There was just a very small bruise on his head.

'He didn't even need a stitch,' Betty said.

'You know why he's in, Mum.'

'For nappy rash!' Betty wasn't having it.

'Mum... He's getting his hearing tested tomorrow.' They were less than impressed. 'Aren't you going to ask where Courtney is?'

'Getting some well-deserved rest,' Betty hissed. 'She must have had the fright of her life last night.' They didn't stay very long. They fussed over Harry for half an hour or so and it was a very weary Bridgette who tried to get Harry off to sleep.

'How's he doing?' Dominic asked as she stood and rubbed Harry's back.

'Fine,' Bridgette said, and then conceded, as she really wasn't angry with him, 'he's doing great. We're going for a hearing test tomorrow. Dr Andrews said we should check out the basics.' Of course he said nothing. He was his 'at work' Dominic and so he didn't fill in the gaps. 'I thought he was autistic or something.' She gave a small shrug. 'Well, he might be. I mean, if he is, he is…'

'You nurses.'

'You'd be the same,' Bridgette said, 'if he was…' Except Harry wasn't his and he wasn't hers either and it was too hard to voice so she gave him the smile that said keep away.

She washed in the one shower available for parents, an ancient old thing at the edge of the parents' room, and pulled on the awful pyjamas her parents had brought and climbed into the roller bed at seven-thirty p.m., grateful that the lights were already down. But she found out that Courtney was right—it was far too noisy to sleep. When she was woken again by a nurse doing obs around ten and by a baby coughing in the next cot, she wandered down to the parents' room to get a drink and nearly jumped out of her skin to see Dominic sprawled out on a sofa.

He'd changed out of his suit, which was rare for him,

and was wearing scrubs, and looked, for once, almost scruffy—unshaven and the hair that fell so neatly wasn't falling at all neatly now.

'Good God.' He peeled open his eyes when she walked in.

'Don't you judge me by my pyjamas,' Bridgette said, heading over to the kitchenette. 'I was just thinking you weren't looking so hot yourself—what happened to that smooth-looking man I met?'

'You did.' Dominic rolled his eyes and sort of heaved himself up. He sat there and she handed him a coffee without asking if he wanted one. 'Thanks.' He looked over at her. 'Bridgette, why didn't you say you were worried about Harry?'

'And worry you too? I haven't been ignoring things. I reported my concerns a few months ago, but I think I might have made things worse. I thought she was on drugs, that that was why she was always disappearing, but they did a screen and she's not. He's always been well looked after. Even now, he's just missed a couple of baths.' It was so terribly hard to explain it. 'They lived with me for nearly nine months, right up till Harry's first birthday.' She missed the frown on Dominic's face. 'And it was me who got up at night, did most of the laundry and bathing and changing. I just somehow know that she isn't coping on her own. Which is why I drop everything when she needs help. I don't really want to test my theories as to what might happen to Harry...'

'You could have told me this.'

'Not really holiday-romance stuff.'

'You've not exactly given us a chance to be anything more.'

'It's not always men who don't want a relationship,' Bridgette said. 'I always knew you were going back to Sydney and that I would stay here. It suited me better to keep it as it was.

'How was your weekend?' she asked, frantically changing the subject. 'How was Chris?'

'Great,' Dominic said. 'It's his twenty-first birthday this weekend, so he's getting all ready for that. Gangster party!' He gave a wry smile. 'I'm flying back up for that.'

'Have fun!' She grinned and didn't add that she'd love to be his moll, and he didn't say that he'd love it if she could be, and then his phone rang.

He checked it but didn't answer and Bridgette stood there, her cheeks darkening as Arabella's image flashed up on the screen.

'Well...' She turned away, tipped her coffee down the sink.

'Bridgette...'

'It doesn't matter anyway.'

Except it did.

He had seen Arabella—she'd found out he was back for the weekend and had come around. He'd opened the door to her and had surprised himself with how little he'd felt.

It would be easier to have felt something, to have gone back to his perfect life and pretend he believed she hadn't meant what she'd said about Chris. Easier than what he was contemplating.

'Bridgette, she came over. We had a coffee.'

'I don't want to hear it.' She really didn't, but she was angry too. It had been the day from hell and was turning into the night from hell too. 'It's been less than a week…' She didn't understand how it was so easy for some people to get over things. She was still desperately trying to get over Paul: not him exactly, more what he had done. And in some arguments you said things that perhaps weren't true, but you said them anyway.

'You're all the bloody same!'

'Hey!' He would not take that. 'I told you, we had coffee.'

'Sure.'

'And I told you, don't ever compare me to him.' He was sick of being compared to a man he hadn't met, a man who had caused her nothing but pain. 'I told you I'd have had this sorted.'

'Sure you would have.'

And in some arguments you said things that perhaps were true, but should never be said. 'And,' Dominic added, regretting it the second he said it, 'I'd never have slept with your sister.'

Her face looked as if it had been dunked in a bucket of bleach, the colour just stripped out of it. 'And you look after her kid—' Dominic could hardly contain the fury he felt on her behalf '—after the way she treated you?'

'How?' She had never been so angry, ashamed that

he knew. 'Did Vince tell you? Did Jasmine tell him?' She was mortified. 'Does the whole hospital know?'

'I know,' Dominic said, 'because most people talk about their break-ups, most people share that bit at the start, but instead you keep yourself closed. I worked it out,' he explained. 'Courtney and Paul both happened to move out around Harry's first birthday…'

'Just leave it.'

'Why?'

'Because…' she said. 'I kicked my sister out, which meant I effectively kicked my nephew out, and look what it's been like since then.'

'Bridgette—'

'No.' She did not want his comfort, neither did she want his rationale, nor did she want to stand here and explain to him the hurt. 'Are you going to stay here? Tell me we should fight for Harry?' She just looked at him and gave a mocking laugh. 'You don't want kids of your own, let alone your girlfriend's nephew.' She shook her head. 'Your holiday fling's nephew.'

And he didn't want it, Dominic realised, and did that make him shallow? He did not want the drama that was Courtney and he did not want a woman who simply refused to talk about what was clearly so important.

'I'm going back,' Bridgette said. 'You can take your phone call now.'

And two minutes later he did.

She knew because she heard the buzz of his phone as she stood in the corridor outside, trying to compose herself enough to head out to the ward.

She heard his low voice through the wall and there was curious relief as she walked away.

She was as lousy at one-night stands as she was at holiday romances.

There was only one guy on her mind right now, and he stood in the cot, waiting patiently for her return.

'Hey, Harry.' She picked him up and gave him a cuddle, and as Dominic walked past she deliberately didn't look up; instead she concentrated on her nephew, pulling back the sheets and laying him down.

It felt far safer hiding behind him.

CHAPTER TWELVE

COURTNEY rang in the morning to see how Harry's night had been and said that she'd be in soon. Bridgette went with Harry for his hearing test and then surprisingly Raymond, the ENT consultant, came and saw him on the ward. 'Glue ear,' Raymond informed her. 'His hearing is significantly down in both ears, which would explain the speech delay. It can make them very miserable. We'll put him on the waiting list for grommets.' It might explain the temper tantrums too, Bridgette thought, kicking herself for overreaction.

By late afternoon, when Courtney still hadn't arrived and Harry was dozing, Bridgette slipped away and up to Maternity, even though she'd rung to explain things. Rita *was* nice and surprisingly understanding.

'We're having a family meeting tomorrow,' Bridgette explained. 'I really am sorry to let you down. I'll do nights just as soon as I can.'

'Don't be sorry—of course you can't work,' Rita said. 'You need to get this sorted.'

Though her family seemed convinced there was nothing to sort, and as Bridgette walked onto the ward, she could see Courtney sitting on the chair beside Harry, all smiles. She was playing the doting mother or 'mother of the year', as Jasmine would have said. Dominic was examining Harry's new neighbor, young Roman, and Bridgette stood and spoke to Tony for a moment. Harry, annoyed that Bridgette wasn't coming straight over, stood up, put up his leg and with two fat fists grabbed the cot, annoyed that with the barrier he couldn't get over it—he was indeed a climber, it was duly noted, not just by the nurses but by Courtney. And Bridgette wondered if she was going mad. Maybe there was nothing wrong with her sister's parenting and she, Bridgette, had been talking nonsense all along.

'Thanks so much for staying last night,' Courtney said. 'I was just completely exhausted. I'd been up all night with him teething. Mum said that that can give them the most terrible rash…and then when he climbed out, when I heard him fall…'

'No problem,' Bridgette said. 'ENT came down and saw him.'

'Yes, the nurse told me,' Courtney said, and rather pointedly unzipped her bag and took out her pyjamas. Brand-new ones, Bridgette noticed. Courtney was very good at cleaning up her act when required. 'You should get some rest, Bridgette.' Courtney looked up and her eyes held a challenge that Bridgette knew she simply couldn't win. 'You look exhausted. I'm sure I'll see you at the family meeting and you will have plenty to say about his nappy rash and that I put him to bed without washing him to Aunty Bridgette's satisfaction.'

Dominic saw Courtney's smirk after Bridgette had kissed Harry and left.

He spoke for a moment with Tony, told him he would see him tomorrow. And Dominic, a man who always stayed late, left early for once and met Bridgette at her car. It wouldn't start, because in her rush to get to see Harry last night, she'd left her lights on.

'Just leave me.' She was crying, furious, enraged, and did not want him to see.

'I'll give you a lift.'

'So I can sort out a flat battery tomorrow! So I can take a bus to the meeting.' She even laughed. 'They'll think I'm the one with the problem. She's in there all kisses and smiles and new pyjamas. She'll be taking him home this time tomorrow.'

'She'll blow herself out soon,' Dominic said.

'And it will start all over again.' She turned the key one last hopeless time and of course nothing happened.

'Come on,' Dominic said. 'I'll take you home.'

They drove for a while in silence. Dominic never carried tissues, but very graciously he gave her the little bit of silk he used to clean his sunglasses. With little other option, she took it.

'I do get it.'

'Sure!'

'No, I really do,' Dominic said. 'For three years after Chris was born it was row after row. My father wanted him gone—he never came out and said it, didn't have the guts, and I can tell you the day it changed, I can tell you the minute it changed.' He snapped his fingers as he drove. 'My mother told him to get out because Chris wasn't going anywhere. She told him if he stayed in *her* home then he followed her rules.' They were at the roundabout and she wanted him to indicate, wanted to go back to his place, but instead he drove straight on. 'She got her fire back.' He even grinned as he remembered his trophy-wife mother suddenly swearing and cursing in Spanish. He remembered the drama as she'd filled his father's suitcases and hurled them out, followed by his golf clubs, as she picked up Chris and walked back in. 'I really want you to listen, Bridgette. You need to think about what you want before you go into that meeting. You will need to sort out what you're prepared to offer or what you're prepared to accept, not for the next week or for the next month but maybe the next seventeen years—you need to do the best for yourself.'

'I'm trying my best.'

'Bridgette, you're not listening to me. My mum could have gone along with Dad—she could have had a far easier life if she hadn't been a single mum bringing up a special-needs child. Chris could have been slotted into a home. Instead he went to one when he was eighteen, to a sheltered home with friends, and my mother did it so that he'd have a life, a real one. She did not want him to have to start over in thirty years or so when she was gone. She thought out everything and that included looking out for herself. What I said was you have to do the best for you—you have to look out for yourself in this…'

Dominic gritted his teeth in frustration as he could see that she didn't understand what he meant and knew that he would have to make things clear. 'The best thing that could happen is that Courtney suddenly becomes responsible and gets well suddenly, becomes responsible and looks after Harry properly—and we both know that's not going to happen. Now, you can run yourself ragged chasing after Courtney, living your life ready to step in, or you can work out the life you want and what you're prepared to do.'

She still didn't get it.

'Bridgette, she could have another baby. She could be pregnant right now!' She closed her eyes. It was something she thought about late at night sometimes, that this could be ongoing, that there could be another Harry, or a little Harriet, or twins. 'Come away with me on Saturday,' he said. 'Come for the weekend, just to see...'

'What about Arabella?'

'What about her?' Dominic said. 'I told her last night the same thing I told her when we had coffee on Saturday. We're through. And I've told her that I'm blocking her from my phone.' He knew he was pushing it, but this time he said it. 'You could be my moll!'

'I've got other things to think about right now.'

'Yes,' he said as he pulled up at her door. 'You do.'

And she didn't ask him in, and neither did he expect her to, but he did pull her into his arms and kiss her.

'Don't...' She pulled her head back.

'It's a kiss.'

'A kiss that's going nowhere,' she said. 'I'm not very good at one-night stands, in case you didn't work it out. And I really think the holiday is over...'

'Why won't you let anyone in?'

'Because I can't stand being hurt again,' Bridgette admitted. 'And you and I...' She was honest. 'Well, it's going to hurt, whatever way you look at it.' And she did open up a bit, said what she'd thought all those days ago. 'My life's not exactly geared to hopping on planes.'

'You only need to hop on one,' Dominic said, and he was offering her the biggest out, an escape far more permanent than her flat.

'Think about it,' he said.

'I can't.'

'Just think about it,' Dominic said. 'Please.'

He wished her all the very best for the next day, then drove down the road and pulled out his phone.

'It's Wednesday,' Chris said. 'Why are you ringing me on a Wednesday?'

'I'm just ringing you,' Dominic said. 'It doesn't only have to be on a Friday.'

'It's about Bridgette?' Chris said, and Dominic couldn't help a wry grin that he was ringing his brother for advice. 'The one with the baby.'

'It's not her baby,' Dominic said, because he'd explained about Harry as they'd walked along the beach.

'But she loves him.'

'Yep.'

'Well, why can't they come and live here?'

'Because it's not going to happen,' Dominic said. 'His mum loves him too.'

'And you can't stay there because you're coming over on Saturday,' Chris reminded him. 'For my birthday.' He heard the silence. 'You said you would.'

'I did.'

'See you on Saturday,' Chris said.

And Dominic did know how Bridgette felt—he was quite sure of that, because he felt it then too, thought of his brother all dressed up with his friends and his disappointment if *he* wasn't there. He thought of Bridgette facing it alone.

'You are coming?' Chris pushed.

'You know I am,' Dominic said. 'I'll see you then.'

'Are you still going to ring me on Friday?' Chris said, because he loathed a change in routine.

'Of course.'

CHAPTER THIRTEEN

'Hi, Tony!' Dominic said the next morning. 'Hi, Roman.' He tried not to look at Harry, who was watching him from the next cot. He'd seen all the Joyce family head off to the conference room, Courtney marching in front, the parents, as Bridgette would say, joined at the hip, and an exhausted-looking Bridgette bringing up the rear.

'Is this your last morning?' Tony said, because it was common knowledge now that he was leaving.

'No,' Dominic said. 'I'm on call tonight.'

'Well, if I don't see you I just want to be sure to thank you for everything with Roman and Esperanza and Maria,' Tony said.

'You're very welcome,' Dominic said. 'How are they both doing?'

'They're amazing,' Tony replied. 'Maria's a bit torn of course. She wants to be here more, but she doesn't want to bring Esperanza here…'

'Better not to,' Dominic said. He finished examining Roman and told his father he was pleased with his progress and that hopefully by Monday Roman would be home.

'It will be nice to have a full house again,' Tony said. 'Thought we couldn't have children—three goes at IVF for the twins, then Roman surprises us and now Esperanza!'

Dominic carried on with his round and tried not to think what was going on in the conference room, tried not to think about the offer he had made last night.

Bridgette couldn't *not* think about it.

She had pondered it all night, had been thinking about it in the car park for the hour she had waited to sort out her battery, and she was feeling neither hopeful nor particularly patient with her family. She sat there and the meeting went backwards and forwards, like some endless round of table tennis, getting nowhere. She listened to Courtney making excuses and promises again, watched her parents, who so badly wanted to believe their youngest daughter's words. She listened to the social worker, who, Bridgette realised, was very willing for Harry's aunt to support her sister—and of course she didn't blame them; but she realised that no one was ever going to tell her that she was doing too much. She had to say it herself.

'This is what I'm prepared to do.' She looked around the room and then at her sister; she took over the bat and slammed out her serve and said it again, but a bit louder this time.

'This is what I'm prepared to do,' she repeated. And when she had the room's attention, she spoke. 'Harry is to attend daycare here at the hospital, whether he's staying with you or being babysat by me—there has to be some consistency in his life. I will pay for his place if that is a concern you have, but he has to be there Monday to Friday from now on.' She looked at the social worker. 'If I can get a place again.'

'I can sort that out.' She nodded. 'We have a couple of places reserved for special allocations.' Bridgette turned to her parents. 'Mum, if I'm on a late shift or working nights and Harry is in my care, for whatever reason, you have to collect him or stay overnight. I can't always work early shifts.'

'You know we do our best!' Betty said. 'Of course we'll pick him up.'

Bridgette looked over at the caseworker, who gave a bit of a nod that told her to go on. 'He's due to have surgery…' She was finding a voice and she knew what to do with it, was grateful for Dominic's advice because she'd heeded it. 'He's on the waiting list for grommets and if that comes up while he's in my care I want to be able to go ahead. I want written permission obtained so that when Harry is in my care, or at any time I'm concerned, I can speak to doctors and I can take him to appointments. And I want—'

'I don't want him in daycare,' Courtney chimed in. 'I've told you—I'm not going anywhere. I decide what treatment he has and who he sees.'

'That's fine.' Bridgette looked at her sister. 'You have every right to refuse what I'm offering. But I can't stand aside any more. If you don't accept my conditions…'

It was the hardest thing she would ever say and could only be said if it was meant. Whether he was serious or not, she was incredibly grateful for Dominic's offer last night. 'Then you can deal with it. I'll move to Sydney.'

'Bridgette!' Her mum almost stood up. 'You know you don't mean that.'

'But I do—because I can't live like this. I can't watch Harry being passed around like a parcel. So it's either you accept my terms or I'm moving to Sydney.'

'You said you'd always be there for me.' Courtney started to cry, only this time it didn't move Bridgette. 'You promised...'

'Well, that makes us both liars, then,' Bridgette said. 'Because I can remember you saying exactly the same to Harry the day he was born.'

'Bridgette.' Her mum was trying to be firm, to talk sense into her sensible daughter. 'You know you're not going anywhere. Why Sydney?'

'I've met someone,' Bridgette said. 'And he's from there.' Betty had seen the happy couple, that were back as Bridgette's screensaver, when she'd had a nose in her daughter's spare room, had tutted at the two faces smiling back, and she had a terrible feeling her daughter might actually mean what she was saying.

'You love Courtney...' Maurice broke in.

'I'm not sure if I do,' Bridgette said, and she truly wasn't sure that she did. 'I honestly don't know that I do.'

'You love Harry.' Betty triumphed.

'Yes, I do. So if she wants my help then she can have

it, but those are my conditions and she needs to know that any time I think Harry is at risk I will speak up.' She walked out of the meeting because she had nothing left to say. It had to be up to Courtney. She walked over to the ward and saw Harry sitting in his cot, building his bricks. She let down the cot side and held out her arms. She had meant every word she had said in that room, had convinced herself of it last night, but there was a piece of her that was hidden apart, a piece of her that no one must ever see, because as she picked up her nephew and buried her face in his curls, she knew she could never leave him. They just had to believe that she might.

Dominic watched her cuddling Harry and he wanted to go over, to find out what was happening, but instead he picked up the phone.

It was the longest morning, even though he had plenty to do, but he could not get involved, or be seen to be getting involved, which surely she knew, but still he felt like a bastard.

'Do you want me to give Harry his lunch?' Jennifer, one of the nurses, offered. 'You can go to the canteen, maybe have a little break?'

'I'm fine,' Bridgette said. 'They're still in the meeting. I'll give him his lunch and then—' she took a deep breath '—I'm going home.'

'Jennifer!' Dominic's voice barked across the ward. 'Can you hold on to Harry's lunch for now, please, and keep him nil by mouth until I've spoken to his mum?'

'What's going on?' Bridgette frowned.

'I've no idea,' Jennifer admitted. 'Wait there and I'll find out.' And she went over and spoke to Dominic, but instead of coming back and informing Bridgette, Jennifer headed off to the conference room. The group was just coming out and it was clear that Courtney had been crying but, along with Jennifer, they all headed back inside.

'What's going on?' She went up to him.

'Someone's coming down to speak to his mother.'

'Dominic!' She couldn't believe he'd do this to her.

'I'd go home now if I were you.'

'You know I can't.'

'Yes,' he said. 'You can.' She looked at him, met those lovely black eyes and somehow she trusted him. 'Go home,' he said. 'I'm sure you've got an awful lot to do.' She just stood there. 'Maybe tidy that bedroom, young lady.'

And she trusted him, she really did, but she knew he was leaving tomorrow, knew that right now he was saying goodbye.

'Go,' he said, 'and when she calls, don't come back.' He gave her a small wink. 'You only answer if it's me.'

'I can't do that. I can't just leave him.'

'You can,' he said. 'I'm here.'

CHAPTER FOURTEEN

WHEN her phone rang fifteen minutes later, she was driving, just approaching the roundabout, and she didn't pull over so she could take the call, as she usually would have. She didn't indicate when she saw that it was Courtney and instead she drove straight on.

Dominic was there.

She felt as if Dominic was there in the car beside her.

It rang again and this time it was her mum. Still, she ignored it.

Then it rang again as she arrived home and she sat at her computer before answering.

'Oh. Hi, Mum!'

'You didn't pick up.'

'I was driving.'

'Where are you?' she asked. 'I thought you'd gone down to the canteen.'

'I'm at home,' she said, as if she was breathing normally, as if home was the natural place she should be.

'Well, you need to get here!' Bridgette stared at her screensaver and tried to shut out the sound of her mother's panic. 'The doctors are here and they say

Harry needs an operation. There's a space that's opened up on the list and they want him to have an operation!' she said again really loudly.

'What operation?'

'He has to have surgery on his ears, and if she doesn't sign the consent, he'll go back on the list...' She could hear the panic in her mother's voice. 'Bridgette, you need to get here. You know what your sister's like— Courtney can't make a decision. She's gone off!'

'It's a tiny operation, Mum. It could do him an awful lot of good.'

'Bridgette, please, they've added him to the list this evening. Courtney's going crazy!'

'Mum...' Bridgette looked into Dominic's eyes as she spoke, and then into her own and wanted to be her again, wanted to be the woman who smiled and laughed and lived. 'It's up to Courtney to give consent. If not, he can go on the waiting list and wait, but it would be a shame, because his hearing is really bad.' She stood up. 'I've got to go, Mum. I've got things to do. Give Harry a big kiss from his aunty Bridgette. Tell him that I'll bring him in a nice present for being brave.' And she rang off.

She took the phone into the bathroom with her and because she didn't have any bubble bath, she used shampoo, put on a load of washing while she was waiting for the bath to fill and every time the phone rang, she did not pick up.

And then she did her hair, straightened it and put on blusher and lipstick too, even though she knew Dominic was on call and wouldn't be coming round. Then when her phone finally fell silent, she tackled her bedroom, worked out how to use a stud finder and put up the shelves that had been sitting in cardboard for way too long. Then the phone bleeped a text and it was from Dominic.

She took a breath and read it.

Op went well—he's back on ward and having a drink. Home tomoz.

She felt the tension seep out of her.

Should I come in now?

She was quite sure what the response would be, that he'd tell her to stay put, that Courtney was there and to let her deal with it, but as she waited for his reply, there was a knock at the door and when her phone bleeped he didn't say what she'd thought he might.

No, stay put—your mum's with him.

She wanted to know what was happening so badly. She had this stupid vision it was him as, phone in hand, she opened the door.

Instead it was her father and Courtney.

CHAPTER FIFTEEN

IT WAS a long night and he was glad when it hit six a.m. and there were just a couple of hours to go.

'Cot Four.' Karan, the night nurse, looked up from the baby she was feeding. 'I'll be there in a minute.'

'I'll be fine,' Dominic said, and headed in.

He took off his jacket, glanced again at Harry, who sitting there staring, and then proceeded to wash his hands. When he turned around, Harry was smiling. Dominic couldn't help himself from looking at the pull-out bed beside him, relieved to see that Betty was there.

He didn't know what had happened.

He'd heard the explosions from the fuse he'd lit when he'd asked for a favour from Raymond and a certain blue-eyed theatre nurse, but he'd been up and down between here and NICU and had never caught up as to what had really gone on.

He smiled back at Harry and then headed over to the cot opposite him, carefully examining the baby who was causing concern, pleased with her progress.

'How's Harry Joyce?' he asked Karan. He had every right to enquire as he was the paediatrician on call that night and Karan wouldn't know that he had stepped aside from the case.

'He's doing well.' Karan smiled. 'You could see the difference in him almost as soon as he came back from Theatre. He must have been struggling with his ears for a while. He's much more smiley and he's making a few more noises, even had a little dance in his cot. He's off home in the morning to the care of Mum.' She pulled out a notebook. 'Hold on a moment. Sorry, he's home with his aunt tomorrow. There was a big case meeting today apparently. Lots of drama.' She rolled her eyes. 'I haven't had a chance to read the notes yet.' She stood up and collected the folder and put it in front of him. 'Should make interesting reading.'

Karan walked back to the nursery to put down the baby she had been feeding and Dominic sat there, tempted to read the notes, to find out all that had gone on. It would be so easy to. 'So this is your last morning.' Tony stopped by the desk, just as Dominic went to open the folder. Tony had been up and used the parent showers before all the others did, was dressed and ready for when Abuela came in.

'It is,' Dominic said. 'I'm flying to Sydney this afternoon.'

'Well, thanks again.' Tony stifled a yawn.

'You must be exhausted.' It was Dominic who extended the conversation.

'Ah, but it's Saturday,' Tony said. 'I'm going home to sleep. That's if the twins and Esperanza let me.'

'You've got a lot on your plate,' Dominic said, but Tony just grinned.

'Better than an empty plate.'

Dominic stood up and shook Tony's hand and when Tony had gone he stepped away from the notes. Bridgette didn't deserve her ex reading up on her private life. If he wanted to know, he should ask her.

CHAPTER SIXTEEN

'HARRY!' She took him into her arms and wrapped him in a hug, truly delighted to have him home. 'I've got a surprise for you.' And she carried him in to what had been her study as well as Courtney's room and spare room. The cot had been folded and put away (well, it had been neatly put away under Bridgette's bed till she hauled it to the charity shop on Monday) and the bed that had been under a pile of ironing now had a little safety rail, new bedding and a child's bedside light. There were new curtains, a new stash of bricks in a toy box and an intercom was all set up.

'You've been busy,' her mum said when she saw Harry's new bedroom. 'Isn't he a bit young for a bed?'

'Well, at least he can't climb out of it. I'll just have to make sure I close the bedroom door or he'll be roaming the place at night.'

'It looks lovely.' Betty smiled at her daughter. 'I'm sorry that we haven't been much help.'

'You have been,' Bridgette said, because she couldn't stand her parents' guilt and they had probably been doing their best.

'No,' her mum corrected. 'We've been very busy burying our heads in the sand, trying to pretend that everything was okay, when clearly it wasn't. We're going to be around for you much more, and Harry too.'

'And Courtney?' Bridgette watched her mother's lips purse. 'She needs your support more than anyone.'

'We're paying for rehab,' Betty said.

'It's not going to be an instant fix,' Bridgette said, but she didn't go on. She could see how tired her parents looked, not from recent days but from recent years. 'We can get through this, Mum,' Bridgette said, 'if we all help each other.'

'What about you, though?' It was the first time her father had really spoken since they'd arrived. 'What about that young man of yours, the one in Sydney?'

'Let's not talk about that, Dad.' It hurt too much to explore at the moment. It was something she wanted to examine and think about in private—when she had calmed down fully, when she was safely alone, then she would deal with all she had lost for her sister, again. But her father was finally stepping up, as she had asked him to, and not burying his head in the sand as he usually did—which was a good thing, though perhaps not right now.

'We need to discuss it, Bridgette.' He sat down and looked her square in the eye. 'We didn't know you were serious about someone.'

'It never really got a chance to be serious,' Bridgette said.

'We should have had Harry more.'

Yes, you bloody should have, she wanted to say, but that wasn't fair on them, because really it wasn't so much Harry who had got in the way; it had been her too—she hadn't wanted a relationship, hadn't wanted to let another close. 'Things will be different now,' Bridgette said instead.

'You could go away for the odd weekend now and then…' her dad said. And teeny little wisps of hope seemed to rise in her stomach, but she doused them—it was simply too late.

After her parents had gone, Bridgette made Harry some lunch and then cuddled him on the sofa. She did exactly what she'd tried not to—she let herself love him. Of course she always had, but now she didn't hold back. She kissed his lovely curls and then smiled into his sleepy eyes and told him that everything was going to be okay, that Mum was getting well, that she would always be here for him.

And she would be.

It was a relief to acknowledge it, to step back from the conflict and ignore the push and pull as to who was wrong and who was right—she wasn't young, free and single, she had a very young heart to take care of.

'You wait there,' she said to Harry as the doorbell rang. They were curled up, watching a DVD. Harry was nearly ready to be put down for his afternoon nap and Bridgette was rather thinking that she might just have one too.

'Dominic!' He was the last person she was expecting to see, though maybe not. She knew that he did care about her, knew he would want to know how she was.

He wasn't a bastard unfortunately. It would be so much easier to paint him as one—they just had different lives, that was all.

'I thought you had a gangster party to be at!'

'I've got a couple of hours till the plane.' He was dressed in a black suit. 'I've just got to put on a tie and glasses—Mum's sent me a fake gun, though I'd better not risk it on the plane.' His smile faded a touch. 'I wanted to see how the meeting had gone...'

'Didn't you hear?' Bridgette said, quite sure the whole hospital must have heard by now. 'Or you could have read the notes.' He saw her tight smile, knew that Bridgette, more than anyone, would have hated things being played out on such a public stage—it was her workplace, after all. She opened the door. 'Come in.'

He was surprised to see how well she looked, or perhaps *surprised* wasn't the right word—he was in awe. Her hair swished behind her as she walked, all glossy and shiny as it had been that first night, and he could smell her perfume. She looked bright and breezy and not what he had expected.

Back perhaps to the woman he had met.

'I didn't want to read the notes,' Dominic said, walking through to the lounge. 'Though I heard that Harry had come home with you...' His voice trailed off as he saw Harry lying on the lounge, staring warily at him. 'Hi, there, Harry.'

Harry just stared.

'What happened to the nice smile that you used to give me when I came on the ward?' Dominic asked, but Harry did not react.

'Do you want a drink?' Bridgette offered, though perhaps it was more for herself. She wanted a moment or two in the kitchen alone, just to gather her thoughts before they had to do what she had been dreading since the night they had first met—officially say goodbye. 'Or some lunch perhaps?' She looked at the clock. 'A late lunch.'

'I won't have anything,' Dominic said. 'I'll have something on the plane and there will be loads to eat tonight. A coffee would be great, though.' It had already been a very long day. 'You've changed the living room.'

'I've given Harry his own bedroom,' Bridgette said, 'and I quite like the idea of having a desk in here.' And she could breathe as his eyes scanned the room, because, yes, she'd changed the screensaver again. Now it was a photo of Harry and his mum, a nice photo, so that Harry could see Courtney often.

'It looks nice,' he said as Bridgette headed out to the kitchen and Dominic stood, more than a little awkward, nervous by what he had to say. He wasn't used to nerves in the least—he always had a level head. He said what was needed and rarely any more. He took off his jacket and looked for somewhere to hang it, settling on the back of Bridgette's study chair. Turning around he saw Harry smile, half-asleep, lying on the sofa. He gave Dominic the biggest grin and then closed his eyes.

'What are you smiling at?' Bridgette asked Dominic

as she walked back in the room carrying two mugs and saw him standing there grinning.

'Harry,' Dominic answered, still smiling. 'That nephew of yours really does love routine.' He saw a little flutter of panic dart across her eyes, realised that she thought perhaps he was there to tell her something. He understood she had an overactive imagination where Harry was concerned. 'He smiles when I take my jacket off. I've just realised that now. Whenever I came onto the ward at night he watched me and frowned and then suddenly he gave me a smile. I could never work out why.'

'It's what you do.' Bridgette grinned, because she'd noticed it too. 'Before you wash your hands. I don't think I've ever seen you examine a patient with your jacket on. Funny that Harry noticed,' she mused. 'I guess when your world's chaotic you look for routine in any place you can find it.'

'Well, it doesn't look very chaotic to me. You've done great,' Dominic said. He waited while she put Harry down for his very first nap in his big-boy bed—Bridgette surprised that he didn't protest, just curled up and went straight to sleep. She gently closed the door. 'So,' he asked when she came back in, 'how did the meeting go?'

'You really didn't read the notes?' She was a little bit embarrassed and awkward that he might be here to question her *plans* to follow him to Sydney, because even though she hadn't given his name, if Dominic had read the notes, the indication would be clear. 'Because I was just bluffing…'

'Bluffing?' Dominic frowned. 'About what?'

'Getting a life.' Bridgette gave a wry smile. 'Moving to Sydney.'

'You said that at the meeting?'

'Oh, I said that and a whole lot more,' Bridgette admitted. 'I did what you suggested. I spent the time before the meeting trying to work out rules I could live with. I said that he had to attend daycare, but I had to be able to take him to a doctor if needed and to take him for any procedures if Courtney wasn't available. I said that Mum and Dad had to help more if Courtney wasn't around…that I was through looking out for Courtney, that I was only on Harry side.'

'You said all that?' He put down his coffee and took her hand. 'Well done. How did Courtney take it?'

'I didn't stay to find out,' she said. 'I just left the meeting. I hope you don't mind, but I said that I'd been seeing someone, that he lived in Sydney—it just made it seem more real to them. It made them believe that I would leave if I told them I had somebody who wanted me to go with them.'

'You did.'

And she'd no doubt cry about it later—but not now. 'Thank you,' she said. 'For getting him squeezed onto the list.' He gave a frown. 'I know you must have…'

'Well, I thought it might buy another night before she dropped her act, and when you came out of the meeting…' He looked at her, didn't want to tell her how hard it had been to step aside, to not be in that room, not as a doctor but sitting beside her. 'I figured she might drop it a little quicker if you weren't there to sort it out for her.'

'Well, it worked. She fell apart when she had to actually make a decision and it all came out. It isn't drugs—it's alcohol. She's just been slowly falling apart since I kicked her out.'

'It would have happened wherever she was,' Dominic said. 'It was probably going on here...'

And she nodded because, yes, it had been a bit.

And she thought of Harry's birthday that should have been about cordial and cake but instead her sister had chosen to party on—and so too had Paul.

'I hate what she did,' Bridgette said. 'I just couldn't have her stay after that.'

'Of course you couldn't.' Dominic thought for a moment, knew he had to be very careful with what he said. Certainly he was less than impressed with Courtney, but even if people didn't like it at times, he was always honest. 'But I think it's something you have to move on from. She's clearly made a lot of mistakes, but if you're going to be angry with anyone—' he looked at Bridgette, who so deserved to be angry '—then I think it should be with him.'

'It was both of them.'

'He took advantage.'

'Oh, and you never have—' She didn't get to finish.

'Never,' Dominic said. 'Not once. My sexual résumé might not be impressive to you, but...' He shook his head. 'Nope, what he did was wrong, and however awful your sister has been, I bet she's been trying to douse an awful lot of guilt about her treatment of you.'

Bridgette nodded. 'She's gone to rehab. It's three months and Mum and Dad are paying. She came over last night with Dad and said she was terrified of letting everybody down…which she may well do, so I'm not getting my hopes up, but I've made a decision to be here for Harry.' She saw him glance at his watch.

'Sorry, I'm rattling on…'

'It's not that. I have to leave in an hour. I can't miss that plane.' He took a deep breath. Really, he was finding this incredibly difficult—she seemed fine, better than fine, as if she wasn't missing him at all.

Wouldn't miss him.

But he would miss her.

Which forced him to speak on.

'What you said about Sydney, about having someone who wanted you there, you weren't exaggerating, Bridgette.' He took her hand and her fingers curled around his. Inside her, those little wisps of hope uncurled too, and it was so wonderful to see him, to have him sitting beside her, to know this was hard for him. 'I want this to work too. I just can't not be there for Chris,' he said.

'I was very unfair to you—it was ridiculous that I couldn't even get away for a single weekend, and it is about to change. I spoke to my parents this morning so maybe I can get away now and then, maybe I could come up on days off, or some of them.' She stared at her fingers being squeezed by his, and she wished he would jump in, would say that was what he wanted, but he let her speak on. 'And who knows what might happen in the future? Courtney might get well—'

'You're not going to leave Harry,' Dominic cut in. 'You might be able to convince them, but you'll never convince me. You're not going anywhere while Harry's so little.'

'No.' She could feel tears trickling down at the back of her throat and nose. She'd been so determined not to cry, to do this with dignity, to let him go with grace. She could see the second hand on his watch rapidly moving around, gobbling up the little time that they had left. 'No, I'm not going anywhere. Well, not long term.'

'And I don't think the odd weekend is going to suffice.'

'No,' she said, because it wouldn't be enough.

And they could talk in the time they had left, but what was the point? Bridgette realised there was no solution to be had, so instead of tears she gave him a smile, not a false one, a real one. And she put herself first for once, was completely selfish and utterly indulgent and just a little bit wild, because as he went to speak she interrupted him.

'Have we got time for a quickie before you go?'

'We need to talk,' Dominic pointed out.

'I don't need anything,' she cut in. 'I know what I want, though.'

And he wasn't going to argue with that.

He didn't know what he had expected to find when

he came over, how he'd expected her to be when he'd knocked at the door, but as always she'd amazed him. Then, as she opened the bedroom door, she amazed him all over again.

'Wow.' As he walked into her bedroom he let out a low whistle. 'You've got a carpet!'

'I know!'

'I'm impressed.' He looked at the shelves and politely didn't comment about five holes she had made in the wall—because he wouldn't know how to find a stud either.

'Just you wait.' She was at his shirt as she spoke. He pulled off her T-shirt and undid her bra and it slowed things down undressing each other, so they stripped off for themselves and then Bridgette peeled back the duvet.

'You get first feel…'

'Of what?' he asked, hands roaming her body, but she peeled off his hands and placed them on the bedding.

'Of my million-thread-count sheets. I was saving them for best…'

Which he was, Bridgette knew that, because he lay on the sheets and wriggled around and made appreciative noises, and then he pulled her in and kissed her.

'I want to feel them now,' she said.

So she lay on the sheets and wriggled around and made appreciative noises too.

And then he kissed her again.

'Don't let me fall asleep after,' Dominic said.

'After what?' She frowned, naked in his arms. 'If you really think you can just come here and have sex…'

She made him laugh and she loved making him laugh. She loved the Dominic others so rarely saw. When it was just the two or them, the austere, remote man seemed to leave—and he understood her humour and matched it. He made her laugh too, turned those cold black eyes into puppy-dog ones. 'I don't want sex, Bridgette. I just want to hold you.'

'Oh, no.' They were laughing so much they would wake up Harry.

'I just want to lie next to you…' he crooned.

'No.'

He straddled her.

'I just want to talk,' he said.

'No talking,' she begged.

It was a whole new realm for Dominic, like swimming in the ocean after a lifetime doing laps in a pool.

He did not know that you could laugh so much on a Saturday afternoon, that she could laugh even now as she lost him.

As she loved him.

It was a different kiss from any they had tasted before, a different feeling from any they had ever felt.

He kissed her slowly and more tenderly and *he* let himself love her—smothered her, physically, mentally, buried her and pressed her against her very best sheets. He wrapped his arms under her and drove into her till she wanted to scream, and she pressed her mouth to his chest and held on for dear life. She didn't know what the future held and she couldn't control it anyway, so she lived in the moment, and what a lovely moment it was. And she could cry afterwards and not be embarrassed or sorry.

It was a wonderful afternoon, and nothing like the one he had intended, the most delicious surprise. His head was spinning that she could love him like that when she considered it over between them.

'I've made some decisions too.' He took a deep breath, dived out of the pool and into the ocean, where it was rough and choppy but exhilarating and wild. 'When I went to resign this week, when I told them I wouldn't be back, I was offered a job.' He looked at her grey eyes that were for the first time today wary. 'Here.'

She felt little wisps of hope rising again, then she moved to douse them. They were guilty wisps. Surely this was wrong.

'I'm going to ring on Monday and take it.'

'You want to work in Sydney, though. Your family's there, your friends, Chris. You always wanted to work there. It's your goal.'

'Goals change,' Dominic said.

'What about your brother?'

'I'm not going to say anything to him yet,' Dominic said. 'It's his birthday.'

He shook his head, because he couldn't do it to Chris this weekend. 'Look, the job doesn't start for a month and I'm taking the time off. I'm not working. You and I will spend some proper time together, do some of that talking you so readily avoid, and we'll see how I go with Harry…'

'You could have told me!'

'I tried,' Dominic said. 'You didn't want to discuss it—remember? I'll be back on Monday and we can talk properly then.' He looked at his watch. 'I'm going to have to get going soon. This is one plane I can't miss.'

She lay in bed and stared up at the ceiling, tried to take in what he was saying. A month…

A month to get to know Harry, to see how they went, and then… She was happy, happier than she had ever felt possible, but it felt like a test. Then he turned around and maybe she should compromise too.

'I could ask Mum and Dad to come over.' She was torn. 'If you want me to come tonight…'

'I think Harry needs a couple of nights in his new bed, don't you?'

And she was so glad that he understood.

'I have to get back.' He smiled. 'Would it wake Harry if I had a shower?'

'Don't worry about that.' And she had a moment of panic, because Harry was being golden and sleeping now, but what about at two a.m. when he decided to wake up, what about when it was six p.m. and her mother hadn't picked him up from crèche? How would Dominic deal with those situations? She wasn't sure she was ready for this, not convinced she was up to exposing her heart just to have Dominic change his mind. 'I'll get you some towels.'

'Could you pass my trousers?' he asked as she

climbed out of bed. 'Oh, and can you get out my phone?' He snapped his fingers as she trawled through his pockets, which was something Bridgette decided they would work on. Sexy Spaniard he may be, and in a rush for his brother's party perhaps, but she didn't answer to finger snaps. 'I can't find it and don't snap your fingers again,' she warned him. 'Hold on, here it is.' Except it wasn't his phone. Instead she pulled out a little black box.

'That's what I meant.' He grinned. 'So, aren't you going to open it?'

Bridgette was honestly confused. She opened the box and there was a ring. A ring that looked as if they were talking about a whole lot more than a month.

'I thought we were going to take some time...'

'We are,' Dominic said. 'To get to know all the stuff and to work things out, but, compatible or not, there's no arguing from me.' He pulled her over to the bed. 'I love you.' He looked at her and to this point he still didn't know. 'And I hope that you love me?'

She had to think for a moment, because she had held on so firmly to her heart that she hadn't allowed herself to go there. And now she did. She looked at the man who was certainly the only man who could have taken her to his home that first night. She really was lousy at one-night stands, because she knew deep down she had loved him even then.

'If I say it,' she said, 'you can't change your mind.'

'I won't.' That much he knew. She was funny and kind and terribly disorganised too—there was nothing he might have thought he needed on his list for the perfect wife, but she was everything that was now required.

'How do you know?' she asked.

'I'm not sure…' Dominic mused. 'Chemistry, I guess,' he said.

'And Chris?' she said as he pulled her back to bed and put his ring on her finger. She realised the magnitude of what he was giving up.

'He'll be fine.' Dominic had thought about it a lot and was sure, because of something Tony had said. He should have thanked Tony, not the other way around, for far better a full plate than an empty one. He didn't want to be like his father, hitting golf balls into the sky at weekends, a perfect girlfriend waiting at home, with not a single problem. 'I'll go up at least once a month and he can come here some weekends. If I'm working you might have to…' He looked at her and she nodded.

'Of course.'

'We'll get there,' he said. 'You're it and I know you'll do just fine without me, but better with me.' He looked at eyes that weren't so guarded, eyes that no longer reflected hurt, and it felt very nice to be with someone you knew, but not quite, someone you would happily spend a lifetime knowing some more. 'And I'm certainly better with you.'

'Hey!' There was a very loud shout from down the hall. 'Hey!' came the voice again.

'Oh, no.' Bridgette lay back on the pillow as Harry completely broke the moment. 'Those bloody grommets. It's as if he's suddenly found his voice.'

Harry had found his voice and he knew how to use it! 'Hey,' Harry shouted again from behind his closed door. It was a sort of mixture between 'Harry' and 'Hello' and 'Have you forgotten me?'

'I'll get him.' Bridgette peeled back the sheet, liking the big sparkle on her finger as she did so.

'If you say you love me, I'll go and get him,' Dominic said, and pulled on his trousers, deciding he had to be at least half-respectable as he walked in on the little guy.

'If you go and it doesn't make you change your mind—' Bridgette grinned, knowing what he would find '—I'll say it then.'

It was the longest walk of his life.

He'd just put a ring on a woman's finger. Shouldn't they be sipping champagne, booking a restaurant, hell, in some five-star hotel having sex, not getting up to a baby?

But with him and Bridgette it was all just a little bit back to front and he'd better get used to the idea.

He pushed open the door.

'Hey!' Angry eyes met him, and so did the smell. Angry eyes asked him how dared he take so long, leave him sitting in this new bed that he wasn't sure how to get out of?

'This isn't how it's supposed to be, Harry,' Dominic said, because surely it should be a sweet, cherubic baby sitting there smiling at him, but it was an angry Harry with a full nappy. The newly engaged Dominic had to change the first nappy in his life and, yes, it was shocking, a real baptism of fire!

'Think of all the cruises I won't be going on,' Dominic said as he tried to work out all the tabs, 'all the sheer irresponsibility I'm missing...'

'Hey!' Harry said, liking his clean bottom and new word.

'Hey,' Dominic answered

And then he picked him up.

A bare chest, a toddler who was still a baby and a mass of curls against his chin, and it *was* inevitable— he didn't just love Bridgette, he loved Harry too. For the second time in twenty minutes he handed over his heart and it was terrifying.

He would never tell, but he thought he was crying. Maybe he was because Harry's fat hands were patting his cheeks. He could never tell Bridgette that he was terrified too.

That the phone might ring.

That there might be a knock on the door.

That Courtney might come back.

That this little guy might have to be returned too soon.

'I'll make this work.' He looked into the little grey eyes that had always been wary and saw the trust in them now. 'I will make this work,' Dominic said again, and his commitment was as solid as the diamond he had placed on Bridgette's finger—his promise to Harry would cut glass if it had to, it was that strong. 'It will all be okay.'

He walked back into the bedroom with a sweet-smelling Harry and did a double-take as he saw his previously sexy fiancée in bright orange flannelette pyjama bottoms and a T-shirt.

'Don't want him having flashbacks about his aunt in years to come,' Bridgette said.

And it was hard, because she was more a mother than the one Harry had.

'I'm just going to wash my hands.'

He was so tidy and neat. As he handed over Harry and headed to the bedroom, she worked something out. 'That's why he smiled,' Bridgette said. 'When you took your jacket off, he knew that you were staying.'

She looked at her nephew, at smiling grey eyes that mirrored her own, and it was easy to say it as Dominic walked back in the room.

'I love you.'

EPILOGUE

BRIDGETTE never got tired of watching a new life come into the world. It had been a glorious morning and had been a wonderful straightforward birth. Kate was watching from the bed, and Michael, the father, was standing over Bridgette as she finished up the weights and measurements, popped on a hat, wrapped up their son and handed him over—the perfect miracle, really.

'We're going to move you back to your room soon,' Bridgette told the new parents. 'I'll come and check on you later, but Jasmine is going to take over from me for a little while.'

'That's right.' Kate looked up from her baby. 'You've got your scan this morning. I'm glad he arrived in time and you didn't have to dash off.'

'I wouldn't have left you,' Bridgette said. 'I'd already rung down and told them I might not be able to leave.' She looked at the little pink squashed face and smiled. 'You have a very considerate baby.'

'You'll have one of your own soon.'

'Not that soon.' Bridgette gave an impatient sigh, because she really couldn't wait. 'I'm only nineteen weeks.' And then she checked herself, because she sounded just like any impatient first-time mum, and then she laughed because that was exactly what she was. She gave a small wink. 'Nineteen weeks and counting!'

She would breathe when she got to twenty-four weeks, she decided, no, twenty-five, she corrected, thinking of the difference those extra few days had made to Francesca. Francesca had been discharged the day Dominic had started his new job—home on oxygen but doing brilliantly. It had been a nice way to start, Dominic had said.

As she walked down to the canteen where she was meeting Dominic, she wondered if he'd be able to get away. She really didn't mind if he couldn't. It was a routine scan, after all, and he'd end up asking the sonographer way too many questions. Still, even if she would be fine without him, she smiled when she saw him sitting at the far end of the canteen, sharing lunch with Harry, and she realised he was going to make the appointment—it was better with him there.

'Hi, Harry.' She received a lovely kiss that tasted of bananas, and asked about his busy morning, because along with building bricks he'd done a painting or two, or was it three? He really had come on in leaps and bounds. 'Any news from Courtney?' Bridgette asked Dominic.

'I was about to ask you the same,' Dominic said. 'She seems to be taking ages. I thought it started at eleven.'

Courtney had an interview this morning at the hospital. She was attending college, and now that she had been clean for well over a year, she was applying for a job on the drug and alcohol unit. But as much as Bridgette wanted her sister to get the job and to do well, she was a little bit torn, not quite sure that Courtney was ready for such a demanding role. Courtney lived in Bridgette's old flat, paid a minimal rent and had been working hard in every area of her life. Although Bridgette was unsure about this job, she was also worried how Courtney would take it if she was turned down when she had such high hopes.

'We're about to find out,' Dominic said, and she looked up as Courtney made her way over.

'How did you go?' Bridgette asked.

'I didn't get it,' Courtney said, which seemed contrary to her smile as she kissed her little boy. 'They don't think I'm quite ready to work with addicts yet. I need more time sorting out myself and they said that there was another course I should think about, but—' she gave a very wide smile '—they were very impressed with me. Apparently there is a position as a domestic. The patients do a lot of the cleaning work, but I would be in charge of the kitchen, sort of overseeing things.' She pulled a face. 'And I have to do the toilets and bathrooms. It's three days a week for now and some weekends, but they'll also pay me to do the course.' She gave a nervous swallow. 'Really, it's like a full-time job.'

'Oh, my!' Bridgette beamed. 'It sounds perfect.' Then laughed. 'Except I can't really imagine you keeping things clean.'

'She's such a bossy landlady, isn't she, Harry?'

Courtney said, and Bridgette admitted that, yes, maybe at times she was. 'I have to go to the uniform room and then down to HR. I'd better get him back.'

'We'll take Harry back to daycare,' Dominic said, rather than offered, because Harry was still eating. 'That way he can finish his lunch.'

He was very firm with Courtney, didn't play games with her, didn't bend to any to her whims, and he didn't let Bridgette bend too far either.

Courtney breezed off and Dominic rolled his eyes. 'She's doing great and everything, but she's still the most self-absorbed person that I've ever met.' He let out a wry laugh. 'She didn't even wish you luck for your scan.'

'That's Courtney.'

With Harry's lunch finished, they headed back to daycare but at the last minute, as he handed Harry over to Mary, it was Dominic who changed his mind. 'Should we bring him?'

'To the ultrasound?' Bridgette frowned at Mary. 'Won't it upset him?'

'It might be a wonderful way to get him used to the idea,' Mary said. 'After all he's going to be like a big brother.'

'I guess,' Bridgette said, because Harry was going to be a brother to this baby, even if not in the conventional way... And that just about summed them up entirely. It was as if Harry had three parents. Even if Courtney was doing brilliantly, it hadn't been the smoothest of rides, and it was an ongoing journey. As Dominic had once pointed out, Harry deserved the extra ration of love and he got it, over and over—from his mum, from his aunt and her husband, from his grandparents too, who made a far more regular fuss of him.

So as Dominic held Harry, Bridgette lay on the bed and the ultrasound started. 'Are we going to find out?' She still couldn't decide if she wanted to know the sex or wanted the surprise.

'I am,' Dominic said, studying the screen closely, and she felt sorry for the sonographer with this brusque paediatrician in the room. 'Don't worry, I won't let on.' He wouldn't; Bridgette knew that much. He was the best in the world at keeping it all in. It had taken ages to work him out and she was still doing it, would be doing it for the rest of her life no doubt—but it was the most pleasurable job in the world.

She heard the clicks and the measurements being taken and felt the probe moving over her stomach. She looked over to where Dominic and Harry were closely observing the screen and then she laughed because there *he* was doing somersaults, a little cousin for Harry, and a nephew for Chris, who would be the most devoted uncle in the world.

'Everything looks normal.' The sonographer smiled and then she spoke to Dominic. 'Did you want to have a look?'

She saw him hover, could almost hear the ten million questions whizzing around that brilliant brain, knew he wanted to take the probe and check and check again that everything was perfect, that everything was just so, but with supreme effort Dominic gave a small shake of his head.

'"Normal" sounds pretty good,' he said, 'and it's not as if we'll be sending it back.'

Already their family was perfect.

*****

THE MIDWIFE'S SON

SUE MacKAY

Thanks very much to Kate Vida for her medical help. Any mistakes are mine.

And to Deidre and Angela, because I can.

CHAPTER ONE

JESSICA BAXTER STARED at the champagne glass twirling between her thumb and forefinger. It was empty. Again. How had that happened? Best fill it up. She reached for the bottle nestled in ice in the silver bucket beside her.

'You planning on drinking that whole bottle all by yourself?' The groomsman sat down beside her, his steady green gaze fixed on her. Eyes so similar to his sister Sasha's, yet far more dramatic. The way they were sizing her up at this moment sent shivers of anticipation through her. But it was more likely she had whipped cream and strawberry compote on her nose rather than anything earth-shatteringly sensual going on.

Her finger shook as she wiped the top of her nose. Nope. All clear of dessert. So what was fascinating Jackson Wilson so much that his head seemed to have locked into position and his eyes forgotten how to move? Maybe if she answered him he'd get moving again.

So she told him, 'Yes.' Every last drop.

'Then I'll have to get my own bottle. Shame to have to move, though.' Jackson smiled at her, long and slow, making her feel as though she was the only person in the marquee. The only woman at least.

Which was blatantly untrue. Apart from Sasha, who was looking absolutely fabulous in a cream silk wedding gown, there had to be half the female population of Golden Bay in this marquee. Hadn't Sasha said she wanted a small wedding? Define small. Jess looked at the bottle in her hand. Had she drunk too much? Not yet. 'This has to be the best champagne I've ever tasted. Your father went all out.'

'Can't argue with that.'

She wasn't looking for an argument. Her mouth curved upwards. Just some more champagne. The bubbles sped to the surface as she refilled her glass. The sight was enough to turn a girl on. If you were the kind that got turned on easily. Which she definitely wasn't. Her eyes cruised sideways, spied Jackson's legs stretched far under the table, and stilled. Well-toned thighs shaped his black evening trousers to perfection. Her tongue stuck to the top of her mouth, her skin warmed, and somewhere below her waist she felt long-forgotten sensations of desire. Maybe she was that kind of girl after all.

She lifted the bottle in Jackson's direction. 'Got a glass?'

'Of course.' He presented one with a flourish. 'I never go unprepared.' That gaze had returned, stuck on her, apparently taking in every detail of her face.

She paused halfway through filling his glass, raising a well-styled eyebrow. 'Has my mascara run or something?'

Jackson shook his head. 'Nope.'

Spinach in my teeth? Except spinach hadn't featured on the wedding dinner menu. So what was he looking at? Looking for? Jackson Wilson had never taken much notice of her before. They hadn't even liked each other much during the two years she had gone to school here; both had been too busy trying to steal the limelight.

The last time she'd seen him had been at their school

graduation party. Thirteen years ago. He'd been the guy every girl had wanted to date. She'd been the girl everybody had invited to their parties because she could supply anything money could buy. They'd never hooked up.

'Hey, stop.' He said it quietly, in that bone-melting voice of his. 'My glass runneth over.'

'What?' Eek. Bad move. She'd been so distracted she'd started pouring again without realising. So unlike her. Worse, he knew exactly what she was distracted by—him. Suck it up, and get over him. He's a minor diversion.

Jackson raised his fingers to his mouth and lapped up the champagne. Had he heard her telling herself to suck it up? She shivered deliciously. The gesture was done so naturally that she had to presume Jackson hadn't meant it as a sexual come-on. But, then, why would it be? She'd be the last female on earth he'd come on to. They probably still wouldn't get on very well; she was a solo mum, he was used to glamorous, sexy ladies who didn't sport stretch marks on their tummies.

Wait up. He'd only been back in Golden Bay for five days and before today she'd only seen him at the wedding rehearsal. She might have that completely wrong. She was open to having her opinion changed. He didn't look so full of himself any more. No, rather world-weary and sad, if anything.

Then Jackson seemed to shake himself and sit up straighter. Lifting his glass carefully, he sipped until the level dropped to a safe place, before clinking the rim of the glass with hers. 'To the happy couple.'

'To Sasha and Grady.' She should be looking for her friends as they danced on the temporary floor in the centre of the marquee, but for the life of her she couldn't drag her attention away from Jackson. When had he got so handsome? Like so handsome she wanted to strip him naked. Back at school, she'd never been as enthralled as all the other girls, but maybe she'd missed something. His body was tall and lean. His face had a chiselled look, a strong jawline and the most disconcerting eyes that seemed to see everything while giving nothing away.

'Has my mascara run?' he quipped.

Her face blazed. Caught. Why was that any different from him scrutinising her? It wasn't, but she never normally took the time to look a guy over so thoroughly. She usually wasn't interested. 'Yes.'

'Wonderful. My macho image is shattered.' His deep chuckle caught her off balance.

That made her study him even closer. There were deep lines on either side of that delectable mouth. More of them at the corners of those eyes that remained fixed on her. What had caused those lines? To avoid getting caught in his gaze she glanced at his hair, dark brown with a few light strands showing in the overhead lights. Grey, yet not grey. She glanced back to those eyes. 'You look exhausted.'

Jackson blinked, tipped his head back to stare at the top of the marquee. His mouth had tightened, instantly making Jessica regret her words. There was no way she wanted to upset him; she didn't want him to think she was probing, being nosey. 'Sorry. I take that back.' She sipped her champagne, the glass unexpectedly trembling in her hand.

'I am totally beat.'

Phew. Still talking. 'Jet-lag?' She supposed it was a longish haul from Hong Kong.

'Nah. Life.' His hand groped on the tabletop for his drink.

'Here.' She pushed it into his fingers.

'Thanks.' Sitting straighter, he took a deep taste of the nectar. 'You're right. This is superb.'

Again she wondered what hiccups there had been in his life to make him look so shattered. From what she knew, he worked as an emergency specialist in a huge hospital in Hong Kong. That would keep him busy, but many specialists put in the long hours and didn't end up looking as jaded as Jackson did right now. He'd be earning big money and no doubt had a fancy apartment and housekeeper, along with the to-die-for car and a string of women to ride alongside him. Maybe one of those women had caused a ripple in his otherwise perfect life? 'Why Hong Kong?'

'To live? I did part of my internship there and was offered a position in the emergency department for when I qualified.' Now he stared into his glass, seeming to see more than just the bubbles rising to the top. 'Hong Kong was exciting, buzzing with people, and completely different from Golden Bay. It was like starting a whole new life, unhindered by the past.'

'You sound like you hated it here.' What had happened to make him want to head offshore?

'I did at times.' Draining the glass, he reached for the bottle, peered at it. 'We need another one. Be right back.'

Jess watched Jackson stride around the edge of the dance floor, ignoring the women who tried to entice him to dance with them. So he was determined to sit with her for a while and share a drink. Why? Why her of all the people here? There had to be plenty of family and friends he knew from growing up in Takaka, people he'd want to catch up with. Come to think of it, she hadn't noticed him being very sociable with anyone in particular all day. Not that he'd been rude, just remote. Interesting. There must be more to this man than she knew.

Was she a safe bet, unlikely to molest him because she sat alone, not leaping up to shake and gyrate to the music?

Well, he'd got that right. She didn't come on to men any more. Not since the last one had made her pregnant and then tossed 'Don't send photos' over his shoulder on the way out, heading about as far north as earth went.

The sound of a cork popping as Jackson returned was like music to her ears. 'What is it about champagne that's so special?' she asked, as he deftly topped up her glass. 'Is it the buzz on the tongue?'

'That, the flavour and the fact that champagne goes with celebrations. Good things, not bad.' Somehow, when he sat back down, his chair had shifted closer to hers.

'I guess you're right.' Goose-bumps prickled her skin and she had to force herself not to lean close enough to rub against his arm. Bubbles tickled her nose when she sipped her drink and she giggled. Oops. Better go easy on this stuff. Then again, why not let her hair down and have a good time? It had been for ever since she'd done that.

'Of course I'm right.' He smiled, slowly widening his mouth and curving those delectable lips upwards, waking up the butterflies in her stomach and sending them on a merry dance. Then he said, 'That shade of orange really suits your brown eyes and fair hair.'

'Orange? Are you colour blind, or what? Your sister would have a heart attack if she heard you say that. It's apricot.' She fingered the satin of her dress. Being bridesmaid for Sasha had been an honour. It spoke of their growing friendship and being there for each other. One of the best things about returning home to Golden Bay had been getting to know Sasha, whom previously she'd only thought of as the girl about the bay who was younger and wilder than her. But that had been then. Nowadays they both were so tame it was embarrassing.

Jackson shrugged. 'Orange, apricot, whatever. You should wear it all the time.'

'I'll remember that.'

'Do you want to dance?'

What? Where had that come from? Dancing had nothing to do with dress colours. 'No, thanks.'

'Good. I'm hopeless at dancing. Always feel like a puppy on drugs.' His smile was self-deprecating.

'Then why did you ask?' She seemed to remember him gyrating around the floor at school dances.

'Thought you might want to.' He chuckled again. Deep and sexy.

'Luckily for you I'm not into dancing either.' She could get addicted to that chuckle. It sent heat zipping through her, warming her toes, her tummy, her sex. Once more her cheeks blazed, when they'd only just cooled down after the last time. What was going on here? She never blushed. It must be the drink. She stared at her glass belligerently and tried to push it aside, but couldn't. Not when she was letting her hair down for the first time in years and enjoying a drink or three. Nicholas was staying with his little friend, Bobby, just down the road at Pohara Beach. Tonight was hers to make the most of, mummyhood on hold for a few hours. Tomorrow reality would kick back in and she'd pick up the reins again. Not that she ever really let them go. But for one day and night it was great to be able to stop worrying.

'How old is your little boy?'

So mindreading was one of Jackson's talents. 'He's four and a handful. A gorgeous, adorable handful who keeps me on my toes nonstop.' He'd looked so cute at the marriage ceremony in his long trousers and white shirt.

'What happened to his dad?'

This man was blunt. 'Which rumour did you hear?' she asked, as she contemplated how much to tell.

'That he was a soldier on secondment who didn't take

you with him when he left. That he was the married CEO of a big company who liked beautiful young women on his arm.' Jackson drank some more champagne. Was that what had made him suddenly so talkative? 'That he was an alien visiting from Mars for a week.'

Her growing anger evaporated instantly and she dredged up a smile. 'Guess you know you're home when everyone starts making up stories about you.'

'Which is why I hightailed it out of here the day after I finished school.'

'Really?' Jess could feel her eyebrows lifting and brought them under control. How much would he tell her?

The steady green gaze locking onto her lightened. 'Really. I hated it that I couldn't sneeze without someone telling me I'd done something wrong.'

Not much at all. Memories niggled of a rumour about Jackson and a pregnant girl, something to do with a set-up. 'It's like that, isn't it? Claustrophobic.' She shuffled around on her chair, all the better to study him again. 'But there's also security in that.'

'You haven't told me which story is true. I'm guessing none of them.'

Persistent man. Or was he just shifting the focus off himself? She didn't talk about Nicholas's father. Not a lot of point. 'I prefer the alien one.'

He nodded. 'Fair enough.'

That's it? He wasn't going to push harder for information? Most people wouldn't care that the subject had nothing to do with them. She could get to like Jackson Wilson. Really like him. 'How long are you home for?'

'Almost three months.'

Her eyebrows were on the move upwards again. Three months? That seemed a long time when Sasha had mentioned this was his first visit in thirteen years. Of course, his mother had MS now. And there was Sasha's baby girl, Melanie, to get to know. 'Amazing how weddings bring people together from all corners of the world.'

'You're fishing.' He grinned at her.

'Am I catching anything?' She grinned straight back.

His grin faded. His focus fixed on her. Again. She was getting used to his intense moods. 'I need a break. A long one.' He stretched those fascinating legs further under the table and crossed them at the ankles. 'And now you're going to ask why.'

Putting all the innocence she could muster into her gaze, she tapped her sternum. 'Me? No way.' Then, unable to hold that look, she grinned again. 'If you don't tell me I'll have to torture you.'

His mouth curved upwards as his tongue slicked over his bottom lip. 'Interesting.'

Idiot. She'd walked into that one. Now he'd make some smutty comment and ruin the easy camaraderie between them. 'Um, forget I said that.'

'Forgotten.' Did he add, 'Unfortunately,' under his breath?

She so wasn't into leather and handcuffs, or whips and ice. At least she hadn't been. Her mouth twitched. Maybe she should head home now, before the champagne made her say more things she shouldn't.

Where were Sasha and Grady? Right in the centre of the floor, still dancing, wrapped around each other as though they were the only people there. A sudden, deep envy gripped her, chilled her despite the summer heat.

She wanted what they had. Wanted a man who loved her more than anything, anyone else. Who'd put her first. A man to curl up against at night, to laugh and cry with. A man like— Her eyes swivelled in her head, away from the dance floor right to the man beside her. A man like Jackson? No. For starters, he was her best friend's brother. Then there was the fact he was only home for a few months. Add his sophistication and Jackson was so not right for her.

Hold that thought. Focus on it. Believe it. Remember how she'd thought Nicholas's father would give her all those things, only to be shown just how wrong she'd been. Instead, she'd found a man incapable of commitment, even to his wife back in the States. A wife she hadn't had a clue about.

Unfortunately for her, right now, all the reasons for not getting involved with Jackson seemed to have no substance at all.

CHAPTER TWO

JACKSON WATCHED JESSICA. Her brown eyes lightened to fudge and darkened to burnt coffee depending on her emotion, flicking back and forth so fast sometimes she must give herself a headache. Talk about an enigma. One moment all shy and unsure of herself, the next flipping a sassy comment at him like she wanted him. Which was the real Jess Baxter?

Suddenly the months looming ahead didn't seem so long and depressing. Instead, they were beginning to look interesting. Could he spend some time with Jessica and get to know her? Have some light-hearted fun for a while and find the real woman behind that sharp mind and sad face? He enjoyed puzzles, but right now he didn't even know where to begin solving this one. They were hitting it off fine. There might be some fun to be had here.

But— Yeah, there was always a but. He didn't want involvement. Especially not with a woman who'd require him to stay on at the end of those months, to become a permanent resident in the one place that he'd decided before he'd turned fifteen wasn't right for him. Too small, too parochial. Too close and personal. Nasty, even. He'd never forget the gut-squeezing, debilitating hurt and anger when Miriam Blackburn had accused him of getting her pregnant. He'd only ever kissed her once.

No wonder big cities held more attraction. Easy to lose himself, to avoid the piranhas.

From the little Sasha had told him, he understood that Jessica had come home permanently. That she'd begun mending bridges with the people she wrongly believed she'd hurt years ago. Apparently she wanted her son to grow up here, where he'd be safe and looked out for. There was no arguing with that sentiment.

He definitely wasn't looking for commitment in any way, shape or form. Commitment might drag him back to the place he'd spent so long avoiding. He wasn't outright avoiding women. But Jessica wasn't like his usual type of woman. Those were sophisticated and well aware of how to have a good time without hanging around the next day. Women who didn't get under his skin or tug at his heartstrings.

Jessica would want more of him than an exciting time. She'd want the whole package. Settle down, have more babies, find a house and car suitable for those children. *And what was so awful about that?* No idea, except it was the complete opposite from what he wanted.

Back up. He mustn't forget why he'd decided to stay on after his sister's wedding. He needed to spend time with his family, to help Mum and Dad as they came to terms with the multiple sclerosis that had hit Mum like a sledgehammer. He'd also like to get to know his niece. Melanie was so cute and, at three months old, had wound him round her little finger. Already, memories of her smile, her cry, her sweet face were piling up in his head to take back with him to Hong Kong.

Then there was the small issue of needing to rest and recoup his energy, to find the drive to continue his work in Hong Kong and keep his promise to his dead colleague. That motivation had been slipping away over the last year, like fine grain through a sieve. The cata-strophic events of last month had really put the lid on his enthusiasm for his work. But a promise was a promise. No going back on it.

Clink. 'Drink up.' Jessica was tapping her glass against his again.

Yeah, drink up and forget everything that had hap-pened in the past month. Let it go for a few hours and have some uncomplicated fun. 'Cheers,' he replied, and drained his glass. Picking up the bottle, he asked, 'More?'

He saw her hesitating between yes and no, her eyes doing that light then dark thing. He made up her mind for her. 'Here, can't let this go to waste.' When he'd filled both glasses, he lifted them and handed over hers, tak-ing care not to touch her fingers as they wound around the glass stem. That would be fire on ice. 'To weddings and families and friends.'

She nodded, sipped, and ramped up his libido as she savoured the sparkling wine, her tongue licking slowly over her lips, searching for every last taste. So much for avoiding contact. She could heat him up without a touch. That mouth… He shook his head. He would not think about her champagne-flavoured lips on his skin. Or her long, slim body under his as he plunged into her. While he lost himself for a few bliss-filled moments. Hours, even.

She was talking, her words sounding as though she was underwater.

Focus, man. Listen to Jess. Ignore your lust-dazed brain. 'What did you just say?'

'Looks like the happy couple are on the move.' Her eyes followed his sister and new brother-in-law as they did the rounds of their guests, hugging and kissing and chatting.

'You and Sasha never used to be mates.'

Jess had been the girl with the rich parents who had bought her anything and everything she could ever have wanted. Yet she'd never seemed genuinely, completely happy, always looking for more. Definitely a party girl, always in the thick of anything going down in Takaka, but at the same time she'd seemed removed from everyone. Like a child looking out the lolly-shop window at the kids gazing in at the sweet treats.

Yet she'd had more than the rest of them put together, having spent most of her childhood apparently travelling to weird and wonderful places. Hadn't she had love? Had that been her problem? It would go a long way to explaining why she'd always bought her pals anything they'd hankered after. Perhaps she had been buying affection and friendship. Talk about sad.

Right now a big smile lit up her face, lightened her eyes. 'The day Sasha walked into the medical centre to start her job we just clicked. Guess that amongst our past friends we're the odd ones out, having left and come back. We've tasted the world, know what life's like on the other side of Takaka Hill, and returned. Though Sasha's done a lot more than I have when it comes to our careers.'

'You didn't work overseas?'

'Nope. I'd travelled a lot with my parents when I was a child. The idea of working in another country didn't appeal. Auckland was enough for me.'

'Are your parents still living here?'

Coffee-colour eyes. And her teeth nibbled at her bottom lip. 'Not often.'

He recognised a stop sign when he saw one. 'Here comes the happy couple.' Jackson stood, placed a hand on Jessica's elbow and pulled her up to tuck her in beside him. Her warm length felt good against his body. The side of her thigh rubbed against his, her elbow nudged his ribs. A perfume that reminded him of Mum's citrus grove teased his nostrils. Her hair, all fancy curls with orange ribbons woven through, tickled his chin when he lowered his head.

I want her. Like, really want her. Not just a five-minute quickie behind the shed either.

Surprise ricocheted through him and he felt his muscles tighten. All his muscles. Especially below his belt. Why was he surprised? Hadn't this need been growing all evening? Against him Jess jerked, looked up with a big question in those pull-you-in eyes.

Don't move. Hold your breath and wish away your out-of-left-field reaction to her before she catches on. Because otherwise she's going to empty what's left in that champagne bottle over your head.

His stomach dropped in time with her chin as she glanced down, over his chest to his waist, and on down. His breath caught somewhere between his lungs and his mouth. She'd have to be blind not to see his boner.

Her head lifted. Her gaze locked onto his. She clearly wasn't blind. Those brown pools were filled with comprehension. Raising herself up on tiptoe, she leaned close and whispered, 'Your place or mine?'

'Yours.' Definitely not his. He was currently staying at his parents' house.

Her hand slipped into his and she tugged him off balance. 'What are we waiting for?'

'I have no idea.' So now he was in the flirty corner of the Jessica puzzle. Fine by him. He'd look into the shy corner another day.

Sasha and Grady stepped in front of them. 'Hey, you two. In a hurry to leave?' Sasha asked, with an annoying twinkle in her eyes. 'Without saying goodbye?'

Jackson removed his hand from Jessica's and carefully hugged his sister. 'You look beautiful, sis. No wonder Grady hasn't moved more than two centimetres away from you all day.'

Then he slapped Grady on the back and stepped away to watch the two women hugging tightly. They'd got so close. Like they shared everything. A small knot of longing tightened in his gut. He wanted that, too. No, he wanted what his sister and Grady had. Wanted to be able to talk about what had happened last month, share his fear and apprehensions, even the promise that hung over him. He would like to know there was someone special to look forward to going home to every night, someone who wasn't the housekeeper.

Jessica? Maybe, maybe not. Though so far tonight she'd been totally in tune with him, not pushing for answers to questions he refused to give, understanding when he wanted to talk and when he didn't. Knowing how his body reacted to hers.

Which reminded him. Weren't they going somewhere? In a damned hurry, too?

'See you two tomorrow,' he told Grady, and grabbed for Jess's hand. He whispered, 'We're out of here.'

And received a big, knowing smile in return. 'Sure are, Doctor.'

As they passed the bar he swiped a bottle of champagne and tucked it under his free arm. 'Neither of us is driving tonight. Let's hope one of those vans Dad organised for transporting inebriated guests home is available.' Like right this minute. Hanging around waiting for a ride and being forced to listen while other guests talked and laughed in their ears would be a passionkiller for sure. Though the beach was a short walk through the flaxes if need be.

They were in luck. The beach could wait for another night. Two vans were lined up so they snaffled one and ten long, tension-filled minutes later Jess was unlocking her front door.

She didn't bother with lights. 'There's enough light from the full moon to see what we need to see. The rest we can do by touch.' Her laughter was soft and warm, touching him in a way none of the sophisticated women he'd bedded had. Was this shy Jessica? Or fun Jessica?

'Where are the glasses?' he asked as he popped the cork on the champagne.

'Come with me.' She reached for his hand. Being tugged through the small house by this gorgeous woman with only moonlight to see by was a breathtaking experience, heightening his senses—and his growing need for her.

Jess's slim outline with those just-right curves outlined by her gown hardened him further. Her backside shaped the fabric to perfection, her hips flared the almost skintight skirt subtly. 'How are you going to get out of that dress?'

They'd reached the kitchen, where she removed two champagne glasses from a cupboard and handed them to him. Her mouth curved into a delicious, cat-like smile. 'That's your job.'

Give me strength. He wouldn't last the distance. 'Right.'

Just then she turned, pressed up against him, her thighs pushing against his, her lush breasts squashed against the hard wall of his chest. Her hands slid around his neck and pulled his head down so her mouth covered his. His pulse went from normal to a thousand in a flash. Wrapping his free arm around her, he hauled her close, so close her lower belly covered his reaction to her, smothered it, warmed it.

'Gawd, Jess. Keep this up and we'll be over before we've started.'

Her mouth pulled back barely enough for her to reply, 'And your problem is?'

'Why did we stop to get glasses?' His lips claimed hers again. She tasted sweet, exciting, sexy. She tasted of what he so badly needed right now. Of freedom and oblivion. Of recovery.

Somehow she began stepping backwards, taking him with her, not breaking their kiss at all, not removing those breasts from his chest. Back, back, until they made it into another room. Thank goodness there was a bed. A big bed. His knees were turning to something akin to badly set jelly as desire soared through him. He was about to explode and that was only under the ministrations of her mouth on his. He lifted his head. 'Turn around so I can free you.'

She spun so quickly she almost lost her balance. 'Oops. I need to slow down.'

'Really?' Jackson reached for her zip. Idiot. He still held the champagne bottle and glasses in one hand. Oh, so carefully he placed them on the bedside table. He had completely lost where he was. All he knew was that Jess stood before him and that he wanted her like he'd never wanted a woman before. He was desperate for her. But first he needed her naked. He concentrated on pulling the zip down with fingers that refused to stop trembling. Desire vibrated through him, everywhere, not just his fingers, like this was totally new to him.

It was hard to understand. He hadn't been living in a monastery. Far from it. There'd been a steady stream of women through his bedroom most of his adult life. Yet now he was losing control like the teenager he'd been last time he'd lived in this place, wanting desperately to bury himself inside Jessica Baxter.

'Jackson. What's going on back there?'

'The zip's caught.' Idiot. Couldn't even undo a simple zip. 'Hang on.'

She giggled. 'Hang on? Whatever you want.' Her hand slid behind her and found him. Her fingers slid up and down his covered erection, while the other hand worked his fly, which she obviously had no difficulty with. His trousers were suddenly around his ankles. 'I'm trying to get a hold.'

'Jess, I'll never get you out of this dress if you keep doing that.' And I'll come before I get my boxers down as far as my knees.

Instantly she stilled, her body tense, but he could feel her heat, knew her pulse was working overtime by the way her breasts rose and fell rapidly. She sucked her stomach in so tight it must've hurt. 'Well?'

'Thank you,' he muttered, as he tugged downwards. 'At last.' He slid his hands inside the soft fabric, his fingers sliding over her hot skin, across her back to her waist, round to her stomach and up to cup those luscious breasts. Free breasts. 'You haven't got a bra on.'

'Would've ruined the look.' She wriggled her butt against him. Sucked in her breath. 'Jackson, your thumbs are sending me over the edge to some place I've never been.'

Music to his ears. 'That's nothing to the storm your hand's stirring up.' His erection felt large, hard, throbbing and ready to explode.

She leant forward, teasing him with her rear end as she shrugged her upper body out of the dress and let it fall to her feet. Then she stepped out of the puddle of

orange fabric and turned to face him. Insecurity and
sass warred on her face, vied for supremacy. 'We haven't
kissed. Not once.'

Jackson wasn't sure he'd make it through a kiss. But
that uncertainty blinked out at him from her dark eyes
and he hauled on the brakes, pulled his hands from where
they'd fallen to her waist, and encircled her with his arms.
He so wanted to get this right for her. For him. Hell, he
knew it would be great for him, but if Jessica wanted
a kiss then she'd get one she'd never forget. When his
mouth covered hers he couldn't believe he hadn't done
this earlier. She tasted of champagne and the promise
of hot sex. She also tasted of honest-to-goodness, trust-
worthy woman with a lot to offer and something to take.

When she pushed her tongue into his mouth to tangle
with his he thought he'd died and gone to heaven. His
jelly knees melted and they tipped onto the bed, neither breaking their hold on the other. As they rolled and
sprawled he continued to devour her mouth. Until now
he'd thought kissing highly overrated, but this moment
had rewritten his ideas. Kissing Jess went so far off the
scale he might never come back to earth.

Then her hand found him again. Forget kissing. His
lungs seemed to fold in on themselves as all the air hissed
over his teeth. Forget everything. Absolutely everything.

Pulling her mouth away, Jess said, 'You mentioned
always being prepared for anything. I guess that means
you've got a condom or two in your pocket.'

He froze. Swore under his breath. No. He'd been going
to his sister's wedding, had not expected to be bedding
a hot bridesmaid.

Hot, shaky laughter filled the room. 'You owe me,
buster. Top drawer by the bed. They're probably out of
date but better than nothing.'

Within moments she had him covered and her hand was back on him, heat rolling through every cell of his body.

He had to touch her. But suddenly he was on his back and Jess was straddling him. Before he'd caught up with her she was sliding over him, beginning to ride him. His hands gripped her thighs, his thumbs slipped over her wet heat to find her core. She instantly bucked and for a moment she lost the rhythm.

But not for long. Her recovery was swift. This woman had to be something else. He kept the pressure on as he rubbed across her wetness.

Above him Jessica let out a long groan and squeezed tight around him and his brain went blank as he lost the last thread of control over his body.

Careful not to wake Jess, Jackson withdrew his arm from around her waist and rolled onto his back. A comfortable exhaustion lapped at him. It would be so easy to curl back into Jess and sleep for hours. Too easy, which was a scary thought. They'd made love again. Slowly and sensually, and just as gratifying. She'd been generous in her lovemaking, and hungry for her own release. He hadn't experienced anything so straightforward and honest in a long time. And he'd enjoyed every moment.

But now he had to be thinking of getting home. Squinting at his watch, he tried to make out the time. Four twenty-four? The sun would soon be clawing its way up over the horizon. He slid out from under the sheet and groped around the floor for his clothes, which he took out to the bathroom to pull on.

He had to get away from here before there was a chance that anyone might see him leaving. He would not give anyone reason to gossip about Jess. It might be harmless but he knew how it could still hurt, ricocheting around the bay and getting more outrageous by the hour. According to Sasha, Jess wanted nothing more than to blend in around here, and to become a member of the community who everyone could rely on for help and empathy. She most definitely would not want to be the centre of idle chitchat at the corner store or in the pub. Jess wasn't as lucky as he and Sasha were, she didn't have her family to believe in her and stand by her.

Biting down on a sudden flare of anger, he dressed and headed to the kitchen to find pen and paper. He wouldn't leave without saying thank you. Or something. Anything but nothing. He did not want her waking up and thinking he'd done a dash while she'd slept because he hadn't had a good time or couldn't face her in the light of day.

Back in the bedroom he quietly crossed to place the note on her bedside table. Then he stood looking down at her in the glimmer of light from the bathroom opposite. Sleeping Jess appeared completely relaxed. No sass, no uncertainty. His heart lurched. And before he could think about it he bent down to kiss her warm cheek. His hand seemed to rise of its own volition and he had to snatch it back before he made the monumental error of cupping her face and leaning in for one of those brain-melting, hormone-firing kisses.

Another lurch in his chest. She was like a drug; slowing his thought processes, making him forget things he should never forget. So, he was already half under her influence. If he didn't leave immediately he might never go away. Which would cause all sorts of difficulties. He and Jessica were light years apart in what they wanted for their futures. Futures that could never blend comfortably. He didn't need the hassle of trying to make it work and failing, and neither did Jessica.

Walking away was hard, and for every step his heart made a loud thud against his ribs. But he had to—for Jess. Making sure the front door was locked behind him to keep her safe—which also meant he couldn't go back to her—he began the ten-kilometre walk back to his parents' house.

Hopefully, if anyone he or Jess knew happened by at this early hour they wouldn't put two and two together and come up with…four. Because there might be gossip about them spending the night together, but this was one story that would be based on truth.

Three hundred metres on and headlights swept over him. A car sped past, the horn tooting loud in the early morning. Again anger flared, sped along his veins. So much for being discreet. It just wasn't possible around here. Increasing his pace, he tried to outrun the temper threatening to overwhelm him. When would these surges of anger stop? It had been more than a month since the attack. He should have got past that terrifying night by now.

The nearly healed wound in his side pulled as Jackson swung his arms to loosen the knots in his neck and back. There was another reason for leaving before the sun came up. That bloody scar. If Jess saw it she'd have a stream of unwanted questions to fire his way. Somehow she hadn't noticed the rough ridge of puckered skin during the night. Amazing, considering he doubted there was a square millimetre of his body she hadn't touched at one time or another.

'So, Jackson,' he muttered, as he focused on the road and not tripping over some unseen obstacle in the semi light of dawn, 'where to from here, eh?'

His lips tightened as he grimaced.

'That's a tricky one. I don't want commitment, gossip

or questions about why I've got an ugly red scar on my body.' That about covered everything.

If only he'd worn running shoes he could be jogging now. Like they'd have been a good match for the wedding clobber he still wore. But who was around to notice? It was weird how quiet it was around here. No hordes of people bumping into him, no thousands of locals talking nonstop as they began their day. Very, very quiet. Peaceful. A complete contrast to Hong Kong.

'Don't get too comfortable. You're heading out of here before the end of April.' He spat the words. 'But I wouldn't mind a repeat of last night with Jess.' Just the mention of her name calmed him, slowed his angry thoughts. A smile began deep in his belly, sending tentacles of warmth to every corner of his body, curving his mouth upwards. 'Oh, yeah. I could do that all over again.'

But would he?

Even if it meant talking about things he preferred buried deep inside his psyche?

Right at this moment he had no damned idea.

CHAPTER THREE

KEEPING HER EYES closed, Jess reached across the bed for Jackson and came up cold. What? She scrambled up and looked around. She was alone.

'Jackson?' she called.

Nothing. No cheeky reply. No deep chuckle. Silence except for the house creaking as the sun warmed up the day.

'Great. Bloody wonderful, even. I hate it when the guy of the night before leaves without at least saying good bye.' Her stomach tightened. Jackson had enjoyed their lovemaking as much as she had. She'd swear to it. 'Maybe he didn't want the whole bay knowing we've been doing the deed.'

Was that good or bad? Did she want the whole of Golden Bay discussing her sex life? Nope. Definitely not. The muscles in her stomach released their death grip.

Did she want to do it again? With Jackson? Oh, yes. Her stomach tightened again. Absolutely wanted that. Which was a very good reason not to. Already she felt the need to see him pulling at her, wanted his arms around her, to hear his sexy chuckle. And that was after one night. Blimey. Was she falling for her best friend's brother? Even when she knew she shouldn't? That was a sure-fire way to fall out with Sasha, especially once

Jackson packed his bags and headed back to his job. But there was no helping those feelings of want and desire that seemed to sneak out of her skull when she wasn't looking.

Throwing the sheet aside, she leapt out of bed. He might've left but, darn, she felt good this morning. Despite the uncertainty of today and, in fact, every other day of the coming months with Jackson in the bay, she felt great. Just went to show what a healthy dose of sex could do for her.

'What's that?' A piece of paper lay on the floor by the bed. Picking it up, she read:

Hey, sleepyhead, thought I'd get away before the bay woke up. Thanks for a great night. See you at brunch. Hugs, Jackson.

Hugs, eh? That was good, wasn't it? Seemed he wasn't hiding from her if he'd mentioned the post-wedding brunch. What was the time? Eight-thirty. Yikes. She was supposed to be at the Wilsons' by nine-thirty and she had to pick up Nicholas. Her boy, the light of her life. She might've had a fantastic night but she missed him.

The piping-hot shower softened those aching muscles that had had a rare workout during the night. Singing loudly—and badly—she lathered shampoo through her hair while memories of last night with Jackson ran like a nonstop film through her mind. Hugging herself, she screeched out the words to a favourite song.

The phone was ringing as she towelled herself. Knowing she had no babies due at the moment, she wondered who'd be calling. Sasha would be too busy with Grady, it being the first day of married bliss and all that.

'Hello,' she sang.

'Is that Jessica Baxter? The midwife?' a strained male voice asked hesitantly.

Her stomach dropped. 'Yes, it is. Who's this?'

'You don't know me, but my wife's having a baby and I think something's wrong. It's too early. Can we come and see you? Like now?'

No. I'm busy. I'm going to have brunch with the most amazingly attractive, sexy-as-hell guy I've ever had the good luck to sleep with. Except, as of now, she wasn't. She swallowed the disappointment roiling in her stomach. 'Let's start at the beginning. Yes, I am Jessica. You are?'

'Sorry, I'm panicking a bit here. I'm Matthew Carter and my wife's Lily. We're up here for the weekend from Christchurch. Staying at Paton's Rock.' The more he talked the calmer he sounded. 'She seems a bit uncomfortable this morning.'

'How far along is your wife?' Why had they come away from home and their midwife when this Lily was due to give birth?

He hesitated, then, 'Nearly eight months. Everything's been good until this morning, otherwise we wouldn't have come away. But my cousin got married yesterday and we had to be here.'

'You were at Sasha and Grady's wedding?' She didn't remember seeing any obviously pregnant women, and as a midwife she usually noticed things like that.

'No, Greg and Deb Smith's.'

No one she knew. There were often multiple weddings in the bay in January. The golden beaches were a huge attraction for nuptials. 'Right. Tell me what's going on.'

'Lily's having pains in her stomach. Personally I think she ate too much rich food yesterday but she wants someone to check her out.'

'That sounds wise. They could be false labour pains.

Can you drive into Takaka and meet me at the maternity unit? It's behind the medical centre. I'll head there now.' She went on to give exact directions before hanging up.

Immediately picking the phone up again, she called the mother of Nicholas's friend and asked if it was all right for him to stay there a while longer. Then she phoned Sasha's mother.

'Virginia, I'm very sorry but I have to bail on brunch, or at least be very late. A pregnant woman from Christchurch is having problems.'

'That's fine, Jess. You can't predict when those babies will make their appearance.'

Yeah, but this wasn't one of hers. Then there was the fact it was coming early—if it was even coming at all. 'Can you tell Sasha and Grady I'm sorry? I really wanted to be there.' And can you let your son know too?

'Sure can. What about Jackson?'

Ahh. She swallowed. 'What about him?'

Virginia's laughter filled her ear. So that's where Jackson had got that deep chuckle. She'd never noticed Virginia's laugh before. 'Seems he had a bit of a walk home at daybreak. We shared a pot of tea when he got in. He doesn't realise how little I sleep these days. It gave him a bit of a shock when he crept in the back door just like he used to as a teenager.'

So much for Jackson trying to stop the town knowing about their night of fun. But his mother wouldn't be one for spreading that particular titbit of gossip. Or any other. She didn't do gossip. And…Jessica drew a breath…*she* didn't need to know what he'd got up to as a teen.

'Tell him thanks.' Oops. Wrong thing to blurt out to the man's mother.

'For what, Jess?' That laughter was back in Virginia's voice.

Too much information for Jackson's mother. 'For...' she cast around for something innocuous to say, came up blank.

Virginia's laughter grew louder. 'I'll tell him thanks. He can fill in the blanks. Good luck with the baby. Come round when you're done. We'd love to see you.'

I'm never going to the Wilson house again. My face will light up like a Christmas-tree candle the moment I step through their door. Apparently Virginia had a way of getting things out of a person without appearing to be trying.

Hauling on some knee-length shorts and a sleeveless shirt, she gave her hair a quick brush and tied it in a ponytail. There wasn't time to blow-dry it now and as she wasn't about to see Jackson it didn't really matter any more.

Pulling out of her driveway, she saw her neighbour, Mrs Harrop, waving at her from the front porch. They both lived on the outskirts of town in identical little houses built back in the 1950s. Mrs Harrop took care of the gardens for both of them while Jess made sure the other woman had proper meals every day by always cooking twice as much as she and Nicholas needed.

'Morning, Mrs Harrop. Everything all right with you today?'

'The sun came up, didn't it? How was the wedding? Who was that man I saw leaving your place in the early hours?' There was a twinkle in the seventy-year-old woman's eyes.

Damn. Usually her neighbour was half-blind in full daylight. 'Mrs Harrop...' Jess couldn't help herself. 'You won't mention anything to your friends, will you?'

'Get away with you, girl. My lips are zipped.'

Now, why did she have to mention zips? Jess's brain

replayed the memory of Jackson undoing the zip of her dress last night. Oh, and then of her hand on his fly, pulling that zip down. Turning the radio onto full blast, she sang some more cringeworthy words and banged the steering-wheel in an approximation of the song's beat, and drove to town.

Jess made it to the maternity unit fifteen minutes before the distressed couple arrived. She filled in the time making coffee and nipped next door to the store to buy a muffin for breakfast. Nothing like the big cook-up she could've been enjoying at the Wilson establishment. But way better for her waistline.

The man she supposed to be Matthew helped his wife into the clinic and stood hopping from foot to foot, looking lost and uncomfortable.

After the introductions, Jess helped Lily up onto the examination bed. 'This is where they used to tell the husbands to go and boil water.'

Matthew gave a reluctant smile. 'Thank goodness the world is far more modern these days. But I admit having something concrete to do would help me right now.'

'You could hold your wife's hand while I examine her.' Try being a comfort to her, rubbing her back. She's the one doing the hard work here.

'Speaking of water, Lily did pass a lot of fluid just before I rang you.'

'You're telling me her waters broke?' What was wrong with letting me know sooner?

Matthew looked sheepish. 'Lily wouldn't let me look and I wasn't sure.'

Jess wanted to bang her head against the wall and scream. These two really weren't dealing with this pregnancy very well. After an examination she told them,

'Baby's head's down, and its bottom is pointing up. You're definitely in labour.'

Lily said nothing, but her face turned white. 'Now? Here? We shouldn't have come.' The eyes she turned on her husband were filled with distress and something else Jess couldn't quite make out. Blame? Fear?

'Matthew told me you're nearly eight months along.' When Lily nodded slowly, Jessica groaned internally. She'd have preferred to be dealing with a full-term baby when she didn't know the patient. 'I need to talk to your midwife. Lily, have you timed how far apart your contractions are?'

'She wasn't sure they were contractions,' Matthew replied.

'So this is your first baby?' Jess asked.

'No, our second.' Matthew again.

So far Lily had hardly got a word in. Maybe that boiling water was a good idea after all. Jess pasted on a smile before saying, 'I really need to talk to Lily for a moment. Have you timed the pains?'

Lily nodded, her face colouring up. 'They're four minutes apart.'

'Okey-dokey, we've got a little lead-in time, then.' Possibly very little, if this baby was in a hurry, but there was no point in raising Lily's anxiety level any further. 'You can fill me in on details. Like who your midwife is and how I can get hold of her for a start.'

I so do not like flying blind. A perfectly normal pregnancy so far, according to Matthew, but that baby was coming early. Too early really. Jess punched the cellphone number Matthew read out from his phone.

'They're where?' the other midwife yelped when Jess explained the situation. 'I warned them not to leave town.

Lily has a history of early delivery. She's only thirty weeks. The last baby didn't survive.'

'Thirty weeks? You're sure? Sorry, of course you are. Damn it. Why would Matthew have said nearly eight months?' Jess would've sworn long and loud if it weren't the most unprofessional thing to do.

'To cover the fact he shouldn't have taken Lily away at all.' The other midwife didn't sound surprised.

'He's brought his wife to a place where there's no well-equipped hospital or any highly qualified obstetricians and paediatricians.' All because he'd wanted to go to a family wedding. The closest hospital by road was Nelson, a good two hours away. Now what? She had to call one of the local doctors. At least she knew where they all were. At the post-wedding brunch. She needed help fast. And probably a rescue helicopter. Those guys would have Lily in Nelson with every chance of saving her baby's life in a lot less time than any other form of transport.

Lily groaned her way through a contraction. It would only get worse very soon, Jess thought after another examination of Lily. 'Your baby has definitely decided on Golden Bay for its showdown.' But she'd do her damnedest to change that. 'Do you know if you're having a boy or a girl?'

'A girl,' Matthew answered.

A discreet knock at the door had her spinning around to see what her next crisis was. Another patient was not on her agenda.

Heat slammed into her tummy. 'Jackson?' Yes, please, thank you. 'Come in.' Perfect timing. 'What brought you here?'

'Mum's truck.' He grinned. 'When she told me why you'd phoned I thought I'd drop by and say hi.'

'I'm really glad you did.' Then Matthew glared at her and Jackson so she quickly made the introductions.

'Good. A doctor is exactly what we need,' the guy had the temerity to say straight to her face.

Lily would've had any number of those if only they'd stayed in Christchurch. 'Lily, Matthew, I need to talk to Dr Wilson. We'll be right back.'

She dragged Jackson out of the room before anyone had time to utter a word. Her hand held a bunch of his very expensive shirt, the likes of which wasn't usually seen around Takaka. In other circumstances, she'd have been pulling that gorgeous mouth down closer so she could kiss him hard and long. But today wasn't her lucky day. 'I know you don't start covering for Grady for a few more days so I can phone Mike or Roz, but I'd like some assistance here.' She quickly ran through all the details the midwife had given her. 'I think it would be best if the rescue helicopter is called. I do not want to risk that baby's life.'

'I'm with you.' Jackson caught her hand to his chest as she let go of his shirt. 'The baby will need all the support it can get right from the moment it appears.'

'She. It's a girl.' Jess spread her fingers across the chest that only hours ago she'd been kissing. 'You need to make the call. I'm not authorised to except in exceptional circumstances.' Which this could arguably be.

'No problem. I'll examine Lily first and then I'll know what I'm talking about when I phone the rescue service. Can you get me the number? And the midwife's? I'd like to talk to her, too.' His green gaze was steady. 'I'm not undermining you, Jess. I prefer first-hand information, that's all. Especially since it's been a while since I delivered a baby.'

The relief that he was sharing the burden swamped

her, although she knew it shouldn't. She had experience in difficult deliveries, though always in places where back-up was on hand. 'Not a problem, I assure you.' She turned to head for her patient. 'Come on, we'll talk to those two again. Together.'

Jackson still held her hand, tugged her back against him. 'I had a great time.' His lips brushed hers. 'Thank you.'

You and me both. But she couldn't tell him because of the sudden blockage in her throat and the pounding in her ears. So she blinked and smiled and then made her way into see Lily.

Jackson made the phone calls and returned to check on baby Carter's progress. He was angry.

Breathe deep, in one two, out one two.

This mother and baby should not be here, jeopardising their chances of a good outcome. His hands fisted.

In one two. Out one two.

Sure, everything could work out perfectly, but at thirty weeks the baby would still need an incubator and special care. The father was a moron. Especially considering the fact their last baby had died. How did Jess remain so calm? Maybe she'd had time to settle down and get on with what mattered most, appearing confident in the current situation and ignoring the if-only's. 'Lily, you're going to Nelson Hospital to have this baby. It's too early for us to be bringing her into the world here.' His tone was too harsh.

In one two. Out one two.

'I'm not driving Lily over that awful hill in her condition. It was uncomfortable enough for her on Friday and she wasn't in labour then.' Matthew stared at Jackson as though it was his fault they were dealing with this here and now.

Jackson ground his teeth and fought for control. Losing his temper would do absolutely nothing to help. Finally, on a very deep, indrawn breath, he managed to explain without showing his anger. 'The rescue helicopter will be here in approximately one hour. Jessica, where do they land?'

'In the paddock out the back of the medical centre. I'll go and see if there are any sheep that need shifting. Matthew, you can give me a hand.' Jess winked at Jackson before she led the startled man out the door.

'Go, Jess.' Jackson grinned to himself, his anger easing off quicker than usual. Starting an examination of Lily, he talked to her all the while, explaining what was happening. And calmed down further. These sudden anger spurts were disturbing. He was usually known for his cool, calm manner in any crisis and he'd hoped taking time away from his job would fix the problem. It seemed he was wrong or maybe just impatient.

'Will my baby be all right?' Lily asked through an onset of tears.

He would not promise anything. 'We'll do everything we can towards that outcome.'

The tears flowed harder. 'I didn't want to come to the wedding but Matthew insisted. He can be very determined.'

Try selfish and stubborn. 'We can't change the fact that you're in Golden Bay at the moment so let's concentrate on keeping baby safe.'

'Grr. Ahhh.' Lily's face screwed up with pain as another contraction tore through her.

Jackson reached for a flailing hand, held it tightly. The contractions were coming faster. All he could do was

prepare for the birth and hope like hell the emergency
crew would get here first. How fast could they spin those
rotors? Where was Jess? She'd be more at ease with the
situation than him. It's what she did, bringing babies into
the world. Admittedly not usually this early or with this
much danger of things going horribly wrong, but she was
still more used to the birthing process.

'Hey, how are we doing?' A sweet voice answered his
silent pleas. Jess had returned, dissolving the last of the
tension gripping him.

Stepping away from the bed and closer to this delightful woman who seemed to have a way about her
that quickly relaxed him, he murmured, 'Remind me to
buy you another bottle of champagne when this is over.'

The fudge-coloured eyes that turned to him were twinkling. Her citrus tang wafted in the air when she leaned
close to whisper, 'I might need some of that brunch first.
My energy levels need rebuilding.'

Jess would drive him crazy with need if he wasn't
careful. And did that matter? Of course it did. Didn't it?
He'd hate to hurt her in any way. 'You'll have to wait.
How was that paddock? Any sheep?'

'Nope, all clear. The windsock is hardly moving so the
landing should be straightforward. How's Lily doing?'

'Starting to panic. And who can blame her?'

Jess crossed to the woman. 'We're all set for that
helicopter, Lily. Ever been in one before?'

'N-no. I—I don't like flying.'

Jackson groaned quietly. This day was going from
bad to worse for the woman. 'They're quite different to
being in a plane. Perfectly safe. The pilot will probably
go around the coastline instead of over the hill so you
won't be too far above ground level.'

Jess added, 'This is definitely the best way to keep

your baby safe. Now, with the next contraction I want you to stand. You might find it easier to deal with the pain.'

Lily's smile was strained as she clambered off the bed. 'Thank you. I know you're trying your best. I'll be okay.' Then all talk stopped as she went through another contraction.

This time Matthew held her as she draped herself over him and hung on. 'You're doing great, Lily.'

Finally, just when Jackson thought they'd be delivering Baby Carter in the medical centre the steady thwup-thwup of the helicopter approaching reached them inside the hot and stuffy room. 'Here we go. Your ride has arrived, Lily,' he said needlessly.

Everyone had heard the aircraft and Matthew had gone to watch the landing. Jackson followed him out and once the rotors had stopped spinning he strode across to meet the paramedic and paediatrician as they disembarked and began unloading equipment.

'Glad to see that incubator.' He nodded towards the interior of the craft. 'You might be needing it.'

'Baby's that close?' the man who'd introduced himself as Patrick asked. His arm badge read 'Advanced Paramedic'.

'The mother has the urge to push. But I'm hoping she can hold off for a bit longer.'

'Let's take a look before we decide how to run with it. I don't fancy a birth in mid-air.'

In the end, Baby Carter made their minds up for them. She arrived in a hurry, sliding out into the bright light of the world, a tiny baby that barely filled Jackson's hand. Handing her carefully to Jess, he concentrated on repairing a tear that Lily had received during the birth.

Matthew stood to one side, stunned at the unfolding events. 'Is Lily okay? What about my daughter? Is she going to make it? At least she cried. That's got to be good, doesn't it?'

The last baby didn't cry? Jackson looked up and locked gazes with Matthew. 'The baby's breathing normally, and Lily's going to be fine. Have you decided on a name for your daughter?'

'Yes, but we were afraid to mention it until we knew if she'd be all right.' Matthew's eyes shifted to the right, where his daughter was being attached to monitors inside the incubator. 'Alice Rose,' he whispered, and brushed the back of his hand over his face.

'Alice Rose Carter.' Jess spared the man a sympathetic glance. 'I like it. Pretty. And so is she. Come over here and see for yourself.'

The paediatrician continued adjusting equipment as he explained, 'Alice Rose is very small, as to be expected. At thirty weeks her lungs aren't fully developed so this machine will help her breathe until she grows some. But…' the man looked directly at Matthew '…everything so far shows she's looking to be in good shape despite her early arrival. I'm not saying you're out of trouble yet. There are a lot of things to watch out for, but one step at a time, eh?'

Matthew blinked, swiped at his face again and stepped closer to his daughter. 'Hello, Alice. I'm your daddy.' Then he sniffed hard.

Jess handed the guy a box of tissues. 'Hey, Daddy, blow your nose away from your baby.' She said it in such a soft tone that Jackson knew she'd forgiven the guy for being rather highhanded earlier. 'You're going to have to learn to be very careful around Alice Rose for a long time to come.'

Jackson helped Lily into a sitting position. 'I'm so sorry you can't hold your daughter yet.' That had to be devastating for any new mother. During many long phone calls last year Sasha had often told him that she could barely wait for Melanie to be placed in her arms and to be able to give her that very first kiss. Lily and Matthew weren't going to have that for a while.

'I'm grateful she's doing all right so far. Not like last time. We knew straight away little Molly wouldn't make it.' Lily's bottom lip trembled. 'No. I'm lying. I want to hold her so much it hurts. By the time I do she won't be a newborn.' The tears flowed, pouring down her cheeks to soak into the hospital gown that she still wore.

'You're going to need to head across to Nelson as soon as possible,' Jackson told her, shifting the subject to more practical matters. 'There's a shower next door, if you want to clean up first.'

'Thank you. It all seems surreal. I've just been through childbirth and there's no baby in my arms to show for it.' Tears sparkled out of her tired eyes as she gathered up her clothes and headed towards the bathroom.

His heart squeezed. For this couple who'd blown into their lives that morning with a monumental problem? Or could there be more to his emotional reaction? Since the attack he'd never quite known where his emotions were taking him, they were so out of whack. Coming home had added to his unrest. Having spent so many years being thankful that he'd escaped Golden Bay, it was difficult to understand why regrets were now filtering through his long-held beliefs.

He'd never really given much thought to having a family of his own. It wasn't that he didn't want one. It was just a thought that had been on the back burner while he established his career and got over his distrust of women enough to get to really know them. Then his career had grown into a two-headed monster, leaving him little time to develop anything remotely like a relationship. The women who'd passed through his life hadn't changed that opinion. Probably because he'd chosen women who wouldn't want to wreck their careers or their figures by having children. He'd chosen women who wouldn't lie to him or about him.

But honestly? He wasn't against a relationship where he settled down with someone special. The problem was, he couldn't see it working in the centre of Hong Kong surrounded by high-rises and very little green space. As that city was where his life came together, where he was the man he'd strived so hard to become, he could see that there'd be no children in his life for a long while.

He looked around and found Jess regarding him from under lowered eyelids. Could she read him? Did she know that if he ever changed his mind she might be the one woman he'd be interested in? Get a grip, Jackson. Until last night he wouldn't even have had these thoughts. One very exciting and enjoyable night in the arms of Jessica Baxter and he was getting some very weird ideas.

Because, love or hate Golden Bay, there was a lot to be said for the outdoors lifestyle and bringing up kids in this district. The district where his career would fizzle out with the lack of hospitals and emergency centres.

CHAPTER FOUR

THE HELICOPTER LIFTED off the paddock, the wind it created whipping at Jess's clothes, moulding her shirt against her breasts. 'Right, I'd better go and pick up Nicholas. I promised he would get to see Sasha and Grady before they left on their honeymoon.' Jess glanced at her watch. 'Brunch is probably well and truly wrapped up by now.'

Jackson's gaze was on her breasts. 'What did you say?' he almost shouted.

She grinned. Deafened by the aircraft or distracted by her boobs? 'I need to collect Nicholas. And hopefully catch Sasha and Grady before they leave.'

Jackson finally lifted his head enough to meet her gaze. 'Okay.' He tossed his keys up and down in his left hand. 'I don't think they were heading off until about one. Their flight leaves Nelson at four and they're staying overnight in Auckland.'

'Two weeks in Fiji sounds sublime.' Jess sighed wistfully and headed inside.

'Not just Fiji, but Tokariki Island. Tiny place, catering for only a few couples at a time. Heaven.' Jackson grinned at her as he strode alongside, sending those butterflies in her stomach on another of their merry dances.

'You are so mean. I'd love to go to the Islands.' With a hot man. Not that it was ever going to happen. She was a mother with a four-year-old who needed her more than anyone. 'Let's get out of here before the bell rings and we're stuck fixing cuts and scrapes for the rest of the day.' Leading by example, she turned off the lights and headed for the outside door.

'Can I come with you to pick up your son?'

Jess stopped her mad dash for freedom and spun round to come chest to chest with Jackson. He'd startled her with his simple request, and judging by the look of surprise in his eyes he'd startled himself as well. 'Did I hear right? You want to share a tiny car with a loud, boisterous little boy who talks nonstop, never letting anyone else get a word in?'

She waited for him to back off fast. But instead he nodded. 'Guess I do. Is Nicholas really that noisy?'

Laughter rolled up her throat. 'Oh, boy. You have no idea.' This would test their burgeoning friendship. Her son was no angel. In fact, she had to admit he was getting very much out of control and she didn't know what to do about it. Loving him to bits meant saying no which didn't come easily for her.

But one day soon she was going to have to grow a backbone when it came to Nicholas or they were in for a very rocky ride as he grew up. It was just that she needed to lavish him with love, show him how much he mattered to her. She would not become her parents, throwing money at every situation when more often than not a hug would have sufficed. No. Nicholas would always know how much she cared about him. Always.

A big, warm and strong hand cupped her chin, tilted her head back so that she stared into Jackson's green gaze. 'Jess? Where have you gone? Something up?'

With an abrupt shake of her head she stepped away from that hand and those all-seeing eyes. It would be too easy to lean into him, burden him with her problems. That would certainly put the kibosh on getting to know him better. He'd suddenly have so much to do she'd not even see his delectable butt departing for all the dust he'd raise on the way out. She mightn't be sophisticated but she knew the rules. She'd invented some of them.

Keep it simple.

Do not get too close.

Don't ask him for more than fun. And great sex.

Her skin sizzled. What they'd shared last night had gone beyond fun, beyond description. She grimaced. What rule had she broken there?

'Jessica, you're going weird on me.' Jackson was right beside her as she punched in the security code for the alarm system.

Pulling the door shut and checking it was locked, she dug deep for a nonchalant answer and came up with, 'Not weird, just pulling on my mother-in-charge persona.'

'You're two different people?' His eyes widened, making him look surprised and funny at the same time.

She couldn't keep serious around him. Bending forward at the waist, one hand on her butt like a tail and the other creating a beak over her mouth, she headed towards her car. 'Quack, quack, quack.'

'Hang on, who are you? Where's Jess gone? Bring her back. I'm not getting in a vehicle with a duck.'

'Quack, quack.'

Jackson chuckled. 'Is this how you bring up your son? The poor little blighter. He'll be scarred for life. I need to save him.'

Jess felt his arms circle her and swing her off the ground to be held against that chest she'd so enjoyed running her fingers up and down during the night. She slid her hands behind his neck and grinned into his face. 'You're not going to kiss a duck?'

He groaned. 'I must be as crazy as you.' Then his mouth covered hers and she forgot everything except his kiss.

Heat spiralled out of control inside her. Her skin lifted in excited goose-bumps. Between her legs a steady throb of need tapped away at her sanity. Sparks flew. Whoever had invented electricity obviously hadn't had great sex.

Without taking that gorgeous, sexy mouth away from hers, Jackson set her on her feet and tugged her hard against him. She could feel his reaction to her against her abdomen. She clung to him. To stop holding him would mean ending up in an ungainly heap on the ground.

His lips lifted enough for him to demand, 'What's that code you just punched in?'

'Why?'

'We need a bed. Or privacy at least.'

He was right. They couldn't stay in the very public car park, demonstrating their awakening friendship. Not when he'd made sure no one had seen him leaving her place early that morning. She glanced down at Jackson's well-awake evidence of their needs and grinned. 'Three-two-four-eight-one.'

'I'm expected to remember that in the midst of a wave of desire swamping my brain?'

Thank goodness he returned his mouth to hers the moment he'd got that question out. She couldn't stand it when he withdrew from kissing her. Could this man kiss or what?

Cheep-cheep. Cheep-cheep.

'What the——?' Jackson's eyes were dazed as he looked around.

Reality kicked into Jess. 'My phone.' She tugged the

offending item from her pocket and glared at the screen. Then softened. 'It's probably Nicholas, using Andrea's phone.' As she pressed the talk button she gave Jackson an apologetic shrug. 'This is another side of being a mother. Always on call.' Then, 'Hello, is that my boy?'

'Mummy, where are you? I want to see Grady now.' He'd taken to Grady very quickly. Perhaps it was a sign he needed a male figure in his life?

'I'm on my way to get you.' She turned from the disappointment in Jackson's eyes. He might as well get used to the reality of her life right from the start. Presuming he wanted to see more of her, and that bulge in his jeans suggested he did.

'How long will you be, Mummy? I want to show you the fish the seagulls stole.'

'Nicholas, you know I can't talk to you while I'm driving so you'll have to wait until I get there to tell me about the seagulls. Okay?'

'Why won't the policemen let you drive and talk to me? It's not fair.'

Jess grinned. 'It's the law, sweetheart.' Knowing Nicholas could talk for ever, she cut him off. 'See you soon.'

Jackson's hands were stuffed into the pockets of his designer jeans as he leaned against the vehicle he'd borrowed from his mother. 'Want me to drive?'

'You still want to come with me?' Now, that surprised her. As far as she knew, Jackson wasn't used to little kids and this particular one had interrupted something fairly intense. 'Are you going to growl at him for his timing?'

'No.' He flicked a cheeky smile her way. 'The day will come when someone interrupts him in his hour of need.'

She groaned and slapped her forehead. 'I do not want to think about that. He's four, not thirty-four.'

'Thirty-four?'

'That's when I'll think about letting him out on his own to see girls.'

'Good luck with that one.' He crossed to the driver's side of her car and held his hand up for the keys. 'Let's go.'

'Um, my car. I drive.'

He just grinned at her. Really grinned, so that her tummy flip flopped and her head spun. So much that driving could be dangerous.

'Go on, then.' She tossed the keys over the top of her car. 'Men.'

'Glad you noticed.'

How could she not? His masculinity was apparent in those muscles that filled his jeans perfectly, in his long-legged stride, in the jut of his chin, in that deep, sexy chuckle that got her hormones in a twitter every time. She climbed into the passenger seat and closed the door with a firm click. Then something occurred to her. 'We're going to Pohara Beach. Shouldn't we take both vehicles, save a trip back into town later?'

'Nah. I'll go for a run when it cools down, pick up the truck then. Mum won't be needing it today.'

'Running? As in pounding the pavement and building up a sweat?' She shuddered. 'You obviously need a life.' But it did explain those superb thigh muscles. And his stamina.

Jackson just laughed. 'You're not into jogging, then? Knitting and crochet more your style?'

Thinking about the cute little jerseys she'd made for Nicholas last winter, she smiled and kept quiet. *If only you knew, Jackson.*

Then he threw another curve ball as they headed towards the beach. 'Who held you while you had Nicholas? Who smoothed your back and said you were doing fine?'

The man wasn't afraid of the big questions. 'No one ever asked me that before.' Not even Mum and Dad. Especially not Mum and Dad.

'Tell me to shut up if you want.'

That was the funny thing. She didn't want to. Jackson touched something in her that negated all her usual reticence when it came to talking about personal things. 'Two nurses I was friendly with took it in turns to hold my hand and talk me through the pain.' She'd trained with Phillip and Rochelle, and when they'd got married she'd been there to celebrate with them. They'd been quick to put their hands up when she'd announced she was having a baby, offering to help in any way they could. It had been more than three years since they'd left to work in Australia, and she still missed them.

'That must've been hard.'

Because Nicholas's dad wasn't there? No, by then she'd known she'd had a lucky escape. 'Not so bad. It was worse afterwards when I wanted to share Nicholas's progress, to talk about him and know I was on the right track with how I brought him up. That's when single mothers have it tough. That's what I've been told, and going by my own experience I have to agree.' It was also probably why Nicholas got away with far more than he should. There was no one to share the discipline, to play good cop, bad cop with.

'So how do you cope with the day-to-day stuff of being a solo mum?'

'Heard of the headless chook? That's me.'

'When you're not being a duck, you mean?'

She giggled. 'That too. I don't think about how I manage, I just do. I wouldn't want to go back to before I had Nicholas. Being a mother is wonderful. Though there are days when I go to visit Sasha or your mum for a bit of adult conversation and to help calm the worry that I'm getting it all wrong.'

'Even two parents bringing up a child together have those worries.'

'Guess it will never stop.'

Jackson turned onto the road running beside Pohara Beach. 'I was watching Lily and Matthew earlier. They were desperate to hold their baby and it hurt them not to be able to.'

Again she thought she could read him. 'Believe me, if you want to be a part of your child's life then you're not going to miss that first cuddle for anything. Sad to say, but my boy's father truly didn't care. He came to town for three months, had a lot of fun, and left waving a hand over his shoulder when I told him I was pregnant. He didn't even say goodbye.'

It was silent in the car for a minute then she pointed to a sprawling modern home on the waterfront. 'There.'

Jackson pulled up on the drive, switched the engine off and turned to her. 'He wasn't interested in his child?'

'There was a wife in Alaska.' It had hurt so much at the time. She'd been an idiot to fall for him.

'The jerk.' Jackson lifted her hand and rubbed his thumb across the back of it, sending shivers of need racing through her blood. Again.

'It's Nicholas who misses out. He'd love a dad to do all those male things with. Apparently I'm no good at football.' She pushed out of the car. All the better to breathe. Despite the conversation they were having, sitting beside Jackson in her minuscule car did nothing to quieten her rampaging hormones.

'Mummy, here I am.' Nicholas's sweet voice interrupted her internal monologue and reminded her who

was important in her life. Here was the only person she
should be thinking about.

'Hey, sweetheart, have you had a good time?' She
reached out to haul him in for a hug but he'd stumbled
to a stop and banged his hands on his hips.

His head flipped back at Jackson. 'What's your name?'
he demanded.

Jackson stood on the other side of the car, studying her
boy in that searching way of his. 'I'm Jackson Wilson.
You saw me at the wedding.' He came round and put his
hand out to be shaken.

But Nicholas hadn't finished. 'Why did you drive my
mummy's car?'

The corner of Jackson's mouth lifted but he kept his
amusement under control. 'I like driving and haven't been
doing very much lately.'

'Mummy likes driving, too.' Nicholas stared at the
proffered hand. 'Are you a friend of ours?'

'Yes, I am. That's why I'm waiting to shake your hand.
Want to put yours in mine, sport?'

Jess could barely contain her laughter as she watched
her son strut across and bang his tiny hand into Jackson's
much larger one. They both shook.

'See, Mummy. That's how it's done.'

'So it is.' What she did see was that Nicholas really
did need some male influence in his life. He picked up
on anything Grady said, and now, if she wasn't mistaken,
he was factoring Jackson into his thinking.

A chill ran through her veins. Not good. Jackson
would soon be going away again, and if Nicholas got
too fond of him, they were in for tears. Some of those
might be hers, too. Already she felt comfortable around
him in a way she rarely felt with men. There were a lot
of hidden depths to Jackson, but she liked the way he

took the proper time with her son. Amongst other things. Then her face heated as she recalled how there'd been no time spared last night when they'd first fallen into bed.

'Do I get my hug now, Nicholas?'

Dropping the strut, her boy ran at her, barrelling into her legs. 'I missed you, Mummy. Did you miss me?'

Swinging him up in her arms, she grinned and kissed his cheek. 'Big time.'

'Hi, Jess,' Andrea called from the porch of the house. 'How was the wedding?'

Andrea's question might have been directed to Jessica but her gaze was fixed on Jackson. He seemed to have that effect on most women. Including her. Even now, when there was no alcohol fizzing around her system, she definitely had the hots for him. She knew that if they were alone with time to spare she'd be requesting a repeat performance of last night's lovemaking.

But she wasn't alone with him. Her son was waiting to go and see Grady, and Andrea was waiting for a reply to her question. 'Sasha looked stunning, and Grady scrubbed up all right, too. They're leaving on their honeymoon shortly so I'd better get Nicholas around there to say goodbye. Thank you so much for having him to stay. I hope he wasn't any trouble.' He could be. She knew that. He hated being told what to do and could throw a paddy that matched the severity of a tornado. It was something she needed to work on.

He wriggled to be set down as Andrea waved a hand in his direction. 'You were very well behaved, weren't you, Nicholas? I wish Bobby could be half as good.'

Huh? Did Nicholas only play up for her? 'Thank goodness for that.' Jess checked he'd put his seat belt on properly before walking around to get back in the car.

Jackson started backing out the driveway. 'What did you get up to with your friend, Nicholas?'

'We played soccer, and Bobby's dad took us in his truck to get a boat. I wanted to go fishing but we weren't allowed because no adults wanted to go with us.' On and on he went, detailing every single thing he'd done since she'd dropped him off after the wedding service and before the reception.

Warmth stole through her, lifting her lips into a smile. 'That's my boy,' she whispered. Though thankfully they were pulling up outside Virginia and Ian's within minutes. Jess didn't want Jackson bored to sleep while driving. But he was the one to unclip Nicholas's belt and help him down. 'There you go, sport. Let's see if there's any of that brunch left for us to enjoy.'

'What's brunch?'

'Breakfast and lunch all mixed together,' Jess told him as she straightened his shirt.

'Why do you mix them?'

'So you only have one meal.' She rubbed his curls and got a glare for her trouble.

'That's a dumb idea.' Nicholas, as usual, got in the last word.

There were still a lot of people milling around, obviously in no hurry to leave. Jess hoped Virginia was coping. Yesterday had been tiring enough for someone with her disease. 'I'm going to see if I can do anything to help,' she told Jackson.

'I'll go and find Dad,' he told her.

'Hey, there you two are.' Grady strode across the lawn towards them.

The way he said it suggested she and Jackson were a couple. That would surely send Jackson off to hide amongst the guests.

'Howdy, Grady. How's married life treating you so far?' she asked.

'No complaints,' he answered, before swinging Nicholas up above his head and holding the giggling, writhing body of her son aloft. 'Hey, Nicholas, how are you doing, boyo? Did you have fun at Bobby's house?'

'Yes, yes,' Nicholas shrieked. 'Make me fly, Grady.'

'Please,' Jess said automatically.

Too late. Grady swooped his armful earthward and up again. How his back took the strain she had no idea. 'Where's Sasha?'

'Inside with Virginia, getting some more food. Man, these people can eat.' Swoop, and Nicholas was flying towards the ground again.

'You okay with Nicholas while I go see what I can do to help?' she asked Grady.

'She thinks I can't look after you, Nicholas. Women, eh?'

'What do you mean, women?' Nicholas's little face screwed up in question.

Jackson laughed. 'Get yourself out of that in one piece, Grady.'

'Better that he knows all he can as soon as possible.' Grady grinned. 'Leave the lad with us, Jess. We'll teach him all our bad habits.'

'That's what I'm afraid of.' She tipped her head to one side. 'You are grinning a lot this morning, Mr O'Neil. I'd better go see what Mrs O'Neil has been up to.' Jess headed to the house, ignoring the ribald comments coming from the two men she'd just left.

Inside she found Sasha and Virginia busy plating up leftover dessert from the wedding dinner. One look at Sasha told her everything. 'Oh, yuk. You look as happy as Grady. Must be something in the water out here.'

Sasha grinned and rushed to hug her. 'Morning. You're not looking too unhappy yourself.'

Uh-oh. Jess looked over at Virginia who suddenly seemed very busy placing slices of fruit on a pavlova. 'Of course I do. I've just delivered a baby. Although she was ten weeks early.'

'Is that why the helicopter went over earlier?' Virginia finally lifted her head. Dark shadows stained her cheeks, and her smile was a little loose.

'Yep. Now, Virginia, I'd love nothing better than a good old chinwag with Sasha before she leaves on her honeymoon. Want to let me finish that while I talk? Jackson's outside somewhere.'

Jess held her breath. She knew better than to out and out insist that Sasha's mum should take a rest.

'Good idea. I've been waiting to have a chat with that boy of mine.' She had the audacity to wink at Jess.

'I think he's with Grady, though he said he wanted to find Ian.'

Virginia hadn't even got to the door when Sasha rounded on Jess, grabbing her arms. 'What's this about my brother staying the night at your place?'

Didn't Sasha approve? She should have known it wasn't wise to get too close to her friend's brother. Hell, none of last night had been wise, but it had been a lot of fun. Though if it would come between her and Sasha then she'd learn to get over Jackson fast. Which wasn't a bad idea. She didn't want a serious relationship. 'Your mother's been talking?'

'Her words were, "Maybe there's enough of an attraction here to keep Jackson from returning to Hong Kong."' Sasha locked her eyes on Jess's, looking right inside her. 'It's okay, you know. In fact, I wholeheartedly approve.'

The air in Jess's lungs whooshed across her lips. 'I'm

glad it isn't going to be an issue between us. But you and your mother are getting ahead of the game. One night doesn't automatically lead to a wedding.'

'Got to start somewhere.' Sasha grinned again.

These lovesick grins were getting tiresome. But, then, hadn't she been smiling and laughing more than normal this morning? 'Great sex does the trick every time.'

'Excuse me?' Sasha's eyebrows rose and her brow wrinkled.

'You and Grady, going around like those clowns at the show with big grins that won't close.'

'Oh. Like the one on your face right now? Bet there's one on my brother's mug, too.'

Jess couldn't help it. She burst out laughing, and grabbed Sasha into another hug. 'Guess we should get these pavlovas done.'

'You always change the subject when it gets too hot for you.' Sasha resumed hulling the bowl of strawberries on the bench beside her. 'By the way, thank you for that painting you gave us. It's fabulous. How does the artist do such intricate work? Looking at that gull on the post with the sea in the background makes me feel the sun on my face and the salt air in my nostrils.'

'He's very good, no doubt about it.'

'Yeah, well, we love it and thank you so much. Of course, I could say you shouldn't have spent that kind of money but then I'd have to give the painting back and I'm not parting with it.'

'Damn. My cunning plan failed.'

They talked about the wedding as they worked, reminding each other of everything that had happened from the moment they'd started getting ready early yesterday morning.

Loud masculine laughter reached them through the

open kitchen windows and Jess stopped to stare out at Jackson as he stood talking with Grady and Ian. Those butt-hugging jeans and a T-shirt that outlined his well-defined muscles made her mouth water. Her heart bumped harder and louder than normal, and those pesky butterflies in her tummy started their dance again. 'Sasha, what does love feel like?' she whispered.

Sasha came to stand beside her and looked in the same direction. Slipping her arm through Jess's, she answered softly, 'It feels like every day is summer, like the air is clearer, and at night the stars are brighter. Love feels as though nothing can go wrong. As though everything is bigger. It makes you laugh and smile more.'

Jess bit down hard on her lip. *I've fallen in love. Overnight. Or did it happen the moment I saw Jackson standing beside Grady as they waited for us to arrive and the wedding ceremony to start? Does it even matter? It's happened. And it's not going anywhere.*

Sasha nudged her gently. 'The sky's very blue today, isn't it? Sparkling with sunlight.'

'Yes,' she whispered. *What the heck do I do now?*

'The colour of love, I reckon.'

CHAPTER FIVE

'WHO'S LOOKING AFTER Nicholas while you're working all these extra hours?' Jackson asked Jessica, as she folded the towels just back from the laundry and stacked them in the storeroom. It was Wednesday and he'd missed her every minute since the weekend. At least working here at the medical centre he got to see her occasionally but most of the time they were both too busy for more than quick snatches of conversation.

'He's at day care until Andrea picks him up after she collects her little boy from school. Bobby started school on Monday and Nicholas is so jealous. June can't come quickly enough for him.'

'I bet. It must be hard to leave him while you work.' She doted on her boy.

'It is. His little face turns all sad, which hurts to see. But it only happens a couple of days a week unless I'm covering for someone here.' Her face was turning sad now.

'You wouldn't think of not working at all?' What was her financial situation?

'Thanks to my parents...' she winced '...I could afford to stay at home, but not having a partner I need some adult contact. The brain needs some exercise, too.'

'I can understand that. It won't hurt Nicholas to be

mixing with other kids his age either.' Do not wrap her up in a hug. Not here at work. 'Do you like doing Sasha's job as well as your own?' From what he'd seen so far, she coped remarkably well. Nothing seemed too much for her. It made him wonder if people took advantage of that.

Jessica shrugged. 'Two weeks is nothing. And I get to keep my other nursing skills up to date.'

'Do you often do the nursing job?'

'First and foremost I'm the midwife, but if either nurse wants time off I cover for her. I like the variety and there are times when I've got no babies due and need to be busy.' The face she lifted to him was beautiful. Those big brown eyes were shining and her mouth had been curved in a perpetual smile all day.

'That chicken dish you dropped at home yesterday was tasty. When did you find the time to make it?' He and Dad had come in from the orchard late to find that Jess had dropped by with the meal. 'Mum was grateful, though, be warned, she's not likely to tell you.'

'I know. Not a problem. The wedding took its toll on her.'

'Which is why I haven't had time to call round to see you since Sunday.' Not for lack of trying. 'Dad's had a lot to do, clearing away everything and getting on with the orchard needs.' He'd ached to visit Jess but knew his priorities lay with his parents for a few days at least. His guilt at not having been here for so long could only be kept at bay by working his butt off, doing chores for them. Leaving in April was not going to be easy. 'My tractor skills have been in demand.'

'I understand.' The hand she laid on his arm was warm, but the sensations zipping through his blood were red hot. 'Virginia's worked nonstop on wedding plans since the day Sasha proposed to Grady. She had to crash some time.'

Jackson grinned. 'Sasha proposed to Grady? Are you sure?'

Nodding, Jess told him, 'Absolutely. She did it minutes after Melanie was born.'

'That's so Sasha. I'd have thought Grady would've been chomping at the bit to ask her to marry him. He's besotted.'

'Isn't he? Sasha had been keeping him at a distance. Afraid he might leave her again, I guess.'

Jackson stepped back, away from the citrus scent, away from that body that he so craved. Otherwise he was going to haul Jess into his arms and kiss her senseless. Something he wanted to do every time he saw her. Something he very definitely couldn't do while at work in the medical centre. But they could catch up out of the work zone. 'I've been checking the tides and it's looking good for a spot of surfcasting. How about we take Nicholas down to the beach when we're done here and he can try some fishing?'

Her eyes were definitely fudge-coloured right now. 'You'd do that? I'd love it, and you'll be Nicholas's hero for ever.' Then the light gleaming out at him dimmed. 'Maybe that's not so wise.'

Jackson stepped back close, laid his hands on her shoulders. 'I promise to be careful with him. And Grady will be back to replace me in my male role model position.' He suddenly didn't like that idea. Not one little bit. For a brief moment he wished he could be the man who showed Nicholas the ways of the world. But he wasn't being realistic at all. It was not possible to be there for Nicholas for more than a few weeks. So having Grady in the background was good. He had to believe that, or go crazy, worrying about the little guy.

Under his hands her shoulders lifted, dropped. 'You're right. But just so as you know, I don't want Nicholas getting high expectations of your involvement with him. Not when you're not staying around.'

At least she hadn't said anything about his involvement with her. While he hadn't worked out where their relationship was headed, he didn't want the gate closing before they'd spent more time together. 'I understand, Jess.'

'Do you?' She locked her gaze on him, like she was searching for something. 'I worry because I know what it's like to have expectations of adults and never have them met.'

'Your parents?' He held his breath, waiting for her to tell him to go to hell. To say it was none of his business.

But after a moment she nodded. 'Yeah. I'm sure they loved me. But they never needed me. I was a nuisance when all they needed was each other and their busy life outdoors, studying native flora and fauna, and how to protect it for generations to come. They tried. I'll give them that. I always had more money than even I could spend. Occasionally they took me on trips to places in the world most people aren't even aware of. All far away from civilisation, from the fun things a kid likes to do. I guess growing up I never wanted for anything. Except hugs, and sharing girl talk with my mother, and being able to brings friends home for sleepovers.'

When she started spilling her heart she didn't stop easily. The pain in her words cut him deep. No one should ever feel that they came second best with their parents. No one. To hell with being at the medical centre. He wrapped his arms around her, held her tight, and dropped kisses on the top of her head. 'You already give Nicholas far more than that.'

'I hope so,' she murmured against him, her warm breath heating his skin. 'It's a work in progress.'

'You think you don't know how to love? From what I've seen, you're spot on.' She exuded love—to Nicholas, to Sasha, his parents, her patients. Did she have any left over for him? Because he really wanted some. Correction, he wanted lots. And what would he give her in return? Love? Full, hands-on love? Or the chilly, remote kind, like her parents'? From afar, in a city that was not conducive to raising a small boy with an apparent penchant for the outdoors.

His hands dropped away and he took that backwards step again. It was too soon to know. Did he want to know? He knew he didn't want to hurt Jess. *Don't forget you're heading out of here come mid-April. No way will Jessica and Nicholas be going with you.*

Jess rocked sideways, regained her balance. Gave him a crooked smile. 'Thanks. I think. Fishing after work would be lovely.' Then she spun round and became very intent on those damned towels again, refolding already neatly folded ones. Shifting them from stack to stack.

'Jackson.' Sheree from Reception popped her head around the corner. 'Mrs Harrop's here to see you.' Her voice dropped several octaves. 'She's not the most patient lady either.'

'On my way.' He stared at Jess's ramrod-straight back, waited for the other woman to return to her desk out front. 'We'll have fish and chips for dinner on the beach. That okay with you? And Nicholas?'

'Sounds great.' Jess turned and he relaxed. Her grin was back. Her eyes were like fudge. 'I'm looking forward to it.'

So was he. A lot. Too much for someone who wasn't getting involved. Face it, taking a woman and her son to do regular stuff like fishing was a first.

'And, Jackson?'

He turned back. 'Yes?'

'Mrs Harrop is a sweetie underneath that grumpy exterior.'

'I'll remember that.' How come Jessica stuck up for the underdog so much? Maybe it was because she'd been the odd one out in those two years she'd been to school here. He'd had the loving, sharing family *and* all the friends at school, and yet he stayed away.

'Mrs Harrop, it's been years since I saw you. Do you even remember me?' Jackson showed the rather large, elderly lady to a chair in the consulting room he was using while Grady was away.

'Could hardly forget the boy who kicked his football through my front window.'

Jackson winced. That had been at least fifteen years ago. He gave Mrs Harrop a rueful smile. 'Sorry about that.'

'You've been away too long, my boy,' she muttered, as she carefully lowered herself onto the seat. 'But you're here now.'

As this was about the fifth time he'd heard almost the exact words since arriving in Golden Bay Jackson didn't react at all. He might even have been disappointed if people hadn't commented on his return, even though it wasn't permanent. After all, since one of his reasons for leaving was that everyone here knew everything about people's business, he'd feel cheated if his actions were no longer justified.

'I wasn't going to miss the wedding. Sasha would

never forgive me.' He wouldn't have forgiven himself. He loved his sister. 'She's so happy, it's wonderful.'

'That Grady was always meant for her.' Mrs Harrop was pulling up her sleeve. 'You going to take my blood pressure, or what?'

'I sure am. But first, how've you been feeling?' He'd read the patient notes before asking Mrs Harrop to come through and knew that she'd had two arterial stents put in six months ago.

'Old, tired, and a lot better than I used to.'

'How's your diet been? Are you sticking to fat-free?' Jackson saw that her last cholesterol test had been a little high but nothing dangerous.

'Your lady makes sure of that.'

'My lady? Mum? Or Sasha?' He wound the cuff of the sphygmomanometer around her upper arm.

'Pssh. I'm talking about Jessica. She's very good to me. Always delivering healthy meals and telling me how she's cooked too much. You'd think she'd have learned a new excuse by now. She's the best neighbour I ever had. Very kind. She genuinely cares about people.'

Alarm bells began clattering in his head. Mrs Harrop was calling Jessica his woman and they'd only spent one night together. Wasn't this why he left Golden Bay in the first place? 'You live in the house next to Jess?' Guess that explained her comment about his woman. At seventy Mrs Harrop might have old fashioned ideas about him spending a night with a lovely young woman.

Without waiting for Mrs Harrop's answer, he stuck the earpieces in and squeezed the bulb to tighten the cuff. Then he listened to the blood pumping through her veins and noted the systolic and diastolic pressures. 'Moderately high. Have you been taking your tablets daily?'

'Yes, young man, I have. But I need a new prescription.' His patient pulled her sleeve down to her wrist and buttoned it. 'She bought both houses.'

'I think you need a different dosage.' Jackson began tapping the computer keyboard. 'She what? Who bought both houses? Jessica?'

Mrs Harrop's chin bobbed up and down, and her eyes lit up with satisfaction. 'Of course, Jessica. She saved my bacon when she bought mine. And now she lets me rent it back for next to nothing. I know I should be paying more but I can't.'

Jackson slumped in his chair. Jess owned both those homes? She hadn't said. *But why should she? She might've talked about her parents earlier but that didn't mean she would be telling you everything. Like you, she can play things close to the chest.* Another vision of that chest flickered through his brain before he had time to stamp on it. Beautiful, full breasts that filled his hands perfectly.

Apparently Mrs Harrop hadn't finished. 'You see, that boy of mine cleaned out my savings and left me with only the house. I wouldn't even have had that if my lawyer hadn't made me get a trustee to oversee any sale I might want to make.'

'I'm sorry to hear that.' But Jess had saved this woman from heartbreak.

'The day Jessica decided to return to Golden Bay was my lucky day.'

'So it would seem.' *Good for you, Jess. You're an absolute star.* Money had never been in short supply in her family, yet she drove a joke of a car and gave her neighbour cheap accommodation. 'Now, Mrs Harrop, here's your prescription. I've upped the dosage a little and I want to see you again next week.'

'Thank you, Doctor. I'll make an appointment on the way out.'

Jess was taking bloods from Gary Hill when he walked back from showing Mrs Harrop out. He asked, 'Hi, Gary. You still into motocross?'

'Gidday, Jackson. Sure am. Though the body's a bit stiff these days and I don't land so easily when I come off. Break a few more bones than I used to.' The guy appeared flushed and lethargic, but had plenty to say. Some things didn't change.

'Maybe it's time to give it up.'

Jess turned to him and rolled her eyes. 'Even when he broke his clavicle and humerus, there was no stopping Gary. You honestly think he'll give up because his body's getting rumpty on him?'

'Guess not.' Jackson was puzzled as to why Jess was taking bloods. 'So what brings you here today? I'm seeing you next, aren't I?'

'I've got a fever. I got malaria last year when I was riding in Malaysia and this feels exactly the same as the previous two bouts.' Gary shrugged. 'Just hope I'm not on my back too long. I'm supposed to be heading away to the Philippines in eight days.'

'Sorry, Jackson, but the courier's due to pick up medical specimens and Roz suggested I take Gary's bloods while he waited to see you.' Jess labelled the tubes of blood for haematology and biochemistry, then made some thick blood smears. Next she stuck a tiny plaster on the needle entry site on Gary's arm. 'There you go. We should hear back tonight about the malaria.'

Back in his room Jackson began to read Gary's file on the computer screen as he asked, 'Any symptoms other than the fever?'

'Hot and cold, hell of a headache, and I keep wanting to toss my food.' Gary eased himself onto a chair, rubbing his left side.

'You're hurting?' Was that his spleen giving him grief, engorged through trying to remove malarial parasites from his blood system?

'That's my old injury from when I came off the bike and broke my pelvis. Still hurts on and off. Guess the arthritis is starting to set in. I was warned.' He yawned deep. 'Yeah, this is familiar. The bone-numbing tiredness.'

Jackson found a thermometer and slipped it under Gary's tongue. 'Seriously, you ever think about slowing down?' The guy was only thirty-four but at this rate he might not make forty in reasonable working order.

Gary kept his lips sealed around the thermometer and shook his head.

'Fair enough. Your call.' Reading more of the file, he commented, 'I see your malaria was diagnosed as falciparum. Common in Asia. Had you taken anti-malarials at the time?'

A nod.

Reading the thermometer, he told Gary, 'That's way too high. I hope you've been taking lots of fluids. Let's get you up on the bed so I can check your spleen.'

Jackson gently felt Gary's abdomen. 'Your spleen's definitely enlarged, which fits the diagnosis.'

'Guess I already knew. Can't blame me for hoping I was wrong.'

'When did you start getting symptoms?'

'Started feeling crook night before last, but I was working up the Cobb Valley and wanted to get the job done.'

'You've got to take care of yourself, mate. This malaria can be very serious if you stall on getting treatment.'

'I live hard,' Gary growled. 'With my family history

of bowel cancer taking my dad and two brothers, I'm packing in as much as I can in case I'm next.'

It made sense in a way. Jackson asked, 'You married, got kids?'

'Kate Saunders and I got hitched ten years back. Got two youngsters. What about you?'

'No, no kids or wife.'

'What are you waiting for? None of us are getting any younger. You don't want to be in your dotage, with anklebiters hanging on to you.'

'I'll remember you said that.' And try not to think about Jess in the same moment. 'I suggest we get you over the hill to hospital today. I don't want you waiting here until we find out those results. You need intravenous fluids ASAP.'

'Figured you'd say that. Kate's packed my overnight bag.'

He remembered Kate from school, a quiet girl who'd followed the crowd around. After signing a referral to hospital, Jackson went with Gary out to the waiting room and explained everything to Kate. 'It's great to see you both again.'

'You stopping here permanently?' Gary asked.

'No.'

'Why not? I travel a lot but this is the greatest little place on earth.'

Exactly. Little. Too little for him.

Thankfully Jessica joined them and diverted Gary's focus as she handed him a package. 'You might as well take your bloods with you. Save time at the other end, and prevent the need to be jabbed again.'

'Jess, line one for you,' Sheree called. 'It's a Lily Carter.'

'Cool. I hope that means good news on baby Alice Rose.'

'Let me know,' he called after her. That had been their first time working together and he'd enjoyed it.

So far, buster, there hasn't been anything you haven't enjoyed doing with Jess.

Five minutes later the woman swamping his brain popped her head around the door. 'Lily says hi and thank you for everything we did on Sunday. Alice Rose is doing very well and we're getting the credit.' That smile she gave him would get her anything she wanted.

'That's good news. I hated seeing her pain, and I'm not just talking about the labour. She's had more than her share of misfortune.'

'If they have another baby, I don't think Matthew will be taking her far from home. She hated her helicopter flight.'

'What a waste.' He grinned.

A light offshore breeze lifted Jess's hair as she sat on the sand, watching Nicholas trying to fling the fishing line into the water. Unfortunately it kept getting stuck in the sand and seaweed behind him as he threw the rod tip over his shoulder. She chuckled. 'Go slowly with that rod, Nicholas. You don't want to break it.'

'I'm doing what Jackson showed me.'

Right, shut up, Mum, and let the men get on with the job of fishing. 'I guess he knows best.'

'I'm a man, remember. We know these things from birth.' Jackson flicked a cheeky grin her way before carefully lifting the tip of Nicholas's rod out of the sand.

Of course she remembered he was a man. A perfect specimen of a man. Why else had she gone to bed with him? *Because you were so attracted to him you couldn't think straight.* Yeah, well, there was that, too. Which only underlined the fact he was male. She lay back on her towel to soak up some of the end-of-day summer warmth, and glanced at Jackson again.

He was still watching her but now his gaze had dropped to cruise over her scantily clad body. She saw his chest rise and his stomach suck in.

Guess her new bikini was a hit, then. Sasha had told her she would be nuts not to buy it when they'd spent a day in Nelson shopping two weeks ago. While they'd gone for last-minute wedding accessories they'd got side-tracked with lingerie and swimwear for Sasha's honeymoon. Bikinis all round.

Jackson croaked, 'What did I tell you? Orange really suits you.'

'You're close. Burnt orange this time.' Pulling her eyes away from that tantalising view of rock-hard muscles and sexy mouth, she tipped her head back to look up at the sky. Bright blue. The colour of love. Gulp. Her gaze dropped back to the man who'd snatched her heart. Thankfully he was now focused on fishing with Nicholas so she could study him without being caught. Tall, lean and as virile as it was possible to get. Yep, this was definitely love. How fast that had happened. So fast she couldn't trust it. Yet.

Four days after that heady night with him she still didn't know what to do. She'd been surprised when Jackson hadn't taken off at the first hint of her talking about something as personal as her misguided parents. He'd even hugged her, reassured her. Yeah, he wasn't hard to love. Too darned easy, in fact.

'Mummy, something's pulling my line. Look. Mummy, come here, quick. It's jiggling.'

Jackson was holding the rod upright. 'Wind the line in as fast as you can, Nicholas. That's it. Keep it coming. You don't want the fish jumping off the hook.'

'Mummy, look. Is it a fish? Jackson?'

'Yes, sport, you've caught your first fish.' Jackson reached for the hand net on the sand and raced to scoop up the flapping trophy. 'Look at that. Well done, Nicholas. You're a proper fisherman now.'

'Can I see? I want to hold it.' Nicholas dropped the rod and ran at Jackson, who scooped him up and carried boy and net up onto the sand.

'If we tip the fish out here, away from the sea, we won't lose it back in the water.' His long fingers deftly unhooked the ten-centimetre-long herring and handed it to Nicholas. 'Put your fingers where mine are, by the gills. That's it.' In an undertone he added, solely for her benefit, 'I hope you brought the camera, Mum.'

She did an exaggerated eye-roll. 'Would I forget the most important thing?'

After at least ten photos, capturing the biggest smile she'd ever seen on her boy's face, she made Jackson kneel down beside Nicholas and snapped a few more of the pair of happy fishermen. Those would look great in her album. Along with the wedding shots of her and Jackson standing with Sasha and Grady.

'I want to do it again, Jackson.'

'Like a true fisherman.' Jackson retrieved the rod, baited the hook and handed it to Nicholas, then took the herring aside to deal with it.

'Can we have my fish for dinner, Mummy?'

Yuk. Herring. But this was her boy's first fish. 'I guess, but it's very small for three people to share.'

As Nicholas's little face puckered up, ready for an outburst, Jackson saved the moment. 'You know, herrings are usually used for bait to catch bigger fish. Why don't we put it in your mother's freezer for when we go out in the boat after big fish?'

'Okay. What's for dinner? Fishing makes me hungry.'

'Now, there's a surprise.' She blew him a kiss before glancing across to Jackson, who was smiling at Nicholas.

'We're having fish and chips as soon as we've finished fishing, sport. What do you reckon? Had enough with that rod yet?'

'No. I'm going to get another he-herring.'

He did. Two more. Then they packed up and headed to the motor camp and the fast-food shop.

'Fish and chips on the beach in the fading sunlight, with sand for extra texture, and lukewarm cans of soda. I can't think of a better meal,' Jess said an hour later, as she unlocked her front door. Behind her Jackson carried Nicholas from the car.

'Talk about picky. What's wrong with a bit of sand crunching between your teeth?' He grinned. 'Bedroom?'

What a silly question. Of course she wanted to go to her bedroom with him. Her body was leaning towards him like metal to a magnet. That dancing feeling had begun in her stomach.

'Which is Nicholas's room?' Jackson's deep voice interrupted her hot thoughts. A wicked twinkle lightened his eyes.

Oh, yes, Nicholas. She gave herself a mental slap and led the way into the second, smaller bedroom. 'Definitely bedtime for my boy.' He was out for the count, had been all the way home, after talking excitedly non-stop about his fish.

'Whatever else were you thinking?' The bone-melting chuckle played havoc with all her thought processes so that she stood waiting for Jackson to lay Nicholas on the bed.

'Jess? The bedcover?'

Blink. Another mental slap. Concentrate. Heat raced up her cheeks as she hurriedly snatched the quilt out of the way. Then her heart rolled over as Jackson placed Nicholas ever so gently onto his bed and reached for the quilt to tuck it up under his chin. It wouldn't take much for her to get used to this. This was what she wanted for her boy, for herself. Sharing parenthood. Sharing everything.

'Thanks,' she whispered around a thickening in her throat. She found Teddy and slipped him in beside Nicholas, before dropping a kiss on her boy's forehead. She sniffed back her threatening tears, and grinned. 'Yuk. He smells fishy.'

'Only a little.' Jackson draped an arm over her shoulders. 'All part of the fun.'

Sniff, sniff. 'How come you don't reek? You handled those herrings more than Nicholas did.'

'I used the bathroom at the takeaway place. I thought Nicholas had, too.'

'Little boys have to be supervised at cleaning time.' She nudged his ribs with her elbow. 'Want a coffee before you head home?'

His finger touched her chin, tilted her head back so their eyes met. 'Any chance I can stay longer than a coffee?'

She melted against him. 'Every chance.'

'What's this?' Jess's fingers were running over Jackson's flat belly, seeking pleasure, hopefully giving pleasure, as they lay luxuriating in the aftermath of great sex.

Under her hand he stilled. 'An old wound.'

Didn't feel that old to her. The scar was still soft with a rough ridge running through the puckered skin. 'Define old.' If he refused to answer she'd back off. Everyone was entitled to privacy.

'Five weeks.'

'That is a long time.' She smiled into the dark.

'Seems like yesterday.' He rolled onto his side and ran a finger from her shoulder down to her breast, flicked across the nipple, sending shards of hot need slicing through her.

Okay, so this was the sidetrack trick. She'd run with it. She might be missing out on something important but amazing sex wasn't a bad second.

Then Jackson said, 'I was knifed.'

'What?' She bolted upright and stared down at him in the half-light from the hall. A low-wattage light always ran in case Nicholas woke up needing the bathroom. 'You must've really annoyed someone.'

'Come back down here.' He reached and tugged at her until she complied, sliding down the bed and finishing up tucked in against him. 'You don't want to know.'

'Wrong, Jackson. I do.'

She felt his chest lift as he drew a breath. Then he told her. 'In Hong Kong there's a group of doctors and nurses I belong to outside the hospital. We look after the poor and underprivileged during the hours of darkness. We mostly visit night shelters but occasionally the police call us to look at someone who refuses to get help.'

'You do this as well as work in the emergency department of a large hospital?' No wonder the guy looked exhausted most of the time. 'This is what you were referring to the other night when I asked why you were so tired.'

'Not quite.' He leaned in and dropped the softest of kisses on the corner of her mouth. Then he lay on his back, hands behind his head, and stared up at the ceiling. 'It was Christmas Eve. Fireworks displays out on the harbour. Plenty of tourists and locals enjoying themselves.'

Jess wound an arm over his waist and laid her cheek on his chest. 'Lots of booze.'

'Lots and lots of booze.' Jackson was quiet for a long time. Under her cheek she could feel his heart thudding. Tension had crept into his body. Her hand softly massaged his thigh. Finally, he said, 'The unit I worked with was doing the rounds of the usual haunts when we had a call from the police to meet them three streets over where they'd found a woman claiming she'd been raped.'

Running her fingers back and forth over his skin, Jess waited. He'd tell his tale in his own time, and she had all night.

'It was a set-up. We were attacked the moment we turned the corner. The nurse with me…' His Adam's apple bobbed. 'It should've been me, not Juliet who got the fatal blow. But she was always a fast sprinter.'

'Your friend ran into the attackers?'

'Slap bang onto the knives they wielded.'

'So you feel guilty because you didn't take the hit.' Her hand smoothed over those tense muscles. 'How were you to know that would happen?' About now he'd go all silent on her. 'Is this why you get angry at times?'

'Yeah.'

She waited quietly, only her hand moving as it swept his skin.

Exhaling, he continued. 'Frustration, guilt, vulnerability all add up to an ugly picture. It's debilitating.'

It took a brave man to tell her that. She wrapped herself around him, held him tight. Just listened.

'She didn't make it. I tried. Believe me, I did everything in my power to save her. But she'd been struck in the heart. There was absolutely nothing I could do but wait for the ambulance, hold her hand and keep talking. Noting the things she wanted me to tell her family, dreading that I might forget even one little detail.'

'She knew she was dying.'

'Yeah.' His sigh was so sad it tugged at her heart. 'I couldn't hide that from her. She was too experienced in emergency medicine.'

'You were wounded, too.'

'Yeah. But I survived.'

With one hand she traced the outline of the scar that ran down his thigh. 'Why did they attack you?'

'No one knows. So far the men who did this haven't been found. The police put every resource they had into finding them but no one's talking. The cops don't think it was personal, in that it wasn't me or Juliet they were targeting but more likely the organisation we worked for.'

'Will you continue with that when you return to Hong Kong?'

'Juliet made me promise not to give up our work on the streets because of this.'

That was a big ask. Jess chilled. No wonder Jackson wasn't staying in Golden Bay. He believed he had to go back even if he didn't want to. That promise would be strong, hanging over him, adding to his guilt if he even considered not returning. 'She didn't say not to quit if you had other compelling reasons.' *Like your mum. Like me.*

'I think I need to go back, if only to get past what happened. I don't mind admitting I'll be scared witless the first time I hit the streets, probably see knife-wielding attackers at every dark corner. At the same time I find myself wondering what it would be like to create a life outside medicine.'

Jess caught her breath. What sort of life? Where? Breathing out, she admitted her disappointment. He hadn't said he intended changing hospitals or countries. 'Guess you've got time to make that decision.'

'True. Doesn't get any easier, though. I don't know if

I'm reacting to the attack or if I'm genuinely ready for a change.'

Her hands began moving up his sides, lightly touching his skin, gentling the tension gripping him. Her lips kissed his chest, found a nipple and she began to lick slowly, teasing him to forget the pain of that night. Gradually his reaction changed from tension caused by his story to a tension of another kind, pushing into her thigh. Shifting slightly so that she held him between her thighs, she slid a hand between them and began to rub that hard evidence of his need.

'Jessica,' he groaned through clenched teeth. 'Please don't stop. I need this. I need *you*.'

She had no intention of stopping. Not when her libido was screaming for release. She had to have him—deep inside her.

Suddenly she was flipped onto her back. Jackson separated her thighs to kneel between them. His hands lifted her backside and then he drove into her. Withdrew. Forged forward. Withdrew. And her mind went blank as her body was swamped with heat and desire and need.

CHAPTER SIX

A VOICE CUT through Jess's dreams, dragging her cotton-wool-filled mind into the daylight. 'Who—?'

'Now for the seven o'clock news. Last night—'

The radio alarm. She shut the annoying drone out, concentrated on why she felt so languid this morning. 'Jackson.' Why else? Who else?

Rolling her head sideways, she saw what she already knew. He'd gone. Sneaked out some time in the early hours while she'd been snoozing, gathering her energy around her. For another round of exquisite sex? Turning to glance the other way, she smiled. A note lay on the bedside table.

'Didn't want to be around when Nicholas woke in case it caused trouble. See you at the medical centre. Hugs, J.'

Thoughtful as well as sexy. Great combination, Jackson. And I still love you. But you are going away again and I can understand why. Unfortunately.

Leaping out of bed, she tugged the curtains open. Yep, the sky was as blue as the lightest sapphire. The colour of love. Love meant letting go and waiting for him to come back.

'Now for the weather forecast.' Behind her the voice droned on. 'Expect showers this morning and if you're thinking of going out on the briny, maybe you should find something else to do. Forty-knot northerlies are predicted from around lunchtime.'

Showers? The day was light and sunny. 'Get a new forecast, buddy.' She clicked the pessimist off and headed for the shower.

Twenty minutes later Nicholas bounced into the kitchen and pulled out a chair at the table. 'I want cocoa pops.'

'Please,' Jess said. Placing the bowl and box of cereal on the table, she did a double take. 'What are you wearing?'

'My fishing shirt. This is the lucky shirt. Jackson told me I should wear it every time I go fishing with him.'

So there were to be more fishing expeditions? 'That's fine, but you're going to play centre this morning, not fishing. Take it off and put it in the washing basket.'

'No. I'm wearing it so my friends can see it.' The cocoa pops overflowed from the bowl onto the table. 'I'm going to tell them all about the three fishes I got.'

Removing the carton from Nicholas's hand, she put it back in the cupboard, out of reach. 'That's more than enough cereal. Let's put half those pops in another bowl before you add the milk or there'll be a big mess.'

Too late. The puffed rice spilled over the rim on a tide of milk. 'Whoa, stop pouring now.' She snatched the milk container away.

'I want more milk.' Nicholas banged his spoon on the tabletop. 'More milk, more milk.'

'Sorry, buddy, but you've got more than enough.' She spooned coffee granules into a mug, added half a teaspoon extra, then two sugars. As she dropped two slices of wholegrain in the toaster the front doorbell rang.

Behind her a chair slammed back against the wall. 'I'll get it.' Nicholas raced out of the kitchen.

'Hello, Mr Fisherman.' A deep, sexy voice echoed down the hallway before Jess had made it to the kitchen doorway. Her stomach turned to mush as she peeped around the doorframe and drank in the sight of this man who seemed to hold her heart in his hand.

'Mummy, it's Jackson,' Nicholas yelled, as though she was already at the medical centre.

'Morning.' Jackson had somehow moved along the hall to stand in front of her. 'You're looking good enough to eat this morning.'

Corny. But nice. 'Want a coffee?'

'Please, ta.'

Nicholas jumped up and down in front of Jackson. 'I'm wearing my fishing shirt. See?'

Jackson flicked a question her way. 'Not your idea?'

She shook her head.

'See, here's the thing, Nicholas. Fishing shirts are special and we men have got to look after them. They need washing after you've caught fish, and then put away in the drawer until next time you go to the beach.'

Nicholas was nodding solemnly. 'Okay. I'll go and change.'

Jess stared after Nicholas as he sped out of the room. 'How did you do that? I could spend ten minutes arguing myself blue in the face about that shirt and he'd still wear it to play centre.'

'Hey. Solo parenting can't be so easy. You've got to make all the calls.' A friendly arm encircled her shoulders, tugged her in against a warm, strong body. 'From what I saw last night, you have a good relationship with Nicholas. Don't be so hard on yourself. It's not like you have family here to support you or give you a break.'

The more she got to know Jackson the more talkative

he got. 'Thanks.' Reluctantly she pulled out of his hold. 'Have you had breakfast?'

'Toast on the run. Sam's sheep got into Mum's orchard overnight. I helped Kevin round them up and get them back in their rightful paddock.'

'Kevin's turning out to be very helpful.'

'Where'd he come from?'

Jess handed him a coffee as she answered. 'He and Tamara had an unexpected baby, which Sasha and Grady delivered. There are some terrible family issues involving Tamara's family. Seems the young couple got so much help when the locals heard about the baby and everything else that they decided to stay here. Your dad offered Kevin work on the orchard, helping Virginia, and since Sam's accident he hasn't been able to go back to driving full time so Kevin fills in for him as needed.'

'That's why they're living in the orchard cottage.'

'Yep. Sasha moved in with Grady after Melanie was born. Kevin and Tamara needed somewhere to stay. Simple.'

'Is this shirt okay, Jackson?' Nicholas bounded back and climbed onto his chair.

After silently checking with her, Jackson gave his approval. 'You'd better get on with your breakfast, sport. It's nearly time to go to play group.'

Jess held her breath. But the kitchen became quiet except for the steady munching of cocoa pops. She shook her head and turned to Jackson. 'That's a turnaround. You sure you're not staying for good?'

His smile faltered then returned. 'Can I take a raincheck?'

Her eyes must have been out on stalks. They'd certainly widened so that they were stretching. Her mouth dried. As she stared at Jackson he shoved a hand through his hair, mussing it nicely.

'You are making it so tempting, believe me.' His chest rose. 'But I have to be very honest here. I can't see me staying. For a start, there isn't an emergency department for me to find work at.'

'There's one two hours away over the hill.'

His lips pressed together and she knew she'd gone too far. But this wasn't a one-sided conversation. Was it?

'Like I've already explained, I don't see myself settling back into such a small community. I didn't much like it the first time round.' His chest rose and fell. 'Not to mention my promise to Juliet.'

She couldn't complain that he hadn't given her the facts. He was more honest than she was. But she had no intention of telling him she'd fallen in love with him. Not when she knew deep down she couldn't start a serious relationship. Her son was more important than her love for any man. So that meant keeping her mouth shut and enjoying whatever happened between her and Jackson. 'Thank you for being honest.'

'Jess,' he called softly. 'Am I asking too much if I say I'd like to carry on with what we've got? Is that selfish?'

'It would only be selfish if you were the only one getting something out of it.' Even to her, the smile she made felt lacklustre. Trying again, she came up with something stronger, warmer. 'I…' I'm stuck for words.

'It's okay. You don't have to say anything.'

But I do. I want to. 'Until Saturday night I never expected to meet a man I'd feel so relaxed and comfortable with. You touch something within me, and—' Oh hell, why wasn't this easy? Maybe she should come out with it, tell him she loved him. Except she had to remember that she carried her parents' genes—she would never be able to trust herself to be a good parent when she was in love with someone else. Mum and Dad were devoted to each other, to the point she'd always felt like a spare part in their lives. She'd never do that to Nicholas. 'Jackson, you're special and you make me feel the same way. So, yes, let's carry on with whatever it is we've got.'

Did that sound like a business arrangement? Nah, who had hot sex with their business partner? She started to giggle. This really was an oddball situation, and she had no intention of dropping it. Her giggles turned to laughter.

'What's funny, Mummy?' Nicholas tapped Jackson on the arm. 'Mummy doesn't like laughing.'

Jackson's eyes widened. 'Must be my fault. She laughs a lot around me.'

'That's because you're funny,' Nicholas told him as he got down from the table.

'Funny ha-ha or funny strange? No, don't answer that, either of you.' Jackson grinned at her boy.

'Funny cool.' Getting herself under control, Jess noticed Nicholas heading for his bedroom. 'Nicholas, come back and put your bowl and spoon in the sink, please.'

'You do it. I'm getting my school bag.'

'Nicholas. Do as I say. Please.'

'No. Too busy.'

Jackson glanced at her then down the hall. 'Hey, sport, that's not the way for a boy to talk to his mother. Better come and do as she says.'

She held her breath, and waited through the sudden silence that descended on her home.

'Okay, coming,' her son called, moments before he bounced back into the kitchen. There was the clatter of his plate dropping in the sink, followed by the spoon.

Then he snatched up the cloth and wiped the spilled milk further across the table. 'There, Mummy, all clean.'

Jess rescued the cloth from sliding off the edge of the bench and rinsed it under the tap. 'Thanks, Nicholas. You can finish getting ready for play group now.' As she re-wiped the table she didn't know whether to be pleased or unhappy at Jackson's help. He'd certainly got a good response from Nicholas. Far more than she'd managed. 'Thank you,' she whispered.

'Like I said, you're a good mum, Jessica Baxter. You're too hard on yourself.' Those arms she was coming to rely on for comfort were winding around her again.

Sighing she pulled back and looked up into those green eyes that reminded her of spring and new growth. New love? Don't think like that. Some time soon Jackson will twig what you're thinking and then where will you be? Out in the cold. 'Guess we'd better get cracking. The centre opens in fifteen and I've got antenatal clinic this morning.'

At the medical centre Jackson sat at the staff kitchen table, a strong, long black coffee in hand, and listened to Roz and Rory discussing their patients. 'Seems there's no end of people needing lots of care.'

Jess hadn't had a moment to spare during the day. Mike was at home, catching up on sleep after a night up on Takaka Hill helping Search and Rescue haul a caver out of Harwood's Hole. The man had slipped and fallen fifty metres, breaking both legs on landing at the bottom.

Rory told him, 'Summer is always busier. The influx of holidaymakers adds to our workload something terrible. Not to mention numerous cavers and trampers getting out into the wilderness.'

Roz added, 'It's as if people leave the cautious side of their brains at home when they pack to go on holiday.'

'You must remember what it was like when you were growing up here, Jackson,' Rory said.

'Sure, but I wasn't a doctor. I got to see a few incidents that occurred amongst my mates. I don't remember anything too serious happening.'

'What about when those guys took a dinghy out with too big a motor for the size of the boat? They flipped the boat and nearly drowned themselves. Saved by another boat going past. And by you swimming out to rescue one of them. He would've drowned if it hadn't been for you and the doctor on board the second boat.'

When had Jess come into the room? When had his antennae failed him? He always knew when she was within metres of him. Or so he'd thought. 'Ben and Haydon. Damned idiots they were.'

'Lucky idiots, by the sound of it.' Rory picked up a printout of a lab result. 'I see it's confirmed Gary's got another bout of falciparum. We need to look into what else can be down to prevent further attacks. Jackson, do you see much malaria in Hong Kong?'

'We get quite a few patients presenting but then they're passed on to the medical team and that's it as far as the emergency department is concerned. But I can give you a contact at the hospital if you like.'

From under lowered eyelids he watched Jess as she filled her water bottle. The movement of leaning slightly forward over the sink accentuated her sweet curves, especially that butt he'd cupped in his hands last night. His mouth dried while below his belt muscles stirred. Was there such a thing as having too much of Jess? Not in this lifetime.

'Have you got many house calls, Jess?' Rory asked.

'Five for this afternoon, which isn't too bad. I'll stop by and see Claire Johnston and baby Max on my way home.'

Jackson sat up straighter. 'I'll give you another prescription for antibiotics for Max. Talking to Claire earlier, she said the baby still has a wheezy cough.'

Jess gave him one of those heart-melting smiles of hers. 'Sure. Send it through to the pharmacy and I'll pick it up on my way.' She pulled a pen from her pocket and scribbled a note on the back of her hand. 'There, shouldn't forget now.'

'Right.' Roz pushed her chair back and stood up. 'Might as well get this show on the road.'

Rory stayed seated, twirling his mug back and forth in his hands, like he was waiting for the others to disappear.

'Baby Carrington's due any day now so I'll be hovering.' Jess shoved her water bottle in the fridge and followed Roz.

Jackson drained his coffee and stood up. 'You want to say something?' he asked Rory.

The mug kept moving back and forth in those big hands resting on the table. 'Are you fixed on returning to Hong Kong at the end of your leave?'

'Definitely. Nothing to keep me here.' Why did an image of a pair of all-seeing, fudge-coloured eyes suddenly dance across his brain?

'Pity.' Rory lifted his gaze from the table to Jackson. 'Will you go back to working on the streets at night?'

How did he know about that? 'Of course. There's no end of work out there.'

'Your near-miss with a knife hasn't changed your attitude?'

Disappointment was a hard ball in the pit of his gut. 'Jess has been talking too much.' So the very thing that had made him wary about being here had come back to haunt him—in less than three weeks.

Rory's eyebrows lifted. 'Jess?' Then understanding dawned. 'Not Jess. Dr Ng Ping.'

What was going on here? Ping was his department head, and probably the closest he had to a friend in Hong Kong. Why had he and Rory been in touch? 'You care to explain?' Jackson's blood started to simmer. If anyone had anything to say about him, they should say it to his face.

'Dr Ng rang to ask after your health. Said whenever he talked to you, you only ever told him you were fine.'

'Wait until I see Ping. He had no right to do that.' The simmer was becoming a boil. How could Ping do that behind his back? He, more than most, understood how important it was to him to be above board in everything.

'He told me he was a concerned friend who wanted to know you were doing as well as you said. That you are getting over the incident.'

Had Ping told Rory about his meltdown in the middle of the department one particularly busy night? Yes, Jackson would bet everything he owned on it. Pulling out a chair, he straddled it and eyeballed Rory. 'I still have small temper surges at the most unexpected moments, but they disappear quickly, and they happen less and less often. Nothing has happened here at the centre, and no patients have any reason to be concerned. Neither do you and your partners.' Bile soured his mouth. And he'd been stupid enough to think loose-tongued people only lived in Golden Bay.

'Relax, Jackson. I have absolutely no qualms about you working with us. No one else knows about that call either. I figured it wasn't necessary.'

'So where's this headed? I'm sure the waiting room is

bursting with people wanting our services.' The threatening temper outburst backed off a little.

Rory got up and shut the door, came back to the table but didn't sit. 'I'm getting antsy, want to head home to Auckland. But my conscience won't let me leave these guys in the lurch. Not before I've tried all avenues I can think of to find a replacement.'

Jackson stared at him. 'You're asking if I want to stay on permanently?' Of course, the man knew next to nothing about him and how he'd left the moment the school bell had rung for the last time on his school life. Hell. How had his parents coped with that? He'd never stopped to ask. Maybe he should. *Only if you can handle the answer.*

'Yeah, something like that.' Rory grimaced. 'Your face tells me all I need to know. But if Jess manages to change your mind, let me know, will you?'

Jackson felt his mouth drop open. Was it really that obvious? Guess so if Rory had noticed. *Grady, the sooner you're home the better for me. And as for Ping—I'm ringing you tonight. Pal.*

His stomach tightened and his hands balled into fists as his head spun. Damn you, Ping. Thankfully Rory had disappeared out the door without seeing this tantrum.

'Hey, what's up? You look ready to shoot someone.' Jess was back. Her hand gripped his shoulder, shook him softly.

'My so-called friend in Hong Kong has been checking up on me. Rory took a call from Ping and now knows about the attack.'

Jess smiled. Smiled? This was serious.

'Jackson, friends do that. This Ping obviously cares about you, wants to make sure you're doing okay.' Her mouth came close, caressed his cheek with the lightest of kisses. 'He's doing the right thing.'

And just like that, the tension disappeared. The anger evaporated. His arms encircled this wonderful woman. 'You are so good for me.' And he kissed her, thoroughly. Until there was a knock on the door.

'Mind if I get a coffee?' Sheree asked.

Jess leapt back and winked at him. 'Just leaving.'

In his consulting room Jackson studied the notes of his first patient for the day. Dawn Sullivan, thirty-nine years old, no major health issues during the five years she'd been coming to the Golden Bay Medical and Wellbeing Centre.

He turned to study the woman sitting opposite. Her cheeks appeared unnaturally pale. 'So, Dawn, what brings you to see me today?'

'I'm so tired all the time I can hardly get out of bed some days. I've got the attention span of a fly, which is great considering school started this week and I'm a teacher.' Even as she spoke Dawn was yawning.

'You don't have any history of anaemia. How are your periods? Heavier than usual? Or do they last longer these days?'

Shaking her head, his patient told him, 'All much the same as ever. But I do get lots of stomachaches. Actually, I ache everywhere at times. It's like I've got the flu full time. I'd planned on finally painting my house over the summer break but hardly got one wall done I've been that short of energy. Not like me at all. Ask anyone around here. I always used to be on the go.'

'How long has this been going on?' he asked.

Dawn looked sheepish. 'Months. At first I went to the naturopath, who gave me vitamins and minerals. Fat lot of good they turned out to be and nearly bankrupted me in the process. Whatever I've got is getting worse. I've lost a bit of weight, which normally would make me happy but right now worries me sick.'

Jackson felt as though he should be sitting in the back of a classroom as Dawn's voice carried loudly across the small gap between them. He read Dawn's blood pressure—normal; checked her eyes—they showed signs of anaemia. 'Can you get up on the bed and I'll examine your abdomen.' After a few moments of gently pressing over the area he stepped back. 'I can't feel anything out of the ordinary.'

'So what do you think is going on?' Dawn sat up and pulled her top back into place.

'I'd say you're anaemic but the cause needs to be checked out. We'll do some blood tests. Any changes in diet? Or are you a vegan?'

Dawn shuddered. 'No, love my meat too much for that.'

'We'll start with these blood tests.' He glanced at the patient notes on his computer screen. Something was bothering him. 'Your house is going to have to wait a little longer for its new coat.'

'Right now I'd be happy to have enough energy to teach all day.'

Jackson tapped his forefinger on the desktop. Checking Dawn's address, he tried to remember the style of houses in that road. 'Your house—how old is it?'

'About seventy years. It's a bungalow. The wide boards and wooden window frames type. Mighty cold in winter.'

'Did you do a lot of preparation for the paint job? Sanding off old paint, for example?'

'Yes, I spent weeks with an electric sander, getting down to bare boards. From what I could see, it hadn't been done properly in for ever.'

Bingo. 'I might be wrong but I have a hunch that what you're suffering from is lead poisoning. The old paints are notorious for having a lead component. Did you wear a mask while you were using the sander?'

'No. I can get lead from inhaling dust granules?' Dawn sank down onto the chair, looking shocked. 'It's bad, isn't it? Lead poisoning? Really?'

The more he thought about it the more certain he was. On the screen he ticked boxes on the laboratory form. 'We won't know for sure until the haematology results come back but I think we're onto something. So let's forget those vitamins and wait for a couple of days. If you do have lead in your system, it has to be removed by chelation therapy.'

'Meaning?' Dawn's voice had grown smaller, no longer the booming teacher's tone.

'You'd be given chelation agents that absorb the lead from your body tissues, which is then passed out through your urine. It's an effective way for cleaning up the lead and then we can treat the residual effects, like that lack of energy, which will be due to an anaemia caused by the poisoning.' Signing the form, he added, 'Take this through to Jess. I don't think she's left for her rounds yet.'

'Thank you, Doctor.'

'It's Jackson, and I'll phone you as soon as the results come through.'

'Again, thank you. Guess this means the house and my job are on hold.'

'Talk to the school board and see if you can take on reduced hours for this term.' He held the door open and ushered Dawn through, before going in search of his next patient.

Kelly Brown walked carefully and slowly into his room and eased her bottom onto the edge of the chair.

Her face, arms and every other bit of exposed skin was the colour of well-ripened tomatoes. She wore a loose dress that barely reached her thighs and probably had nothing on underneath.

Jackson sat down and said, 'You're here for that sunburn?'

Kelly nodded. 'It's awful. Can you do anything to stop the heat? Or the pain? I can't wear clothes or lie under the sheet. It hurts all the time.'

'I'll give you a mild painkiller. I hope you're drinking lots of water.'

'Mum nags at me all the time.' Kelly moved, grimaced.

'Where did you get so much sun? It was overcast here yesterday.' Or so he'd thought.

'A group of us went over the hill to Kaiteriteri Beach. Everyone got a bit of sunburn but nothing like this.'

Jackson typed up details on her notes. 'Do you have naturally fair skin?' When she nodded he added, 'You should know better, then. Lots of sunscreen all the time. Any blisters?'

'On my back and all down the front. I've always been sort of careful but yesterday I forgot to take the sunblock with me and thought I'd be safe if I got out of the sun after an hour. But I fell asleep sunbathing.'

'Cool showers, lots of fluids and a mild analgesic is all I can recommend, Kelly. And stay out of the sun in future.'

Taking the prescription he handed her, she said, 'Think I'll move to Alaska. Should be safe there.'

He laughed. 'Might be eaten by a bear.'

'At least that'd be different.' Kelly hobbled to the door. 'Thanks, Doctor. I hear you're only here while Grady's away. Can you tell Jess I won't be able to babysit this week?'

'Your cellphone not working?' Why the hell did this teen think he should be passing Jess her messages?

'Nothing wrong with it. Thought you might like an excuse to talk to her.' With a cheeky wink the minx left his room.

Jackson stared after her. Small towns. There was no getting away from the fact everyone knew everyone's business. How many weeks before he caught the big tin bird back to Asia? Too many.

Then he thought of the woman he was supposed to pass Kelly's message on to and took back that thought. Not nearly enough days left.

CHAPTER SEVEN

JESS HELD BABY Carrington while his mother wriggled herself into a comfortable position on the bed.

'Is this going to be hard? Painful?' Anna asked, anxiety in her voice, as she reached for her baby.

'No and no.' Jess carefully placed the baby in Anna's arms. 'But remember I told you your milk mightn't come in for the first few days. You'll most likely be feeding him colostrum, which is full of goodies he needs.'

'How do I hold him? Oh, hello, gorgeous. Aren't you the most beautiful baby ever?' Anna beamed as she studied her son.

'He's a little cracker, absolutely beautiful.' As they all were. When Nicholas had been placed in her arms for the very first time she couldn't believe her overwhelming sense of love for her son. She'd seen exactly the same reaction in every mother she'd delivered before and since Nicholas's birth, only nowadays she understood how deep the bond ran. How it was the start of something that stayed with mothers for the rest of their lives. Life-changing, empowering. Frightening.

Anna finally raised her gaze. 'Show me how to hold him so I can feed him.'

Tucking the baby in against Anna so she supported his shoulders, Jess then placed Anna's hand on his head.

'Holding him like that means he can access your nipple easily. That's it. Now rub his mouth against your nipple to encourage him to suck. That's it. Perfect.'

'Wow, that's awesome. Oh, my goodness, I'm feeding my baby.' Anna's eyes grew misty. 'Danny, look at this.'

The baby's father was transfixed, watching his son. A bemused expression covered his face. 'That's amazing.'

Jess felt a similar sense of wonder. This was always a wonderful sight, mum bonding with baby. Memories of Nicholas tugged at her heart again. *I'd love to do it all over again. Have a brother or sister for Nicholas.* And where on earth had that idea come from?

Jackson. Of course. Loving him had sparked all sorts of weird ideas. Ideas she wouldn't follow through on. Nicholas needed all her attention. It wouldn't be fair to expect him to share her with Jackson. *What about that baby you suddenly want? Can you spread your love between two children without depriving one or the other?* Surely that would be different? A mother's love was very different from the love she felt for Jackson.

Besides, it was one thing to find herself a solo mother of one, but of two? That would be plain irresponsible. Jackson wouldn't be staying, baby or no baby. That was unfair. He was a very responsible man. But she wouldn't be wanting a loveless—make that one-sided—relationship.

Anna's question cut through her turmoil. 'How will I know when he's hungry?'

Jess dragged up a smile. 'Believe me, he'll let you know. His lungs are in good working order.'

Danny grinned. 'Just like his dad.'

'I feel so much happier now that I've tried feeding him. It isn't the nightmare I'd thought it might be.' Anna gazed adoringly at the baby. 'He's looking sleepy.'

'Carefully take him off your breast. You need to wind

him now. Place him on your shoulder and rub his back gently. That's it. You're a natural at this.'

'Who'd have believed it, huh? It's not like my day job as a gardener gave me any clues.'

'I'm going to leave you two to get to know your son. What are you naming him, by the way?'

'Antony.'

'Michael.'

Jess grinned. 'Right, you definitely need to sort that out. Call the nurse if you have any problems with anything, otherwise I'll be in to see you later.'

She went to find Sheryl and hand over her patient. 'I'm off. I doubt you'll be needing me, though I'll drop by later. That baby might've been two weeks late but the birth was straightforward and Anna's already managing feeding.'

Sheryl waved her out the door. 'Go and enjoy the weekend. It's a stunner of a day.'

It certainly was. Summer had turned on its absolute best for the weekend, which had brought people in droves from Nelson and other towns to their beach houses. At home Jess stood on her deck with a glass of icy water and looked around. Bright blue skies—the colour of love—sparkled above and not a whisper of wind stirred the leaves on the trees in the neighbour's yard. The sparrows and finches were singing while the tuis were squabbling over the last few yellow flowers of a kowhai tree.

'Mummy, can I go swimming at the beach?'

'After lunch has settled in your tummy I'll take you down to Pohara.' She'd picked him up from Bobby's on the way home. Studying him now, that feeling of awe that had struck her as she'd watched Anna and her baby bonding returned in full force.

Was Nicholas missing out because he didn't have a sibling? When she'd been young she'd pestered her mother about why she didn't have a sister like her friends did. Her mother had always told her that she got more love being the only one but somehow that had never washed with Jess. There hadn't been much love. She'd grown up fast, only having adults around to talk to most of the time. She hadn't spent a lot of time in places where there were other kids for her to play with.

'Why can't Jackson come with me?' Nicholas rode his bike round and round the lemon tree, making her feel dizzy watching him.

'He's busy picking the avocados for Virginia.' Nicholas definitely missed out by not having a father. Balancing that against what he'd miss out on if the man she loved lived with them, she suddenly didn't know what was best for them all.

'Actually, I've finished that chore,' a familiar deep voice said from the corner of the house. 'Got up with the birds to do the picking. I've even graded and packed the avocados, ready to go to the markets.'

'Jackson, look at me,' Nicholas shouted, and pedalled faster than ever until he forgot to watch where he was going and rode into the lemon tree.

Jess winced and rushed to lift him back onto his bike. 'Nicholas, be careful, sweetheart.'

'Okay, Mummy.'

Jackson moved up beside her. 'Hey, you're looking great.' Sex oozed from that voice, lifting bumps on her skin.

'Go easy around you know who,' she warned, at the same time noticing how his gaze cruised over her legs. She'd pulled on very short shorts and a singlet top the moment she'd got home, feeling the need to make the most of the sun after hours shut inside that small delivery room. 'Anna Carrington had her baby this morning.'

Jackson's eyes softened. 'So you've been up most of the night?'

'All of it.'

'You don't look like you're wilting.' He ran a finger down her arm. 'What did she have?'

'A boy.' She couldn't help the sigh that slid across her lips.

'That cute, eh?'

'Yes. I never get tired of seeing new babies.'

'You sound as though you're yearning for another of your own.' Jackson's finger hovered over her wrist.

Her feelings were too obvious if Jackson was picking up on them. 'It's easy to wish for another baby when they're brand-new and behaving and I'm not at home alone trying to balance everything like a one-winged bird.'

Jackson turned to stare across her lawn, his eyes following Nicholas as he again rode faster and faster, happily showing off. 'You'd have to choose a father.'

She sucked in a breath. Odd way of putting it. 'Not doing that. I do not want to have another child on my own, no matter how cool it would be for Nicholas to have a sibling. It's not fair on the children.'

'Or you. It's hard work, for sure.' He still watched Nicholas, but what was going on in his head?

'It's not about the hard work. It's about having two role models, a male perspective as well as mine. Anyway, I don't know why we're having this conversation. It's not going to happen.'

Jackson turned then, his hands reaching for her arms. 'You sound so certain.'

Because I am. Because you're going away. Because I

couldn't trust myself not to be able to share my love between you and Nicholas and any other child even if you did stay. 'I'm being practical. No point wishing for the impossible. Takes too much energy.' She stepped back, pulling her arms free. 'Want to go to the beach with us?'

Disappointment blinked out at her. 'You're changing the subject.'

'Are you staying on in Golden Bay come April?'

He hesitated, and she held her breath. Until, 'No.'

Now it was her turn to feel disappointed, despite knowing the answer before he'd enunciated it. Swallowing hard, she said, 'Then of course I'm changing the subject. We're going to the beach. Want to join us?'

'Yes, Jackson, you've got to come.' Nicholas let rip with another shout as he spun around on his bike too fast and tipped over. 'I want you to,' he yelled, through the too-long grass covering his face.

'How can I refuse that demand?' Jackson shrugged in her direction, puzzlement in his eyes. So he'd picked up on what she hadn't said. That she'd be interested if he was hanging around.

'I guess Nicholas has a way with words.' If only it was that easy for her to get Jackson to do what she needed. Because it was slowly dawning on her that she wasn't going to be able to let him go as easily as she'd first thought. For a moment there she'd almost wished he'd said he was staying and that they might make their relationship more permanent. For a moment she thought she could see past her fears and take a chance. For a moment.

Jackson went to right the bike and held it while Nicholas climbed back on. 'You're going to need a bigger bike soon.'

'I told Mummy but she said I had to wait.'

A bigger bike meant further to fall. 'There's no hurry.'

'Have you got sun block on, sport?'

'Yes.' Nicholas nodded gravely. 'Kelly got burnt at the beach. She said it hurt a lot.'

'That's right, she was bright red. You don't want to look like a fried tomato.'

Jess watched the two of them: Jackson so patient and Nicholas so keen to show off his skills. They looked good together. If only this relationship could last as it was, but the weeks were cranking along, disappearing unbelievably fast. The first of March was only a couple of days away, and that heralded the end of summer. Then it would be April and some time during that month it would be the end of her affair with Jackson. Swallowing down on the sudden sadness engulfing her, she vowed to make the most of whatever time she had with him. For someone who did not want a permanent relationship with any man she was making a right hash of keeping Jackson at arm's length.

'You're daydreaming again.' Jackson stood in front of her.

'Must be the heat.' She poured the last of her water down her throat.

'Shucks. Here I was thinking I might be the reason you had that far-away look in your eye.'

'Nope. That was pollen from the lemon flowers.'

His finger ran along her bottom lip, sending zips of heat right down to her toes. 'Is that why you always smell of citrus? You spend a lot of time hauling Nicholas out of the lemon tree?'

Rising onto her toes, she nudged his hand out of the way and kissed those full, sexy lips that knew how to tease and tantalise her for hours on end. 'Try reading the label of my shampoo bottle. Less exotic but more practical.'

He took over the kiss, deepening it until she had to hang on to keep her balance. Pressing her body up against his, she felt the hardening of his reaction to her. Not now. Not here. Hands on his chest, she pushed back. 'Nicholas.'

His sultry eyes widened. 'God, I'm like a crazed teen around you, forgetting everything except what you make me feel, want.' Jackson stepped back, tugged at his shirt to cover the obvious reaction to their kiss. 'Better do something else before the trouble really starts.'

'I'll get towels and things for the beach.' How mundane was that? It should dampen their ardour.

Jackson followed her inside. 'I came around to ask you what you think about camping.'

'As in a tent? Sleeping bags and air mattresses? That sort of camping?' It had been years since she'd done that and then it had been in the Australian outback with her parents. She'd spent her whole time sitting up with the thin sleeping bag zipped right to her throat, terrified a snake would come into her tent and bite her.

'Is there any other sort?' Jackson grinned. 'A friend from way back has a bit of land by the beach out at Wainui Inlet. There's a shed with bathroom and cooking facilities. I figured we could go out there and pitch a tent, go swimming and fishing. Nicholas can take his bike and ride around the paddock when we're tired of the beach.'

Jess grunted. 'Like that's going to happen. It's usually a battle to get him out of the water. A prune is wrinkle-free compared to what he ends up looking like.'

'I've got steak, potatoes wrapped in foil to bake, lots of salad stuff, and fruit for afterwards. How can you refuse?' Jackson implored, looking at her like a little boy intent on winning his case.

'Steak? You don't have any faith in your fishing skills?'

'Fishing? Are we going fishing?' Nicholas leapt between them, looking excited already.

Jackson locked eyes with her. 'Are we? Fishing and camping?'

There wouldn't be any snakes or other creepy-crawlies for her to worry about. 'What are we waiting for?'

Of course, it took nearly an hour to pack clothes, towels, more food, toys and the bike into the truck. Nicholas hindered progress but as he was trying so hard to be helpful Jess didn't growl at him once. His excitement level escalated until it was almost unbearable, and then Jackson stepped in.

'Hey, sport. Take it easy, eh? You need lots of energy to go fishing and swimming, and the way you're going now you'll run out before we leave.'

'Sorry, Jackson. I'll be good, promise.'

Jess shook her head. 'How do you do that?'

'I'm very good at getting my way. With little boys and their wicked mothers. Okay, make that singular. One boy and his mother.' Jackson's hand cupped her butt, squeezed gently. 'Nicholas will go to sleep tonight, won't he?'

Finally she let go of the hurt that had sprung up when Jackson had told her he wouldn't be staying. 'Come on,' she teased him. 'The kid's never been in a tent before. He's going to be wide-eyed all night long.' Chuckling when disappointment darkened Jackson's eyes, she added, 'You can leave behind any condoms you've packed.'

'Which reminds me. Be right back.' He headed outside to the truck. Returning, he handed her a parcel the size of a book.

'What's this?'

'Open it before your young man comes back inside.'

She tore the paper off, became even more baffled at seeing the plain cardboard box. With her fingernail she slit the tape holding down the lid and flicked it open. 'Bleeding heck.' She stared at the condoms. 'You planning on staying around for a while, or just being very busy?'

'That first time? You told me I owed you and I always pay my debts.' Leaning in, he kissed the corner of her mouth. 'Now put them out of sight. I hear small footsteps coming this way. I won't complain if you put a handful in your pocket for later, though.'

'A handful? Yeah, right.' Laughing all the way to her bedroom, she slid the box into the drawer of her bedside table and, yes, shoved some condoms into her overnight bag.

Jess slipped the air-filled bands up Nicholas's arms. 'These'll help keep you afloat in those waves.' Tiny waves that suddenly seemed big compared to her wee boy. 'Hold my hand.'

Small fingers wrapped around hers. 'Will there be fish in the water, Jackson?'

'Not around you. They'll see your legs and swim away fast.' Jackson took his other hand. 'You like swimming, sport?'

'I only like the pool.'

Uh-oh. How did I not know that? Jess bit her lip. 'We'll stay on the edge where it's shallow.' She sank to her knees in the water, the waves reaching the top of her thighs, and reached for Nicholas.

He leaned against her, studying the waves, worry darkening his eyes. 'Why does the sea go up and down like that?'

'Sometimes the wind makes it happen.'

'But there isn't any wind.' Nicholas stared around the small bay.

Jackson squatted down beside them, those well-honed thighs very distracting. 'There might be further away. Or a big boat might've gone past. Engines on boats stir the water like when Mummy makes a cake, and that sends waves inshore.'

'My cakes resemble the sea?'

Jackson grinned and lifted a strand of hair off her face. 'Don't know. You've never made me one.'

'Be grateful.'

Nicholas sank down lower, sucking in his stomach as the water reached his waist. 'It's not cold, Mummy.'

Right. So why the shivers? 'Let's play ball.' Hopefully a game would distract him enough to relax and have fun. She made to take the beach ball from Jackson and came up against hard chest muscles, the hand holding the ball well out of reach. Her gaze shot to his face, caught the cheeky grin. Right, buster. Carefully removing her other hand from Nicholas she turned and shoved at Jackson, toppling him into and under the water.

'Nicholas, help me. Your mother needs controlling.' Jackson coughed out salt water, that grin wider than ever. 'Let's show her she can't play dirty tricks and get away with it.'

Her son didn't need any more encouragement, leaping onto her, wrapping his arms tightly around her knees. Jackson showed no sympathy, helping Nicholas dunk her.

She leapt up, shaking her sodden hair, water streaming down her body. 'Right, who's next?'

'You can't catch me, Mummy.' Nicholas forged through the water, parallel to the shore, shrieking at every splash he made.

Jackson took her hand and they pretended to chase

him hard, keeping close enough to reach him quickly if needed but letting him think he was winning. Inevitably he tripped himself up and went under. Jess felt the air stall in her lungs. He'd panic and choke.

Jackson lunged forward, caught Nicholas and stood him on his feet. 'You okay, sport?'

Wide-eyed and grinning, Nicholas shouted, 'Yes. Look at me, Mummy.' He jumped up, tucking his knees under his chin and dropped into the water again.

'Guess he likes the sea as much as the pool, then.' She was relieved. Living in Golden Bay meant he'd spend a lot of time on or near the water and if he feared it then he wouldn't learn to master it.

'What happened to that ball?' Jackson looked around. 'Oops, it's heading out. I'd better retrieve it before it gets too far away.' He dived in and swam for it, his strokes strong and powerful, pulling his body quickly through the water.

'Mummy, I want to swim like Jackson.'

Thank you, Jackson. Until now, learning to swim had been the last thing Nicholas had wanted to do. The pool had been about splashing and jumping. She ruffled his wet hair. 'I'll sign you up for lessons this week.' And thank Jackson in an appropriate fashion once her boy was asleep.

'Help me collect driftwood for a bonfire, Nicholas.' Jackson threw an armful of wood down on the damp sand. The tide was receding fast and they'd be able to light a small fire before darkness set in.

'Why are we having a fire?' the boy asked.

'So we can toast marshmallows on sticks and eat them after dinner.'

'Won't they melt?'

Sometimes Nicholas was smarter than he should be for his age. 'Not if you're quick.'

'Are we all sleeping in the tent?' Nicholas picked up the end of a huge piece of wood and staggered along the beach, dragging it behind him.

'Yes.' Damn it. He hadn't thought that far ahead when he'd had this camping brainwave. Hadn't considered the frustration of lying with Jess and not being able to make love to her because Nicholas would be with them. It had seemed like a brilliant idea to come out here and give the boy a new experience. Guess he'd have to rein in his hormones for the night. Unless they found a secluded spot away from the tent but close enough to hear if Nicholas woke and got frightened.

'Hey, you two,' Jess called from down by the water's edge. 'Come and help me collect some cockles to cook for dinner.'

'What are cockles?'

'Shellfish,' Jackson told him. 'They're yummy.' If you got rid of all the sand in the shells.

'Why don't we catch them with our rods?'

'Because they live in the sand and mud. You've got to dig for them. See, like Mummy's doing.' Jess looked stunning in that orange bikini she wore. All legs and breasts. His mouth dried. When she'd asked if he intended staying on at Golden Bay he'd struggled to say no. Which meant he should be hightailing it out of the country now, not planning a way to get into her sleeping bag tonight.

There was no denying Jess had sneaked in under his skin when he'd been busy looking the other way. Leaving her was going to be incredibly difficult. But he couldn't take her and Nicholas with him. His eighteenth-floor apartment was definitely not conducive to raising a young child. No, Nicholas was in the perfect place for a boy—

swimming and fishing on his doorstep, farms with real animals just as close in the other direction.

'I want to do the digging, Mummy.' Once Nicholas got started there was no stopping him. Finally they had to drag him into the water and clean off the mud that covered him from head to toes. 'Why are you throwing them away?' he asked when Jackson tipped half their haul back into the mud.

'Because we're not allowed too many.'

'Will the policeman tell us off if you don't put them back?'

'Yes. It's so that we don't use them all up and can get more another day.'

'Okay.'

Okay. Life seemed so simple for Nicholas. Give him an explanation and he was happy, not looking for hidden agendas. 'How about you and I cook the cockles so that Mummy can have a rest?' Jess's all-night haul at the birthing unit appeared to be catching up with her. He'd seen her hiding a yawn more than once. 'Jess, why don't you curl up in the tent and have a snooze?'

'Because I'd probably not wake up till morning. I don't want to miss out on anything.' Her smile was soft and wistful.

'I promise to call you for dinner.' He knew what all-nighters with patients were like. They drained you so that putting one foot in front of the other became hard work. 'Go on. Nicholas and I will put our rods in the water and see what we can catch. On your way to the tent can you put those cockles in fresh water so they spit out the sand?' He wasn't giving her a chance to argue.

'You promise to call me?'

'Promise. I'll have a glass of wine waiting. The potatoes will be cooking and the steak ready to sizzle.'

Another yawn stretched her mouth and she shrugged. 'Guess I can't argue with that.' Picking up the bucket of shellfish, she trudged up the beach and across the road to their camp site.

Jackson only tore his eyes away from her when she reached the tent. His heart ached with need. With love. Love? No way, man. He hadn't gone and fallen in love with Jessica. No way. So why the pain in his chest? Why the need to wrap her up and look after her? Why spend time with her little boy, teaching him things any father would do if he wasn't in love with Jess?

No, he couldn't be. It wasn't meant to happen like that. Lots of hot sex, and plenty of fun; that was how it went. Harmless, enjoyable, no ties, no future.

He dropped to his haunches and picked up a pebble to hurl it across the water. Where had he gone wrong? How had he made such a monumental error? Right from that first night he'd had no intention of getting too close to Jess. Because no matter what happened, what she hoped for, he was going home to Hong Kong. To his frantic life, his orderly life. His now frightening life—and that damned promise.

Another pebble skimmed across the wavelets. Dropped out of sight under the water. And another, and another. A lonely life it may be, but at least he wasn't letting anyone down by being too busy for them.

What about Ping's words of wisdom last week when he'd finally caught up with him on the phone? *You are ready to return home. Hong Kong isn't home for you.* Ping had sounded so certain that he'd found he couldn't argue with his friend. Not that he'd done anything stupid like hand in his notice. No way. But he hadn't been able to shut Ping out of his brain, especially in the early hours while he lay in bed, waiting for the sun to lift above the horizon so he could go for a run. Ping often came out with Chinese proverbs or other wise bits of advice, but this time Jackson would ignore him.

He might be falling for Jess but he wouldn't be doing anything about it. He wasn't prepared to live in the back of beyond where his medical skills would be wasted. And he couldn't ask Jess to move when she'd only recently settled here and begun making a secure environment for Nicholas to grow up in.

'Look at me. I can throw stones in the water like you.' Nicholas stood beside him, his little face earnest as he tried to toss his pebbles as far as the water's edge.

Might be time to head away, get out of here earlier than planned, save any further heartache that being with Jess would cause. Then there was this little guy who took everything at face value and had accepted him as a part of his life.

'You're doing great, Nicholas.' Jackson stood up and moved behind him, took his elbow and gently pulled it back. 'Swing your arm back like this. Now fling it forward as hard as you can.'

They continued throwing pebbles until Nicholas tired of that game. 'Can we go fishing now?'

'Sure. I'll go and get the rods and bait.'

'I'll do it.' Without waiting for Jackson, Nicholas raced up the beach. 'I know where the rods are.' He was nearing the road too fast.

'Nicholas, come back here now.' Panic had Jackson charging after him. 'Don't you go on that road, Nicholas,' he roared. He thought he could hear a vehicle approaching at speed. 'Nicholas. Stop.'

'I'm looking both ways.'

'Wait for me.' Jackson skidded to a stop beside him at the road's edge. His hand gripped the boy's shoulder.

'Never run towards a road, sport,' he gasped around his receding fear. 'Cars go a lot faster than you do and the driver might not see you.'

'Mummy told me that.' Nicholas wriggled his shoulder free and looked right, left, then right again. 'See. Nothing's coming. Can I cross now?'

That vehicle had to have been in his imagination because now he'd stopped his mad dash up the beach Jackson couldn't hear it. Quickly checking both ways, he said in an uneven voice, 'Yes, you can. Let's go quietly so we don't wake your mum.'

Over an hour later Jackson and Nicholas returned from their fishing expedition with all the bait gone and no fish to show for it.

'I wanted to catch a fish.' Nicholas pouted. 'It's not fair.'

'That's the way of it, sport. If fish were too easy to catch, there'd be no fun in it.' Jackson stopped at the tent entrance and peered in. Jess lay sprawled face down across the bigger of the two air beds, her hair spread over the pillow. How easy it would be to curl up beside her and push his fingers through that blonde silk. Fishy fingers, he reminded himself.

He turned to Nicholas. 'Let's go clean ourselves up. Then we'll get dinner cooking and wake your mother.'

'I'm hungry now.'

'Wash your hands first. You smell of fish bait.'

'I want something to eat first.'

Jackson sighed. No wonder Jess gave in to Nicholas so often. Otherwise she'd be sounding like the big, bad wolf all the time. 'You can have a banana as soon as you're clean.' He swung Nicholas up under his arm and carried him to the ablutions block, tickling him and getting ear-piercing shrieks for his efforts. So much for keeping quiet, but at least the temper tantrum had been avoided.

With the potatoes baking on the barbecue hot plate and the cockles in a pot ready to steam, Jackson poured a glass of wine and headed for the tent. 'Wake up, sleepy-head.' His heart blocked his throat at the sight inside. Jess had rolled onto her back and spread her arms wide, like an invitation. In sleep she had lost that worrying look that had him wondering if she'd got too involved with him, making it easier for him to believe they were merely having an affair that he would shortly walk away from unharmed. Except he already knew it would hurt, that he was too late to save his heart. But he would still have to go.

'Jess.' He nudged her foot with his toe. 'Time to wake up, lazybones.'

'Go away,' she mumbled, and made to roll over.

'Mummy, you've got to get up now.' Nicholas bounced onto the bed and dropped to his knees so close to Jess that Jackson feared she'd be bruised.

Her eyes popped open. 'Hello, you two.' Her voice was thick with sleep. Rubbing her hands down her cheeks, she yawned and then stretched her feet to the end of the bed and her hands high above her, lifting her breasts as she did.

His breath caught as he ogled those sweet mounds pushing against her singlet top. The glass shook in his hand, spilling wine over his fingers. 'I'll see you outside. Do you want this wine in here?'

'No, I'll join you in a minute.' Already she was scrambling onto her knees and delving into her bag to haul out a jersey.

Nicholas had arranged the outdoor chairs so that they could see down the grass to the beach. Jackson sank down on one and picked up his beer. His hand still shook. He knew how it felt to hold Jess in his arms and make love to her, the little sounds she made in pleasure, the way she liked to wind her legs around his afterwards. He wanted to know all those things again and again.

Making love to Jess was nothing like the sex he'd had with those women he usually dated. But he hadn't really dated Jess. They'd just got together. At work, at his parents' place, and mostly at her home, where they enjoyed each other whenever Nicholas wasn't around or was tucked up in bed, sound asleep.

'Where's the TV?' Nicholas asked as he crossed over to Jackson.

Laughter rang out, sweet and clear, from the tent. 'There's no TV out here, sweetheart. When you go camping you don't have power for things like that.'

As the boy's face began to pucker up Jackson reined in his smile and said, 'Think about telling your friends how you spent the night in a tent and that you ate food cooked outside, and how you dug for shellfish. Isn't that more exciting?'

'Can I catch a fish tomorrow?'

'We'll give it a darned good try, sport.'

Jess slid onto the chair beside him, her light jersey covering those tantalising breasts. 'You have a knack with him.' She sipped from her glass. 'Perfect.'

'Should've got champagne, knowing how much you enjoy it.'

'You'd better stop spoiling me. I might get used to it.' She stared out across the water, seeing who knew what. The glass shook in her fingers, as it had moments ago in his.

Laying a hand on her thigh, he squeezed gently. 'Jess, I can't—'

She turned, placed a finger on his lips. 'Don't say anything, Jackson. I know this has to come to an end, have known it all along, but I don't want to spoil our time together talking about things we can't change.'

He could not argue with that, so he didn't.

CHAPTER EIGHT

'So MELANIE'S GETTING a little sister or brother. That's cool.' *And I'm fighting something very like jealousy here.* Jess watched Sasha's face light up with excitement, felt her own heart thump harder. *A baby—with Jackson— would be perfect.* She breathed in deep, exhaled slowly. *Get real.*

'Yeah, isn't it? I can't wait. So unlike last time, when I was dealing with the defection of Melanie's father and coming to terms with returning here, this time I've got Grady right beside me.' Sasha grinned and wrapped her arms around Jess in a big hug. 'Know a good midwife?'

'I might.' She squeezed back. 'A summer baby.'

'Not like Melanie. She kept me warm through last winter.' Sasha stepped away and opened the fridge, where she found the salmon Jackson had placed there earlier. 'Did Jackson go out to Anatoki for this?'

Anatoki was a salmon farm where customers could fish for their dinner in large holding ponds. 'He took Nicholas and let him catch the salmon. In fact, Jackson let him catch and release two before bringing this one home. I don't think my boy will ever stop talking about that. I'm surprised he hasn't told you every minute de- tail. I couldn't get his fishing shirt off him so he does reek a little.'

Sasha shook her head. 'I haven't spoken to him yet. He's following Jackson everywhere, glued to his hip.'

'There's a certain amount of hero worship going on, for sure.' Which would soon turn into a big problem. The weeks were speeding by and when Jackson headed away she'd be left to pick up the pieces. As well as deal with her own broken heart.

Sasha looked up from stuffing the salmon with herbs. 'You're worried?'

'Big time. Maybe I should've stopped seeing Jackson right after your wedding and kept him out of Nicholas's life.' Like she'd have been able to manage that easily. She'd fallen for him so fast she'd been spinning.

'Maybe you should tell Jackson how you feel about him.' Sasha cocked her head to one side. 'Hmm?'

'No way. We've been up front right from the start. No commitment, no demands on each other. Have a good time and sign off come April.' Why did that sound so flippant? Because it was. Casual maybe, but not normal. 'But I haven't, and won't, tell him I've fallen for him. It would ruin everything.'

Her friend's lips pressed tight for a moment and Jess knew she was about to get a lecture. 'Leave it, Sasha. I'm not asking Jackson to stay on when he obviously doesn't want to. Don't forget I'm not interested in tying myself to anyone either. It wouldn't be fair on Nicholas.'

'That's getting a little monotonous, Jess. You've got a big heart, big enough for more than your son. You've spread it around the community and he hasn't suffered.' Hadn't she already heard that from Jackson? Unfortunately, Sasha wasn't finished. 'There are still a few weeks for you to talk to him, lay your feelings on the line.'

Jess shivered. She couldn't do that. Too scary. 'Do we want to make the salads now?'

Sasha wasn't about to be sidetracked. 'Think about it. What have you got to lose? A broken heart? That's coming anyway, regardless. But you might find my brother has changed his mind about his mighty Hong Kong hospital and lifestyle. He was moody when he first arrived home, got angry at the smallest things, but that's not happening so much now. Mum says he sometimes sings in the shower. That's unheard of. You've got a role in all this. He's keen on you, really keen.'

Jackson hadn't told his family about the stabbing. He didn't want them worrying about him when he returned to Hong Kong. Opening the fridge again, Jess removed the vegetable bin containing everything needed to put together a crisp, healthy salad. Jackson might be keen on her, as Sasha put it, but he didn't want her trailing after him all the way to Asia. That also would mean putting her needs before Nicholas's. How could she explain to her boy that living in an enormous city was as good as being in Golden Bay with beaches and fishing?

Loud laughter rolled through the open windows. Jackson and Grady were playing soccer with Nicholas on the front lawn. Her son wore a huge grin as he charged after the ball and stole it from under Jackson's foot. He dribbled it towards the makeshift goal until he fell over the ball and landed on his face. Jess held her breath, waiting for an explosion of tears, but Nicholas bounced back up and took off after the ball that Grady had stolen while he was down. Her boy was lapping up the male attention. 'Grady will still have some time for Nicholas, won't he?'

'You know he will, though it won't be the same as having Jackson's undivided attention.' Sasha handed her a glass of champagne. 'You'll have to drink my share now that I'm pregnant. Let's join Mum and Dad on the deck. The salmon will take a while.'

Jess continued to keep one eye on Jackson, filing away memories of how athletic he looked, how his long legs ate up the ground as he chased the ball, how his laughter sneaked under her ribs and tickled her heart. She collected even more mental images during dinnertime.

But. Nothing was going to be the same ever again. Grady might be there for Nicholas when he had time, but he had his own children to put first. She'd do anything to make her son's life perfect—except tell Jackson she loved him.

But as Sasha had pointed out, what did she have to lose? Honesty was good, wasn't it? What if Jackson had already guessed her feelings for him? Was he waiting for her to say something? Or crossing his fingers she'd keep silent?

'You're very quiet tonight.' Jackson leaned close.

Unnerved that he might read her mind, she shivered. 'Sorry.'

'You're cold. I'll get your jersey.'

She let him go and find it. Cold had nothing to do with that shiver. But—but all to do with cowardice. She was afraid if she told Jackson she loved him he'd laugh at her or, worse, commiserate and beat a hasty retreat. So she'd remain silent. Coward. If her heart was big enough for more than Nicholas, as people kept telling her, then what was holding her back? Nothing ventured, nothing gained, as they said. Or nothing lost.

But. She was hanging onto her belief that she'd turn out to be like her parents. Did Sasha have a point? Was this belief just an excuse to hide behind because she was afraid of putting her heart on the line? It had hurt when Nicholas's father had done a bunk, and now, compared with her feelings for Jackson, she saw she hadn't been as invested in that relationship as she'd thought.

'Here.' Jackson held out her jersey. 'Have you taken to buying everything you wear in orange since the wedding?' Those delicious lips curved upwards, sending her stomach into a riot of fluttering.

'No, but I have bought things in apricot shades.' Underwear, two shirts and the sexiest pair of fitted jeans. 'Online shopping is an absolute boon when living here.'

Jackson did an eye-roll. 'Women will always find a way to shop, even if they're living on Mars.'

'Sexist.' Jess and Sasha spoke in unison.

Virginia added her bit. 'So says the man with the biggest, most expensive wardrobe I've ever seen.'

'Nicholas. Want another game of soccer, sport?' Jackson grinned.

'After dinner. I want to eat more salmon. It's yummy, Mummy. Can you take me to catch more?'

Giving Jackson a mock glare, she answered, 'You've been spoiled today. This is a treat.'

'We'll go next time I come home, sport.'

She'd have sworn she was trying not to look at him, but she was—staring. 'You might come home for another visit?' she croaked in a squeaky voice that had everyone staring at them both. Don't. It won't be fair on Nicholas. Or me.

'We'd love it if you do.' Ian filled the sudden silence. 'But we understand how busy you are over there.'

Jackson looked embarrassed, like he'd made a mistake. 'I've got more leave owing but it's hard to get away. There's always a shortage of temporary replacement staff.' Backpedalling so fast he'd fall on his butt if he wasn't careful.

Jess forced her disappointment aside. What had she expected? Glancing around the now quiet table, she saw that Jackson's statement had taken a toll on everyone. Of course Ian and Virginia wanted their son staying home. Now that Virginia was ill it would be more important for them. Sasha would want her brother on hand to help out on the orchard and to be a part of her children's lives. Everyone was affected by Jackson's decision and yet he should be able to continue with the career path he'd chosen.

Her gaze stopped on Jackson, noted the way his jaw clenched, his lips whitened. This was the first time he'd got angry in a couple of weeks. Was he angry at himself for hurting his family? Reaching under the table, she laid a hand on his thigh and softly dug her fingers into those tense muscles. 'Do they make apricot-coloured fishing rods?'

Green eyes locked with hers. Recognition of how she was trying to help him flickered back at her. His Adam's apple bobbed. Then his mouth softened. 'No, but I'm sure I can find you an orange one.'

The chuckles around the table were a little forced but soon the conversation was flowing again, this time on safer topics.

Not all the questions buzzing around inside Jess's head retreated. Instead, they drove her loopy with apprehension, making her feel like she was on a runaway truck, with no hope of stopping, and only disaster at the end. When Jackson offered to drive her home, she shook her head. 'Not tonight. My boy's exhausted and so am I. An early night is what we need.' She needed space to cope with the growing fear of how she'd manage when he left.

'You're mad at me for saying earlier I'd go fishing with Nicholas again some time.' He stood directly in front of her, hands on hips, eyes locked on hers.

'Not mad, Jackson, disappointed. Nicholas is young.

He only sees things in black and white, and everything happens now.' That was only the beginning of her turmoil.

'Yeah, I get it. I'm very sorry. I'm not used to youngsters and how their thought processes work.'

'Says the man who has been absolutely brilliant with Nicholas these past two months.' She dug her keys out of her bag. 'Just so you know, I'm not going home alone because of what you told him. I'm bigger than that. I really do need some sleep.' *Some space in my bed so I can think, and not be distracted by your sexy body and persuasive voice.*

His lips brushed her cheek. 'I get that, too. I think. Let me put Nicholas in his car seat.'

She watched with hunger as he strode into the lounge where Nicholas was watching TV with Ian. She watched when he came back with her boy tucked against his chest, Nicholas's thumb in his mouth as he desperately tried to stay awake. Her hunger increased as he carefully clicked the seat belt around her son and brushed curls off his face. She shouldn't have turned him down. Climbing inside her car, she watched as he bent down and kissed her, long and tenderly. So tenderly he brought tears to her eyes. And a lump to her throat. She needed to be with him. She needed to be alone.

Jackson watched Jess drive out onto the road for the short trip back to her place. It took all his willpower not to run after her, to follow her home and slip into bed to hold her tight.

How the hell was he going to leave Jess? His heart ached now and he still had four weeks left to be with her. Impossible to imagine how he'd feel once he stepped onto that plane heading northeast.

Don't go. Stay here. Everyone wants you to. That much

had been painfully obvious at dinnertime. Surprising how easy it might be to do exactly that. Stay. Become a part of the community he'd been in such a hurry to leave when he'd been a teen. If he stayed, what would he do for work? On average he'd have one emergency a week to deal with. Unless he worked in Nelson. Only two hours' drive away. He could commute or get a small apartment, return home on his days off. Not the perfect way to have a relationship but it had worked for Mum and Dad. Nah, he did not want that for him and Jess.

As the taillights of Jess's car disappeared he headed for the deck and some quiet time. Inside, Sasha and Mum were arguing light-heartedly about who had the best chocolate-cake recipe. Dad was still watching TV. Or was he catnapping, as he often did when he thought no one was looking?

Family. He loved them. Leaving Golden Bay back then hadn't been about them. Being young and brash, he'd always believed they would be around for ever. That whenever he chose to return, family life would be as it had always been. And it was. Yet it was different. There were additions: Grady, Melanie and the unborn baby. Dad no longer disappeared to the other side of the world every second week. Then there was Mum. His rock when he'd been growing up, always there with a ready ear and a loving word. Now he should be here for her. That promise shouldn't keep him from those he loved, yet he was afraid to ignore it. His word was important.

He was avoiding the real issue. Jessica Baxter.

Jess hadn't had what he and Sasha got from Mum and Dad, yet she'd slotted into his family: best mates with Sasha; a surrogate daughter to his parents. Often she could be found helping out in the orchard or doing the ironing or scrubbing the floor. If anyone was the outsider in his family it was him. Only because he lived so damned far away, but it was reason enough.

'Want a beer?' Grady's question cut through the crap in his head.

'Thanks.' He took the proffered bottle, dropped onto a chair and swung his feet up onto the deck railing. The cold liquid was like nectar. 'That's bloody good.'

'Nothing's ever easy, is it?'

He presumed Grady was talking about the things going on in his head. 'Nope.'

They sat in a comfortable silence, drinking their beer, replenishing the bottles when they dried up, not bothering with unnecessary talk. They both knew the situation. Why keep talking about it? As far as brothers-in-law went, Sasha had got him a good one.

The temperature had cooled, and the air felt heavy with dew. Summer was giving way to autumn and the temperatures were beginning to reflect that, day and night. Soon the holiday homeowners would clean down their boats and put them away for winter. They'd lock up their houses and go home. What would Jess do over winter? Would she hunker down for the cold months or get out there, continuing to visit people: checking they had enough firewood to see them through; taking food and books to the older folk living outside the township boundaries; keeping an eye on their health?

No guesses there. He knew the answer. Jess was generous beyond generous. No matter that she thought it was about repaying folk for the bad things she'd done as a wild teenager. It wasn't that at all. Jess was kind and generous to a fault. Couldn't help being so good to others.

'Time we went home, Grady.' Sasha stepped into the light spilling from the windows. 'Melanie has finished feeding and needs to be tucked up in her cot.'

'Not a problem, sweetheart.' Grady unwound his long body and stood up. 'You want to do a spot of fishing tomorrow, Jackson? We could put the tinny in before breakfast and go find ourselves something for brunch.'

'I'm on. See you about six?' Fishing always relaxed him. Unless he was with Nicholas and had to spend the whole time baiting hooks and untying knots in the line. Which was kind of fun, in its own way.

'Six? Just because you're sleeping solo tonight, you want to drag me out early.'

'Five past?' Jackson laughed, but inside he felt lonely. Grady was a good bloke, but he wasn't what he needed right now, at night, in bed. No, she had elected to go home alone.

Jess might've desperately wanted to sleep, but that didn't mean she got any. At two o'clock she gave up and went out to the kitchen to make some chamomile tea. Sitting in the lounge, she switched on the TV and watched the second half of some out-of-date rerun of something she'd first seen when she'd been about fourteen. And still the thoughts about what she should tell Jackson before he left went round and round her skull.

'Hey, Jackson, I love you. So if you ever change your mind about coming home or wanting a life partner, you know my number.'

Yep, that would work. She could see him rushing up and kissing her and telling her that was the best news he'd had in a long time. Not.

Okay, what about, 'Jackson, I love you and would love it if Nicholas and I could move to Hong Kong to be with you.'

He probably wouldn't bother packing his bags, just run for the airport.

What about just shutting up, keeping her feelings to herself, and getting on with enjoying the remaining weeks?

Yep, that might work.

Except she'd heard Sasha loud and clear. It was time to risk her heart, lay it out there for Jackson to do with as he pleased. At least she'd know exactly where she stood with him.

Thought I knew that already.

They were having an affair; no more, no less. She'd fallen in love with him the night it had started but she'd known from the beginning that the fling had no chance of becoming anything else. It'd be breaking the rules to tell Jackson her true feelings.

Rules were made to be broken, weren't they?

Apparently, but…she drew a deep breath…this could backfire so fast, so badly, she daren't do it.

She had to do it. It was eating her up, not being honest with him.

Why had she fallen for him? Why Jackson, of all men? Because he was out of reach and so she'd be safe? Wouldn't have to relinquish her long-held beliefs that she couldn't love more than one person thoroughly?

Newsflash. You already do love Nicholas and Jackson, and you haven't once let your boy down in the weeks you've been seeing Jackson. You are so not like your parents it's a joke.

The annoying voice in her head hadn't finished with her yet. 'You love Jackson because he's Jackson, because of all the little things that make him the man he is. The good things and the not-so-good things.' Huh? 'The immaculate clothes that are so out of place here, the need to be in charge.' Oh. 'Remember the colour of love is sky blue. Happy blue with bright yellow sunshine.'

CHAPTER NINE

THE COLOUR OF love was absent the next morning as Jess drove to the Wilson household. The sky was grey with heavy, rain-filled clouds and they were going nowhere. The moist atmosphere felt chilly after such a hot summer.

Her heart was out of whack, like it didn't know what rhythm it should be beating. It sure clogged her throat any time she thought about her mission.

'So don't think about it.' Yeah, sure.

'What can't I think about, Mummy?'

'Sorry, sweetheart. I was talking to myself.' Turning into the long driveway leading up to Ian and Virginia's house, her foot lifted off the accelerator and the car slowly came to a halt. *What am I doing? Is it the right thing?* The resolve she'd found at about six that morning had deserted her. *Turn around and go home. No. That's cowardly.*

Before she could overthink what she'd come to do, she pressed her foot hard on the accelerator and the car shot up the drive like she was being chased.

'Hi, Jess, Nicholas. You're out early.' Ian sauntered over to them from his packing shed. 'Just like the boys. Grady was around here before the sparrows woke to take Jackson out fishing.'

Her heart stopped its erratic tattoo as relief whooshed

through her. *Coward. This is a delay, not the finish of your mission.* 'Isn't it a bit rough out on the water today?'

Ian shook his head. 'No. Flat calm at the moment. Perfect conditions. Though it is forecast to kick up early afternoon, but they'll be back long before then. Hopefully with a bin of fish for lunch.'

'Fishing? I want to go, too.'

'No, Nicholas, you can't.' Thump-thump went the dull pain behind her eyes. The last thing she needed was Nicholas throwing a paddy because he hadn't gone with Jackson. Picking him up, she hugged him tight. 'Sorry, sweetheart.'

Ian ruffled Nicholas's hair. 'Sorry, boyo, but Grady and Jackson were having some man time. None of us were invited.'

'What's man time?' came the inevitable question.

Jess held her breath as Ian answered, keen to know what this fishing trip was all about if not catching fish.

'It's when close friends want to spend time talking or not talking and doing something together that they enjoy.'

What did Jackson and Grady have to talk about that they hadn't already discussed last night around the dinner table?

'Guess we'll go back home, then.' She sighed. Home, where she could pace up and down the small lounge. Or make herself useful and bake cookies for her neighbours. Or, 'Think I'll go see Sasha.'

Ian frowned. 'Don't go before you've seen Virginia, will you? She's a bit shaky this morning and I don't mind admitting she worries me. I never know how she's really feeling, she's so intent on hiding the truth from me.'

Guilt assailed her. She'd become very selfish recently, putting her own concerns before those of her friends. See, loving Jackson did divert her from the other people in her life. 'Of course I'm going to see Virginia. Is there something you want me to check out?'

'No. There are two doctors in the family taking good care of her. Driving her insane with all their questions if you want to know the truth. But while I can sympathise with Virginia, I need those boys doing the doctor thing.' Ian looked glum as he ran a hand through his hair. Like father, like son. 'Just give her some cheek and pretend everything's normal, will you?'

'Come on, Nicholas. Let's go say hello to Virginia.'

'He can help me in the shed, if you like.' Ian looked at Nicholas. 'We've got boxes to make up for the avocados.'

'Yes, please. I want to help.'

'Guess that's decided, then.' Jess headed for the house, torn between being relieved Jackson wasn't around to talk to and being disappointed she hadn't got it over and done with.

Jackson wound hard and fast, bringing the line in before the barracuda bit into the blue cod he'd hooked. 'Get lost, you waste of sea space.'

'You've got two cod on those hooks.' Grady grinned. 'Talk about greedy.'

'Saves time.' Jackson swung the straining line over the side of the boat so that his catch landed in the big bin they'd put on board. 'Nothing wrong with either of them either. Definitely not undersized.' He grinned. Not like Grady's last two.

'Next you'll be saying you've caught the biggest of the day.'

'Too right.' One of the cod had swallowed the hook, making it tricky to remove. He found the special pliers and wrenched it free. The other fish was foul-hooked around the mouth and didn't take much to undo. 'Got my brunch. How're you doing?'

'I'm onto getting enough for the rest of the family.' Grady wound in a fish and Jackson nearly split his sides laughing.

'Not even Nicholas would get enough to eat from that.'

'Says the expert,' Grady grumped, and carefully slid the undersized cod back under the water. 'You and that boy get on okay.'

'He likes fishing.' Hopefully Grady would take him out occasionally. 'I'll miss him.'

'What about his mother? Going to miss her, too?'

'Definitely.' More than he'd have believed possible. Hell, he missed her now, missed her whenever they were apart. It had hurt last night when she'd wanted to go home alone. But she was entitled to her space. He didn't want to encroach on everything she did. Not much, anyway.

'There's a job going at the Nelson Hospital ED.'

That he did not want to know. It added to his dilemma about heading away, leaving everyone behind. 'I've got one, thanks.'

Grady dropped his line back in the water. 'Just thought you should know.'

A tug at the end of his line gave Jackson the distraction he needed. Winding fast, he soon had another cod in the bin. 'One to go and we've got our limit.'

And we can head home to the family. My family. And Jess and Nicholas.

Jess placed the tray of shortbread in the oven and set the timer. It was quiet in her house. Nicholas had stayed on with Ian, doing man stuff apparently. Thank goodness there were men like Ian to give her boy a male perspective. Jackson was Nicholas's firm favourite. Unfortunately. His little heart would be broken soon. Had she done wrong, encouraging Nicholas to get on with Jackson? Probably. But, then, life was like that and the sooner Nicholas learned he had to look out for himself the better.

Her cellphone vibrated on the bench. 'Hello?'

'I think I'm in labour.'

'Constance? Is that you?' The thirty-six-year-old woman wasn't due for ten days.

'Yes.' Grunt. 'Can you hurry? You know how fast my babies like to be.'

'On my way.' Turning the oven off, she ran for her car, whilst phoning Virginia. 'I've got an eminent birth. Can Nicholas stay there until I'm finished?' She hated asking when Virginia had enough to deal with, but right now she didn't have the time to collect her boy and deposit him with Andrea and Bobby. 'I can phone Andrea and see if she'll pick him up later.'

'Nonsense. We love having him here. Don't worry about him at all. Just go and deliver that baby safely.'

Nicholas waved furiously as they turned up the drive. Jackson looked around, felt a tug of disappointment when he didn't see Jess's car. 'Hey, sport. What have you been up to all morning?'

'Making boxes. Did you get any fish?' Nicholas jumped up and down by the boat, trying to get high enough to see what they'd caught.

Jackson swung him up and into the boat. 'Take a look in that bin.'

Nicholas's eyes popped out wide. 'That's lots. They're very big.' He delved into the bin, ran his hands all over the cold, wet fish. Jess would be thrilled when she caught up with her stinky boy.

'Where's Mummy?' The question was out before he'd thought about it.

Grady rolled his eyes and hefted the bin out of the boat.

'She's getting a new baby.' Nicholas picked up a rod and handed it to him.

Grady's eyes widened and his mouth twitched. 'Interesting.'

'Careful of those hooks, sport.' Jackson took the rod and stood it against the side of the boat and waited for the second rod to come his way. Jess was at a birth. He remembered when Baby Carter had been born and the misty look of longing that had filtered into her eyes. Did she really want more children? Or did she get like that with every birth she attended?

'You're looking dewy-eyed.' Grady nudged him.

Jackson snapped his head around. 'What? I don't think so. I am definitely not interested in babies. Not when I've got to go back to Hong Kong anyway. No, sir.'

'The man protests too much. Come on, Nicholas. Help me clean up these fish.' Grady strolled off to the outside sink and table to fillet the fish, Nicholas stepping along beside him.

Do I want children? Now? With Jess? Turning the hose on, he began hosing down the boat and trailer to remove any traces of salt water.

Yes. Someday. Yes. Cold water sprayed down his trousers, filled his shoes. Damn. Concentrate on the job in hand. Stop asking himself stupid questions. Whatever he wanted, it wasn't going to happen.

So whose baby was Jess delivering?

'Abigail is absolutely beautiful.' As Jess handed Constance her daughter she heard a vehicle pulling up outside the house. 'You've got a visitor, Tim.'

Tim groaned. 'Bad timing.' He didn't move from

where he sat on the edge of the bed his wife had just given birth in.

'Want me to go give whoever it is a nudge?' Jess figured these two needed time alone with Abigail and it was an excuse to take herself out of the room.

'Would you mind?' Tim looked hopeful. 'Though I guess if it's one of our parents there's no stopping them.'

'Leave it to me.' She was already halfway out of the room. The doorbell chimed before she reached the front of the house. Pulling the door wide, the breath stuck in her lungs.

Jackson stood there, beaming at her. 'Thought I'd drop by and see if you needed any support.'

Leaning against the doorjamb for strength, she waited for her breathing to restart. 'You're too late. Abigail arrived ten minutes ago.'

His brow creased. 'That was fast. From what Mum said, you've only been gone a little over an hour.'

'Constance has a history of short labours, hence the home birth. She didn't fancy giving birth in Tim's truck on the way to town.'

Nodding, Jackson said, 'So you're all done here? Heading back to town now?'

'I've got some cleaning up to do, and I like to hang around for a while in case there's anything not right. Though Constance is a seasoned mum, this being her fourth baby.' But she wasn't about to leave because of that. 'I'm about to make coffee. Want one?' Hopefully the caffeine wouldn't set her heart racing any faster than it already was. One sight of Jackson and it lost all control over its rhythm.

'Sounds good.'

Pushing away from the jamb, she straightened. 'How was the fishing?'

'Brilliant. You've got blue cod for dinner.' He caught her elbow, held her from moving away. 'Did you get any of that sleep you wanted? You're looking more peaky than ever.'

'Flattery will get you anything.' She tugged free, only to be caught again.

'What's bothering you, Jess?' Those green eyes bored into her, seeing who knew what? Probably everything she was trying to hide from him.

So stop hiding it. Get it over and done. Stepping past him, she tugged the door shut and went down the steps to the path. Rotating on her heels, she faced him, locked eyes with him again. 'You. Me. Us. That's what's keeping me awake at the moment.'

He froze, stared at her like he was a deer caught in headlights. His Adam's apple bobbed. The tip of his tongue slid across his bottom lip. Fear tripped through that green gaze. 'Us.'

Nodding slowly, she added, 'I know we agreed to an affair for the duration of your time here.' Damn, that sounded too formal, but how else did she say what needed to be said? *Try coming straight out with it.* 'But I fell in love with you.'

His face paled. Not a good sign. At all. Might as well give him the rest. Might help put him at ease. 'You're safe. I said at the time I had no intention of ever getting into a permanent relationship with anyone. That hasn't changed.' *You are so wrong, Jess. You'd settle down with Jackson in a flash, given the opportunity.* Yes, now she understood she would. No argument.

The next thing she knew his arms were around her, holding her tight against his chest. Under her ear his heart was speeding faster than a rabbit being chased by hounds. 'I'm so sorry, Jess.'

'I think that should be my line,' she muttered. But why? What had she done wrong? It wasn't as though she'd been able to avoid falling for him. It had happened in an instant. Yet she repeated in a lower voice, 'I'm sorry.'

'Ahh, Jess, this is all my fault. I've been so selfish. But I couldn't stay away from you.' Still holding her around the waist, he leaned back to lock eyes with her. 'You are beautiful, inside and out, Jessica Baxter. I've never known anyone like you.'

'Yet you're still going away.' Wanting to pull away before she melded herself to him so he had to take her with him, but needing to stay in his arms for as long as she could, she stood irresolute, fighting threatening tears.

'I'm sorry.' His voice was low, and sad, and trembling. 'Very sorry for everything.'

Jess spun out of his arms and tore down the path out onto the roadside, gulping lungful after lungful of air as she went. Get a grip. She'd known this would hurt big time. Yeah, but knowing and experiencing were poles apart. This hurt so bad she felt like she might never be able to stand straight again. She loved Jackson. End of story. There'd be no happy ever after. Funny how now that she knew that for real, she realised how much she actually wanted it. Desperately.

'Jess.' Jackson had followed her, stood watching her through wary eyes. 'Are you all right?'

'Oh, I'm just peachy.' She gasped, tried to hold onto the words bursting from her throat, and failed. 'Of course I'm not all right. I've spent days agonising over whether to tell you or not, but honesty got the better of me, and now I've spoiled what we might've had left before you head away.' The floodgates opened and a deluge poured down her cheeks, and there was nothing she could do to stop them.

Strong arms wrapped around her, held her close to his hard body. The rough beating of his heart against her ear echoed her own. Jackson's sharp breaths lifted strands of her hair and wafted them over her face. 'I'd like to promise I'll be back, but that'd be selfish. I honestly don't know what's ahead.'

Lifting her head just enough to see his face, she told him, 'I understand. Truly. It's not as if you lied to me. Golden Bay has never been big enough for you.'

'It will be a lot harder leaving this time than it was at eighteen. There's so much that's important to me here.' His hand rubbed circles over her shoulder blades.

She raised a pathetic chuckle. 'At eighteen you left in such a hurry you scorched the road.'

'True. If only I hadn't made that promise to Juliet.'

She pulled out of that comforting hold and slashed a hand over her wet cheeks. 'I'd better go check on Constance and Abigail.'

He looked hesitant.

She put him out of his misery. 'Go home, Jackson. I won't be long and then I'll be doing the same thing.' Which meant collecting Nicholas from his parents' house. This just got harder and harder.

'Jess…' He hesitated. 'It might be in both our interests if I leave for Asia sooner than I'd planned.'

She gasped. She hadn't seen that coming. 'What about Virginia? She'll be upset.'

Wincing, he replied, 'I'll talk to her, explain, hopefully make her understand. After all, it was Mum who taught me to be honest and to live by my beliefs. But I will come home often, no more staying away for years on end.'

She had no answer to that. Her heart ached so badly it felt as though it was disintegrating inside her chest. 'Will I see you before you go?'

Shock widened his eyes, tightened his mouth. He reached for her, took her shoulders and tugged her close. 'Most definitely. I won't walk away without saying goodbye.'

For the second time since he'd turned up here she spun away and put space between them. Goodbye? A cruel word. A harsh reality for her future. A bleak future without Jackson in it. Behind her the truck door slammed shut and the engine turned over. She didn't look as he drove away. If she did she'd have started running, chasing the truck, begging him to stop and talk to her some more.

She didn't even know his feelings for her. Somewhere along the way she'd started to think he might care for her a lot, even love her a little. Not that knowing would have changed what happened, but it might've been a slight salve for her battered heart.

At seven o'clock on Tuesday morning Jess woke with a thumping headache. The alarm was loud in her quiet bedroom. She'd lain awake until about four then drifted into a fitful sleep. Now all she wanted to do was stick her head under the covers and go back to sleep, where she wouldn't notice Jackson leaving.

'Mummy, I got myself up.' Nicholas bounced onto her bed, creating havoc inside her skull.

'Good for you, sweetheart. What are you going to have for breakfast today?' She wouldn't be able to swallow a thing. When would her appetite return?

'Toast with honey. Can I cook it by myself?'

That had her sitting up too fast, her head spinning like a cricket ball in flight. 'Wait until I'm out there with you.' Slipping into her heavy robe, she tied the belt at her waist and followed him out to the kitchen.

While Nicholas made toast, along with the usual mess,

she drank a cup of tea that threatened to come back up any moment.

A knock on the back door sent Nicholas rushing to open it. 'Mummy, it's Jackson.'

She tried to stand up, she really did, but her legs failed her. Her hands gripped her mug of tea as her eyes tracked Jackson as he entered the room and came towards her. Dressed in superbly cut trousers and jacket, he looked like something out of a glossy magazine, not the man in shorts and T-shirt she'd been knocking around with for the last couple of months.

'Jess.'

'Jackson.'

He'd dropped in last night to tell her he was flying out today, bound for Auckland, and on to Hong Kong on Saturday. Said it was for the best. That's what she'd spent most of the night trying to figure out—how could it be good for him or for her?

'Jackson, I made my own breakfast.' Nicholas seemed impervious to the mood in the room.

'That's great.' He looked down at her boy, and swallowed. 'Nicholas, I'm leaving today, going back to where I live.'

Her eyes blurred, her hands were like claws around the mug. *Give me strength.*

Nicholas stared up at the man he'd come to accept as part of his life. 'You can't. I don't want you to. Mummy, tell him to stay.'

There were tears in Jackson's eyes as he hunkered down to be on Nicholas's level and reached for him. 'I'm sorry, sport, but I have to go.'

'No, you don't.' Nicholas began crying, big hiccupping sobs that broke her heart as much as Jackson's leaving would.

'Can I send you emails? You can answer, telling me how your swimming lessons are going, how many fish you catch with Grady?' Sniff, sniff. Jackson studied her boy like he was storing memories to take with him.

Nicholas nodded slowly then his eyes widened in panic. 'I don't know how to email. Mummy?'

'I'll show you.' Was it a good idea to let these two stay in touch? Would Nicholas feel let down, or would he slowly get over Jackson's disappearance?

Jackson stood, Nicholas in his arms. 'I want you to look after Mummy, for me. She's very special, you know.'

Stay and look out for me yourself. 'That doesn't give you licence to do what you like around here, Nicholas.' Her smile was warped, but at least it was a smile.

'What's licence?'

'I think your mother means you can't do whatever you like without permission.' Jackson squeezed him close then dropped a kiss on his head before handing him to her. 'See you later, alligator.' His voice broke and he turned away.

She cuddled her little boy, comforting him, comforting herself. 'Ssh, sweetheart. It's going to be all right.' Like hell it would be, and now she'd lied to Nicholas. She kissed the top of his head. 'Jackson, you'd better go.' *Before I nail you to the floor so you can't. Before I fall apart, the way my boy is.* 'Please,' she begged.

He turned back to face her. 'Sure.' But he didn't move. Just stood there, watching her, sadness oozing out of those beautiful green eyes.

'Go. Now. Please.'

He stepped up beside her, his hand took her chin and gently tilted her head back. His kiss was so gentle it hurt. Her lips moulded to his, fitted perfectly, for the last time.

She breathed in to get her last taste of him, a scent to hold onto and remember in the dark of the night.

And then he was gone. Her back door closed quietly behind him. Nicholas howled louder. Jess sat there, unable to move, and let the tears flow.

Jackson had gone.

CHAPTER TEN

JESS PULLED THE bedcovers up to her chin and listened to the rain beating down on the roof. It hadn't let up all night. She'd never heard rain like it. And according to the radio it wasn't about to stop.

'Heavy rain warnings for the Cobb Valley and lower Takaka' had been the dire message, again and again.

'Not a lot I can do about it. Might as well stay snug in bed. At least until Nicholas decides he wants up and about.' The rain suited her mood. The mood that had hung over her, keeping her gripped in misery, for the two days since Jackson had walked out of her life.

It was time to get over that. Yeah, okay, time to paste a smile on her face and pretend everything was fine in her world. Going around looking like someone had stolen her house when she hadn't been looking didn't help. Starting from now, she'd enjoy these quiet moments before Nicholas demanded her attention. She flicked the bedside light on and reached for her book. 'Bliss,' she pretended.

The light flickered. Dimmed, came back to full strength. Went off.

'So much for that idea.'

'Mummy, it's gone dark,' Nicholas yelled from his bedroom. 'I'm getting up.'

'Me, too, Sweetheart.' Jess leapt out of bed and quickly

dressed in old jeans and T-shirt. It didn't matter that she looked like a tramp; Jackson wasn't around to notice. The familiar tug of need twisted at her heart, tightened her tummy. She missed him. So much. Let's face it, she'd already been missing him before he'd left.

The moment he'd said goodbye and walked away she'd shut down, squashing hard on the pain threatening to break her apart. She'd gone through the last two days at work like a robot. One day she'd have to face up to the end of her affair with Jackson, and deal with it. But right now it was a case of getting through the minutes one at a time.

With a smile on her face. No matter how false that was.

'Hey, Mummy. Can I go outside and jump in the puddles?' Nicholas appeared in her doorway, dressed in his favourite shirt—his fishing one, of course.

Another tug at her heart. At least she could be thankful that after his first outburst of disappointment Nicholas hadn't been as sad as she'd expected. But that could be because her son didn't get what goodbye really meant. Up until now anyone who said that to him always came back—from Nelson, from school, from just about anywhere. But not from Hong Kong.

'Let me see what it's like outside first. There's been a lot of rain and those puddles might be very deep.'

Jackson would still be in Auckland. He'd left Golden Bay with days to spare before the first flight he could get to Asia, running out as though dogs had been snapping at his gorgeous butt. He was staying with an old med-school pal he'd kept in touch with over the years since graduation. Or so Sasha had told her as she'd handed Jess the tissue box. There'd been a lot of tissues used in the past two days. Who'd have believed one person could produce so many tears? She could probably singlehandedly meet Golden Bay's salt requirements.

Pulling the curtains back, Jess stared at the sight of her front yard with puddles the size of small swimming pools. A trickle of concern had her heading out the front door to check what was happening with her neighbours and the road. Wet, wet, wet. Water was everywhere, and rising. She'd never seen anything like this. It looked like her house had been transplanted into the sea.

Back inside, she reached for her cellphone. At least that was working. 'Hey, Grady, just checking everything's all right over your way. We're inundated with water here. The power's out as well.'

Grady sounded calm as he told her, 'Sasha and I are with Ian and Virginia. Might be a good idea for you and Nicholas to join us. The area is copping huge runoff from the hills. That's probably what you're getting. About an hour ago it started coming across the farms, over the road and through the properties on this side.'

'I'm sure we're safe but, yeah, I might come over before it gets worse. I don't want to be stuck here with Nicholas. At the moment he thinks this is all for his benefit but if we have to wade out it won't be pretty.' Besides, there was safety in numbers and all that.

'Take your phone and call if you think you're going to get stuck. Actually, no. Stay there. I'll come and get you in the four-wheel drive. That little hybrid thing of yours won't stand a chance if there's more than a few inches of water on the road.' Click, and Grady had gone.

'Nicholas, put a jersey and your shoes in a bag. Get your rain jacket and gumboots ready too. Grady's coming to pick us up.'

'Ye-es, Grady's coming.' He leapt up and down all the

way down the hall to the laundry, where his bag hung on the back of the door.

Quickly stuffing some warm clothes in another bag for herself, she slipped into her heavy-duty jacket and went around making sure all light switches were off and everything was locked up tight. Then she grabbed another handful of Nicholas's clothes. There was no way her boy would stay dry today. Too much temptation outside.

'Nicholas…' She waited until she had his full attention. 'When we get to Mrs Wilson's you are not to go outside. It's dangerous out there. Do you understand?'

'Yes, Mummy.' He looked so innocent that she crossed her fingers. But thanks to Jackson he was more amenable these days.

Jackson. What she wouldn't do to have him walking in the front door right now.

'Grady's here.' Nicholas raced for the door to drag the poor guy inside.

Once aboard the four-wheel drive, she told Grady, 'Thanks for taking us to your in-laws'. I didn't fancy hanging around watching that water getting higher by the minute.' Mentally she crossed fingers that her house would be safe.

'No problem. The situation's going to get worse before it's over.'

Less than an hour later Jess heard from the police that her house had a torrent of water pouring through it, as did the other few houses in her immediate neighbourhood, including Mrs Harrop's place. Thankfully the old lady had gone to Nelson for a few days. The cop told her, 'Half a kilometre back the road has been undermined with a deep and wide cut made by the force of the ever-increasing volume of water. That caused it to build up and surge forward through your area.'

Her heart sank. 'At least we're safe. Thank goodness Grady came and got us.' But what about her home? All her things? Nicholas's favourite toys and books? Tears spurted down her cheeks. 'They are only possessions,' she muttered, slashing at her cheeks with the back of her hand. 'But this has turned into the week from hell.'

Sasha hugged her. 'Those things are *your* things. I get it. It isn't fair. Maybe it won't be as bad as you think.'

Jess looked at her friend and shook her head. 'You reckon?'

Then Ian burst in through his back door yelling, 'The water levels are rising fast. I need to shift the sheep out of the orchard into the yard around the house. All hands on deck.'

Virginia said, 'I'll look after Melanie and Nicholas while you're all outside.'

Sasha yelled down the phone. 'Jackson, get your butt back home. You're needed. The whole area is flooded. It's serious.'

His heart stalled. 'Is Jess all right? Nicholas?' He looked around the crowded bar, found the TV screen. A rerun of last night's rugby game between the Auckland Blues and the Hawkes Bay Magpies was in full swing. He needed the news channel. 'What about Mum and Dad? I know you said the house was high and dry, but how are they dealing with this?' The orchard had gone under water before but they'd always pulled through. Of course, they hadn't been dealing with other things like MS before. But Jess? How would she fare? Her house was closer to the hills. *Oh, God, Jess, I've let you down.*

Sasha ramped up her yelling. 'Mum and Dad are great. It's Jessica who needs you. Her house's been flooded.

She's probably lost just about everything. Including you, you big moron.'

The expletives spitting out of his mouth copped him a few unwanted glares from people sitting at the next table. For a moment he'd forgotten he was in the pub. Up until five minutes ago he'd been having a quiet beer and early brunch with his friend Simon from med-school days and pretending everything was okay. Now he couldn't deny it any longer. He shouldn't be here. Neither should he be going to Hong Kong. 'Tell me about Jess. Is she safe?' His heart finally started working properly and he could hardly hear for the thumping in his ears.

'She's out helping rescue people, patching others up, making sure they've got somewhere to go for the duration of the flood.'

Typical, big-hearted Jess. The woman he hadn't had the courage to tell he loved her. Jackson stood up abruptly, his chair crashing back. He needed to see the flood for himself, to get a grip on reality. 'Has this been on the news?'

'Where have you been, Jackson?' Sasha sounded completely fed up with him. As she had every right to be. He'd been an idiot, thinking he could walk away from them all. Especially from Jess, the love of his life.

'What's up, Jackson?' Simon stood up too, righted the chair and apologised to the people sitting behind them.

'I need to get the bar owner to change to the news channel. It's flooding at home. Badly.' With the phone still glued to his ear, he began picking his way through the crowd.

Simon grabbed his elbow. 'You want to get us lynched? Every single person in this bar has their eyes fixed to that game.'

'Tough. This is important.'

'That's all relative. Come with me. I have a better idea. Besides, I want to live a while longer yet.' Simon was nothing if not persistent. Jackson's elbow was grabbed in something resembling a rugby hold and he was quick-marched outside.

'Where are we going?' he demanded, as fury began roaring up inside him. 'I need to see the news channel.'

'What did you say?' Sasha demanded in his ear.

He'd forgotten all about his sister. 'Sorry, Sasha. Got to go. Simon's dragging me halfway around the city and I need to stop him.'

'Whatever. I got it wrong, didn't I?' Sasha sounded disappointed—in him.

'Got what wrong?' He tugged free of Simon's grip, then stopped as understanding hit. They were outside an appliance store. A store where hopefully someone would listen to his request. 'Thanks, Simon.'

'I thought you cared.' Sasha spoke so softly he nearly missed her words. 'I've got to go. We're dealing with an emergency down here.'

'Wait. Sasha, please. Is the road over the hill a go?'

'Nope. Landslides closed it around lunchtime.'

Jackson opened his mouth to swear again, glanced around the store and saw the row of televisions—all playing the news. Showing Golden Bay like he'd never seen it before. Showing his home town besieged by water. 'Crap.'

Water ran amok, taking trees and kennels and dead cattle with it. Brown, swirling water decimating everything in its path. Suddenly the only place on earth he wanted to be was in Golden Bay, in the thick of it, with Jess, helping her while she helped everyone else. And it had taken a damned disaster to wake him up to that fact.

Simon said, 'I'll run you to the airport.'

'I'll have to hire a private plane when I get to Nelson.' Hell, he hoped he could get on a commercial flight from Auckland to Nelson at such short notice. He didn't fancy the extra hour and a half by road if he had to land in Blenheim. He wouldn't consider the time delay if Christchurch was his only option.

Five hours later Jackson dumped his bags in the corner of the Pohara Motor Camp office and headed for the communal kitchen/dining room being used as an emergency centre. The moment he walked through the door his eyes scanned for Jess, came up blank.

'Where's Jess?' he demanded the instant he saw Grady.

'Hello to you, too. She's seeing to Sam. He's injured himself while trying to dig a ditch to divert water from the house.' Grady reached for a ringing phone. 'She's fine, Jackson.'

Jackson picked his way around people and bags and boxes of food, heading for the white board on the wall. Lists scrolled down the board. Properties damaged by the flood, people being evacuated, injured folk needing house calls. He'd seen some sad sights on his way in from Takaka airstrip, travelling first by four-wheel drive then by boat and lastly on foot.

Jess's house was listed in the flooded properties, as was her other place, where Mrs Harrop lived. Yet Jess was out there doing what she did best—looking out for others. She was magnificent. And he'd been going to walk away. Idiot. He wanted to run to her, stick by her while she went about her calls. But she'd hate that. Anyway, he could be put to better use, attending patients himself.

Impatience gripped him as he waited for Grady to finish his call. Sounded like someone out past Pohara needed urgent attention from a medic. 'I'll go,' he announced the moment Grady hung up.

'Take my truck. There's a medical kit and hopefully anything else you'll need inside. Tom Gregory, Tarakohe, had his arm squashed while trying to tie his fishing boat down.'

Jackson snatched the keys flying towards him. 'I'll be in touch.'

'Good, because I've already got another call for you out at Wainui Inlet after you're done with Tom.'

Jess shivered. Under her thick jacket her clothes were soaked through. On her way to the truck that she'd hijacked from Ian she'd slipped in the mud and gone into a ditch to be submerged in sludge. It would be weeks before the foul taste of mud left her mouth.

It was well after seven and as dark as coal. This had been the longest day of her life, and it wasn't anywhere near over. Too many people needed help for her to put her feet up in front of Virginia's fire. But what she wouldn't give for a hot chocolate right about now.

Not going to happen. If she was lucky she'd get a lukewarm coffee and a droopy sandwich at Pohara before heading out somewhere else. She wouldn't be the only one feeling exhausted. All the emergency crews had been working their butts off throughout the day. The damage out there was horrendous, taking its toll on people, animals and buildings.

Buildings. As in houses. Her home.

No. She wasn't going to think about that. Wasn't going to consider the damage she'd seen briefly when the police had taken her home to collect some things. At least she'd managed to grab some clothes, a few photos and a couple of Nicholas's favourite toys. The rest didn't bear thinking about.

Hunched over the steering-wheel to peer through the murk and hoping like crazy the vehicle stayed on the road, she drove cautiously towards the temporary emergency centre. Shivering with cold, yawning with fatigue, it was hard to concentrate.

Focus. The last thing the emergency guys needed was her driving into a ditch and having to be rescued.

Finally she pulled up outside the well-lit building, got out and immediately pushed open the door. If she sat still she'd fall asleep. She'd fall asleep walking if she wasn't careful.

The heat exploded as she stepped through the door into the chaos of emergency rescue. Hesitating while her eyes adjusted to the bright lights, she could feel her hands losing their grip on the medical bag she'd brought inside to replenish. She heard it hit the floor with a sickening thud and couldn't find the energy to bend down and pick it up again.

Someone caught her, led her to a chair and gently pushed her down. A cup of tea appeared on the table in front of her. 'Get that inside you, Jess. I bet you didn't stop for lunch.'

Her stomach rumbled in answer. Lunch. What was that? 'The store was shut.' She'd never get that cup to her lips without spilling most of the contents.

'I'll get you a sandwich.'

The rumble was louder this time. She blinked. Looked up at this kind apparition hovering over her. That's when she knew she'd lost her mind. Exhaustion had caught up, obviously tipping her over the edge of sanity. She dropped her eyes, focused on the cup until it was very clear in her mind, no blurring at the edges of her sight. Looking up again, her breath snagged in the back of her throat. Jackson? If this was what not eating did then she'd schedule meals every hour from now on. Seeing Jackson at every turn would put her in the loony bin.

'Hey, sweetheart, you need to eat while Sheree finds you some warm, dry clothes.' A lopsided smile kept her from looking away.

Funny how her lungs seemed to have gone on strike. 'Is it really you?' How could it be? He should be somewhere over Australia by now. The tremors that had been racking her turned into quakes that would knock the socks off the Richter scale.

'Yes, it's me. I'm home, Jess. For good.' Steady hands held the cup to her lips. 'Now get some of this inside you.'

Her lips were numb with cold and the liquid dribbled down her chin, but some ran over her tongue and down her throat. It was good, sending some warmth into the chill. She took another mouthful, this time most of it going in the right direction. 'Define "for good",' she croaked.

'As in for the next fifty years at least.'

She couldn't do the sums. Her brain was struggling with drinking tea, let alone anything else. But she figured he meant he'd be here for a long while. 'Great.'

Now she really looked at him, concentrating as hard as she had while driving from Sam's. Really, really saw the man hunkered down in front of her, those beautiful deep green eyes fixed on her. Need laced that gaze. So did apology. And concern. Could that be love lingering around the edges, too? Or was she hallucinating?

'I heard your home has taken a hit.'

Oh. Not love. Just everyday concern for someone he knew well. That gave her the strength to murmur, 'Got a bulldozer out in your dad's shed? I'm going to need it.'

Her lips pressed together, holding back her returning bewilderment. This was too much. First her home had been all but destroyed. And now the man who had walked away from her two days ago, taking her heart with him, was in front of her, his hand on her knee, looking like he… Like he… That was the problem. She didn't understand any of this. Why had he suddenly reappeared?

Whatever the reason, she really didn't need this right now. She was busy helping folk in the bay. It was what she needed to do, it was how she atoned for being a brat teenager. Had she been even more badly behaved as a young woman than she'd imagined? Was that why all this was happening to her? Would she never pay for her mistakes?

On a long, steadying breath, she told Jackson, 'Glad you're here. They need all the medics they can get.'

'I've been helping for the last four hours. Seems we're all caught up for a while.' He took the plate of sandwiches Sheree arrived with and handed her one. 'Eat.'

'Your jersey's wet.' So was his hair. She hadn't noticed.

'Last time I looked, it was still raining.'

'I need to top up my bag.' Chew, chew. Concentrating on more than one thing at a time was too hard right now.

'I'll see to it in a minute.' He didn't move.

'Jackson,' she growled around another mouthful of bread and ham. 'Why are you here?'

'Because I couldn't leave.' He pulled another chair around and sat in front of her, still holding the plate of sandwiches. 'I was wrong to think I could go, Jess. No, let me rephrase that. I knew I wanted to stay but that bloody promise kept getting in the way, doing my head in.'

Chew, chew. 'Okay.' Was it? Jackson was back, whatever that meant.

'Jackson,' Grady called. 'Got a minute? We've got a

young boy needing stitches in his hand waiting in the other room.'

'Sure.' Leaning close, he kissed her cheek so softly she probably imagined it. 'Don't go anywhere.'

Jess watched him stride to the back door and remove his sodden jacket before heading down the hall to the bathroom. 'Did I just see Jackson in here?' she whispered.

Sheree placed a pile of clothes on the chair beside her. 'Definitely Jackson. No one else around here looks so cute in his city clobber, even when it looks like he's been swimming in it.'

'That's because no one else around here wears city clothes.' But Sheree was right. He looked downright gorgeous. Sexy and hot and warm and caring. Even when he was so bedraggled. Jackson. Had he brought her heart back to put her all together?

'Why has he come back?' she asked no one in particular.

'Go and change into those dry clothes, Jess. They'll be too big for you but at least you'll feel warmer.' Sheree could be bossy when she put her mind to it. 'Jackson isn't going anywhere tonight. You'll get your answer, I'm sure.'

Who'd have believed tears would feel so hot when your cheeks were frozen?

CHAPTER ELEVEN

JACKSON TRIED TO watch Jess as she carefully drove the short distance to his parents' place, avoiding racing water as best she could, driving around fallen trees and bobbing logs. Why had she insisted on driving when she was shattered? Trying to regain some control? Over herself? Or him?

He could barely see her outline in the dark but as they'd pulled away from the emergency centre he'd noted how tight her mouth was, how white her lips were. Her eyes had stood out in her pale face. Worry had turned their warm brown shade to burnt coffee. Now her fingers were wrapped around the steering-wheel so hard he thought he'd be peeling them off for her when they stopped.

'You're staring.'

Yes, he was. Drinking in the dark shape of her in the gloom. She was all mussed, her damp hair fizzing in all directions. Adorable. He'd only been gone a couple of days but he'd missed her every single second of the time. He'd had to fight himself not to return. How bloody stupid was that? Thought he knew what he was doing? Yeah, right. Think again, buddy.

Her voice squeaked as she asked, 'How did you get through? I heard the hill's closed.'

'Hired a plane out of Nelson. I'm glad the airstrip is on higher ground.'

'It's worse around here.'

'Shocking. I haven't seen anything like it before. The orchard's a disaster area, avocado and citrus trees standing deep in the swirling water. Fortunately the house is safe on the higher ground, unscathed by the flood, and full of people Mum and Dad are taking in and feeding.' People that included Jess and Nicholas.

'It's what people do for each other.' He thought Jess glanced at him. 'This isn't the first time this has happened in the bay.' Her tone was sharp, fed up. The turn into Dad's drive was equally sharp.

'Yeah, but I've always been somewhere else.' There lay his problem. He'd done a damned fine job of avoiding being a part of this place when the bad times were going down. Only ever here for some good times. But not any more. 'Jess, there's something I—' He jerked forward as she braked too hard for the conditions.

'Here we are. I can't wait to put on dry, clean clothes, my clothes. And to hug Nicholas.' Slam. Her door banged shut.

'No hugs for me, then.' What had he honestly expected? The band playing 'Welcome home, lover'? Jackson sat shivering from the bone chilling effect of his wet clothes and Jess's avoidance. He watched her stomping across the yard to Mum's back door. Every step sent up a spray of water. Every foot forward, away from him, accentuated the fact she couldn't deal with his return. Didn't want to, more like.

Finally he shoved the door open and dropped to the ground. Tonight wasn't the time for deep and meaningful conversations. Not when Mum and Dad's house was full of neighbours. Not when Jess had her own house situation to deal with. Not when Nicholas would want her attention.

He drew a breath and dug deep for one attribute he didn't have. Patience. Somehow he had to hold back and not rush in waving a flag, demanding that Jess listen to him. Somehow he had to take the time to show he would stand by her no matter what. Help her fix the home she'd been so proud of and that now stood full of muddy water. Wrecked. Not that anyone really knew how vast the damage would be. It'd take a few days before assessors and builders could even begin evaluating the situation.

One thing he knew with absolute certainty—whatever it took, he'd do it to win Jess's heart. For ever.

'Hey, you coming in?' Dad yelled from the back door. 'I've still got some of that bourbon left.'

'That's my dad.' His heart lifted a fraction as he went to join him. But as he approached the porch he noticed how grey Dad had turned, almost overnight. He wasn't coping with Mum's illness, and this situation would have exacerbated everything. His leaving wouldn't have helped matters either.

And I thought I could leave. His gut clenched. 'Dad, I'm sorry.' He wrapped his arms around the man who'd been there for him when he'd stubbed his toe, when he'd caught his first fish, when he'd wanted to know about sex, when he'd shouted he was leaving Golden Bay for ever. 'I'm not leaving again.'

'Tell that to Jess, not me. I'd already worked that out. Even before you had. But that young lady inside is going to take a lot more persuasion.' Dad locked gazes with him. 'She needs you, son. Badly. From what Jonty says, it's really bad news about her property. Both houses are wrecked.'

'Yeah, I saw that on the board at Pohara.' No wonder Jess didn't have time for him.

Dad nodded. 'You're onto it.'

The bottom dropped out of Jackson's stomach. He should be shot. He'd been so sure of himself, acting strong and supposedly doing the right thing. It had taken an act of nature to bring him to his senses. It was going to take a lifetime to prove to Jess he could change, and get it right the second time round. If she even gave him a chance.

Jess forced her feet forward, one slippery step at a time, through her kitchen into the lounge. The mud and sludge was above her ankles, but overnight the water had at last dropped to ground level. Everything dripped moisture. Brown goo stained the walls higher than her waist. Furniture sat like sodden hulks, ruined for ever. The smell turned her nose, curled her stomach.

On the wall photos were buckled from moisture. Seeing one of Nicholas, grinning out at her as he rode around the front lawn, snagged her heart, threatened to break her determination to be strong. She'd sneaked out of the Wilsons' home the moment it was light enough to see her hand held out in front of her. The night had been long and stressful and sleep evasive as she'd tossed and turned on the couch. She'd desperately wanted to see her house, the place she'd made into a home for her and Nicholas. A safe haven where she knew she finally belonged.

Of course she'd known it would be bad, but she had to see it, to know by touch, smell and sight just how bad it really was. She needed this short time alone to absorb it all. That way she'd be able to hold herself together and be strong in front of everyone else, no matter how generous they were with offers of help and new furniture.

Tracking through the mess, she made her way to Nicholas's room and swiped at her cheeks. So much for not crying. The quilt she'd bought at the local fair when Nicholas was two now had a distinct brown tinge but the appliquéd zoo animals were still clear, just dark brown.

'Will I ever be able to wash that clean?'

Pulling open a drawer, she gasped, still able to be surprised at the mess inside.

'Guess we're going shopping for clothes in the next few days, my boy. Thank goodness you wore your lucky fishing shirt yesterday.' The tears became a steady stream.

Another ruined photo caught her eye. How had she missed this one yesterday? There hadn't been time to collect them all, but this one? Reaching out slowly, she lifted it by the frame and stared at the excited face of Nicholas with his first fish. Jackson squatting beside him, an equally big grin on his gorgeous face.

The stream became a torrent. Jackson. Nicholas. The two most important people in her life. The life that had turned into one big mess.

'Hey.' Strong arms wrapped around her, turned her to hold her tight against that familiar, strong body she'd missed so much for the last three days. No, make that since the day she'd told Jackson she loved him.

The torrent turned into a flood, pouring onto Jackson's jersey, like the floodwaters that had soaked his clothes yesterday.

All the time she sobbed he held her against him, his hands soothing her by rubbing her back, his chin settled on the top of her head. Letting his strength soak into her. Calming her with his quiet presence. Not trying to deny that she had a problem but showing he'd be there as she sorted her way through the debris that had become her life.

Finally the tears slowed, stopped. Her heart felt lighter and yet nothing had changed. The house was still a wreck. Jackson would still return to Hong Kong. He might've said he was staying but she couldn't take a chance on that. Time to toughen up. She pulled away, moved to stand in the middle of the room, the photo still in her hand. Wiping her other hand over her cheeks, she told him, 'Thank you. As if there isn't already enough water around the place.'

Jackson winced, but he didn't turn round and hightail it out of her house. 'Let's see what we can save. Throw anything not ruined into the truck and take it back to Mum's to clean before storing. Then we'll check out Mrs Harrop's place.'

It was a plan and she desperately needed something to focus on. Nodding, she walked through to her bedroom and stared around. Looked at the bed where she'd had so much fun with Jackson. Her wardrobe door stood ajar, her shoes everywhere. Bending down, she picked up one of the apricot silk pair she'd worn at the wedding. 'Ruined. But I guess they're only shoes.'

She didn't realise Jackson had followed her until he said, 'No such thing as *only* shoes for women.' When she looked up, he gave her a coaxing smile. 'I'll take you shopping when we've had time to work out what's going to happen with all this.'

That's what she'd said about Nicholas's things. Throw 'em out and get new ones. That didn't seem so easy now. 'I'll get some bags to put things in.'

'Have you called your insurance company yet?' Jackson seemed determined to stick with her.

'Hardly. Too busy yesterday and it's still too early today.' Where were those large black bin liners? They'd be perfect for the damp clothes she needed to take away for washing.

'Jess.' Jackson stood beside her as she poked through a drawer of sodden plastic bags and cling wrap.

'Here we are.' She snatched up the roll and kneed the drawer closed.

'Jess.' A little louder. And when she turned to head to Nicholas's bedroom he put both hands on her shoulders. 'Jess, I don't know if this is the right time to tell you but I love you.'

'Right.' *He loves me. That's got to be good. But it doesn't fix a thing. I need to sort clothes and stuff before the day gets started and I have to go to work.*

Those big hands gripping her gave her a gentle shake. 'I am not going back to Hong Kong. I'm here to stay.'

'That's good. We need another doctor in the bay. Rory's busting to go live with his girlfriend in Auckland.' See, some things did work out if everyone was patient.

Her foot nudged something in the mud covering the floor. Bending down, she retrieved Nicholas's stuffed giraffe, Long Neck. The original yellow and black colours looked decidedly worse for their night in the mud. 'This is one of Nicholas's favourites.' She dropped it into one of the black bags.

Jackson took the roll of bags and tore off a couple. 'I'll deal with Nicholas's room if you like, while you go through your drawers and wardrobe.' He sounded very upbeat. Why? It wasn't like she'd acknowledged his statement.

Some time later she wound a plastic tie around the neck of the last full bag from her room and dumped it on the bed, on top of the beautiful quilt that apparently Sasha's grandmother had made years ago. Jess considered it antique and now it was destined for the trash. What a shame. Hands on hips, she stood at the end of the bed and looked around at what had been her pride and joy. She'd painted the whole place, but here in her bedroom she'd let loose with her creative side, buying beautiful little knick knacks for the top of her dressing table, bedside lamps that matched colours in the quilt and the curtains she'd made. She'd been so damned proud of those curtains and now look at them—sodden, muddy and hanging all askew.

Water dripped onto her breasts. Tears? Surely she'd run out by now. Apparently not. They didn't stop. Her hands began shaking and she had to grip her hips tight to keep them under some sort of control.

'Hey, you're crying.' Jackson suddenly appeared before her with a box of tissues that was miraculously dry. 'Here, let me.' Oh, so gently he sponged up the tears, only to have to repeat the exercise again and again.

Her bottom lip trembled. 'I know it's only little, and very ordinary, but this is my home. I made it how I wanted it to be, a place for Nicholas to grow up in feeling secure and loved. I've been happy here, settled for the very first time in my life.'

Those long, strong fingers touched her cheeks, lifted her face so she had to look into his eyes. 'You think that you've lost all that because your house is a write-off?'

Her head dipped in acknowledgement. That's what she'd been trying to say, yes.

'Sweetheart, the love that permeates this home doesn't come from the paint and curtains and flower vases and books on the shelves. It comes from in here.' He tapped her chest gently, right against her heart. 'From within you. That love goes where you go. It's who you are, and always will be. Nicholas is going to be secure and loved by you all his life, even though he mightn't grow up in this particular home. Even when he eventually heads out into the world on his own, he'll know you love him. Whether you get this place put back together or buy another one with the insurance money, it will be filled with your personality, your love, fun and laughter.'

For Jackson that had to be a record speech. She blinked as the tight knots in her tummy began letting go some tension. The trembling in her hands eased, stopped. 'You really, really think so?' she whispered.

'I know so.' His head lowered so that his mouth was close to hers. 'I really, really know.' Then he kissed her. A quiet kiss filled with understanding, with that love he'd not long ago declared, with his generosity. He was giving her something back after all that had been taken from her since the moment he'd walked out of her life three days ago. 'I love you,' he murmured against her mouth.

Jess leaned forward so that her breasts were crushed against his chest, her mouth kissed his in return, her hands finally lifted from her hips to his neck and held onto him. 'I don't know what to do. I love you so much and yet I can't ask you to stay. You hate it here.'

'I'm staying. End of story. I don't hate it here any more. You taught me what this community is all about.'

'Me? How?' Surprise rocked through her. 'All I do is try and make up for the mistakes I made when I was young and in need of friends who'd love me.'

'Jess, Jess, you don't get it. Yesterday, when you were dealt a blow here, what did you do? Stand around bemoaning your bad luck? Not likely. You went out caring for other people. That's community spirit in spades.'

'I'm a nurse. That's what nurses do.'

And right on cue her work phone beeped. 'Jessica, I think my waters just broke.'

'Lynley? Is that you?'

'Yes. Ouch. That wasn't nice. I'm having some light pains every ten minutes or so. Guess this is it. Do I go to the centre now?'

A grim smile twisted her mouth. 'You can wait until those contractions are closer, about six minutes between them. Unless it's going to be difficult getting there after yesterday's flood, then I'd suggest making your way there now.' It was going to take some effort for her to get there given the road this side of town had been underwater last night.

'It's a clear run from here. What about you?' Lynley asked.

'I'll be there as soon as possible. You concentrate on that baby's arrival.' She closed the phone and glanced at Jackson, to find him watching her closely.

'Guess we're headed for town, then. Have you got time to pick up some breakfast from Mum's first?'

'The baby's not rushing but I have no idea if the road is manageable.' And why are you coming with me?

'Let's go and find out.' He took the bags of clothes she'd dumped on the bed and headed out to the truck he'd borrowed.

Nothing else for her to do but follow.

When Jackson had seen Jess's shocked reaction to the state of her home he had wanted to pick her up, hold her close and transport her away from it all. He'd wanted to run her a hot bubble bath and let her soak away her desolation. Not that she'd have let him if he'd even tried. Had she heard him say he loved her? Really heard? Or had his declaration been like words on the wind? Not connecting with her?

He'd been disappointed at her lack of reaction but he figured it had been the wrong time. At least, if she knew how he felt she'd know she wasn't on her own with this. Not that she was. Mum and Dad had had to be restrained from rushing over the moment they'd known where she'd gone this morning. Only by explaining that he'd be helping Jess and that he wanted to tell her why he was home had he managed to make them stay put.

He pressed some numbers on his phone, got hold of Jonty at the fire station. 'Hey, man, how's our road this morning? Is it passable? Jess has a patient in labour in town.'

'It's open but slippery as hell. There's a temporary fix where the road was washed away. Don't let her drive that thing she calls a car. It won't hold on the tarmac.'

'That thing, as you put it, has been submerged most of the night. It's not going anywhere.' He didn't know if Jess had looked in her garage yet, and he'd try to keep her out of there for now.

Jonty groaned. 'Jess has had more than her share of knocks in this flood.'

'She sure has. I'm heading in with her so if anyone needs a doctor over the next few hours I'll be at the medical centre.' He snapped the phone shut, went to find Jess. 'Road's open so let's grab some breakfast and take it with us. We can leave those bags of your belongings at the house.' Mum would probably have everything washed by the time Jess got back.

'You're coming with me? It's a normal birth, Jackson.'

'Sure, but I might be of use at the centre. Besides, there're enough people milling around at home to drive me to drink. It's too soon to start clearing the orchards, so I'm superfluous.' I want to be with you, supporting you, because I don't believe you're totally back on your feet as far as the shock is concerned.

She flicked him a brief smile. 'You're starting to think like a local. You know that?'

'If you'd said that two months ago I'd have run for the hills.'

'Didn't you do just that three days ago? Figuratively speaking.' Those eyes that always got to him were totally focused on him right now.

'Guilty as charged.' His stomach clenched, relaxed. Of course she'd want to take a crack at him. He'd hurt her by leaving like he had. Somehow he was going to make that up to her. But he wasn't barrelling in on this one. They had their whole lives ahead of them. He'd take it slower than he was used to doing with anything.

Parking outside Mum and Dad's house, he pulled on the handbrake. 'I'll tell you something. What you just said about me thinking like a local made me feel warm and fuzzy, not cold and panicked. Guess I'm improving.'

Jess actually chuckled. There was even a hint of mischief in her eyes. 'Watch this space. You'll be standing for mayor before we know it.'

'Get outta here.' Not that Golden Bay had a mayor. There were plenty of people who liked to think they were running the district, but official business was down over the hill.

'Don't let me forget my kit.' She dropped to the ground and reached into the back for two bags. 'Wonder if any of the beach houses are vacant.'

'You thinking of renting one for a while?'

She nodded. 'Got to find somewhere to live fairly quickly.'

Now he had something practical he could do for the woman he loved. 'Leave it with me. I'll ring round, or go online, while you're bringing that baby into this wet world.'

Her gaze lit up as she looked skyward. 'The sun's peeking out, most of the sky's blue, and the rain has stopped everywhere.'

And Jess had started looking a tiny bit more relaxed. Relief nearly made him swing her up in his arms to kiss her soft lips. But as his foot came off the ground to move towards her, caution held him back. Patience, man, patience. Do not rush her. Not today, anyway. He smiled and lifted out two more heavy bags of damp belongings before following that gorgeous butt inside.

Virginia handed her a steaming mug of tea even before she'd got her boots off. 'Here you go, Jess. Get that in you. I tried to get you to have one before you left at sun-up but you weren't hearing anything.'

Jess apologised. 'I had my mind on my home, nothing else.'

'That's what I thought.' Virginia's arm draped around her shoulders. 'You and Nicholas stay here for as long as it takes to sort everything out. No arguments.'

'I'm not arguing. I'm just too exhausted to do anything much about finding somewhere to live today. So, thanks very much.' She laid her cheek against the other woman's arm for a moment, absorbing the warmth and care. 'Thank you,' she whispered again.

Jackson strolled through the farmhouse-sized kitchen and smiled at her and his mother. 'We're heading into town shortly. Anyone here who needs to go that way?' He was definitely sounding more and more like most of the other caring people in the district.

Virginia dropped her arm and handed Jackson a mug. 'Not that I know of. Want to take some food with you? Can't imagine any shops being open today.'

Ten minutes later Jess sat in the passenger seat watching Jackson skilfully negotiate a small washout just past her house. 'It could take months to get everything back to normal.'

Her work phone buzzed in her pocket. 'Hey, Lynley, that you?'

'My contractions are down to five minutes apart and we're waiting at the birthing unit.'

'Nearly there.' She closed the phone. 'That girl is so calm for a first baby.'

'What were you like when you had Nicholas?'

'Terrible. My baby was the first baby ever to be born. No one could've possibly understood what I was going through. I'm surprised I had any friends left by the time I'd finished.' She grinned. 'Labour hurts, big time. And mine went on for thirty-one hours. I swear it's the only time Nicholas has been late for anything.'

'Would you do it again?'

Talk about a loaded question. 'You going somewhere with this?'

'Yep.' He slowed behind a tractor towing a trailer laden with broken trees. Driving patiently, he kept back from the mud sent into the air by the trailer wheels. 'I'd love to have kids.'

And that had something to do with her? Though he had said he loved her—three times. 'Yeah, I'd do it again. The pain's quickly forgotten when you hold your baby in your arms for the first time.'

Jackson didn't say any more, just concentrated on getting them through the mud and debris littering what used to be a perfectly good road.

The medical centre was surprisingly quiet. 'I think everyone's too busy cleaning up to be bothered with visiting us,' Mike theorised, when they tramped inside with their plastic box of breakfast.

'Where are Lynley and Trevor?' she asked.

'Over in the maternity wing.'

Jackson continued walking through the centre. 'I'm over there if you find you're suddenly rushed off your feet, Mike.'

'You don't have to come with me.' Jess hurried after Jackson.

'I'll make breakfast.'

'You have an answer for everything,' she muttered under her breath.

He leaned close, placed a soft kiss on her cheek. 'Better get used to that.'

Lynley had already changed into a loose-fitting hospital gown. 'Can't stand anything constricting me at the moment,' she told Jess the moment she turned into the birthing room. 'Ahh, Trevor, hold me.' Her pretty face contorted as vice-like pain caught her.

Trevor stood rock solid as his wife clung to him, his hands around her waist. 'Glad you got through, Jess. I heard about your place being flooded. Hope it's going to be all right. If there's anything I can do, give me a call, okay?'

'Thanks. It's too soon to know what'll happen with it. This is Jackson Wilson. He's an emergency doctor and, no, Lynley you're not having an emergency.'

Jackson waved a hand at the couple. 'If you don't want me hanging around just say so, otherwise I'm here to watch and learn.'

When the contraction had passed Jess indicated for Lynley to sit back on the bed and then wrapped the blood-pressure cuff around the mother-to-be's arm. 'Baseline obs first and then I'll listen to baby's heartbeat.'

'Any idea how long this is going to take?' Lynley asked.

'It's like the piece of string. Every baby is different. Your BP's good.' She listened through the stethoscope to the baby's heartbeats, counting silently. 'All good there, too.'

'Now we wait, right?' Trevor said.

'We certainly do. And be grateful that wee boy didn't decide yesterday was the day to arrive.' Jess sat on a low stool and filled in patient observations.

Jackson said, 'I'll make our breakfast. Can I get you anything Lynley? Trevor?'

Another contraction, and again Trevor held Lynley. And again. Jackson returned from the kitchen with a tray laden with toast and jam, and four cups of coffee. More contractions, more observations noted on the page. The morning groaned past and Lynley began to get tired.

'I'm fed up with this pain,' she yelled once.

'Why did you get me pregnant?' she demanded of Trevor another time. 'Do you know what you're putting me through?'

Jess sympathised, while thinking that at least Lynley hadn't resorted to swearing at the poor guy, like some women did.

Jackson stood behind her and rubbed her back when she rose from the stool. How did he know she ached just there? And did he understand he was knocking down her resistance towards him?

Finally, some time after three o'clock, Lynley suddenly announced, 'I want to push. Now.' She sank onto the bed and leaned back against the stack of pillows Jackson had placed there earlier in case she got tired of standing.

'Let me take a look at you.' Jess pulled on another pair of gloves and squatted on her stool again. 'Push when you're ready. There you go. The head has appeared. Keep pushing, Lynley. That's it. You're doing brilliantly.'

Lynley's attention was focused entirely on pushing her baby out into the world.

Then the baby slipped out into Jess's waiting hands. 'Welcome to the world, baby Coomes.' Jess wiped the little boy's mouth clear of fluid and draped him over his mother's breasts.

'Oh, my goodness. Look at him, Trevor. He's perfect.' Tears streamed down the new mother's cheeks. 'Didn't we do great?'

Trevor was grinning and crying, staring at his son like he was the most amazing sight ever.

Which he was. Jess blinked rapidly. It didn't matter how many babies she'd delivered, today baby Coomes was the most special. Next week there'd be another for her to get all soppy over.

'Isn't that the most beautiful sight?' Jackson spoke quietly beside her, emotion making his voice raw.

Maybe he really did mean to settle down here. 'It is. Once I've dealt with the cord and afterbirth let's take a break and give these two time alone with their son before the families descend. There'll be no peace when they all arrive.' Which was why Lynley had said right from the outset she didn't want anyone knowing she was in labour.

Mike had locked up the medical centre and gone home, no doubt crossing his fingers he'd get a few hours to himself and his wife, Roz. Today everyone's focus would be on clean-up and less on health issues. Tomorrow might be different as reality settled in.

Jess switched on the lights in the kitchen and filled the kettle for a cup of tea. She automatically got out two cups. Then she found the tin of chocolate biscuits Sasha kept hidden in her locker and sprang the lid, quickly stuffing a biscuit in her mouth. 'I need sugar.'

Pulling out a chair, Jackson sat and sprawled his long legs half across the room. 'You must be exhausted. Did you sleep much last night?'

'Next to nothing. My mind would not shut down.'

'I've found three houses for rent that you can look at. Two at Pohara and one at Para Para. You can see see them any time you want. You've got first dibs on all three.'

Leaning back against the bench top, she folded her arms under her breasts. 'Para Para would be lovely. That long, wide, sweeping beach is stunning, though a bit dangerous for Nicholas when it's windy. Which is often.'

'Not too far out of town?'

'Unfortunately, yes. So I'm already down to two.' She gave him a tired smile. 'Thank you for doing this. I do appreciate it.'

'Just want to help.'

Her forefingers scratched at her sleeves. He'd told her he loved her and she hadn't said a word. Yet he hadn't stalked off in a sulk. Far from it, he'd stayed by her side all day. Helping with the birth, making endless rounds of sandwiches and coffee, looking up rental properties, rubbing her back when it got sore.

Raising her head from where she'd been staring at the tips of her running shoes that were never used for running, she looked directly at him and said, 'Jackson, I love you, too.' When he made to stand up she held up a hand. 'But that doesn't mean I'm going to do anything about it.'

It hurt just to say the words. A deep hurt that twisted in her stomach. She wanted him so much, would do almost anything to give in and accept his love and make a life with him.

'Want to elaborate, Jess?' he asked, bewilderment lacing his tone.

'My parents.' This was hard. So hard. 'They love each other very much.' Too much. 'To the point they are selfish with it.' They don't even realise it. 'They excluded me from a lot. Anything that money couldn't buy, really.' Her eyesight blurred. 'Yes, I love you, Jackson. But what if I love you so much I cut Nicholas out of the picture, forget to give him hugs and kisses, miss school plays, send him on expensive holidays to get him out of the way?' Her voice had got quieter and quieter until she could barely hear herself. 'You want kids, but what if I neglect them, too?'

'You won't.' Two little words and yet there was the power of conviction in them. 'I know you, Jessica Baxter. I've seen you with Nicholas. You totally love him. You'd never be able to avoid hugging him. You'll never want to miss seeing his first proper fish.'

'You're missing the point.' That had been when it had only been her and Nicholas, before she went so far as to admit Jackson into her life properly.

'No.' He stood up and reached for her. With his arms around her waist he leaned back and looked down into her eyes. '*You're* missing the point. You're a natural mother. You'll never be otherwise. But you've got a big heart, Jess, big enough for me as well. And for our children, if we have them. You can love us all. You do love Nicholas and me already. What has Nicholas missed out on since that very first night when we went to bed together? Go on. Tell me.' His mouth was smiling, like this wasn't the issue she'd believed it was. His eyes were brimming with love for her.

'I can't think of anything.' Nicholas certainly seemed

as happy as ever when Jackson was around. In fact, he loved Jackson and the things they had done together.

'Do you trust me to give you a nudge if I think you're not getting the mix right? Because I certainly would. But, Jess, I don't believe it will ever come to that.'

He truly believed she wasn't like her parents. Wow. 'I do love you both and I hoped I was getting it right. But it's hard to know. Mum and Dad don't have a clue what they've excluded me from. They honestly believe they've been great parents.'

'I know you're an awesome parent. I wouldn't want anyone else to be my children's mother.' Jackson lowered his head, his lips finding hers. His kiss, when it came, was tender and loving and understanding, and it fired up her passion. 'I love you, Jess. Will you take a chance and marry me? We could have so many babies you'd always be inundated with their demands, and I'll be making arrangements for date nights so I can have you all to myself.'

The eyes that locked with hers held so much sincerity and love her doubts evaporated. For how long she didn't yet know, but she now knew that she could always discuss them with this wonderful man. He'd help her through. 'Go on, then.' At his astonished look, she laughed. 'That's a yes. I will marry you, Jackson. And love you for ever, as well as all those children. Jessica Wilson, here I come.'

This time his kiss wasn't so gentle. More like demanding as he sealed their promise. 'Thank goodness,' he sighed between their lips. 'Thought I'd be spending the next year trying to sweet-talk you into a wedding.'

When Jackson drove up to his parents' house Nicholas was waiting on the veranda. He immediately began waving and leaping up and down.

'Mummy, I've been watching for you for ages.'

Her heart squeezed painfully. Her boy. She loved him beyond reason. Reaching to lift him into her arms, panic struck and she spun around to stare at Jackson.

'No, Jess, you haven't neglected him for other people. You were doing your job and now you're home to hug and hold and love your son. That's normal for most parents.' Jackson stood beside her, lifting strands of hair off her face.

'Thank you.' She sucked in the sweet smell of Nicholas as he wriggled around in her arms. She felt his warmth warming her. Knew he'd always come first with her.

'Mummy, there was a very big eel in the packing shed. Ian said the flood brought it here. I touched it and it was cold and yucky.'

Jackson took her elbow and led them inside. 'Let's get changed into something clean and warm and I'll break out the champagne. We've got something to celebrate.'

Her mouth stretched so wide it hurt. 'Yeah. We do. But first I need some time with Nicholas. I've got something to discuss with him.'

Jackson nodded his understanding. 'Why don't you go through to Mum's office? I'll make sure no one disturbs you.'

In the office she sat in the one comfortable chair and settled Nicholas on her lap. 'We're going to live in a different house for a while, Nicholas. Our one was flooded.'

His little eyes widened with something like excitement. 'Really? Can I see it with the water in it?'

How easy things were for a child. 'We'll go there tomorrow, but the water's gone now.'

Disappointment replaced the excitement. 'I wanted to see it.'

Drawing a deep breath, she continued with the other

important piece of news. 'Nicholas, how would you like Jackson to live with us? All the time?'

The excitement rushed back. 'Yes. When? Now?' His face fell. 'But he can't. We haven't got a house to live in.'

'We'll find another house. Mummy and Jackson are going to get married. You'll have a daddy.'

'Like Robby's daddy?' Hope radiated out of his big eyes.

Shame hit her. She'd held out on Jackson because she'd feared she'd be hurting her son, yet all along the best thing she could've done for him was accept Jackson's love and go with it. 'Just like Robby's father.'

She kissed her boy. 'I love you, Nicholas.'

'I love you, Mummy. I love Jackson.' He slid off her knees. 'Is he really, really going to be my daddy?'

'Yes, darling, he is.'

A whirlwind of arms and legs raced for the door, hauled it open and Nicholas took off to charge through the house. 'Where's my daddy? Jackson, where are you? Mummy and Jackson are getting married. Jackson? There you are.'

Jess made it to the door in time to see Jackson swinging Nicholas up in his arms, both of them grinning like loons.

'Guess everyone in the bay's going to know in no time at all.' She shook her head at Nicholas, her heart brimming with love. 'Quiet has never been one of your attributes, my boy.'

Jackson rolled his eyes. 'It's funny, but I'm happy if the whole world knows I'm marrying you.'

CHAPTER TWELVE

SIX MONTHS LATER, on a perfect spring day, with a sky the colour of love, Jess walked down the path leading through Virginia's garden to the marquee once again set up on the Wilsons' front lawn. Jess clung to Ian's arm, her fingers digging in hard as her high heels negotiated the newly laid pebbles. 'Thank you for standing in for my father,' she told Jackson's dad.

True to form, Mum and Dad hadn't been able to make it home for the wedding. Something about the gorillas in Borneo needing their attention. Jess swallowed her disappointment. She was about to get a whole new family: one that would always be there for her, as she would be for them.

'I'm thrilled you asked me.' Ian looked down at her with tears in his eyes. 'I'm getting to be a dab hand at it. Two weddings in less than a year. Who'd have believed it? And before we reach that son of mine, who's looking mighty pleased with himself, can I just say thank you for bringing him home for us.'

'Thank goodness he didn't have long to go to finish his contract.' She'd have gone crazy if he'd been away much longer than the four months he'd had to do. Now he worked three days a week in Nelson and the rest of the time at the Golden Bay Medical and Wellbeing Centre.

Sasha spoke behind them. 'Come on, you two. We've got a wedding to get under way, and Nicholas and I can't stand around all afternoon listening to you both yabbering.'

Jess turned and grinned at her soon-to-be sister-in-law. 'Yes, ma'am. By the way, you looked lovely in blue.'

'Why do my friends get married when I'm looking like a house in a dress?' For the second time Sasha was standing up for a close friend while pregnant.

Jess grinned and glanced down at Nicholas. He looked gorgeous in his dove-grey suit and sky-blue shirt that matched Jackson and Grady's. 'Let's get the show under way. What do you reckon, Nicholas?'

'Hurry up, Mummy. It's boring standing here.'

Jess grinned. 'Love you too, buddy.' Then she faced the end of the path, where Jackson stood watching her take every step along that path. When she placed her hand on his arm he blinked back tears. 'You are beautiful,' he murmured. His eyes glittered with emotion.

She couldn't say a word for the lump clogging her throat, so she reached up and kissed him lightly.

'Seems we need to get you two married in a hurry.' Diane, the marriage celebrant, chuckled. She looked around at the family and friends gathered on the lawn. 'Jessica and Jackson stand here today in front of you all to pledge themselves to each other.'

Jess heard the words and yet they ran over her like warm oil, soft and soothing. Not once on that day in January, when she'd stood up with Jackson, watching her best friend marry Grady, had it occurred to her that she'd be getting married in this same place, with the same people surrounding them. She hadn't known love like it—the depth, the generosity, the bone-melting sweetness. She hadn't known the colour of love—summer blue with sunshine lightening it. Okay, today it was spring blue, but that was close enough.

In fact, it was brilliant, as Jackson said the vows he'd written himself, declaring his love for her, promising her so much. Her heart squeezed tight with love. This wonderful man was becoming her husband. Handing Sasha her bouquet, she held her hands out to him. The diamond-encrusted wedding ring he slipped onto her finger gleamed in the sunlight.

'Jess, would you say your vows now.' Diane caught her attention.

Taking Jackson's strong, warm hands back in hers, she managed a strong voice. 'Jackson Wilson, today I promise before our family and friends to always love you with all my heart, to share my life with you, to raise our children alongside you. I acknowledge you as my son's father in the truest sense of the word. I love you. We love you.' And then she couldn't say any more for the tears in Jackson's eyes and the lump in her throat.

Sasha placed the gold band she and Jackson had chosen into her shaking hand. Her fingers trembled so much Jackson had to help her slide the ring up his finger. And then he kissed her. Thoroughly. No chaste wedding kiss.

'Okay, that's enough, you two,' Ian interrupted. 'There are children present,' he added, with a twinkle in his eye.

Diane smiled. 'I declare you man and wife.'

'Good, then I can kiss the bride,' Jackson said.

There was a general groan and many quips from the people seated around them, but none of it stopped Jackson placing his lips on hers again.

Once more Ian interrupted by pulling her out of his son's arms into his. 'Welcome to the family, Jessica.'

Then Virginia and Sasha were hugging her, quickly

followed by Nicholas, Grady, Mike and Roz, Rory and Mrs Harrop. Time sped by until Ian tapped a glass with a spoon and got everyone's attention.

'Champagne is being brought around. Let's all raise a glass and drink to Jessica and Jackson.'

Champagne. That's where this had all started. Her smile was met by one from her husband. 'Yep, it's the same champagne.'

As they were handed glasses of her favourite nectar, Jess grinned. 'I won't be drinking as much of this as I did the last time. I want all my faculties working on my wedding night.'

Jackson ran his hand through his hair, instantly mussing it up. 'I seem to remember they worked fine that other time.'

He slipped his free hand through her arm and tugged her away from the crowd and through the rose garden that was Ian's latest hobby. 'I want a few moments alone with my wife.'

'You sound very smug, Mr Wilson.'

'Why wouldn't I? I've just achieved a dream. You look absolutely beautiful. That dress with the orange flowers suits you to perfection.'

'Apricot, not orange.' She leaned against him and pressed a kiss to his mouth. 'I love you.'

For a moment they were completely alone. No voices touched their seclusion and nothing interrupted the sense that they were in their own little world. Then Jackson pulled his mouth free. 'I hope you've packed that orange bikini for our honeymoon.'

She'd done what she'd been told to do. Jackson had kept their destination a surprise, only saying that she'd need bikinis, lots of them. 'Of course.' And two other new ones he hadn't seen yet. Not apricot in colour, either of them.

'Our flight to Auckland leaves tomorrow afternoon.'

'Right.' Like she'd be wearing a bikini in Auckland in spring.

'Then on Monday we fly to Fiji.' That smug look just got smugger.

Secretly she'd hoped that's where he'd chosen. 'Fiji?' She grinned. 'You remembered.' Her kiss smothered his chuckle.

'We're away for two weeks, sweetheart.'

'Our house will be finished by then.' There was only the paintwork to be completed and the carpet to be put down in their new home before they were handed the keys.

'That will make you happy. Being back on your piece of dirt where you planned on bringing up Nicholas.'

That was one of the things she loved about this man. He understood her need to put down roots for herself, and how she had done that when she'd bought her little home. Which was why, when the insurance company had elected to bowl over both her houses and pay out the money, they'd had the two sections made into one and started building a house big enough to cope with the children they intended on having very soon.

'Mummy, Jackson, come on. Everyone's hungry and we're not allowed to eat until you sit at your table.' Nicholas burst through the bushes they'd hidden behind. 'Come on.'

'That means you're the hungry one.' Jackson swung his son up into his arms, and nudged Jess softly. 'Guess we'd better return to our wedding.'

She followed her men back to the front lawn and into the marquee, decorated in apricot and sky blue: the colour of love.

* * *

As they sat down at the top table Jackson pinched himself. It had happened. He'd married his love. His beautiful Jessica. She'd changed him, saved him really. Shown him that the important things in life were family, community, generosity. She'd brought him to his senses. But most of all she'd shown him love.

'Didn't I tell you it was time for you to return home?' Ping stood in front of them, nodding sagely.

Standing, Jackson reached over to shake the hand of his best buddy. 'Yes, Ping, you did. Took me a while to hear what you were saying.'

'Jessica's a good woman, that's for sure.' Ping draped an arm over the shoulders of the petite woman standing beside him. 'Like my Chen.'

Chen smiled and elbowed her husband. 'You're talking too much again, husband.'

Ping laughed. 'I can see why this Golden Bay brought you back. It's beautiful. All that land with only cattle on it. And the sea that's so clean.'

'You'll be moving here next,' Jackson told him.

Ping and Chen shook their heads at the same time. 'We've got family that we'd never leave back in Hong Kong. More important than green paddocks and sparkling waters.'

Exactly. Family. There was nothing more important. So important that he would soon quit his days in Nelson and become a full-time partner in the medical centre in town. There was no way he'd be leaving Jess and Nicholas for three days at a time every week. Absolutely no way.

Beside him Jess was talking and laughing with Sasha, as happy as he'd ever seen her. Her eyes were fudge-coloured today, matching that orange ribbon wound through her fair hair. A lump blocked the air to his lungs. He'd do anything for this woman who'd stolen his heart. Blinking rapidly, he looked around the marquee at all their friends and family, here to celebrate with them.

Lifting his eyes, he noted the decorations. Blue and orange ribbons festooned the walls. Orange. He grinned as he heard Jess growling, *It's apricot*. Apricot, orange. Whatever. For him, this was the colour of love.

* * * * *

GOLD COAST ANGELS: ANGELS: TWO TINY HEARTBEATS

FIONA McARTHUR

Dedicated to my cousin John, who is toughing it out, so proud of you, and to Aunty Yvonne, Lee, who is also awesome, Gay and Eveline.

CHAPTER ONE

LUCY PALMER WAS so excited even the ride up in the lift made her feel queasy. She'd thought she'd grown out of that.

Today, officially, she could say she was a part of the state-of-the-art Gold Coast City Hospital and she'd done it all herself. Her excitement had been building since graduation fourteen weeks ago.

This wasn't just three years of hard study and unpaid practical placements, this was the start of a mission she'd lived and breathed for ever.

Lucy couldn't wait to be allocated her first birth suite caseload because she was going to be the best midwifery grad they'd ever seen.

The midwifery floor manager, Flora May, ex-air force medic with a gruff voice and, Lucy suspected, a well-camouflaged heart of gold, had met Lucy in one of her placements during her training. Flora's assessment of Lucy's aptitude for the profession had helped very much in her successful interview and Lucy couldn't have asked for a better role model than Flora.

As the orientation tour ended Flora snapped her heels together and waved to the busy floor. Unexpectedly her angular face changed and she smiled with genuine warmth.

'And welcome, Palmer. I've given you Monday to Friday shifts for the first month, so I'll be here if you need advice.'

A friendly face while she settled in. Lucy decided that sounded blissful. 'Thank you.'

'Hmph.' Sentiment should be set aside, obviously, Lucy thought with an internal smile as Flora went on. 'Take Sally Smith, she's a teen mum admitted for threatened premature labour at thirty-three weeks. She needs someone she can relate to.'

This was accompanied by a dry look. 'Night staff will give you Sally's handover in birth suite one.' Flora raised an eyebrow. 'You'll be fine. Let me know if you need help and I'll be your wing man. Any questions, find me.'

The boss would be her wing man? Lucy grinned at the funny wordage and resisted the urge to salute.

Flora marched off and Lucy felt for the first time that someone other than her fellow ex-students was willing to believe she had the makings of a good midwife.

It would have been nice if her mother had been supportive instead of bitter and twisted, but she wasn't going there because nothing was going to spoil this day. Or her confidence, because Flora believed she could do this well.

Her stomach fluttered uncomfortably again and she sucked in a breath. Forget nerves, this was what she'd been born for.

When she knocked and entered the first birth suite and the night midwife didn't look up from writing her notes, Lucy faltered, felt tempted to cough or go back and knock again, but she didn't.

The pale young woman lying curled on her side blinked so Lucy stepped just inside the door and smiled, but the girl on the bed rolled her eyes, and then looked away before shutting them. Tough room, Lucy thought ruefully before, with another deep breath, she crossed to the bed.

The night midwife still didn't look up, so Lucy passed her by and smiled at her patient as she tried to imagine what it would be like to be seventeen, pregnant, and now scared her baby would be born prematurely, in a place where she knew no one.

'Hello, Sally, I'm Lucy. I'll be looking after you today when your night midwife goes home.' Lucy glanced around the otherwise empty room, and no boyfriend or mother was tucked into any corner she could see. Maybe Sally's mother had trained in the same school as hers, Lucy thought, and she knew how that felt. Lack of family support was not fun at all.

The young mum-to-be opened her eyes briefly, nodded, and then rolled carefully over onto her other side, stretching the leads that held the monitor on her stomach.

Really tough room, Lucy thought with a gulp.

Finally the night midwife put down her pen and looked across. 'I'm Cass. I've just done my fifth night shift and can't wait to get out of here.'

Lucy blinked and glanced at Sally's rigid back. Not a very nice intro, she thought, or what Lucy expected from a hospital she'd only ever heard praise about.

To make it worse, Cass didn't look at anything except her notes or, occasionally, the graph of contractions on the machine. 'So this is Sally, seventeen, thirty-three weeks, first baby, and has had intermittent back pain since three this morning. No loss on the pad she's wearing and the CTG is picking up the contractions as five-minutely.'

The lack of emotion sat strangely in a room where emotion was usually a big factor and Lucy began to suspect why Flora May had sent her in here. Lucy wanted to care for Sally, not treat her like an insect in a jar.

Cass sighed as if the story would never end and Lucy wished the midwife would just go home and let her read the notes herself. But of course she couldn't say that, especially on her first day. But she was feeling less timid by the second. Something she'd discovered inside herself when she'd discovered midwifery.

Then Cass went one worse. 'The foetal fibrinectin test for prem labour couldn't be done because she's had sex in the last twenty-four hours.'

Brutal. Lucy saw Sally's shoulder stiffen and winced in sympathy for the callousness of a clinical handover that lacked sensitivity. Lucy vowed she'd never be like this. And now she seriously wished the other midwife gone.

Cass certainly didn't notice and went on in the same bored tone as she read from her notes. 'No urinary symptoms or discharge but we've sent swabs and urine away for microscopy.'

Okay, Lucy understood that she needed to know it had been done, because infection was the most common reason for early labour and miscarriage.

Cass went on. 'She's had three doses of oral tocolytic, which has slowed the contractions, been started on antibiotics four-hourly, and the foetal heart trace...' She glanced at the long strip of paper cascading from the monitor that evaluated baby heart rate and uterine contractions without looking at the patient. Lucy hated impersonal technology. It was too easy for staff to look more at machines than the patient.

Cass shrugged. 'I think she's more stable than when

she arrived. First dose of steroids was given at three-thirty a.m., so she's due another that time tomorrow morning, if she's still here.'

Cass looked up. 'Any questions?'

No way did she want to prolong Cass's stay. Where did you *not* learn your people skills? Lucy thought, but instead she asked, 'What time did the doctor last see Sally?'

'It's all in the notes.' Cass glanced down. 'The registrar at four a.m., but her obstetrician, Dr Kefes...' For the first time some emotion heightened the colour on Cass's face and she looked almost feline. 'Nikolai's delicious.' She sighed as if he was there in front of her and Lucy cringed.

'Nikolai will see her at rounds this morning. He's always punctual at eight so be ready. I'm off.' She snapped shut the folder and uncoiled herself from the chair. 'Bye, Sally.' She handed the folder to Lucy and left without waiting for her patient's reply.

Lucy frowned at the door as it shut, decided even the mention of the doctor as delicious was unprofessional, glanced around for inspiration on winning Sally's confidence after the nurse from hell had departed, and set about changing the dynamics of the room.

She spotted a little black four-wheeled stool and pulled it around to the other side of the bed to see her patient's face before sitting down.

The stool brought her not too close but just under the level of Sally's eyes so she wasn't crowding or looking down at her. After a few moments Sally opened her eyes. 'So how are you feeling, Sally?'

'Crap.'

Lucy smiled. Succinct. 'Fair enough. Can you be

more specific? Your back?' Sally nodded and Lucy continued, 'Worse or better than when you came in?'

'A lot worse.' Sally blinked suspiciously shiny eyes and Lucy wanted to hug her. Instead, she considered their options.

'Okay, that's not good. Let's sort that first. I'll take the monitor off for a few minutes while I check your observations, and have a little feel of your tummy before we put the belts back on more comfortably. Then we'll see if we can relieve some of the discomfort.'

Lucy glanced at the little watch that her friends had all pitched in for her on graduation. Pretty and practical, like her, they'd said, and she still winced because they'd known her mother wouldn't show for the event and she'd be disappointed.

That might even have been why she'd made that dumb choice with Mark after one too many unfamiliar mojitos, but it had been nice to bask in appreciation for a change.

She shook off regrets because they were a waste of time. She'd learnt that one the hard way by watching her mother.

Seven-thirty a.m., so she had half an hour before the obstetrician arrived to assess her patient's condition. Lucy wanted an overall picture of Sally's general health and mental state before then. But mostly she wanted Sally to feel comfortable with her so she could best represent her concerns when more new caregivers arrived. She'd better get started.

Nikolai Kefes, Senior Obstetrician at Gold Coast City Hospital, discreetly named Adonis by his female colleagues, had a strong work ethic. Seventy per cent of his life centred on work, twenty per cent went to his sister, Chloe, and the other ten per cent was divided equally between sport and brief affairs with sophisticated women.

Nick hated being late for ward rounds but there was no way he could have ignored the distress call from his sister, and by the time he'd parked his car at the hospital it was half an hour after he'd expected to start.

Chloe worried him. She had worried him since she was sixteen and in more trouble than he could have imagined, so much so that she'd changed both their lives. But he could never regret giving her the support she needed when she needed it.

Not that she'd always appreciated his attempts to shield her from the hardships that arose when two young people were suddenly cast out in the world without a penny. He still cringed to think how she would have survived if he hadn't followed her.

It was a shame their parents hadn't felt the same, but he'd given up trying to fathom them years ago.

But this morning Chloe had been adamant she would do things her way, despite this last disastrous relationship, and he wished she'd just swim to the surface and avoid becoming involved for a while.

He could only be glad he was in control of his own brief affairs. Short and sweet was not just a concept, more like a mantra for his life, because emotion was best left out of it. That way nobody got hurt.

The lift doors opened and he stepped out on the maternity floor. His eyes narrowed as he noted the arrival of his registrar at the nurses' station just ahead of him. If he wasn't mistaken, Simon had got dressed in a hurry, because his shirt showed the inside seams and the shadow of a pocket.

He guessed he should be thankful the majority of

his own nights were left undisturbed at this stage of his career, so he smiled, and cleared his mind of everything but his work. The familiar focus settled over him and his shoulders relaxed as he zeroed in on his junior.

'So, Simon. Tell me what's happening this morning.' He paused, looked him up and down and smiled. 'Then perhaps you could retire into the staffroom and turn your shirt the other way?'

Eight thirty-five a.m. In the past fifteen minutes Lucy had decided Sophie would definitely have her baby today. Around eight-fifteen the contractions had become strong and regular and Lucy had slipped out and rung the registrar because the eight a.m. arrival of the consultant hadn't occurred.

Neither had the arrival of the registrar, Lucy fumed, and twenty minutes' time lag wasn't good enough. She wasn't happy as she looked for Flora May again to let her know her patient still hadn't been seen.

Instead, she saw a tall, very athletic-looking man arrive at the desk, his immaculate suit dark like his short wavy hair, but it was his air of command that convinced Lucy he could be the person she expected. She diligently ignored the fact he was probably the most handsome man she'd ever seen and that maybe the horrible night midwife hadn't been far off.

'Dr Kefes?'

Both men turned to face her but she went straight for the one who obviously held the power.

'Yes?' His voice was low with a husky trace of an accent that was delightfully melodious, Mediterranean most likely, but she'd think about that later when she had a chance.

'I'm sorry to interrupt. I'm the midwife looking after

Sally Hill. She's seventeen years old and thirty-three weeks gestation in prem labour. I believe she's establishing active labour as we speak and you need to see her now.' She handed him the notes and said over her shoulder, 'This way, please.'

As he opened the notes and followed, Nikolai wondered briefly why he had allowed himself to be steered so determinedly when he usually had handover by his registrar and then did his rounds.

Of course, the young midwife seemed concerned, so that was a good reason, and she had made it difficult for him to refuse, he thought with an internal smile as he watched her reddish-brown ponytail swing in front of him.

He was more used to deference and suggestion than downright direction, but this day had started unusually, and it seemed it was going to proceed that way.

Ten minutes later Lucy stood beside the bed as she watched Dr Kefes and the respectful way he talked to Sally, and she could feel the ease of the tension in her own shoulders.

Thankfully, he was totally opposite from the way the night midwife had been. This tall man with the accent seemed genuinely empathetic with the young mum's concerns and symptoms. Even the tricky business of the physical examination was conducted with delicacy and tact.

Afterwards Nikolai removed his gloves and washed his hands then came back to the bed, where Lucy had helped Sally to sit up more comfortably. The two young women watched his face anxiously.

Dr Kefes smiled. 'It seems your baby has decided to have a birthday today. You are more than half-dilated and we will let the special care nursery know to expect a new arrival.'

Sally's face whitened and the first real fear showed in her eyes. He sat down on Lucy's stool and smiled gently at the young mum. 'This is a shock to you?'

Sally nodded but didn't speak. Lucy could see her lip trembling and she reached across and put her hand out. To her relief Sally grabbed her fingers and clung on while the doctor addressed her fears.

'You are in a safe place. Your baby is in a safe place. If you are worried, listen to your midwife.' He gestured at Lucy. 'This one, who was so determined I would see you first she practically dragged me in here before my round began.'

He smiled at Lucy and she could feel her cheeks warm with embarrassment, and something else, like pleasure that this gorgeous man had complimented her on her advocacy. But the best result was that Sally smiled as well.

He went on. 'We will all work towards this being a very special day for you and your baby.' He stood up. 'Okay?'

Sally nodded, and Lucy could tell she wasn't the only person in the room who had decided Nikolai Kefes was a man to put your faith in.

And Sally's birthing was special. Her baby was born three hours later. Dr Kefes was gentle and patient, and Sally was focused and determined to remain in control.

Lucy had borrowed the ward camera and captured some beautifully touching shots soon after the birth, because the neonatal staff were there for the baby, Dr Kefes managed the actual delivery, Flora May unobtrusively supervised, and she didn't have much to do herself.

The stylish bob of the neonatal specialist, Dr Callie Richards, swung as she paused and spoke to Sally while her staff wheeled tiny Zac out the door on the open crib towards the NICU. 'I think he'll be promoted to the special care nursery very quickly, but we'll check him out first in the NICU.'

Her eyes softened. 'You come and visit him as soon as you're up to it or I'll come to see you if he misbehaves before then.' Her gentle voice was warm and compassionate and Sally nodded mutely. Her eyes met Lucy's as her baby was wheeled away.

'He'll be fine,' Lucy whispered. 'He looks little but very strong.'

Sally sniffed and nodded and Lucy squeezed her hand. 'Let's get you sorted so you can go and see what he's up to.'

Afterwards, when Sally had showered and the two young women had had a chance to look at the photos, Lucy was very glad she'd taken them.

The luminous joy on Sally's face as she gazed at her tiny son—a close-up of a starfish hand, a tiny foot lying on his mother's fingers, and one of him snuggled against his mother's breasts before he'd been whisked away to the neonatal nursery, were all a comfort to a new mother whose baby had been taken for care somewhere else.

Even on the poor-quality prints in black and white that Lucy printed out on the ward computer Sally looked a beautiful mum.

As she waited in the wheelchair, Sally's finger traced the distinguishing features of her tiny son's face and body on the images.

'I'm glad I had you looking after me.'

Lucy squeezed Sally's shoulder. 'I'm glad I was here. Thank you for letting me share your birth.'

Her first birth as a proper midwife had been as em-powering for Sally as she could make it. And she could tell that the young mum was pretty chuffed at how she'd managed everything that had been asked of her.

Lucy had never felt so proud of anyone as she was of Sally. She glanced around to see that they had col-lected everything from the room and pushed the chair forward. 'We'll drop this stuff in your room and then we'll go and see this gorgeous son of yours.'

Five hours later, at the end of the shift, a shift that had held her first prem birth, a quick catch of another impatient baby keen to arrive before the rest of the staff were ready, and a smile from a very senior obstetrician for a job well done, Lucy picked up her bag from the staffroom.

She should be feeling ecstatic as she walked past the sluice room on the way out but, in fact, she felt dreadful.

The nausea that had been building all day suddenly rushed up her throat in an imminent threat—so much so that she had to launch herself at the sluice-room sink in desperation.

Nikolai, too, was on his way out the door when he saw the sudden acceleration of the new midwife who'd been so diligent today.

He frowned as he realised the nature of her distress, and glanced hopefully left and right for someone else in scrubs, but saw nobody he could call on to assist her. He sighed, shrugged, and approached the doorway.

'Are you okay?' By the time he reached her it seemed it was over.

Her forehead rested on the tips of the fingers of one hand as she rinsed the sink. The fragility of her pale neck made him reach for his handkerchief and he leaned past her and dampened it under the cold running water. He wrung it out before handing it to her to wipe her face.

To his amusement she was so intent on patting her hot cheeks that she muttered thanks without turning. Later, perhaps it would be different, but at the moment it seemed she was just glad she'd made it to somewhere manageable.

Then she glanced back and he saw her glance hesitantly past him and he wondered if she expected the whole staff to be lined outside, watching her.

'Nobody else saw.'

Her shoulders sank with relief and he bit back a smile. So transparent.

'Thank goodness. It's crazy.' He could just catch the words because she seemed to be talking to his tie. 'I've been feeling nauseated all day and it just caught up with me.'

'Not pregnant, are you?' He smiled, in no way expecting the startled look of shock that spread over her face as she glanced up at him. Oh, dear me, Nikolai thought, and couldn't help flashing back to his sister all those years ago.

No doubt it was that connection that caused his sudden surge of protective feeling towards this wilting poppy in front of him, but the sudden urge to hug her disconcerted him. He hadn't wanted to drop a bombshell like that, neither had he had any intention of ruining her day, but it was far too late now. He resigned himself to waiting for her to gather herself.

'I can't be.' But even in that tiny whisper Nick heard the thread of perhaps. Perhaps. Perhaps?

She lifted her gaze to his again and he could see the intriguing green flecks in the hugeness of her horrified hazel eyes.

He'd put his foot in it, obviously. 'So you haven't tested for pregnancy?'

'Hadn't given it a thought,' she mumbled, and blushed. 'I didn't consider that precautions might let me down during my first and only ever one-night stand. And that was ages ago.' Her bitterness was unmistakable. She leant back over the sink to cover her face.

Nick winced at the vagaries of fate. Here was a woman anything but pleased by her fertility, while his sister would give anything to be able to fall pregnant again.

He didn't know how he could help, or even why he wanted to, but he couldn't just leave.

Maybe he was wrong. He knew nothing about her. 'Perhaps you're not pregnant. Could be gastro. Lack of food. You could try a pregnancy test. I have some in my rooms. Might even be negative.'

She looked at him, he saw the brief flare of hope, and she nodded. 'That seems sensible. Of course I'm not...' She blushed, no doubt at the blurting out of the indiscreet information she'd given him. He'd have liked to have been able to reassure her he could forget her indiscretion—no problem—but he wasn't sure how.

She didn't meet his eyes. 'It could just be the excitement of the day. Would you mind?'

'It's the least I can do after scaring you like that.' He smiled encouragingly and after a brief glance she smiled back tentatively. 'Follow me.'

He glanced sideways and realised she'd had to skip a little to keep up. He guessed he did take big steps compared to hers, and slowed his pace. 'Sorry.' He smiled down at her. 'It's been a busy day and I'm still hyped.'

Lucy slowed with relief. She'd been hyped, too, until

his random suggestion had blown her day out of the water.

Neither of them commented as she followed him to the lift, luckily deserted, an ascent of two floors and then along the corridor to the consultant's rooms. Lucy's lips moved silently as she repeated over and over in her head, *I am not pregnant, I am not pregnant!*

CHAPTER TWO

TEN MINUTES LATER that theory crashed and burned.

Lucy sank into the leather chair in Nikolai's office with the glass of water he'd given her in hand and tried to think.

She shook her head and closed her eyes for a moment. 'I'm my mother all over again.'

When she opened her eyes he was smiling gently. 'All mothers are their mothers.'

She sat up with a sigh. 'Well, I really am mine. On the brink of a career I've worked so hard for and I've ruined my life.' She could not believe this.

'It's been a shock. Can you remember when…?' He paused delicately and Lucy felt her cheeks warm again. This just got worse and worse. 'The night of our graduation.' Her hand crept over her stomach. This could not be happening, but the tiny bulge of her belly, something she'd been lamenting over the last week and blamed on the huge box of rocky road chocolate she'd been given, suddenly took on an ominous relevance to her queasiness.

How could she have been so stupid not to notice? She was a midwife, for pity's sake! But she'd been so excited about her job, and the house-sitting opportunity that would allow her to save money. She'd always been someone who got car sick, plane sick, excitement sick, thanks to an anxiety to please she'd thought she'd beaten.

It was a wonder she hadn't been throwing up every morning if she was pregnant, the way her stomach usually reacted to change. 'I can't be pregnant. It must be something else.'

He had such calm, sympathetic eyes. But she could tell he thought the test was valid. She guessed he had experience of this situation. Well, she didn't.

'Would you like me to run a quick ultrasound to confirm the test?'

She wanted to say, no, that would be too real. She knew a little about ultrasounds in early pregnancy. She had seen obstetricians during her practical placements using the machines on the ward when women were bleeding.

Find the sac. Foetal poles. Heartbeat if far enough along. She didn't want to know how far she had to be along. Somewhere around fourteen weeks, seeing as that had been the only time she'd ever had sex. Did she want more proof?

Maybe it was something else. Yeah, right. Fat chance. And she may as well face the reality until she decided what she was going to do and how she was going to manage this.

He was asking again, 'Would you like me to ask a nurse to come in? My receptionist has gone home. Just while we do this?'

God, no. 'No, thank you, if that's okay. Please. I don't want anyone to know.' She covered her eyes. *She* didn't want to know, but she couldn't say that.

'I understand.' His voice was low, that trace of accent

rough with sympathy, and she had the sense he really did understand a little how she was feeling.

Maybe she was even glad he was there to be a stabiliser while she came to grips with this, except for the fact she'd have to see him almost every day at work, and he'd know her secret.

'Just do it.' Lucy climbed up onto the examination couch in his rooms, feeling ridiculous, scared and thoroughly embarrassed. Lucy closed her eyes and the mantra kept running through her head. This could not be happening.

Nikolai switched on the little portable ultrasound machine he kept in the corner of his rooms. This must have been how his sister had felt when she'd found out the worst thing a sixteen-year-old Greek Orthodox girl could find out. He just hoped there was someone here for this young woman.

He tried not to notice the unobtrusively crossed fingers she'd hidden down her sides as he tucked the towel across her upper abdomen to protect her purple scrubs from the gel. He didn't like her chances of the test strip being disputed by ultrasound.

He tucked another disposable sheet low in her abdomen, definitely in professional mode, and squirted the cool jelly across the not so tiny mound of her belly. She had silky, luminous skin and he tried not to notice.

When he felt her wince under his fingers, he paused until he checked she was okay, and she nodded before he recommenced the slide of the ultrasound transducer sideways. He couldn't help but admire the control she had under the circumstances. He wondered if Chloe had been this composed.

He glanced from her to the screen and then everything else was excluded as he concentrated on the fascinating parallel universe of pelvic ultrasound.

An eerie black-and-white zone of depth and shadings. Uterus. Zoom in. Foetal spine. So the foetus was mature enough for morphology. Foetal skull. Measure circumference. Crown-rump length. Placenta. Cord. Another cord?

He blinked. 'Just shutting the blinds so I can see better.' He reached across to the wall behind her head and the remote-control curtains dulled the brightness of the Queensland sun. Zoomed in closer. Uh-oh.

The room dimmed behind Lucy's closed eyelids and then she heard it. The galloping hoofbeats of a tiny foetal heart. No other reason to have a galloping horse inside her belly except the cloppety-clop of a baby's heartbeat.

She was pregnant.

It was true. She couldn't open her eyes. Was terrified to confirm it with sight but her ears wouldn't lie.

She couldn't cope with this. Give up her hard-won career just when it was starting. Throw away the last three years of intense study, all the after-hours work to pay for it, all her dreams of being the best midwife GCG had ever seen.

Cloppety-clop, cloppety-clop. The heartbeat of her baby, growing inside her. Her child. Something shifted inside her.

She had to look. She opened her eyes just as Dr Kefes sucked in his breath and she glanced at his face. She saw the frown as he swirled the transducer around and raised his eyebrows.

What? 'Has it got two heads?' A flippant comment when she was feeling anything but flippant. Was her baby deformed? Funny how the last thing she wanted was to be pregnant but the barest hint of a problem with her tiny peanut and she was feeling…maternal?

'Sort of.' He clicked a snapshot with the machine and shifted the transducer. Clicked again.

Her stomach dropped like a stone. There was something wrong with her baby?

'What?'

'Sorry. Not what I meant.' He was looking at her with a mixture of concern and…it couldn't be wonderment surely. 'Congratulations, Lucy.'

That didn't make sense. Neither did a second heartbeat, this one slower than the other but still a clopping sound that both of them recognised. 'The measurements say you have two healthy fourteen-week foetuses.'

'I'm sorry?' He had not just said that. 'Two?'

'Twins.' He nodded to confirm his words. Held up two fingers in case she still didn't get it.

Lucy opened and shut her mouth before the words came out. 'Twins? Fourteen weeks?' Lucy squeaked, and then the world dimmed, only to return a little brighter and a whole lot louder than before—like a crash of cymbals beside her ear. She wasn't just pregnant. She was seriously, seriously pregnant.

She watched the screen zoom in and out in a haze of disbelief. Followed his finger as he pointed out legs and arms. And legs and arms. Two babies!

'I don't want twins. I don't want one,' she whispered, but even to her own ears there might be a question mark at the end of the sentence. She couldn't really be considering what she thought she was considering.

She thought briefly of Mark, her midwifery colleague already settled in Boston at his new job, a good-time guy with big plans. Their actions had been a silly impulse, regrettable but with no bad feelings, more a connection between two euphoric graduates than any kind of meeting of souls.

They'd both been sheepish after the event. The whole 'do you want coffee, can I use your bathroom', morning-after conversation that had made it very clear neither had felt the earth move—friends who should never have been lovers.

Dr Kefes broke into her thoughts and she blinked. 'If you are going to think about your options you don't have much time. In fact, you may not have any.'

Think about what? Terminating her babies that she'd heard? Seen? Was now totally aware of? She didn't know what she was going to do but she couldn't do that.

'Do they look healthy? Are they identical?' From what she'd learned about twin pregnancies there'd be more risk with identical twins than fraternal and already that was a worry.

'Looks to be one placenta but it's hard to tell. Early days, to be sure. They look fine.' His accent elongated the word *fine* and her attention zoned in on something non-traumatic—almost soothing—but he was forging on and she needed to pay attention. 'Both babies are equal size. Nothing out of the ordinary I can see.' He smiled and she was distracted for a second again from the whole tragedy. He was a serious darling, this guy. Then his words sank in.

Relief flooded over her. Her babies were fine. Relief?

She didn't know how she would manage. Certainly with no help from her own mother—how on earth would she tell her?—but she would manage. And no way was she going to blame her babies like her mother had always blamed her for ruining her life.

But that was for home. For quiet, intense thought. And she'd held this kind man up enough with her sudden drama that had blown out of all proportion into a life-changing event. Events.

She was having twins.

Holy cow.

On the first day of her new job.

She had no idea where to start with planning her life but she'd better get on with it. 'Thank you.'

Nikolai removed the transducer and nodded. As he wiped her belly he watched in awe as this slip of a girl digested her news with fierce concentration.

She was thanking him?

Well, he guessed she knew a lot more than she had half an hour ago because of him. And she seemed to be holding together pretty well. He thought of his sister again and his protective instincts kicked in. He didn't stop to think why he felt more involved than usual. But it was all a bit out of left field. 'Will you be all right?'

He wasn't sure what he'd do if she said no, and as he caught her eye, her delightful mouth curved into a smile and he saw her acknowledge that.

'Not a lot we can do if I'm not, is there?' She sat up and he helped her climb down. 'But, yes, I'll be fine. Eventually.'

He thought of his sister and the disastrous decisions she'd made in the heat of her terrifying moment all those years ago. And the ramifications now.

He thought of this woman under the care of a less-than-proficient practitioner like his sister had been, and his mind rebelled with startling force. 'I realise it's early, but if you'd like me to care for you through your pregnancy, I'd be happy to. There'd be no additional cost, of course.'

'Thank you, Dr Kefes. I think I'd like that when I

get used to the idea of being pregnant. That would be most reassuring.'

She straightened her scrubs and he gestured for her to sit in the office chair.

'Wait one moment and I'll print out a list of pathology tests I'd like you to have. The results will come to me and we'll discuss them when they come back.'

The little unexpected catches of his accent made him seem less formidable and Lucy could feel the relief that at least she wouldn't be cast adrift with the bombshell all alone.

She watched his long fingers fly across the keyboard as he opened a file on his desk computer. He made her feel safe, which was dumb because she was just a silly little girl who'd got herself pregnant, and she almost missed it when he asked for her full name, date of birth and residential address.

Luckily her mouth seemed to be working even if her brain wasn't and she managed the answers without stumbling.

He stood up. Darn, that man was tall. 'The rest we will sort out at your next visit.'

Lucy nodded, took the form, and jammed it in her bag. 'Thank you. It's been a huge day.'

'Enormous for you, of course.' Nikolai decided she still looked dazed and he resisted the urge to give her a quick hug. He would have given Chloe one but he wasn't in the habit of hugging patients or staff.

'And…' he hesitated '…may I offer you congratulations?'

'I guess congratulations are in order.' She shook her head and he didn't doubt she was only barely comprehending what her news would entail.

There was an awkward pause and he searched around

for something normal to say. 'Sister May tells me it was your first day of work. You did well and I look forward to working with you.'

He sounded patronising but had only intended to try to ease her discomfort about seeing him on the ward tomorrow.

He tried again. 'Of course your news will remain confidential until you decide to say otherwise.'

She nodded and he saw her draw a deep breath as she faced the door. She lifted her chin and he leaned in front of her to open the door. 'Allow me.'

He actually felt reassured. She would be fine. He now had some idea how strong this young woman really was. He would see that she and her babies remained as healthy as possible, he vowed as he watched her walk away.

But she did look heartbreakingly alone.

Lucy had always been alone.

Half an hour later she pushed open the door to her tiny cabana flat and the really bizarre thing was that it looked the same as when she'd left that morning.

It was she who'd changed. Drastically. And she was alone to face it. But then again when hadn't she been alone to face things? Luckily she had practice at it. The upside was that in about six months' time she'd never be alone again.

Upside? There was an upside? Where was the anxiety she should be feeling? She'd lived her whole life with that. Trying to do the right thing. She searched her feelings for anger and blame for the life-changing event that had just been confirmed, but she didn't find any.

Why aren't I angry with my babies? Didn't my mother get this feeling I'm feeling now? Almost—

no, not almost, definitely—a real connection with her babies. Maybe this was what she was meant to be. A mother.

But twins. Fourteen weeks pregnant was ridiculous. Her first pregnancy was going to be over in twenty-six weeks' time, because she'd already gone through more than a third of it.

She'd better get her head around it pretty darned quick. Let alone the known fact that twins often came earlier than expected.

She guessed she'd had her official first antenatal visit with the delicious Dr Nick.

She had to snap any of those thoughts out of her brain. Not only had he been there to see her throw up but to hear her whole sordid story of a one-night stand resulting in an unwanted pregnancy. Times two.

She frowned, and her hand crept to her tiny bulge. 'It's okay, babies, I do want you now that I know about you, but you could have waited for a more opportune time.'

Lucy rolled her eyes. 'Like in about ten years, when I'd found a man who wanted to be your father. Preferably after the wedding.' Someone like Dr Kefes?

She straightened her shoulders and patted her belly. 'But don't worry. I'll give you all the love I never had and there will be no string of uncles staying over. If I don't meet a one hundred per cent perfect daddy for you, we'll do this ourselves.'

Her voice died away and she glanced around the empty room. She was going mad already. She'd bet Dr Kefes thought she was mad.

Twenty-two, single and taking on twins instead of the career she'd worked so hard to achieve.

She had almost been able to feel his soothing persona. He'd been very kind. Incredibly supportive considering he didn't know her. She could understand why women fell a little in love with their obstetricians if they were all like him.

Though she didn't think there could be a lot of tall, dark and dreamy docs out there with such a delicious hint of a foreign accent.

But at the end of everything, she would be the one holding the babies, and she'd better stop thinking that some demi-god was going to swoop in and lend her a hand.

This was her responsibility and hers alone.

She glanced at the tiny cabana she'd been lucky enough to score in exchange for house-sitting the mansion out front, and she was thankful. *Be thankful.* She needed to remember that. If the owners decided to sell, something else would turn up. She had to believe that.

And she would find a way to support her babies. She'd just have to save every penny she could until she finished work.

At least she'd get maternity leave—or would she if she was fourteen weeks pregnant on her first day? More things to find out.

But they did have a crèche at the hospital so eventually she'd be able to go back. If Flora May would have her after she told her the news. She put her head in her hands.

And how would she tell her mother?

A kilometre away, Nikolai threw his keys on the hall table inside the door of his flat and pulled off his tie. What a day. And not just with work.

He wasn't sure why he was so rattled by his encounter with Lucy the midwife, and her news, but he guessed it had to do with the day starting with his sister's phone call. He'd obviously associated the two women in his mind.

That explained his bizarre feeling of connection with young Lucy. And that was what she was. Young. Barely over twenty, and he was a good ten years older so it had to be an avuncular or older-brother protectiveness. He'd just have to watch it in case she got any ideas.

Because he certainly didn't have any.

Maybe it hadn't been so clever to offer to look after her during her pregnancy, but it had seemed right at the time. And he genuinely wanted her to have the best care.

But when the next day at work he only saw Lucy in the distance, she waved once discreetly because both of them were busy with their own workload, and by the end of the day his concerns had seemed foolish.

He wasn't piqued she hadn't made any effort to speak to him. Of course not. His concerns were ridiculous. But it seemed he had no worries that she might take liberties with his offer.

Then the day suddenly got busier and Lucy and her problems disappeared into the back of his mind.

The busyness of the ward continued for almost a fortnight, so much so that the staff were counting back in the calendars to see what had happened around this time ten months ago. Solar eclipse? Power blackout?

There was an unofficial competition to see who could come up with the most likely reason for the surge in births.

It was Lucy's fifth shift in a row and she was finding it harder to get out of bed at six in the morning.

'Come on, lazybones,' she grumbled to herself as she sat up on the side of the bed. 'You've got no stamina. You think it's going to be easier when you've got to get two little bodkins organised every three hours for feeds?'

She stood up and rubbed her back. 'They all say it's going to get quieter at work again soon. You can do this.' And she still hadn't told her mother. She'd told Mark and he'd offered money. And no strings. That was a good thing because she knew in her heart an unwilling Mark wasn't the answer for either of them. The last thing she wanted was her babies to see her in an unhappy relationship.

When Nikolai saw Lucy he could tell she was starting to feel the frenetic pace. Her usual determined little walk had slowed and he didn't notice her smile as often.

The next time he saw her he decided she looked far too pale and he couldn't remember any results from the blood tests he'd ordered a fortnight ago.

He added 'Follow up with Lucy' to his list of tasks for the day and tracked her down towards the end of the shift.

'One moment, Lucy.'

She stopped and smiled tiredly up at him. 'Yes, Doctor?'

He felt like offering her a chair. Wasn't anyone looking after this girl? It had been hard enough for him to look after Chloe and he'd been the same age as Lucy was now. And a man, not a slip of a girl.

It was tough making ends meet when you were trying to get through uni and feed yourself. He wondered if she was eating properly before he realised she was waiting for him to finish his sentence.

'Sorry.' He glanced around but no one was near them. 'I wondered why I haven't seen those results yet.'

Lucy racked her brain. An hour of the shift to go and

she was finding it hard not to yawn. Now he wanted results and she had no idea whose he was talking about.
For which patient? She frowned. 'Was I supposed to
give you some results?'

'Yours. Antenatal screening.' He looked so hard at
her she felt like he'd put her under the microscope.
'You look pale.'

She felt pale, if that was possible. She'd forgotten the
tests. She ran back over that momentous day, back to
his rooms. Yes, he'd given her forms, and the form was
still scrunched in the bottom of her bag. Maybe there
was something Freudian about that.

She sighed. 'I keep meaning to get them done. Maybe
I'm not ready to tell the world.'

She saw him glance at her stomach and raise his
eyebrows. She looked down, too. And didn't think it
showed much yet.

He was frowning and he rarely frowned. That was
one of the things she liked about this guy. One of the
many things.

'I'd like you to do them today, if you could, please.
Outside the hospital if you want to. But if you have
them done internally there will be no charge for the
pathology.'

And pathology tests could be expensive. Expenses
she needed to cut back on. 'Big incentive.' She nodded. Just so he knew she meant it. 'I'll go after work.'

He stayed where he was. Looking so calm and collected and immaculate. She felt like a dishrag. Her back
hurt. What else did he want?

'And could you make an appointment to come and
see me in two days? I'll let my secretary know.'

Lucy laughed for the first time that day. It actually
felt good. She could even feel the tension drop from

her shoulders and reminded herself she needed to shed a few chuckles more often. She didn't want to forget that. Her mother had rarely laughed while she had been growing up.

But two days? It seemed she wasn't the only one who was tired. 'Two days is a Sunday. I don't think your secretary will be take an appointment on that one. But I will make it for Monday.'

Nick smiled back at her and she felt her cheeks warm. She frowned at herself and him. He shouldn't smile at emotional, hormonal women like that. Especially ones who were planning to be single mothers of twins.

She was never going to feel second best again and he made her feel like she wanted to be better than she was. The guy was just too perfect. For her anyway.

'Thanks for the reminder. Have to go.' She turned and walked back to the desk and she could hear his footsteps walking away. She could imagine the sight. The long strides. The commanding tilt of his head. Not fair.

'You okay there, Palmer?' Flora May was staring at her under her grizzled brows. She glanced at the receding back of Dr Kefes. 'Is he giving you a hard time?'

'No. Of course not. He's been very kind.' Though she smiled at her fierce protector. 'I'm just tired.' Flora May did not look convinced. Lucy tried again. 'Not sure if I'm not coming down with something.'

Flora and Lucy were very similar in the way they viewed their vocation, and Lucy appreciated having Flora on her side. Never warm and fuzzy, Flora's no-nonsense advice was always valid, and usually made Lucy smile.

'You do look peaky. Pale and limp probably describes you.'

Lucy had to smile at the unflattering description. 'Thank you, Sister.'

'If you're unwell, go to the staff clinic at Emergency. Nobody else wants to catch anything. Either way, you can leave early. I'll do your handover. You get here fifteen minutes early every day and you're the last to leave. You've earned some time in lieu.'

The idea was very attractive.

Flora's lips twitched. 'But don't expect it every week.'

'I certainly won't.' Lucy looked at her mentor. Maybe now was a good time. She'd hate Flora to find out from someone else or, worse, through a rumour. 'Can I see you for a moment, Sister? In private.'

'Of course.' Flora gestured to her office.

Lucy drew a deep breath and Flora frowned at her obvious trepidation. 'Spit it out, Palmer.'

'I'm pregnant.' Lucy searched Flora's face for extreme disappointment. Anger. Disgust. She'd suspected Flora had plans for her training and knew she had been instrumental in choosing Lucy over other applicants. But Flora's expression didn't change. Except to soften.

She stepped forward and put her arm around Lucy's shoulders and gave her a brief, awkward hug before she snapped back into her professional self.

'That explains a lot,' she said gruffly. Cleared her throat. 'You've been a little more preoccupied than I expected.' To Lucy's stunned relief she even smiled. 'When, in fact, you've been a lot more focused than you could be expected to be.' Flora gazed past Lucy's shoulder while she thought about it.

Then she concentrated on Lucy again. 'And Dr Kefes is looking after you? He knows?'

Lucy blinked and nodded. How did Flora know this

stuff? 'I forgot to have some tests and he was reminding me.'

'He's a good man.' Then she said something strange. 'Don't go falling for him. Easy people to fall for, obstetricians.'

Didn't she know it! A mental picture of Dr Kefes, five minutes ago, smiling down at her and her own visceral response highlighted that dilemma. No way was she going down that demoralising path. 'I won't. I'm not that stupid.'

Flora sniffed. Her piercing gaze stayed glued on Lucy's face. 'Is there a man on the scene? Some help coming?'

Lucy shook her head. She wasn't anxious to go into it but, judging by the sigh, it seemed Flora had expected that. 'Your family?'

Lucy shook her head again. She could dream her mother would turn into a supportive, caring, helpful shoulder to lean on but it was highly unlikely. She so dreaded that conversation but after surviving telling Flora today, maybe she could even hope a little that it would be as bad as she dreaded.

'I've got your back, Palmer. Go home now. Rest. You still look peaky. And if you want help or advice—ask!'

Lucy nodded past the lump in her throat. How had she been so lucky to end up with Flora as a boss?

Flora smiled at her. 'Look after yourself, Palmer. I still have big plans for you.'

Now she felt like crying, and if she didn't get out of here quickly she'd disgrace herself by throwing her sobbing self onto the starched front of her boss.

Lucy almost ran from the ward, past Cass who was on day shifts for a few weeks, and in her hasty departure she didn't see the speculative look that followed her.

She also forgot all about the blood tests she was supposed to get as she pressed the button for the lift and escape.

The doors opened. When she stepped in Nikolai was standing at the back of the lift like her nemesis. 'Are you going to Pathology now?'

Lucy blinked. She felt like smacking her forehead but instead refused to be goaded into saying she'd forgotten again. 'Are you following me?'

Thick, dark, eyebrows lifted. 'I imagine that would be difficult from the inside of a lift. Not being able to see through the walls.'

She played the words back in her head and winced. Impolite and ungrateful. It wasn't Dr Kefes's fault she felt physically and emotionally exhausted. 'Sorry. And, yes.' She sighed. 'I'll go to Pathology now.'

The lift stopped on another floor and two intense, white-coated doctors entered, and the conversation died a natural death.

Lucy recognised one of the newcomers, Callie Richards, the paediatrician who was looking after Sally's baby. They both nodded at Nick but the tension between them was palpable to the other two in the lift and, fancifully, Lucy decided the air was actually shimmering.

It seemed other people had dramas, too. The man raised his eyebrows at Nick, who didn't change his expression, and Callie offered a forced smile to Lucy, who smiled back awkwardly.

One floor down the late arrivals stepped out and as the doors shut Lucy let out the breath she hadn't realised she'd been holding in a little whistle. She looked at Nikolai. 'Who's the guy?'

Nick smiled. 'Cade Coleman, prenatal surgeon from Boston. And you've met Callie Richards, the neonatal specialist. She's in charge of the NICU here and is looking after Sally's baby.'

'Yep. I remember her. She seems nice. It was just him I didn't know. I guess I'll recognise everyone soon.'

They reached the ground floor and the lift light changed to indicate 'up'. Lucy realised she hadn't directed the lift to take her further down to the laboratory.

Nikolai shook his head and pressed the lower-ground button for Pathology to override the person above. He put his hand across the doors to hold them open. 'Are you working on Monday?'

'One in the afternoon.'

'Perhaps you'd like to see me to get your results before you start. My rooms. Twelve-thirty? In case you forget to make the appointment.'

Ooh. It was her turn to give him the look. 'Fine. Thank you.' As he took his arm away from the doors she said, 'Are you this helpful to all your pregnant ladies?'

He shrugged and she couldn't read the expression on his face. 'Only the really vague ones who forget to have their bloods done.'

'Touché,' she said cheekily, and he smiled. She watched him walk away until the doors shut and the lift sailed downwards. Well, she had been vague to forget again but she needed to sleep. As soon as she got home she was going to bed and sleeping the clock round.

Nick's hand tightened on his briefcase as he strode to the doctors' car park. She had a point. But the memories of Chloe, gaunt and drawn, haunted him and when he'd seen Lucy was looking so tired it had brought it all back. He needed to stop worrying about her. She wasn't Chloe, neither was she his responsibility. Although even

Chloe would have a fit if she thought he still felt the need to keep her under his wing.

His phone rang. His registrar. Thoughts of Lucy shifted to the back of his mind again as he turned back to the hospital.

CHAPTER THREE

THAT NIGHT, AFTER a nap and crossing her fingers after her less-than-traumatic disclosure to Flora May, Lucy decided to talk to her mother. She glanced at the clock. It was too early for the dinner date her mother always had before clubbing with her friends on Friday nights but hopefully late enough to be after the ritual bath and nail preparation that took place prior to departure.

'Mum? It's Lucy.' There was a vague affirmative and Lucy bit back a sigh. One day she was going to stop hoping for a shriek of pleasure from her mother that she'd rung.

'I know you're going out. Can I talk for a minute?'

The conversation went downhill from there. If being told she had always known she would let her mother down, done the exact thing her mother had told her not to do, been called an immoral, stupid little girl, being told that no way was she ever minding her brats or even admitting to being a grandmother counted as a conversation going downhill.

Lucy was pretty sure it was, because she could feel herself curling into a protective ball as the tirade continued. She just got more numb and wasn't even aware of the tears as they rolled down her cheeks.

When her mother paused for breath, Lucy finished

by whispering, 'And by the way, I'm having twins.'
There was a further stunned silence and Lucy decided
to put the phone down gently. Enough.

Yep. It had been as bad as she'd feared. Probably
worse. She sucked in a breath and forced her shoulders
to loosen from the deathlike squeeze she had them in.

Her hand crept to her belly. She wasn't having brats.
She was having gorgeous babies and maybe they would
be better off without a vitriolic grandmother. Maybe she
would finally be able to separate her mother's idea of
who she was from her own version. It might take a bit
of practice but she had six months to do it before her
babies were born.

Surprisingly, or perhaps not surprisingly given her
exhaustion and mental distress, Lucy slept most of the
night for the first time in ages.

On Saturday she did the bare minimum of housework
and lazed and snoozed all day, recharging her batteries
for next week's onslaught.

She started a journal, wrote down her thoughts and
all the things she had to be grateful for, and began to
talk to her babies. It was amazing what a difference a
small change like that made.

By Sunday morning she was rested and felt more like
her old self. In fact, she felt better than better. Maybe
it was knowing that the dreaded call, despite being as
horrific as she'd dreaded, was over. Done.

Some time in the night she'd felt the first real joy
of what was to come. So this was her path. What she
couldn't change, she would just do better.

Her midwifery would be put on hold, but at least it
might have prepared her a bit for what was ahead.

Pregnancy, birth, maybe not twins but, hey, twice

the joy. She'd been chosen for that double blessing for a reason, she just hadn't figured out what that reason was.

So, it was a beautiful day, her stomach growled with hunger for the first time in weeks, and she lived in a fabulous part of the world with the ocean right outside her landlord's front door. What wasn't to celebrate?

Filled with new vigour, Lucy tidied her cabana and afterwards scooted around the big house, plucked dead leaves off ornamental ferns, cleaned the aquarium filter and steam-mopped the outside terrace because the salt was crusty underfoot from the storm a few days ago.

Besides, she loved the front terrace, where she could look out over the white sand just behind the boundary fence, watch the paddle-boarders and hope to catch a glimpse of a whale or a dolphin.

As she hummed a country ballad the gate screeched as she took the garbage out, so she hunted out the lubricant spray, sang a few words and patted her stomach as she wandered back to fix it. 'We'll be okay, kiddos.'

Nick's Sunday morning wasn't going as planned. He'd knocked on Chloe's door to see if she was interested in them having breakfast together. It was handy having a sister in the flat next to his. He was starving and maybe they could catch up.

But after the third knock nobody came to the door, so she was either out or not answering. He'd go for a jog and see if she was there when he came back. He tried to check the impulse to find out where she was or who she was with. Just check she was okay, he reminded himself.

Nick was sick of his own company—which was almost unheard of—and just a little bored. As he set off he reminded himself that exercise often worked to shut the voices down.

The beach felt great under the soles of his runners but while the long jog along the sand had helped his restlessness it had also stoked up his appetite for that iconic Sunday breakfast—one of his favourite times on the Gold Coast. With so many great places showing off the ocean, choice was a problem but the idea of eating alone, again, was less than appealing.

Not that there wasn't activity and people everywhere. Kids were learning to be lifesavers on the beach with their little tied-on caps and colourful swimmers. Paddle-boarders skimmed the backs of waves and made him wish he'd bought one. Apparently it was a useful and not sexually orientated exercise diversion—as his sister had wryly commented.

He didn't know why Chloe had a thing about his carefree love life. He wasn't promiscuous, he just didn't feel the need to belong to anybody.

He was happy to concentrate on his work and have fun with like-minded women. He wasn't out to break anybody's heart, and relationships were for dalliance, not drama.

Still, a diversion would be nice, he thought as his shoes slapped the footpath and he finally spied a shapely little surfer girl in a tiny bright skirt and floaty top ahead, kneeling beside the driveway of one of the mansions. She was doing something to a gate. He couldn't help his appreciative smile as he jogged closer.

The sunlight danced in a deep auburn cascade of hair that hid her face and the way she was leaning over promised the sort of shapely curves men liked and women didn't.

So it was a shock when she looked up to see hazel

eyes and a rosebud mouth he already knew. Not a babe. It was Lucy. Pregnant-with-twins Lucy.

His social skills dropped with his confusion. 'Hey, stranger.'

She grinned at him. Looked him up and down and shook her head. 'Ha. I'm not the strange one. I'm not wearing shorts and joggers with black socks.'

'Ouch.' He looked down at his trunks and runners, and decided to throw away the socks, even though they barely showed above his shoes. He'd thought he looked okay. 'I'll have you know this is the latest in trendy jog wear.'

'My bad, then.' She didn't look sorry. She sat back and wiped her hair out of her eyes and the thick mane flashed like fire in the sunlight. Funny he hadn't noticed her hair that much at work. 'So, where do trendy joggers run to?'

He blinked. 'Mostly to and from the beach. And back to the hospital apartment building where a lot of the trendy staff stay.' He sounded like an idiot, so he glanced away and pointed to a tall building a block back from the ocean.

'Wondered where that was.'

He looked back at her and the slight breeze rippled her hair as she turned her head to look. He'd never had a thing for redheads before—but now he could see the attraction. He'd heard they had a tendency for fire and passion and he could just imagine young Lucy letting fly. The thought made him smile even more.

'I didn't know it was so close to the hospital,' she said. 'Been there long?'

His mind was five per cent on the conversation and ninety-five on admiring the view. 'Not that long. I live next door to my sister, Chloe. Two years now. Very convenient.'

'Someone said you had a sister who was a nurse at the hospital.' She nodded, and everything on the top half of her body wobbled a bit. He tried not to stare at her cleavage.

Things were getting foggy. 'Bless the grapevine. Yep.' Why was he brain dead? 'We used to share but she wanted her own place and couldn't see any reason to shift.' He was rambling. 'It's close enough to the hospital that I can walk if I want to. Or run in an emergency. Most times I drive because usually I'm going somewhere later.'

She nodded again and this time he made sure he didn't look south.

His mouth was dry. From the jogging, of course. He could seriously do with a drink. 'Is this your house?' He couldn't keep the surprise out of his voice but when she laughed he acknowledged relief. The last thing he wanted to do was offend her. She was having things tough enough.

Her lips curved. 'Yeah, right. I'm a closet millionaire.'

She raised her eyebrows haughtily and grinned. 'I'm the house-sitter. These people are friends of an older couple who used to put up with me visiting a lot when I was a kid. They were the first people I told about the babies. Nearly time to go public.'

He thought about that. About the hospital and the rumours, and he consoled himself it would blow over in a week. He'd try to make sure he checked she was okay when it all blew up. 'Seems a very nice place to stay. You living in the house?'

'No.' When she shook her head it was better than nodding because everything really jiggled.

He should go but he enjoyed the way she talked. Bubbly and relaxed. Not like the women he usually hung out with, who were always on their best behaviour. He knew that Lucy wasn't trying to attract him. Which was a good thing because she needed a fling like she needed a hole in the head. And he didn't do relationships, and you couldn't have much else with a woman who was pregnant by someone else.

'I have the cabana out back, which suits me fine. I just open the house up every couple of days, let the breeze blow through, water the indoor plants. Feed the fish. That kind of stuff.'

She was sort of restful, too. He could picture her pottering around. Maybe humming off key. 'Spray the rusty gate kinda stuff?'

She waved the can. 'That's me. Handy Lucy.'

'Nice.' He refused to think about where he wanted to put his hands. Instead, he said, 'Would you like to go for breakfast?'

Where the heck had that come from? Nick couldn't believe he'd just said that. Hell, and he'd told himself he was going to be careful to keep it professional.

But apparently that thought couldn't stop him from embellishing the offer. 'Maybe bacon and eggs down at the surf club near Elephant Rock? My shout. We could try and get a table on the veranda and soak in some Vitamin D.'

He didn't even recognise what he was saying. Some devil inside was using his mouth. Didn't it know she was going to be a patient of his as well as a work colleague? This was an invitation with disaster written all over it.

Lucy's face lit up with the happiest smile he'd seen all week. Too late to back out, then. So maybe having a devil using his mouth was worth it if she got that much of a kick out of company.

Her chin jutted as if she expected an argument. 'I'll pay my own way, thanks, but I love that place.'

Independent, then. He'd already guessed that. But he'd bet she was lonely, too.

'And I understand sunlight is very important for pregnant women.' She grinned. 'Gee. Breakfast on the beach and my appetite's back.'

A glow expanded in his chest, because he could have a cooked breakfast and not have to eat it alone, and he'd made a girl happy. Three good things from one action. 'I'll grab my car and meet you back here, in...' he glanced at his watch '...say, fifteen minutes?'

'Perfect.'

Nick lifted one hand as he jogged off towards the tall building Lucy could see further up the road. She recognised the bulk of the hospital behind and how it could be useful to have the consultants' units so close.

So it seemed Dr Kefes jogged by her door regularly. This morning she'd had her headphones in and hadn't heard him approach so it had been a shock when he'd stopped. She'd thought him just a well-built jogger and had been happy to admire the fitness machine, until she'd recognised him, then she'd been bowled over by the sheer physical presence of him.

That must have been where the black-sock comment had come from. She'd felt like smacking her forehead when that had popped out.

'Just trying to make him human,' she muttered, and bit back a giggle. She should be aghast at herself for teasing him—but she wasn't, and he hadn't seemed to mind. He probably had women sucking up to him everywhere. She'd never been a toady—except to her

mother, but she was going to train herself out of that—
and wasn't going to start now.

Lucy gave the gate a final generous spray of lubricant and stood up.

And she darned well refused to feel nervous about
going for breakfast with him. Dr Kefes. Nikolai. He
hadn't actually said she could call him Nick but she'd
worry about that later. She hadn't felt this good for
weeks so she may as well enjoy it, and now there was
a bit of unexpected excitement in her day.

Who knew when the next pregnancy ailment would
strike? And she was in for double dose when it did
come.

As for having breakfast with a consultant at her
work who'd also offered to be her obstetrician, well,
she wasn't going to get out of line, and there was no way
he would. No reason they couldn't be friends.

By the time Nick arrived to pick her up Lucy was
standing at the gate in a yellow sundress, complete, he
couldn't help noticing, with bra. He saw the straps and
stifled his disappointment. Stop it.

He leaned across and opened the passenger door for
her because he could see she wasn't going to wait for
him to get out and do the job properly.

She slid in, accompanied by a drift of some light and
spicy perfume that smelt like the spring flowers Chloe
kept around her flat, and she must have felt comfortable because she slid her sandals off.

Suddenly his car took on a new life. There was
something earthy and incredibly sexy about bare brown
toes rubbing over each other as she settled back in the
leather seat.

She sighed blissfully and his day got better. 'Always
fancied a convertible.'

He laughed. She made him laugh. 'Me, too.'

'This car would go with my house.'

He nodded sagely. 'Hell with a stroller, though.'

'Especially a twin stroller.' Their eyes met and he was pleased and surprised to see the serenity in hers. He admired her more each time they talked.

He'd have to watch that. 'I see you're at peace with your decision.'

'Yes. Thank you, Dr Kefes.'

'Nick.' He pulled over into a parking space right outside the restaurant that someone had just pulled out from, parallel to the beach. 'You must be very lucky to have around. I usually park twenty minutes away from this place.'

Her head was back against the headrest and her eyes were shut as the sun bathed her in bright yellow light. 'Lucky Lucy. That's me.'

He soaked the sight in for a few seconds, shook his head at her ability to just enjoy the moment and then leaned forward and removed his keys from the ignition. 'Handy and lucky? Worth cultivating.'

She opened her eyes. 'Hopefully someone will think so one day.' There was no self-pity in the statement. Just truth. 'I'm starving.'

He laughed again. 'So am I.' Typically, she was out of the car before he could get to her door.

They scored a table right on the corner of the big verandah overlooking the beach. 'More luck,' Nick murmured, and Lucy just smiled.

The salt-laden breeze blew their big umbrella backwards and forwards a little so that most of the time they were in the shade but every few seconds a brief wash of sunlight dusted her shoulders with golden light. Nick decided the view was great in every direction.

'So, have you thought about what you'll do when the babies are born?'

She rested her cute chin on her fingers. She made him feel so relaxed. 'My next-door neighbour used to say, "Planning to make a plan is not a plan", so, yes. I have a plan.'

He was intrigued. 'And that is?'

She straightened. 'I'll work as long as I can then hopefully I'll get maternity leave from work. It won't be paid but from what Flora May said I think I get to keep my job. The hospital has a crèche, so I'll go back to work one day a week part-time as soon as possible, and that's only eight hours away from them. That's not unreasonable.'

She shrugged. 'When we all get used to that I'll do two days and so on. Not quite sure how I'll survive financially with that but that's a few months ahead. And I've saved a little money.' She grinned at him. 'Luckily, I'm not a material girl.'

It sounded pretty shaky for a plan but she hadn't had much time. 'What about your parents?'

Her face changed and he wondered if she really was shrinking into the chair or if he was just imagining it. She looked away out over the waves and he seriously regretted having asked the question, judging by her response.

'Parent.' She shrugged and still didn't meet his eyes. 'Only ever had Mum, though she's a two-edged sword. She always said I ruined her life.'

'Your mother?' He tried to imagine an older Lucy with a nasty mouth.

She shrugged and he decided she had the best shoulders in the restaurant.

'Imagine one of those anxious-to-please, quiet little

girls who could never get anything right?' She forced a smile and Nick decided it actually hurt to watch. Maybe she wasn't so together after all.

He couldn't quite put this girl together with the one who had dragged him in to see her patient on her first day.

'Anyway. That little girl was me. The only time I ever felt like a winner was when I accepted my midwifery degree. And Mum didn't make it to see that.'

But, still, her mother? Nick thought. 'So she won't help you?'

'Mum?' Lucy laughed but it wasn't the sound he'd heard before. Surprisingly there was no bitterness in the sound, just the scrape of raw nerves. 'She taught me to rely on myself. That's a pretty helpful trait.'

He guessed his own parents had done that to Chloe and him as well. 'And you're not bitter?' He certainly was. Not for himself now but for the young teen his sister had been when they'd cast her off, and him for supporting her.

He guessed his parents had hurt him the way he could see Lucy's mother had hurt her, but he hadn't really had time to worry about it. He'd been more worried about getting food on the table and pushing Chloe to study.

Lucy was staring over the waves and fancifully he wondered why the sun wasn't playing with her any more.

'Mum managed as well as she could with her own disappointments. Now she is a material girl.'

She straightened and he saw a little more of the mid-wife advocate he'd seen on the ward. 'If there's one thing I know, it's that my children won't feel a burden. I'm ambitious for my midwifery, but I'll be there for them no matter what.' It seemed she could fight for others but not for herself. He'd think about that later.

'My mother told me she'd left it too late to get rid of me, and I'm so pleased I can say I made the choice to keep my children.'

Hell. Her mother had told her that? Nick had thought his parents were insensitive but he couldn't imagine what being told that would do to the psyche of a young woman.

But she'd moved on. At least in this conversation. 'I'd hoped that by the time I had kids my husband would have a warm and fuzzy mother who would tuck me under her wing and do girl things with me. Looks like that's not going to happen.'

He didn't usually mention it, in fact, he couldn't re-member ever mentioning it, but maybe it would help if she knew other people had failures as parents. 'Or you could end up with a mother like ours who just wiped Chloe and me out of her life and broke off all contact.'

'What do you mean?'

They'd behaved as though their two children hadn't existed. My word, he remembered that, the way he'd pleaded with them to soften towards his sixteen-year-old sister, when all he'd wanted to do had been to tear strips off them for their unforgiveable behaviour.

He'd taken too many bitter rebuffs for Chloe to ever forgive them.

It had been a defining moment in his life to learn that people could choose to exclude others regardless of how much pain they'd caused. It was also the perfect reason not to become emotionally involved, and that mantra had worked for him very well.

And Chloe was suffering because she still couldn't

do the same. 'Refused to communicate. Didn't answer calls when I tried to get them to talk to Chloe.'

'That sucks. I'm sorry.' Then she looked away and he almost missed her further words. 'But you have your sister. I had no one.'

She lifted her chin. 'Sorry. I'm spoiling your breakfast with my complaining. I didn't mean to. And I'll have my babies soon.' She lifted her chin higher. 'I'm tough. I'll give up whatever I need to for my babies to have a good life and I will always be there for them. Money and possessions aren't important. Love is.'

This had got pretty deep pretty fast, but he'd asked for it. He shifted in his seat. Contrarily, now he wanted out of this discussion. He tried for a lighter note. 'Money buys you sports cars.'

She raised those haughty brows. 'Yeah, but you can't fit twin strollers in them.'

The waitress arrived to take their orders, the conversation bounced back to impersonal, and thankfully the sun came back and danced on her. He didn't know if he'd directed it that way or if she had, but seagulls wheeled overhead, and the breeze made him want to push the hair out of Lucy's eyes.

They talked about the hospital, the great facilities the birth suites had, their young mum's baby's progress and how the young mum had been so diligent in the special care nursery after her own discharge. They were both careful not to mention anyone's names, and it made it more intimate that only the two of them knew who they were talking about.

To his disappointment, the meals were on the table in no time.

For the first time he wished the usually 'snowed under with orders' staff were not so efficient because by the way Lucy was tucking into her meal they'd be out of there in half an hour.

They ate silently until Lucy sat back with an embarrassed smile. 'Wow. I even beat you.'

He admired her empty plate. 'I can see you were hungry.'

She shrugged. 'Rather feed me for a week than a fortnight, eh? But up until today I haven't been eating well.'

She was too cute. 'I think you're cured.'

She patted her round stomach. 'Not too cured, I hope. I don't want to look like a balloon by the time these babies are born.'

His eyes slid over her appreciatively. 'I don't think you have to worry. But I'll mention to your obstetrician to keep an eye on your weight.'

She wagged a finger at him. 'You do that.' Then she began to fiddle with her teaspoon and he wondered what was coming. You never knew with this woman. 'I need to thank you.'

He shifted uncomfortably. 'What for.'

Hazel eyes caught his. 'For looking after me on the day the bomb dropped.'

He glanced at the children playing in the surf. 'My pleasure.'

She laughed and he looked back at her. Couldn't avoid the urge at the sound. 'I'm sure it wasn't. I fell to pieces.'

Her eyes crinkled and her white teeth were just a little crooked. That tiny unevenness made her seem more real than other women he'd dated. Seriously delightful. 'I didn't see any pieces. I though you held up remarkably well.'

She threw back her head and laughed and he saw a

man at another table look their way with an appreciative smile. Nick stared and the guy looked away.

Lucy was oblivious to anyone else. 'Come on. I threw up in front of you.'

That made him smile. 'But very tidily.'

He shrugged. 'I didn't actually see anything…' He shook his head mournfully. 'And have tried not to think about it.'

She laughed again and he enjoyed that he'd made it happen this time. 'I had no idea you were mad.'

'I hide it.' He shrugged.

She pretended to clap her hands. 'Very well, if I may say so. Anyway. Thank you. If it wasn't for you I would have been alone.'

She shouldn't have been. It made him wonder just where this one-night stand was now. It took two to tango. 'What about the father?'

She brushed the unknown man away and, contrarily, now Nick winced in sympathy for the mystery sperm donor. 'I don't expect anything more from him. My mother managed when my own father walked out.'

'But does he know?' Nick still had issues with that. He'd certainly want to know if a woman he'd helped make a baby with hadn't told him.

Almost as if she'd read his thoughts, she said, 'I've told him. He had a right to that information. He suggested termination.'

'Did that offend you?' He'd sort of put it out there, too, not that he was an advocate, especially after Chloe's disaster. Did she hold that against him?

'It clarified his level of commitment. Although he sent a generous amount of money for a termination and said to use it as emergency fund if I didn't use it for that. I won't be putting him on the birth certificate, or expect financial assistance again, unless the babies want that sometime in the future.'

Some conversation that must have been. 'Is that wise?' She was so clinical. 'Won't you need more financial help?' Judging by her 'plan', he thought she might.

'He's a friend. You don't ask friends for money. Even ones you accidentally sleep with. He has his own life and these are my children.'

In this sense she was so tough. So focused. And if he admitted it, just a little scary in the way she seemed to have taken this momentous news in her stride.

It was in his culture to expect women to need help. Greek heritage was all about family. Except for his own toxic parents.

Chloe had allowed him to be there when she'd needed him, but she was his sister. And she was less amenable now. This woman was nothing to him and he was nothing to her. He should be glad she could stand on her own feet.

Lucy heard the brave words leave her mouth and almost believed them. She pushed away the tiny ache for someone else to share some of the responsibility at least. It certainly wasn't this lovely doctor's problem. A shame, that.

She needed to man up. The thought made her smile. Like one of those insects that changed sex once they were pregnant, except she was going the other way. Actually, quite a disquieting thought. 'Thank you for bringing me with you for breakfast.'

Ouch, Lucy thought, she sounded like a little girl after a party. But he was too sweet. Too darned handsome and masculine and eminently capable of carrying responsibility. She rummaged in her purse and brought out the correct change for her meal and slipped it discreetly under her napkin.

Thankfully he didn't say anything. Just picked it up and put it in his pocket. 'I gather you're ready to go?'

'Yes, please.' She picked up her bag and stood before he could come round to her chair. She had the idea she was frustrating his attempts to treat her like a lady but she wasn't his date and she wanted to make that clear.

Judging by his face, he got it. 'I'll fix this up and meet you outside, then.'

Good. She'd have time to go to the ladies' room. She smiled to herself. Being pregnant certainly affected her bladder capacity.

Nick tried not to watch her scurry off and he remembered she was pregnant. How could he have forgotten that? There was no reason they couldn't be friends but the sooner he dropped her home the better. Afterwards he might go and buy himself a paddleboard and take some of that frustration out on the waves.

CHAPTER FOUR

BEFORE LUNCH ON Monday Nick had a strange conversation with Callie Richards, ostensibly a neonatologist discussing a case with attending obstetrician.

Nick wasn't sure how Sally's baby in NICU had somehow ended up with Cade Coleman, the prenatal surgeon, who was apparently giving Callie a hard time. Which was a bit of a joke because Callie loved to straight-talk, too, and the whole hospital was buzzing with the sparks those two were striking off each other.

Callie was a good friend, but there was no chemistry between them, despite their pretty similar outlooks on relationships and no-strings sex.

He thought to himself with amusement, as Callie raved, that any chance of that was out there amongst the waves, with Cade now on the scene.

He put up his hand to stem the flow. 'You fancy him.'

Callie stopped. Shocked. 'I do not.'

Nick raised his eyebrows. 'So this is you being oblivious is it?'

She glared at him. 'I'm just sick of being growled at.'

'I've seen him work in prenatal surgery.' Nick shrugged. 'The guy's intense, he cares, and he's even great with the parents. He's allowed a little growling.'

'I'm whining, aren't I?' Callie drooped.

'A little.' Nick couldn't help but smile.

Callie lifted her head and drew in an audible breath. 'I needed that.' She picked up her briefcase. 'You're right. Thanks.' And she sailed out.

Nick shook his head and glanced at his watch.

Lucy should be here in a minute. He'd given her the time slot he usually reserved for completing the paperwork from the morning and he guessed he could start it now.

He sat down at the desk and tried to concentrate to stop himself opening the door to see if she'd arrived yet. Obviously she hadn't because his secretary would have rung. He picked up his pen again and his eyes strayed to his watch.

Lucy turned up for her first real antenatal appointment at the hospital and despite the fact she was going straight to work from there, she'd tried to be inconspicuous by dressing in loose civilian clothes.

It didn't work. The first person she saw as she opened Nick's office door was the Callie Richards, who was just leaving.

'Hello, there, Lucy isn't it? You're the midwife who looked after Sally, aren't you?'

'Yes, how is little Zac?' Lucy could feel the heat in her cheeks as she smiled and nodded, pretending it was wonderful that the senior paediatrician had recognised her entering an obstetrician's office. On one level it was, but on the other, not so great.

Callie must have picked up her discomfort because her expression changed. 'Great.' And then, cryptically, she said, 'No problem, by the way.' She smiled reassuringly. 'Have a good day.'

This was silly, feeling embarrassed. It was all going to come out pretty soon anyway. 'You, too.'

Callie left and as Lucy crossed to the reception desk, her cheeks only got pinker. This was terrible.

Nick opened his door. 'Lucy?'

The receptionist looked up and waved her through and as she walked past him into his rooms she started to feel better.

Nick seemed so broad and tall and she realised she really liked that about him. It was reassuring for some reason. He was a man to have beside you in a dark alley. Or a single-parent pregnancy.

At five feet seven she wasn't short, but he made her feel tiny as he shut the door behind her. She crossed the room, sat in the seat she remembered from nearly three weeks ago and tried to relax.

So much had changed in that time. She looked up at him, fighting the urge to stare, and wasn't so sure it was going to work, having Nick as her obstetrician. She remembered Flora's words and promised herself she wouldn't fall for her obstetrician.

Having lunch with Nick yesterday, he with his flash convertible and trendy clothes, and she a single-parent house-sitter with no assets, had shown her how big the distance was between them. It had also shown just how easily he could get under her skin.

She did not have the head space for that.

'Thank you for seeing me so quickly.' Being friends might prove a little dangerous but she owed him at least that for being so kind to her.

He settled behind his desk and opened her file. 'You're welcome. I know you're on your way to work.' He glanced at her clothes. 'And need to get changed as well.'

Yeah, well, that had been a non-starter. 'I was trying to be discreet but that failed dismally when I ran into Dr Richards.'

His face softened and she knew he got that. 'If you're worried about people finding out, Callie won't say anything. But it's going to happen soon. Just remember it will all blow over.'

Yeah well. 'It's fine. I was being silly. I'm not ashamed, I just don't want to answer a lot of questions and talk about stuff I haven't had much time to think about. I've told Sister May, anyway. She was the only one I'd worry about finding out from someone else other than me.'

'What about your mother? I meant to ask yesterday. Have you told her about your pregnancy?'

He saw the look that crossed her face, and the intensity of it shocked him. He hadn't picked that up yesterday. He had thought she was safer behind the wall she'd built than she really was.

He wanted to find Lucy's mother and shake her. But as he watched, the look faded and Lucy lifted her chin.

Lucy did not want to think about her mother. It had swamped her for a moment when Nick had asked. She hated sympathy, it always made her want to weep, and she wasn't doing that here.

It was nice he cared but what was her mother to him? 'Yes. But I haven't spoken to her since. I'm not in the mood for a lecture and it's not like listening to her rage is going to change my life.'

He sat back and studied her. She tried not to squirm. 'So how are you feeling in yourself?'

'Still great.' She nodded and glanced at her watch. 'So, did the blood tests all come back okay?'

Nick pushed his less-than-professional questions

away. What was he doing anyway? He should be going through the motions. A normal antenatal visit. Not thinking about yesterday. Not thinking about it really hard.

And she was impatient to be gone. So typically Lucy. He should have guessed from the first morning she'd herded him into Sally's birth unit. No beating around the bush. She was a bit driven, like Callie Richards, and he'd always admired Callie.

The difference was that Lucy refreshed him and he didn't know why. 'The tests were, on the whole, fine. You're a little low with your haemoglobin, so taking iron tablets won't go amiss. Your white cells are a little elevated, so I just wanted to check you're not feeling the effects of any symptoms of infection.'

Her ponytail flipped from side to side. 'Nope. Since yesterday morning I've never felt better.'

Nick smiled and he remembered her appetite from the restaurant. He smiled. 'The second trimester of pregnancy is often the most enjoyable healthwise.'

Lucy reminded herself that she was going to be thankful for everything. 'I'm determined to enjoy it.'

'Good on you. Hold that plan.' He stood up and glided the BP machine over to her chair. 'That sounded patronising but I was sincere. I see a lot of women who expect to be really ill, for some reason, like their mother was, and not surprisingly they are.'

When Nick leaned towards her she could smell that aftershave he'd worn yesterday and she was transported back to sitting with him in his car.

The aftershave had been part of that lovely drive to the beach with him. The whole lovely morning.

But this was now. She watched his big hands wrap the blood-pressure cuff around her arm and pump it up, and she tried not to think about his fingers on her skin.

Before he put the stethoscope into his ears he murmured, 'I just wonder if some women subconsciously programme their bodies to suffer more than they need to.'

She concentrated on his words. Intensely, so she didn't think about his hands. 'Interesting idea and guaranteed to stir up a hornet's nest of debate. My mother hadn't even noticed she was pregnant until too late.'

Déjà vu, then, she thought, and closed her mouth.

That will teach you to stop rabbiting on when he was trying to listen. She kept forgetting he was the senior consultant and she was a new grad midwife—but he was so easy to talk to.

'It's not silly.' He let the blood-pressure cuff all the way down and entered the result on the computer, as well as writing it on the yellow antenatal card he'd started. 'Blood pressure's normal.'

She looked at the card. Something she'd seen so many times held by pregnant women in antenatal clinics everywhere. Funny how something simple like that could bring it all home to her. She was going to have her own babies. 'I'm going to get my own yellow card with my whole pregnancy documented. I never thought I'd have one of those so soon.'

'Yep.' He smiled. 'Don't lose it.'

As if she would. 'Do many women lose their pregnancy records?'

He shook his head. 'No. It's funny really. They lose scripts, ultrasound requests forms, consult letters, but even the dottiest of my patients knows where her card is. I think of it as the first maternal instinct.'

Lucy grinned. 'That's pretty cool, actually.'

'I think so.' He gestured towards the couch with a smile and she knew he was remembering the first sight of her babies up there with his portable ultrasound. Not something she would forget either.

When she'd climbed up onto the couch she pulled up her shirt and they both looked at her belly. It seemed a lot bigger already.

She chewed her lip as she lay down. 'Lucky I wear scrubs at work to hide this.'

He smiled. 'Soon it won't matter what you wear because these little people are going to pop out in front for everyone to see.'

Nick felt above her belly button and gradually moved the heel of his hand down until he felt the firm edge of her uterus. 'You're already above the level of eighteen weeks.'

'Is that good?'

'Expected to be a little over dates.' He slid the little ultrasound Doppler across her belly and they heard one of the baby's heartbeats and then to the left the other one for a brief few seconds. They both smiled. 'We're very lucky to have found them both. It's hit and miss this early to find a single pregnancy heartbeat unless you're using the full ultrasound machine.'

It was incredible how warm and excited just hearing her babies made her feel. Like Christmas was coming. Along with the most expensive credit-card bill yet when she finished work.

He helped her climb down and she could feel the leashed strength under his fingers. There was a funny little knot in her stomach as their hands parted. Uh-oh. She stood on the scales so he could write down her weight and surreptitiously wiped her palm down her jeans.

She looked down at the digital readout. 'I've put on a kilo!'

'I'll mention that to your obstetrician.' They smiled at each other, both remembering Sunday's conversation about ballooning in pregnancy.

She stepped off the scale and sat down again in the chair, and he entered the weight in his computer. 'Everything looks fine.'

'Good.' She glanced at her watch. She had plenty of time to get changed.

'Excellent. Then I'll just send you for a formal ultrasound towards twenty weeks and I'll see you after that. If you have any problems or concerns, you can contact me on this number or just ask if you see me.'

She took his card and glanced at where he'd written his mobile phone number in bold numbers across the back.

'Thank you.' Did he do that for all his women? Not like she could ask. She slipped it into the back of her purse. So it was over. She was back to being just a little new midwife on the ward. Well, that was a good thing.

Nick felt he'd let her down in some way but he couldn't think how so he went back to impersonal mode. Lucy was the same as any other pregnant patient of his. 'You're welcome. Just ask my secretary for an appointment in four weeks.'

He imagined the changes that would happen between now and then. She would be over halfway. She'd be able to feel her babies move. He'd always been fascinated by that.

He watched her jump up. No gentle, ladylike rising for Lucy. Always in a hurry and usually with a smile. He admired her coping ability very much.

'I'll do that.'

'Have a good shift, Lucy.'

The next two weeks passed and Lucy went to her ultrasound appointment when she was just under twenty weeks pregnant with the surprise support person of Flora May.

Flora's enthusiasm was such a pleasure. They smiled with mutual excitement as the ultrasonographer pointed out legs and arms and movements. The babies jiggled about with every move of the ultrasound wand, and Flora laughed and said, 'They'll be a handful.'

Once she'd found out about Lucy's predicament Flora had proved to be her greatest champion, without mollycoddling her.

Unlike Lucy's mother, who'd had only negative comments to offer when Lucy had steeled herself to call, Flora had useful tips and hints on some of the common and less comfortable aspects of pregnancy.

Uncharacteristically, Flora had also quizzed her on how she liked Nick as her doctor, and Lucy had been a bit flustered about that under Flora's knowing gaze.

Coincidentally or not, she'd found herself looking after patients who weren't under the care of Dr Kefes and it actually became easier not having to see Nick all the time because the last thing she needed on top of everything else was a crush on a man who was just being kind.

Nick saw very little of Lucy despite a small unobtrusive effort to keep an eye on her. He found himself thinking often about how Lucy's mother had hurt her.

He could see the shame and hurt of abandonment— it was exactly how Chloe had looked all those years ago when he'd had to tell her their parents hadn't asked about her. Chloe was still affected by the things she'd done because she'd thought she'd had to for their parents' approval. What a disaster that had been.

Initially he'd thought Lucy a confident and independent young woman. She'd certainly made a strong stand on her first shift, but, in fact, he suspected she was vulnerable, and that underneath that bravado she was insecure. That had changed the way he looked at her. Pregnant and fragile, she needed someone to keep an eye on her.

So when he did his morning rounds he tried to check on her, but lately she seemed to melt into the background, and at the end of the day, when he'd taken to visiting the ward one more time before his afternoon appointments, he only caught glimpses of her in the distance.

He was starting to wish he'd made that next antenatal appointment a bit closer, but the latest guidelines were leaning heavily towards fewer visits, not more, for pregnant women, and he didn't want to draw attention to her.

She still hadn't told anyone else except Flora and he was surprised the gossip mill hadn't found out and run with the news. When it did he hoped he was around to make sure she was okay.

In fact, Nick was there when it broke. He rounded the corner just as the night-shift midwife passed the news to the oncoming staff.

'Did you know Flora May's little pet is pregnant? No boyfriend. And twins! What sort of mother will she be?' The words hung in the air as Nick approached and both young women shut their mouths as Nick descended on them.

He actually needed to count to ten before he said

something because what he wanted to say would have caused a much bigger furore than just the announcement. 'Gossiping again, Cass?' He shook his head. 'You'll get a name for it.'

The blonde flushed with embarrassment but Nick was still trying to control his protective reaction. 'By the way, I'm not happy with the observations in birth room one either. Can you do them again before you go off? I'll drop by and check them in the chart later.' He glanced over both women without smiling. 'Thank you.'

He walked away, still fuming, and didn't see Flora May step out of her office into his path.

'Excuse me, Dr Kefes?'

Nick stopped. He refocused, not sure why he was so upset. Focused on Flora. 'Yes?'

Flora watched his face and he tried to lose any expression that would give away his thoughts. 'Do you have a problem with my staff?'

Did he? He was calming down now. He blinked and let his breath out. 'No. Of course not.'

Flora nodded. 'I didn't think so.'

Nick nodded and prepared to move on. Maybe head back to his office to think about what he'd just overreacted about.

'And, Dr Kefes?'

'Yes?'

'Most people are supportive.'

'Good.'

On the Sunday morning, four weeks after her last appointment, the sun was beating down and Lucy was using the leaf blower to clear the path down to the fence that backed onto the beach.

The blower seemed heavier than last week and her

back ached a little and she wished the palm trees gave her a little more shade. She knew she had to be careful because her body was designed to stretch but there was increased risk of pulling a muscle or over-stretching a ligament thanks to the pregnancy hormones.

She could imagine Flora May saying, 'When you have twins there is even more pregnancy hormone and you have to be careful.'

So she stopped, leaned on the gate in front of the beach, looked over the fence towards the waves and just breathed in the salt-laden air. Her backache eased and the breeze helped. As she began to feel better, she tried to ignore the little skip to her breathing when she thought about seeing Nick tomorrow.

Tried to bring down her silly euphoria by reminding herself her days off were nearly over and the new week ready to begin. Could she do this for another three months?

At least everyone knew she was pregnant now. It was too hard to hide even with the baggy scrub uniform, and Maternity was the best place to work when you were having a baby yourself because it was the place with the least germs.

There'd been a few snide comments, mostly originating from Cass, but a lot of unexpected support from others. Especially Flora May.

She'd be okay. Nick would make sure of that, her inner voice said with a shimmy.

A tall paddleboard rider lifted his hand and waved and instinctively she waved back. Now even the board riders looked like Nick. She needed to settle before tomorrow.

She glanced back at the rider and gulped when the

unknown man turned the board towards her and rode the next wave to the beach opposite her fence.

Good grief, she thought as she watched him pull his board onto the sand, and was about to beat a hasty retreat when she realised that it really *was* Nick.

Nick couldn't believe his luck. He'd known it would be a good idea to buy this board. He trod through the hot sand up to her gate. 'Morning, Lucy.'

Lucy leant on the fence. 'Morning, Nick. I thought I'd accidentally given the come-on to a stray surfer for a minute there.'

He was surprisingly glad she hadn't waved at a stray surfer. He'd known exactly whom he was waving at.

She was dressed in red and green, vibrant like one of the lorikeets feeding off the bottlebrush, but her face was strangely pale. 'Sorry if I scared you.' He wondered if she'd guessed he'd been looking out for her.

'All good. So, what made you paddle by?'

He glanced down at the board under his arm. 'To show off my new toy, and see how you are.'

She gave his board a thorough inspection. 'Your board is very sleek and…dark.'

It had been the best one he could buy. 'I've got a thing for black.'

'I noticed.' She glanced pointedly at his bare feet and raised her brows as if to say, 'Where are your socks?' 'And as for how I am, won't you see me tomorrow?'

He ignored the tomorrow comment and looked a bit closer. 'You look a little tired.'

Her brows shot up. 'You should know women hate being told that!'

'You still look good.' She did, but she wasn't her usual robust self.

'I got hot. Probably need a drink, actually. The owners are coming down tonight and I'm sprucing up the house. Don't want to get kicked out. Especially now.'

He frowned. She did too much. Days off were for her to rest. 'Want a hand? You don't need to work every day.'

Lucy looked at Nick, semi-naked, barefoot, with an extremely cumbersome board hooked under his arm like it was a matchstick, and thought about having him follow her around while she tidied.

It would be much, much easier on her own. And she still felt that little thrill his comment had left her with about looking good. That had been unexpected.

So it wasn't sensible to invite him in, and she was practising sensible. 'Thanks, but, no, thanks.'

She could see Nick hadn't expected the knock-back. She watched him try his special, come-on smile—she'd bet that usually got him the response he wanted. 'I may look like a distinguished obstetrician, but I can mow, trim and clean gutters.'

She could feel a smile inside growing with his determination to get her to change her mind. He was like a stubborn little boy who wanted to play.

'Luckily, I'm not responsible for any of those things, but thanks for the offer.'

She could see that had not been the response he wanted. In fact, he'd crashed and burned, and she watched him assimilate that.

Safety sucked but she needed to stick to her guns.

'The last thing I want is to be a nuisance.'

'As if you could.'

He shrugged easily. 'No problem. I'll see you tomorrow.' He picked up his board and turned back to the sea.

She couldn't believe she'd given the most gorgeous guy she knew the brush-off. But it had been the right thing to do. Depressed, she picked up the blower and her back reminded her it was heavy.

Maybe she should have taken up his offer. She flicked a wistful glance his way but she could see his strong thighs as he strode towards the water and the bulge in his biceps as he carried the board back towards the waves. It was too late. It was actually hard, watching him walk away.

Unexpectedly she felt a strange cramp low at the front of her abdomen and her annoying backache took on a more sinister significance. What if it wasn't just the heaviness of the leaf blower?

Then she realised her babies hadn't moved much that morning, and a deep unease expanded in her chest.

When the cramp came back, this time intensified into a painful drag in her belly, she had to drop the blower and clutch at the fence.

'Nick,' she said in a small scared little voice. Not surprisingly, he couldn't hear because he was almost into the waves. She edged towards the gate and opened it as if her voice would carry further. She just needed the pain to stop so she could call out.

To Lucy's intense relief, before he climbed onto his board, Nick looked back and waved. She waved, signalled him back, a little frantically, and he stopped.

Stared at her.

She saw him tilt his head as if wondering if he'd misunderstood. The pain came again and she put both hands on the fence.

When she looked up Nick was through the gate and beside her. His board was halfway up the sand where he'd dropped it. All she could think was how good it was he'd come back.

The concern in his voice made her eyes sting. 'You okay?'

'I'm not sure.' Her voice cracked.

Nick saw the tears at the corners of her eyes. What was this all about? Somewhere inside a voice mocked him, told him to watch out, and he panicked that she was getting needy for him. He did not do needy.

Then she said the unexpected. 'I've had a few cramps in my back this morning and thought it was because I was carrying the blower. But now they've moved to the front.' Big worry-flecked eyes searched his face for reassurance.

What?

All thoughts of himself disappeared.

She chewed her lip. 'I'm scared it's the babies.'

His mind went blank except for the big words, 'miscarriage', 'prem labour', and they were suddenly unpalatable thoughts. She'd be twenty-two weeks.

That was too early for the babies to have a fighting chance. He didn't ask himself how it was he knew exactly how far along she was. But instinctively he stepped in, gathered her against him and his arms went around her.

Surprisingly she fitted into his body like a jigsaw piece he'd always been missing and he soaked in the warmth of her as if he'd been chilled.

'It's okay,' he murmured into her hair as he breathed in the scent of herbs and spring and Lucy.

He squeezed her gently. His hand came up and smoothed her hair and he suddenly connected with what he was doing and his relationship force field snapped back into place. He did not do emotional.

He loosened his arms. Stepped back.

Steered her to the wrought-iron seat while his mind beat him up with reminders not to get involved.

'Sit. Take it easy. It might be nothing.' He hoped it was nothing.

He hadn't picked the amount of investment he had in these babies already. He needed to snap out of that and get back to the person with the medical degree. 'Have you had any bleeding?'

'Not that I know of.' She'd wrapped her arms around her lower belly, protecting her children, and it did strange things to his chest to see her so panicked.

Distress vibrated off her in bigger waves than those in the nearby ocean.

She sat as directed, as if it would all be all right if she did everything she was told, as if he held her fate in his hands. No pressure. Not.

'Okay. No bleeding. That's good. It might have just been a warning sign for you to take it a little easier. Have you any pain now?'

She shook her head and her hair fell into her eyes. He resisted the urge to brush it back.

'Just a tiny ache in my back.'

Her back. Still suspicious. 'Is it coming and going or there all the time?'

'There all the time.'

Best of the bad. 'Again, that's good. Maybe you have a low-grade kidney infection. Very common with pregnant women and a big player in causing premature labour.'

He saw her wince when he said it but she needed to know he wasn't joking. Maybe he should have tested her again for infections, even though she'd said she was fine.

There was that raised white cell count. He didn't stop

to ask why he was beating himself up about something he would have done for anyone else. But this was Lucy.

Lucy was in shock. From two things—the stark terror of risk to her babies and the absolute comfort she'd gained from being wrapped up in Nick's arms. All that salty skin and muscle around her had felt like a shield from the world.

As if nothing in the universe could go wrong as long as she was snuggled into his arms. So it had been a nasty reality when he'd disentangled himself and sat her away from him.

Now he expected her to take in what he was saying when her mind felt like she was inside a big ball of cotton wool and danger was waiting if she peeked out.

'Sorry?' She concentrated and the cotton wool thinned a little. 'Kidney infection?'

Yep, maybe. She had been dashing for the ladies more often this week. She should have picked that up. They could fix that. Everything would be okay if she took it easy until antibiotics sorted that irritation.

Maybe she'd take Monday off. Thank goodness she'd told Flora May about the pregnancy. And Nick could take her aside and explain as well. Or was that presuming too much?

He glanced up towards the house. 'You go to bed. I'll write you a script. In fact, I'll get the antibiotics from the chemist for you. We'll get a sample from you before you take your first dose so we can make sure we've targeted the right bug.'

Lucy listened to him laying out the strategy and she couldn't help thanking whatever lucky stars had directed Nick to paddle past her door today. She had no idea what she would have done if he hadn't been around. And she'd sent him away.

'I'll get my sister to bring a sterile container from work for the specimen. She's at work this morning and she won't mind dropping in.'

Lucy's stomach sank. She hadn't met Nick's sister. What would she think about a pregnant junior midwife latching onto her brother and asking for family favours?

Cringe factor of ten. 'It's okay. I can get one of the girls from work to do that.'

Nick shook his head decisively. Not the easygoing Nick, this was the consultant—Dr Kefes, Nick. 'Too much organising when you're going to bed to rest. I'll sort this.' He looked past her. 'Where's your place?'

'Down behind the pool.'

'Do you want me to carry you?'

Oh, my word, she could picture it. Feel his arms. 'No. I'll be fine.'

'You sure?'

Sob. 'Yep, sure.' She stood up and the pain was there at the back but the front was okay at the moment.

Nick followed her closely along the narrow path, as if she was going to faint or something.

Halfway down the path the contraction pain came again and this time she really got scared. She stopped and swayed and then his arms came around her gently and he pulled her back against his chest.

'I've got you.'

Then he lifted her—like she wasn't a tall girl with two passengers, but a tiny wisp of nothing—and cradled her against his chest, but sadly she was too focused on the grinding ache low in her belly to enjoy the ride.

CHAPTER FIVE

NICK PUSHED OPEN the screen with his shoulder and angled Lucy through the door still in his arms. She pointed to her little room that had come furnished, all designer white cane furniture with hibiscus quilt and pillow covers and Hawaiian surf photos, and he carried her through.

When he put her down, tears threatened and stung her eyes but she was darned if she was going to let them fall—while he was here anyway. 'I'm fine.'

'Mmm-hmm.' He glanced around. 'Much more of this and I'll admit you to the hospital.'

Too real and scary. 'Seriously. It's gone now.'

He narrowed his eyes at her. 'So that pain was in the front?'

'Yep.' She looked at him, dwarfing her little room, so out of place amongst the white doilies and spindly cane. 'But I'll rest.'

'I'll go to the chemist.' He glanced at his watch. Calculating which chemist would be open probably. 'But I'll have to go home first. Is it okay if I go out the road entrance?' He was so full of purpose. She wasn't used to people taking control. Being a back-up for her. It felt dangerously good, and she needed to snap out of it.

'Sure. The gate will lock behind you.' She reached

onto her bedside table and gave him her keys. 'Use these to get back in. The blue key is for the gate.' She consoled herself that he wouldn't listen anyway if she said she'd be fine on her own.

He glanced back into the other room—lounge, kitchen, dining all in one—and focused on the fridge. 'You look like the kind of girl who keeps bottles of water in the fridge.'

He crossed the room in a few steps and peered into the refrigerator. 'Knew it.' She had to smile as he grabbed a pink plastic drink bottle, picked up her mobile phone from the table, and put them beside her bed.

He pointed his finger at her. 'Stay!'

She sank back on the pillows and to be honest it felt good not to be standing up. 'Yes, sir.' Yes, sir?

He raised his brows. 'Now she gets cheeky. Ring me if you need me.'

'Thanks, Nick.' He was such a hero. But not her hero. The tears got closer.

His face softened and she needed him to go. Now. 'Thank me later,' he said, and left.

Nick frowned at himself as he trod back to the beach entrance, hopped down onto the sand and picked up his paddleboard and paddle. As he locked the gate and retraced his steps past her little bungalow he berated himself. Thank me later? What was that? Asking for a what? A kiss? Get a grip.

The driveway gate clanged shut behind him as he set off along the road for his flat. The board and paddle were bulky and a nuisance under his arm. The path was hot under his bare feet and her keys felt strange in his other hand.

He was getting way too involved here. If he wasn't

careful there'd be emotion involved and he didn't want to go there. He knew where that led. To people being able to stamp on you when you were at your weakest. No way was he going there. But what could he do? She didn't seem to have a friend in the world. He was here. What else could he do? He'd ring Chloe when he got home.

Chloe wasn't as supportive as he'd hoped she'd be. His sister didn't take it lightly. 'So she's a patient?'

What was with the suspicion? 'Yeah. But she's a friend. A colleague.'

There was a definite worried tinge in her voice. What was with that? 'She's your patient, though. You're caring for her during her pregnancy?'

He'd already answered that. 'Yes. She's a midwife on the ward.'

He could hear the frown in her voice. 'It's not like you to become involved. Be careful, Nick.'

Nick lifted the phone away from his ear. He did not want to hear this. He put it back. 'Hell, Chloe. Just get me the container and drop it off here when you come home.'

There was a pause. Then, 'I finish work in twenty minutes.'

'Thank you.' He disconnected and threw the phone on the bed. Stripped off his board shorts and trod across to the shower.

Sisters. When had he ever tried to tell her what to do? He paused with his hand on the tap.

Maybe a couple of times, or more if he was being honest, but that didn't give her the right to go jumping to conclusions about him and Lucy.

He turned the cold tap on with controlled force and stepped underneath the spray. Sucked his breath in and forced himself to stand there.

Not that he needed to have a cold shower because he was thinking about Lucy, but it was hot outside. And he wanted to get back to her as soon as he could. He hoped she wasn't going to miscarry her babies.

He'd been going to wait for Chloe to come first before heading out to the chemist's but if he got a wriggle on he reckoned he could get there and back before she finished work. Then he could go straight to Lucy's.

He hoped to hell she didn't get stronger contractions. As long as she didn't bleed it looked okay. Antibiotics should take care of the irritation and with a little rest she'd be fine. Her babies would be fine.

He'd see if he could do something practical in the yard for her or she'd be lying there worrying that the house wasn't perfect for the owners. No. She didn't want help. She was too independent.

He turned the water off and grabbed the towel. Dried himself quickly and dragged on underwear, some shorts and a shirt.

Lucy's crisis had taken over his day and he didn't stop to think why this threatened miscarriage was any different from the dozens he'd dealt with in the past.

During his time when he'd mostly concentrated on IVF, dealing with bereaved parents had been a part of almost every day, and his own sadness had been one of the reasons he didn't do as much of that these days. But this was different.

He grabbed his wallet and keys and a script pad and pen. It would be fine. He could deal with this.

Back at her house Lucy told herself she was starting to feel better.

What more could she ask for? If she'd gone into the emergency department there was nothing they could do for her except what Nick was doing. And that would be after a long wait in the waiting room.

She was only just pregnant enough for it to be noticeable in the obstetric ward. They probably wouldn't even have done an ultrasound unless she bled.

That had been the first thing she'd done when Nick had left. She'd jumped up and checked she wasn't bleeding. The relief that she wasn't had been immeasurable.

So if she'd gone to the hospital all anyone could have done would have been to check for an infection that could be irritating her body into contractions, treat any infection that was there, and send her home to rest. She didn't want to think about what would happen if she progressed into full premature labour.

It would be termed a tragic loss of an unviable twin pregnancy. They'd tell her to hang on for another week. As if she wouldn't do anything to hang on.

Her abdomen tightened ominously and she sucked in her breath and forced herself to breathe out. Be loose. Be relaxed. Don't get stressed.

She tried to swallow the lump lodged in her throat. Even the wonders of medical science couldn't help her babies if they were born. Dreadful odds for a healthy outcome.

In the last few weeks she hadn't even contemplated losing them. 'Very premature birth' were three terrifying words. Why would she have thought this could happen?

She stroked her tight little mound gently and sniffed back the tears. 'Come on, babies. Stop frightening your mummy.'

She had the top obstetrician in the hospital looking after her, at her home, sending off samples, procuring her antibiotics, all without her having to leave the comfort of her bed. And without the whole hospital rampant with curiosity.

Maybe Nick was right, and she just needed to be more careful. Had she been doing too much in the garden? Or maybe she shouldn't have reached up for those overhanging fronds?

Guilt swamped her and it didn't help that she knew, rationally, she hadn't done anything wrong. 'I'm so sorry, babies,' she whispered.

As if in answer a tiny knee or elbow rose in her stomach and poked her as if to reassure her. She smiled mistily. It was incredible, the bond she felt to these tiny pods of humanity who had slipped into her heart so unexpectedly. Her whole life was affected by their now planned-for arrival in around four months' time and she realised, far too belatedly, that she'd be devastated if she lost them.

She looked imploringly at the ceiling. 'I promise I'll be more careful, God. Honest.' A tear trickled down her cheek.

'If I can just keep my babies.' She glanced around the room, feeling slightly guilty with the fact that she only thought of praying when she wanted something. And she hadn't realised how much she really wanted these babies.

A knock on the door had her reach for a tissue and she blew her nose just as Nick poked his head in. 'How are you doing?'

As he approached the bed Nick saw the traces of tears on her cheeks and her eyes were suspiciously bright. But her voice was normal so he hoped nothing too catastrophic had happened while he'd been away. He put down the backpack he'd brought stuff in.

'You okay?' She looked damp but tragically beautiful. It was the first time he'd thought of her as beautiful, didn't know why he hadn't seen it before. But it wasn't helpful in this situation.

'I'm fine.' She sniffed and sat up straighter. Squared her shoulders and smiled bravely. 'And no bleeding.'

'Good.' Relief warmed his belly. 'Let's keep it that way.' He lifted out the paper bag his sister had given him and the packet of antibiotics he'd picked up. 'Start the antibiotics as soon as you visit the bathroom.'

He saw her blush and he knew that she felt embarrassed about all this. But it all needed to be done and done properly.

'I brought you a mini-quiche and a yoghurt, in case you were hungry.' He took them from the bag, too. It had seemed a good idea at the time but now he felt a bit dumb about it. She was in her own home and of course she'd have food in the refrigerator.

She didn't look like she thought it was dumb. 'Thank you. That's very kind. And I just ran out of yoghurt.'

He handed her the yoghurt. 'It's acidophilus. Always a good idea if you're on antibiotics.'

She frowned and then her face cleared as he guessed she got the homeopathic connection of antibiotics and yeast infections and the natural fighting abilities of acidophilus. Because she laughed.

He wasn't sure if it was a good thing to be laughed at for thinking about things like that but he was a gynaecologist, too. He actually saw the tension fall from her face and decided it was a good thing even if it was at his expense.

She grinned at him. 'Not a lot of girls get that kind of service.'

'Well, you're special.' And she was. But just because she didn't have anybody else and she did still remind him of the sort of support Chloe should have had when she'd had her teen pregnancy. Not that Lucy was a teen. Far from it, but it explained the affinity he felt with her. And the fact that he knew she was more vulnerable than she let on.

'Thank you, kind sir.' She looked past him to the kitchen. 'Did you want a cup of tea or anything?'

'Nope.' He paused. 'Look. I know I've already asked but things are a little different now. If you rest up here, is there anything you really need me to do outside before the owners come?'

He thought she was going to refuse again, but saw the tiny hesitation. 'Come on. Spit it out.'

Her cheeks were pink and he could see she hated to ask. It seemed he needn't have worried she'd abuse his help. Not that he'd really thought she would, but Chloe had mentioned it again, and he mentally poked his tongue out at his suspicious sister.

'I left the blower down by the beach gate. Could I ask you to put it back in the garden shed for me, please?' She chewed her lip and he wanted to ask her not to do that. It made him feel uncomfortable.

He nodded. 'I'll do that and poke around to see if there's anything obvious to tidy up then I'll be back. Don't stress if I take a while. Do you have a computer here?'

'No, unfortunately. It's getting fixed.'

'I brought my tablet computer if you want to go online and search the web.' He reached into the backpack and withdrew it.

'Wow.' She peered over the edge of the bed and pointed to his pack. 'Mary Poppins, eat your heart out. What else have you got in there? Maybe a lampshade and an umbrella?'

He didn't get it. A lampshade? Why would he want an umbrella? 'Who's Mary Poppins?'

She grinned and he had to smile back. She had a great smile. 'Didn't you watch Disney movies when you were a kid?' She smiled. 'My mother was always going out and I was left with a big pile of Disney movies to keep me company.'

He really wasn't liking the sound of her childhood. But, then, his had been the opposite. Too strict. 'Disney must have been too commercial. Not on our Orthodox parents' video list.' He glanced at the almost empty bag. 'Nothing much left in there.'

He didn't want to tell her he had a Doppler for listening to foetal heartbeats because he didn't really want to go there. He wasn't quite sure why he'd brought it. Maybe just for his own peace of mind in case she asked.

'I'll just slip out and sort the blower. Take the antibiotics as soon as you can, won't you?'

She blushed again. It was kind of cute the way she did that. 'Yep. Will do.'

Nick blinked and stepped back. Whoa. Stop that thought. 'Right. I'll sort outside, then.' He spun and headed for the door like the hounds of hell were after him. Maybe Chloe wasn't so dumb after all and he did need to be careful.

By the time he'd used the blower around the pool, fished out some palm fronds and cleaned the filter box, he decided he'd devoted enough of his Sunday to Lucy. But when he went back to say goodbye she was asleep.

And he couldn't leave until he made sure she and her babies were okay.

So he sat down beside her bed on the spindly cane chair and watched her sleep.

Once she mumbled, as if talking to someone, and her

hand drifted to her belly as she smiled the softest, gentlest smile, and it tore unexpectedly at the wall he'd built so successfully around his heart so many years ago.

When she rested her hand over the babies inside her he had to stifle the urge to reach across, lay his hand over hers and feel what she was feeling, assure himself these tiny beings who had somehow pierced his armour were healthy and happy.

Instead, he reminded himself that this family was not his family—and they needed someone with a heart to give, not someone moulded by callous parents who could cast off their children without a backward glance.

Nikolai forced his eyes away and checked his email. Browsed the web. Closed his eyes.

When Lucy woke up, Nick was asleep in the chair beside her bed.

Was this guy for real? She'd never had anyone care about her like he had. Except maybe Lil and Clem next door, when she'd been a kid and had got lonely while her mother had been out.

Which reminded her, she needed to let the kind older couple know how she was doing. They were thrilled she had twins coming. Had promised her all manner of equipment they'd finished with. They'd had their own IVF twins the year before she'd moved out and started her training. They'd understand about twins. But that was for after all this worry went away.

She felt her belly and it seemed softer than before. There were no pains in her back or low in her belly. Maybe it was all going to be okay anyway. She hoped so. When she looked back at Nick he had woken up and was watching her. He smiled and she smiled back.

'Hey, sleepyhead,' she said.

'Hey, sleepyhead, yourself. I was on my way out

and your snoring was so loud I thought I'd better wait till you woke up.'

As if. 'I do not snore.'

'So I've found out.' He smiled at her. 'And you look better. Less tense.'

She gently touched her belly. 'And no pain that I know of.'

He stood up and the chair creaked a little. She had to smile. 'That's great. I still think you should have tomorrow off.'

She'd been thinking that, too. 'It scared me. I'll do whatever you recommend, Nick.'

'I'll talk to Sister May. You've still got my number?'

She nodded and he picked up his backpack and the paper bag she'd left there for him. He raised his brows as he picked it up, checking she'd done the deed, and she nodded.

Her ears felt hot. 'I tightened the lid as tight as I could get it.'

He grinned. 'Good.' He slid his tablet in after the paper bag and zipped up the rucksack. 'Ring me any time and I'll drop in if you need me. Or even if you just have a question. It's okay, Lucy. You can ring me and if it's not a good time I'll have my phone on silent and will ring you back. Okay?'

She nodded. 'Otherwise I'll see you for our appointment tomorrow.'

That was good. They could do another check. 'Why don't I arrange for you to have another scan beforehand? We can compare it to the one you had two weeks ago. That way you can be sure everything is fine.'

She'd been going to ask him for that. Her shoulders dropped with relief. 'Thanks. That would be good.'

'I'll ring you with a time when I find out tomorrow.

See you then,' he said, and she could tell he wanted to get going.

Of course he did. The poor guy had had his whole Sunday hijacked by her and she felt terrible. And special. He'd said she was special but she'd better not get any ideas.

Because she didn't want to get all gooey and mushy over a certain obstetrician, one who probably thought of her as the biggest nuisance out, because no man would want to hook up with a pregnant, single mother of twins.

But seriously! What wasn't there to love about Nikolai Kefes?

The guy had created calm out of her sudden plunge into uncertainty, had tidied up the outside of her house-sitting mansion so she wouldn't feel like she'd let the owners down, and had even run to the chemist's and now the pathology department for her.

But in reality the last thing she needed was a broken heart to carry along with two babies, because even a twin stroller wouldn't be big enough to carry all that.

So she definitely wasn't going there.

CHAPTER SIX

NICK HAD RUNG to say Lucy's new ultrasound appointment was at twelve o'clock and as she dressed, she wondered who was missing out on their lunch to do the favour for Nick.

When she was shown into the little room and directed to climb up on the couch in her patient gown, the bombshell blonde ultrasonographer, a different technician from last time, wasn't behind in letting her know. 'Dr Kefes wouldn't take no for an answer so let's see why these babies of yours are causing him such concern.'

As she dimmed the lights there was a knock on the door and BB opened it to Nick. 'Hello, there, Nikolai.' She laughed and signalled for him to come in. 'I wondered if you'd show up for this.'

Lucy blinked at the familiarity in her tone and couldn't help wondering if these two had been more than just professional colleagues. Not that it was any of her business.

'Hi, Jacqui. Thanks for this. I owe you one.' Nick followed the woman into the small room, which suddenly became much smaller, and Lucy didn't like the way he smiled back at the technician. Not that she even had the right to notice who Nick looked at.

Jacqui seemed pretty happy. 'Oh, goody. Dinner.'

He grinned and nodded at Lucy. 'How are you, Lucy? No more pain?'

'I'm fine, thanks.' Except for this ridiculous feeling of exclusion she should not be feeling. An exclusion she had no right to complain about when Nick and Jacqui were both going out of their way to help her. She was an ungrateful wretch.

And they were going out to dinner.

'So let's see what these kids are up to.' Jacqui tilted the screen so Lucy, and now Nick, could see the pictures, and thankfully Lucy could concentrate on the still unfamiliar excitement of actually outlining the shapes of her babies. Thankfully, everything else disappeared from her mind.

With the extra power of the large machine, Lucy could even see their little faces. Could hear and watch the chambers of their hearts all moving as they should. Gaze with wonder as a tiny hand clenched and unclenched. Then a tiny leg kicked.

They were so tiny, and fragile, and vulnerable. She could have gone into proper labour yesterday, and with lungs too small to breathe for long they would have been gone today.

An explosion of fear ballooned in her chest and she drew a breath. They were her family. Her babies, who would always love her, and she would always love them. What if she'd lost them?

Nick must have sensed her distress because he drew closer and rested his hand on her shoulder. Pressed down. With his fingers sending reassuring vibes, she could feel her panic subside a little. 'It's okay, Lucy. They look great.'

She tore her eyes from the screen to search his face.

His eyes met hers, intense, reassuring. He nodded. Wordlessly he told her he was telling the truth and she breathed out.

Suddenly exhausted by the fear that had come from nowhere and was so slow to ebb away, she sank back into the pillow. Okay. It was okay. Nick said everything would be fine.

'Good two-week growth from last time. Do you want to know the sex?' Jacqui was intent on the screen and had missed the byplay. Probably a good thing, Lucy thought with a tinge of guilt, judging by the way this hospital picked up scandal.

Nick's hand lifted away but it was okay. Lucy dragged her mind back to what Jacqui had said. Sex? Not sexes? 'Are they identical?'

'It looks like it to me.'

Lucy grinned at that. Identical twins. Awesome, and how cute! And her babies would never be alone because they would have each other. Lucky babies. Did she want to know what sex? 'No. I don't think so. I like the idea of a surprise.'

Jacqui was very good at her job. In no time she'd done all the measurements, estimated both babies' weights and checked all around the edge of the big placenta to see if there was any sign of bleeding or separation.

'Nope. All looks good. Nice amount of fluid around the babies. Good blood flow through both umbilical cords. Nothing out of the ordinary except there's two of them. Measure at twenty-two weeks.' She put the ultrasound handpiece back on its stand and handed Lucy a towel to dry her belly while she concentrated on Nick. 'Satisfied, Dr Kefes?'

'Very. Thank you, Jacqui.' Lucy swiped the jelly off her belly and tried not to look at the way Jacqui leant towards Nick. It was none of her business.

She swung her legs over the edge of the couch but before she could jump down, Nick was there with his hand to help her. 'Can you follow me to my office, Lucy, and I'll chase up the results of those tests?'

She kept her voice upbeat with an effort. 'Great. That saves me waiting till the later appointment.'

'That's fine.' He opened the door for her. 'I'll meet you there in a minute.'

Lucy went past him into the ultrasound waiting room and he shut the door. She wondered with just a tinge of acid just how he was thanking Jacqui until she smacked herself. None of her business.

Whatever appreciation he'd offered, it didn't take long because Nick caught up with her outside the lifts.

Meanwhile, above Nick and Lucy and inside the lift that sailed towards them, Callie Richards ground her teeth, silently but no less effectively as she stewed. Cade Coleman! Grrr.

She could see him in her mind's eye without turning her head. She didn't want to look at him. Dark brown, wavy hair. Those light brown eyes assessing her. Always assessing. Coldly. As if she came up short every time. Well, she wasn't short, she was five feet ten, for heaven's sake, and she was damn good at her job.

This last case had been gruelling. Nick had called them in at three a.m. and it hadn't finished until an hour ago, but by the time she'd spent eight hours trying to ignore Cade Coleman in a room full of people she'd had enough.

Her nerves had been shredded and the worst part was she didn't know why she couldn't just rise above him. Build a bridge. Get over him. All the things that grown-up, footloose women did.

She jumped when he spoke. 'How come you didn't stay long in the recovery room? Those parents will have more questions.'

'Don't tell me my job. I'll go back again later.' She shook her head. 'Soon.'

I just need a few minutes to calm down first, she thought despairingly. If this stupid lift could get its act together and get her to the ground floor before she burst into tears.

She seriously needed sleep. There'd been a long session in the NICU the previous evening and her eyes felt grainy. That was the only reason she was feeling fragile.

'Really?'

She turned her head in time to see him look her up and down and her blood pressure escalated again.

There was censure in his tone. 'I heard you were the real heart of this hospital. Hearts don't leave.'

Oh, yeah? Not that she thought about it much, but her heart had left years ago. And so apparently had his. Even his brother had warned her when he'd suggested Cade for the job.

He'd been the one who'd said that happily ever after wasn't for people like them.

Those words haunted her. If he wasn't interested, why didn't he just leave her alone and stop pushing her buttons?

But he didn't. 'Is this to do with me knocking you back for a dance at the wedding? When you were tipsy?'

Callie winced. Now, that had been a dumb dare from the girls. 'Don't be stupid.' She certainly regretted draping herself all over him but that was why she hadn't had a glass of wine since.

He looked her up and down. 'Because we could make

a date. Dance the night away and more. No strings, no expectations. Get it out of our systems.'

After being an absolute horror to her all night. Was he joking? 'Strangely, I decline.'

He shrugged and she wondered if he was as laid back about it as he looked. 'Have to find someone else, then.'

The doors opened and Cade and Callie moved back against the wall. Callie forced a smile and nodded at the little midwife, Lucy. With Nick again?

She frowned slightly. These two seemed to end up in the same space a fair bit. She glanced at Nick and he barely looked tired, despite the long night.

He grinned at them both. Where did he get his energy? 'Thanks for the big night, guys. You were incredible. The parents are still coming to grips with things and I said you'd see them again later. That right, Callie?'

'Half an hour. Just have to sort something first.'

'Great. That's what I told them.' He glanced at Cade. 'Amazing job, Cade.'

'But tense. I think I need some heavy exercise to get the kinks out of my neck.' He glanced sardonically at Callie and then at Nick. 'You up for a game of squash later, Nick?'

'What time?'

'Six-thirty and I'm going to flog you.' What a poseur, Callie thought as she listened, but Nick didn't seem fazed. She hoped he wiped the floor with Cade.

Nick just smiled. 'Make it seven, and meet your match.'

She gave Lucy a look that said *Men!* and Lucy grinned as the lift stopped and she and Nick got out. 'I need to catch up with you later, too, Nick.' Callie saw Nick pause and he turned back, saluted her, and the lift doors shut.

Cade looked thoughtfully at the closed door. 'You think Nick is having an affair with that girl?'

'No.' She hoped not because she'd heard the girl was pregnant. 'There's enough gossip in this place already, without making up more.'

'Makes me wonder if they sail up and down the lift together all day.'

The lift finally made it to ground level and the doors opened. 'As long as they don't think we are, it's all good,' Callie muttered, and hurried off.

She could feel his eyes drilling into her back and she picked up more speed.

Back on the level of the consultants' rooms, Nick ushered Lucy through the door into his office and Lucy passed the empty secretary's desk. She'd forgotten it was lunchtime for everyone else because she'd arranged this before she'd known she'd be off sick.

Lucy took her usual seat while he opened up the screen for the results and she thought about the conversation in the lift.

They must have all been in Theatre together. He didn't look tired. 'Were you up all night, operating?'

'Half the night. Complicated triplet pregnancy.' He clicked the mouse. 'Ah, here they are. Yep. Right antibiotics for the bug and a probable cause for your irritable uterus.'

Lucy was still thinking about the three babies. Gulp. 'So there's people out there who are more complicated than me.'

'Always. And lots that are simpler. People forget that twins are tricky. With IVF we get a lot more twins and triplets than normal and it's a serious pregnancy we need to keep a close eye on.'

They did the blood-pressure and weight check and skipped the abdominal palpation because the ultrasound had shown them both the babies were growing well. Nick handed back the card he'd filled out. 'Don't hesitate to call me if you have any concerns.'

He was in doctor mode and she needed to remember that's who he was. He was her doctor, not her friend.

She stood up. 'Yes. Thank you. I'd better get home and put my feet up or I'll be feeling guilty I didn't go to work.'

CHAPTER SEVEN

AT THREE-THIRTY that afternoon Flora May dropped by at Lucy's house to check that she was okay. The company was appreciated because Lucy felt strangely flat.

Flora glanced around at the secluded alcove with palm trees overhead and birds flying in and out. 'It's like being on a little tropical island. No wonder you like it here.'

Lucy watched a lorikeet dart past and tried to lift her mood. Yes. She was lucky. It was a great place to live. 'Plus it's rent-free for very little maintenance of the big house. And nice and close to the hospital.'

Actually, Lucy wanted to throw herself on Flora's motherly chest but she'd been stifling those urges since she'd been a little girl. She'd thought she was pretty good at it but lately her reserves seemed to be running low.

She felt Flora's scrutiny. 'How are you, Lucy?'

'I'm fine. Nick arranged for another ultrasound. The babies are fine. We're just being careful.'

Flora's eyes it up. 'So how was the ultrasound? Did they move much? And that was very sensible.' She'd brought a cake and they set up the little table outside Lucy's door.

Lucy remembered that moment when she'd thought

about losing them, and how Nick had reassured her. 'They looked good. Kicking well.' She didn't know what she'd have done without him the last few days but she didn't want to get used to relying on him. It was nice having Flora visit, too. Almost like a family, but who was she kidding? She needed to get better at going it alone, not worse.

Flora poured the tea. 'So when do you think you'll be back at work?'

'Tomorrow.'

'Good.' Flora sat back. 'Dr Kefes is looking after you well?'

Lucy smiled at the question in Flora's voice. As if she would have words with him if he wasn't doing his job well. 'I wouldn't be going tomorrow if he thought it was dangerous.' She could just imagine Flora taking Nick to task for being negligent. 'In fact, he's been great.'

She couldn't tell Flora how great or the rumour mill would go into overdrive. Not that Flora gossiped. That wouldn't be in her psyche, but it could be awkward if Flora thought she and Nick had something going on when, of course, they didn't. 'I'd like you to try and come with me to the next ultrasound if you're not busy?'

Flora's face softened and she smiled. 'I'd like that.'

Flora stayed another hour and then left, but not before Lucy promised to phone in sick if she felt unwell.

She was so glad she'd told Flora, who'd suggested she allow the news to spread so people would understand and be a little more thoughtful in what they asked Lucy to do.

The next day at work Lucy felt as good as new. Maybe it was because she had slept in that morning, and starting work after lunch instead of before breakfast seemed to suit her better.

The ward was busy, and after checking Lucy was okay Flora glanced at the clock.

'Right, then.' Back to business. 'I'll get you to care for Bonny Shore. Her husband can't be here because they have no one to mind their two toddler daughters.'

'Oh, poor thing.'

'Yes. Meg's in there and I don't think she'll go home before the birth so the two of you will be there. The exciting thing is that Bonny's having twins, too.' Flora smiled and Lucy wanted to give Flora a hug because this was just what she needed—an insight into the happy ending of a twin pregnancy.

'The neonatal nursery is aware we're close but ready to come when we think they'll be needed. Dr Richards and Dr Coleman have been to see Bonny and explain that two neonatal teams will be there just in case either baby decides to be naughty.'

Lucy had to smile at that but inwardly she quailed at the thought of so many consultants in the room. Especially the terrifying Dr Coleman.

But she'd have to get used to it. This was her world and she vowed she would become a valuable part of the network at Gold Coast City Hospital.

Flora went on. 'Of course, Dr Kefes and his registrar will be there also, so the room will become very busy when the time comes.

'Until then…' she looked at Lucy from under her stern brows '…try and give Bonny some reassurance that despite the cast of thousands she does have some control over her birth and that she is still doing what she is designed to do.'

Lucy grinned. 'Absolutely.' She looked up at her mentor. How she wished she'd had someone like this kind woman as her mother or even her aunt. Her dream had been that one day she'd get a warm and fuzzy mother-in-law who would be the kind of mother she'd never had but that dream had slipped further away. He'd have to be some man to want a wife who already had twins.

Maybe that would never happen but Flora was becoming her friend.

'And thank you.' She looked away because her silly hormones were filling her eyes with tears again. 'For caring.'

For a moment Flora's eyes softened and then she looked towards the birthing suites. 'Away you go.'

As Lucy knocked and entered, her patient, Bonny, was shaking her head and pushing the straps off her belly. 'I need to go into the shower.' Her voice cracked. 'I can't sit on this bed any more.'

Bonny Shore was thirty years old, this was her third pregnancy, and she'd had normal births with her two little girls who were waiting at home. By the strained look on Bonny's face, this was all very different.

Lucy suspected her patient was stressed by the extra observations needed for twins, plus she was heading into late active labour.

Lucy had seen that this could be the most challenging time, transition between the first and second stages of labour, before the pushing became compulsive, a time that often left a woman agitated, fearful and sometime quite cross.

As she learnt more each day, Lucy was starting to realise that mums needed extra-calm support right about now. She could remember Flora telling her in her training that this was the usual time for women to abuse their husbands, if they weren't at home minding the other children.

Lucy wondered briefly if she would have anyone to be cross at when she had her babies then scolded herself for being self-absorbed and crossed over the room to Meg. The other young graduate midwife looked up from the foetal monitor as Lucy appeared.

They smiled at each other, acknowledging silently the excitement of the impending birth. They both glanced at the two resuscitation cots set up together at the side of the room.

'Well, here's Lucy come to help you into the shower, too,' Meg, said reassuringly. 'This is the midwife I told you about who's expecting twins as well.'

Bonny looked across and rolled her eyes at Lucy. 'Hi, there. And poor you.' She glanced down at her large rounded belly and then suddenly smiled softly. 'And lucky you.'

As they helped Bonny down from the bed, Meg quietly went through her patient's progress. 'Bonny began her contractions this morning at home about six a.m. She came to us at ten, once she had her girls sorted, and was four centimetres dilated already by then.'

'Wow.' Lucy was impressed. 'That was great progress at home.'

'My husband was a mess by the time he dropped me off and I got into trouble from Dr Kefes for not coming earlier.' Bonny grinned as she shuffled across the room towards the bathroom, her hands under the swell of her huge abdomen to support it.

Lucy could tell she was not at all abashed at the scolding. Then the next contraction took hold and they all stopped as Bonny leant against Lucy and breathed through the contraction.

As they stood quietly and gently breathed together, Lucy realised there was no tension in the room, just a feeling of solidarity, and she thought again how lucky she was to have found her niche in life.

The contraction eased and Bonny went on as if she hadn't stopped. 'He listened when I said I didn't want an epidural. Though he did get an intravenous pin in when I didn't want one.'

Bonny looked up under her hair at Lucy. 'Though it's coming to that point in this labour when you tell yourself you'd forgotten how strong it gets.' She pushed forward grimly and held onto the doorpost as the next contraction rolled through, then she sighed again and forced herself to relax.

'Getting to the business end,' Lucy said gently.

'Precisely.' Bonny's eyes were fixed on the shower nozzle as if it was calling her. 'Which is a good thing.'

They settled Bonny into the shower and Meg completed her handover quietly as Bonny closed her eyes with relief as the warm water cascaded over her stomach. 'Bonny had progressed to eight centimetres dilated when Dr Kefes came in half an hour ago.' Meg stopped as the next contraction hit.

'We've negotiated a short time off the monitoring from Dr Kefes just so she can move around a bit before the birth, but we have to head back to bed as soon as she feels any urge to push.'

Lucy had to agree. 'With twins that's understandable.' The two midwives grinned at each other. It could be tricky balancing two babies and eight people in the bathroom.

Twenty minutes later Bonny looked up with a startled expression on her face. 'It's time.' She turned to face Lucy. 'But I don't think I can move.'

Meg blinked and her face paled but Lucy had a little more experience of this and knew what to do. She leant in and turned off the shower. 'I know. But it's safer for your babies if you do, so we're going to move anyway. Okay?'

She put her hand on Bonny's arm and motioned to Meg to do the same on the other side. 'And I'll buzz so that someone will come and start ringing the troops while we get you back to bed.' She leant across Bonny's body to the wall and pushed the call button. 'Let's go.'

Meg's eyes widened in relief as Bonny stood up and suddenly took off nearly at a run for the other room so that the midwives were almost left behind. She climbed up onto the bed as if she was being chased and by the time Flora arrived they were drying her off and slipping on her open-backed gown.

By the time Nick arrived and Bonny was giving her first push, the foetal monitor was back in place and two baby hearts were making clopping noises.

Nick saw Lucy as soon as he entered the room and forced himself to ignore her.

For some reason, today she distracted him and he wondered if it was because he didn't want to think of Lucy as the patient in a few months' time. The twin thing. He focused on where he should be. 'How are you doing, Bonny?'

'Business end.' Brief and to the point, Bonny wasn't wasting energy on small talk.

Nick nodded and headed over to the basin with a small smile and washed his hands. While he pulled on his gloves, he looked across at Meg and raised his eyebrows in a silent request for an update. Meg was fiddling with the foetal monitor and Lucy stepped in and filled in the blanks, so he couldn't ignore her.

'Bonny went to the shower and about five minutes ago felt the first urge to push. She's had three pushes since then and both foetal hearts have been reassuring.'

Good. Another woman brief and to the point. He liked that. He nodded and snapped his second glove into place.

Bonny groaned as the next powerful urge took over and when they lifted the sheet a tiny dark head of hair slowly appeared like magic between her legs. He stepped in next to the bed. 'You're doing an amazing job, Bonny. Nice and gentle.'

Nick glanced at Lucy. 'Get the paeds, thank you.'

Lucy nodded, sped over to the phone and passed the message to the neonatal staff. A few seconds later she put down the receiver. 'They're on their way.'

At that moment Cade and Callie and two experienced neonatal nurses slipped unobtrusively into the room and he nodded. Not that he expected trouble but he wanted to be prepared for it.

Bonny groaned again, and he looked back at his patient.

Women never failed to amaze him with their strength in these situations. He couldn't help just one quick glance at Lucy, who was holding Bonny's hand as they all waited for the birth. In the not-too-distant future he'd be here to see Lucy give birth.

Lucy watched Nick's large capable hands as they supported the first baby's head as it lifted and turned. She didn't think she would ever forget this moment.

The room calmed as a tiny shoulder appeared, Nick murmuring praise as Bonny silently and unhurriedly eased her baby out. The first of the twins had arrived safely to a sigh of relief from in the room.

Cade stepped up next to Lucy, not saying anything, but she could feel the concentration he was directing her way as Nick passed baby one up to his mother. Lucy rubbed the little body dry until the baby grimaced and then made no bones about complaining loudly.

Bonny's firstborn son screwed up his little face until he was bright red and roared his disapproval and he kicked his legs, exposing his impressive scrotum and penis to everyone except his mother.

Lucy felt Dr Coleman step back and she had to admire his unobtrusive readiness. Maybe he wasn't so bad after all, because he'd certainly achieved what he needed with very little impact on Bonny's birth experience.

Lucy liked that. A lot.

One of the neonatal nurses replaced him and helped Lucy settle the baby between his mother's breasts, mouth and neck nicely positioned for ease of breathing, skin to skin, with a warm bunny rug over them both.

'So what have you got?' Nick smiled at Bonny, because everyone else in the room knew but hadn't said the words.

Lucy lifted the blanket and then the baby's rear end to show his mother, who lifted her head to glance down, and then Bonny laughed. 'A boy. We have our William.'

As they all waited for the next contraction the relief in the room gave way to the tiniest rise in tension. It was always tricky to see how the second twin settled in its mother's uterus after the first had made more room.

Hopefully the baby would turn head first towards the big wide world, but Lucy knew that often second twins would settle into breach position, which was less straightforward for the birth.

What they didn't want was the baby not making a firm decision between the two and lying across the mother's uterus to block the cervix with a shoulder or arm. Such a position became incompatible with a normal birth and Caesarean of the second twin would have to be considered.

'Start the syntocinon, please, Lucy. We want a few more contractions.' Lucy uncapped Bonny's IV cannula and connected the infusion.

Nick's big hands gently palpated Bonny's stomach until he found the hard, circular head of the second twin, who was apparently still undecided on the direction of the exit. Nick kneaded gently downwards along the baby's back through the mother's soft abdomen until the next contraction halted his progress.

After several contractions and Nick's gentle persistence Bonny began to push again.

This time the baby wasn't in so much of a hurry to be born, and the tension crept up until Lucy found herself holding her breath and Nick quietly urged Bonny on.

'Come on, baby,' Bonny muttered. 'If it's a boy, he's called Benjamin.'

Finally the baby's hair and then rest of the head was born, and during what seemed an eternity, but which after Lucy's third glance at the clock she knew was only ninety seconds, the flaccid little body of a slightly smaller twin boy was born in a flurry of floppy arms and legs.

'It's Benjamin,' Nick said. 'We'll take this little one over to Dr Richards for a few minutes, Bonny.' Nick cut and clamped the cord and Callie swooped in, dried the limp baby with the warmed towel and then gath-

ered up the tiny scrap in her confident hands to carry
him across to the heated resuscitaire.

'He's a bit stunned so he hasn't taken his deeper
breaths to start off,' Lucy said quietly in Bonny's ear.
'Needle,' she warned as she gave the injection to help
separate the placenta and reduce the risk of bleeding
after birth.

She glanced across to where the two neonatologists
were working quietly on Bonny's second twin.

The neonatal nurse who'd stayed to observe William
began to explain to Bonny what was happening and
Lucy's attention was drawn that way, too.

Within thirty seconds the tiny oxygen saturation
probe had been taped to Benjamin's tiny hand and they
were puffing little bursts of air into his lungs.

From where she stood she could see his heart rate
was reading eighty and that wasn't too bad if it crept up
over a hundred with the inflation of his lungs.

But that didn't happen. In fact, the heart rate slowed
agonisingly and dropped to fifty.

She heard Dr Coleman's comment to Dr Richards.
'So, secondary apnoea. Change from air to oxygen. I'll
do the cardiac massage.'

Smoothly Dr Coleman changed position, circled the
baby's chest with his big hands and began to compress
the little rib cage three times to every breath from the
face mask Callie held over the nose and mouth.

They began inflating baby's lungs with more oxygen
and immediately his blueness seemed to wash away.

'He needs a little oxygen until he gets the idea of this
new breathing business,' Nick said in answer to Bonny's
worried look. 'Pinking up now.' He glanced back at the
sudden gush of blood that was forming a ruby puddle
in the bed.

The placenta came away and Nick passed it swiftly to Meg in a dish. 'Check it's all there because we've got some bleeding.'

'Fundal massage, Lucy.' Lucy leant over and rubbed Bonny's soft belly firmly until the underlying uterus contracted under her hand to slow the bleeding.

Swiftly Nick checked for any trauma that could be contributing to the blood loss while Meg carried the placenta over to the bench and made sure none of the lobes of tissue were missing from the circle. Lucy knew that sometimes lobes or even membranes from the bag of waters left behind could cause bleeding after a birth.

Nick pulled the spare drape from the trolley and tossed it up onto Bonny's belly. 'I'll do the massage now, Lucy, if you draw me up another five units of syntocinon and get two fifty micrograms of ergometerine ready just in case.'

His big hand came in over Lucy's with the drape between them and Lucy stepped back to assemble the drugs. Nick went on, 'I'm afraid your uterus has gone on strike, Bonny. I have to rub it until it contracts and stops the bleeding. Sorry if it's uncomfortable.'

Lucy held up the first drug to check with Nick and he read the name, dose and expiry date out loud. 'Fine. Give it slowly intravenously. Then start the forty units in a new flask of saline in the line.'

Meg was back. 'Placenta looks complete.'

'Good.' He looked over his shoulder at his registrar. 'Simon, put another cannula in, please, and draw some bloods as you do. Repeat coags and full blood count. We already have blood cross-matched if we need it. You can run normal saline through that as a replacement fluid. I think this bleeding is settling now.'

Lucy leaned towards her patient and took her wrist.

Amazingly, Bonny's pulse was only slightly raised. 'You okay, Bonny?' she asked as she strapped the blood-pressure cuff to the woman's arm.

Bonny nodded. 'I'm more worried about my baby.' At that moment a little wail came from the second re-suscitaire. 'But I think he's getting the hang of it.'

Lucy watched the unhurried way Nick moved through the mini-crisis. She tried to estimate the blood loss and decided it would have been around a litre or two pints. 'Blood pressure one ten on sixty, pulse eighty-eight.'

'Thank you,' Nick said to acknowledge he'd heard, he looked at Bonny. 'You lost an amount of blood that would certainly have caused problems for most adults but thankfully you pregnant ladies have mechanisms in place to cope with extra blood loss at birth.'

He smiled reassuringly a Bonny. 'You still look the pink-cheeked and bright-eyed mum we started with, though tomorrow might be a different story.'

He went on quietly, 'Tummies that have carried twins are notorious for being tired after birth, Bonny, but it's all settling now.'

He gestured to the two IV lines now hanging above her. 'Sorry about the two drips but one can come down when we've replaced a little of the fluid you've lost. We'll run this new flask over four hours and see how you're doing then. Might be able to just put a cap over your IV lines after that.'

Bonny nodded. 'I'll forgive you,' she said, and stroked the little body that still lay across her chest. 'I just want Benjamin.'

Nick glanced across at the team, who only needed to observe her baby now. 'I know. He'll be across here as soon as we can.'

By sixty minutes after birth everything had settled. Benjamin, the second twin, spent a little time with oxygen near his face while he lay on his mother, but soon he was sucking as robustly as his brother from his mother's breast. He'd go to the nursery as soon as he'd finished so he could be watched for another hour.

Nick had gone. Meg had gone home. One of the neonatal nurses had stayed to help Lucy with the babies and they'd been weighed—both had come in at just under seven pounds—and the neonatal nurse was in the process of dressing them.

Lucy took Bonny into the shower and helped her freshen up and climb into her pyjamas, all the time alert in case Bonny began to feel faint, but to her relief the new mum just kept going.

It was incredible how reassuring the whole experience had been for her on a personal level, Lucy thought.

Ten minutes later she finally helped Bonny into bed with her two little guys beside her in the twin cot.

The room was peaceful for five minutes until Bonny's husband arrived with their two little girls, and excited pandemonium broke out.

There were squeals, bed-jumping and excited tears as Bonny's husband squeezed his wife tightly in relief that she and the babies were well.

Lucy was still smiling as she walked away with a promise to return in fifteen minutes to make sure the bleeding remained settled and to check that Bonny had survived the onslaught.

Three hours later, after another emergency trip to Theatre, Nick walked down the corridor to his rooms and deliberately loosened his shoulders.

He was mentally tired but there really wasn't any reason for him to be this drained.

Last night had been torrid in Theatre but ultimately successful.

Today, there had been another good outcome, and he was glad everything had worked out fairly smoothly for Bonny because they'd had many long talks during her pregnancy about her preference for as little intervention if possible. In the end they'd achieved most of that.

But mentally he was distracted, and he didn't do distraction, so where the heck had that come from?

Lucy's worried face at the ultrasound yesterday slipped into his mind. It wasn't a certain little midwife causing all this, he hoped.

He ran his hand through his hair. He guessed he hadn't slept well on Sunday night after Lucy's scare and then they'd been up most of the night after that.

And he'd spent a bit of mind space hoping the scan would come back normal, to the point that he'd made sure he had been there for the appointment yesterday, which, when he thought about it, hadn't really been necessary.

Because Lucy was only a colleague. And a once-only pleasant breakfast companion. And a patient of his. Nothing else.

Not a sister he could put up in his flat until her world righted itself. Not someone he had to go in to bat for when other people let her down. But she was vulnerable and she didn't have anyone else.

Was that why he'd wanted to take her aside after Bonny's birth and make sure she was okay? Maybe give her a hug and reassure her that her own birth would be fine? Her babies would be fine.

This was getting out of hand.

The only ironically amusing part about this was how horrified his parents would have been at his involvement, and how fortunate for Lucy that he didn't speak to them.

He was developing an interest in a non-Greek, pregnant nurse with twins by another man! Well, he knew she was a midwife and not a nurse, but it would be the same to them. Anyone less than a specialist would be a failure to them.

He could hear his mother now. 'This woman, she is after your money. You are a doctor. You are too good for her.'

In fact, he had a sneaking suspicion that Lucy was too good for him. But for some reason she just had to look his way, smile in that cheeky, sexy way of hers, and he was hot. What was that about?

Lust, his inner demon suggested sardonically. He laughed out loud and then glanced around. A hospital orderly dragging a garbage bin looked at him strangely and he pulled himself back under control.

But it was darkly humorous and the joke was on him.

Because lust wasn't going anywhere with a woman pregnant with twins.

Not like he could drag her off to bed for goodness knew how many months so he'd be better casting his gaze elsewhere and scratch that itch with a woman who understood that he was footloose and fancy-free and staying that way. Plenty of those around.

Somehow it just wasn't an attractive thought. But what was most important was that he keep everything under control.

'Would Dr Kefes please phone Emergency. Dr Kefes, please phone Emergency.'

The page boomed overhead and Nick ducked into the

nearest nurses' station to pick up the phone, actually a little relieved to be called to an emergency. Looked like he was going to miss the squash game with Cade as well.

At eleven that night Lucy pushed open the night exit at the front of the hospital and stepped out into the balmy evening.

She was limp with exhaustion but exhilarated by the way Bonny was managing with her babies, and how well both little boys were.

She'd felt so reassured about how Nick had agreed to less intervention, how calm and wonderful he'd been with Bonny, and if everything went well she was going to have babies like that. With Nick as her carer.

She wanted to ask Flora to be her support person because her senior was certainly taking an interest in her well-being and Lucy didn't really have any other friends she could ask to be with her.

It was all months away but she guessed in another couple of months she'd have to start looking for ante-natal classes. And going to those alone, too. She lifted her chin.

A car stirred the warm air as it flew past with its headlights on and she stepped up onto the path towards home.

The bonus of living close to the hospital was that it was quick to walk to and fro, but the disadvantage was that at night it could be a little creepy, heading along a street that comprised of mainly driveways and garages behind big walls.

Another car started up and she waited for the acceleration of sound but unexpectedly this one rolled up beside her and Lucy's heart rate soared.

She stared doggedly ahead and refused to look at the driver. It was even harder not to glance round when the passenger window was wound down, and her heart rate bumped up another notch.

'You're not walking alone at night, are you?'

Nick. She blew out the breath she'd been holding in a long stream. Grrr. 'Hell, Nick! You frightened me half to death.'

'Sorry.' He didn't sound it and her irritation went up another notch. 'Would you like to hop in and I'll run you the rest of the way?'

She could guess what had happened. He'd obviously seen her and decided to go all interfering on her. But now her nerves were shot it would be a horrible walk until she was safely inside her own yard.

So she'd look pretty silly if she said no. Especially when her feet were killing her. But there was no use getting used to it.

He wouldn't be waiting every night so what was so special about tonight? The last thing she needed was to feel let down after every shift because Nick wasn't there to pick her up.

Lucy sighed and opened the door but after she'd climbed in she frowned at him. 'Aren't you going the wrong way?'

The seat felt fabulous as she rested back and took the weight off her feet, and that only made her feel more cross. 'Do you have any idea how bossy you sound?'

'Sorry again.' He didn't sound it and she was glad someone was amused. Not. 'It's the Greek in me,' he said mildly. 'I don't like to see a woman walking alone at night.'

Bully for him. 'It's not my preference, but the Australian in me says get over it and get home.'

'I'm Australian,' he said mildly. 'But I'm also second-generation Greek.'

'Hmm.' As in not my problem, Lucy thought, still grouchy from her fright. 'And this is my house. Thank you for the lift.'

He pulled on the handbrake. 'I'll walk you in.'

'No, thank you.'

Nick tamped down his frustration. He was sorry he'd startled her but he hadn't been able to believe it when he'd seen her head off in the dark. He didn't know why he hadn't thought of it before. He guessed he'd assumed she caught a taxi home or something.

But she was so darned independent he should have known she'd put him on the back foot. He forced himself to relax and smile at her as he leant across to open the door. 'Our first fight.'

She didn't smile back. 'It was fun. Goodnight.' She pushed the door wider and climbed out and he watched her walk to the gate, and hated it that nobody would be there to greet her when she got home.

He thought for a moment she was going to just march away but when she took out her key she looked back. Shook her head and sent him one of those ray-o-sunshine smiles he could live off if he had to.

'Sorry. You scared me.' She shrugged. 'I was cross with myself for being nervy and you copped it. Thank you for the lift.'

He let out his breath. At least she didn't hold grudges, though he'd done nothing wrong by wanting to see she was safe. 'In penance you should have breakfast with me on Sunday.'

She grinned at him. 'Now, that would be a hardship. Love to. But I'm—'

He finished the sentence for her. 'Paying for yourself. Excellent. I'm broke.'

She looked startled for a moment and he patted himself on the back. It had made her smile again. Keep 'em guessing, good motto. 'I'll pick you up at eight?'

'Eight's perfect. See you then.'

Lucy closed the gate behind her as the automatic lights came on then she heard Nick's car accelerate away.

The night noises surrounded her. The owners had only stayed for two nights and now she was back to being home alone.

CHAPTER EIGHT

ONE OF THE fronds from the palm trees crashed down somewhere along the path near the pool and Lucy jumped at the noise and spun around before her brain recognised the familiar sound.

Her babies wriggled and fluttered and she patted her stomach. 'Sorry, guys.' Leftover nerves from the fright Nick had given her.

For the first two weeks she'd house-sat she'd been sure someone had been outside the house when that had happened, but she could have done without it tonight.

She glanced up at the big house and then frowned at the flicker of unexpected light she could see in the lounge room.

There was a small tinkle of glass and this time she knew it wasn't normal. Her hand edged into her bag and she felt around for her phone as she backed towards the gate.

As soon as she was out of sight of the house she pressed the button for contacts and Nick's name lit up. Without hesitation she pressed his number and he answered it on the second ring.

'Lucy? You okay?'

'I'm coming back out,' she whispered. 'Someone's in the house.'

'I'm on my way and I'll ring the police as I come. Get out into the street and under a streetlight.'

By the time Lucy had crossed the street and hurried away from the driveway Nick's car was roaring up the road towards her, and she'd never been so glad to see anybody.

Nick saw her a hundred yards down the street under a lamppost, her arms wrapped around her belly and shaking.

He screeched to a halt and was out of the car in seconds with his arms wrapped around her and her face buried in his shirt. 'You were quick,' she mumbled into his shirt, and he stroked her hair. Poor Lucy.

'I should have walked you into your house.' His arms tightened. 'I'm so sorry.'

'I said no. And I'm not your responsibility.' She eased back as she looked up at him, chin thrust forward and her eyes showing she was bravely determined not to crack. All the conversations, concern, downright worry and now this scare twisted in his gut.

Maybe that was why he tilted her chin with his finger and murmured against her lips, 'It's sure starting to feel that you should be.' And then he kissed her.

It was intended as a gentle salute, a comfort peck, sympathy even, but that wasn't what it turned into.

As soon as she melted against him he lost it, lost where, why, everything except how much he'd wanted to taste this woman, feel her against him.

Her instant response, to open under him and hotly welcome him in, lit a desire that flicked along his arms, tightened his hold and fanned a deep need he hadn't realised he had. He wanted more. He wanted Lucy. He wanted it all.

Lucy was lost. Nick's mouth against hers was intoxicating, hot, hungry and totally in charge. And she wanted more. Wanted to push the boundaries into the world she'd always wondered about. It wasn't safety she wanted at this moment, it was danger.

Apparently 'lost in a kiss' was the way it went with Nick. Swirling sensation, swirling red colours against her closed eyelids.

It wasn't until he was gently pulling away that she caught on to how lost they'd been.

Nick's arm slid over her shoulder and pulled her against him as he faced the uniformed patrolman that had answered Nick's call.

Lucy came slowly back to the real world.

And Nick's voice. 'I'm sorry, officer.'

Officer? Someone else was here? Real red lights were flashing.

Nick's voice again. 'Yes, it was me who called.'

So they'd been sprung in mid-kiss by the patrol car. Embarrassing. Lucy bit back a giggle, still drunk with the sensation of Nick making no bones about the fact that he desired her. Or maybe he'd just been kissing her for comfort and it had been her hormones that had screamed sex. Either way she was a wanton, bad woman and bad mother—so why was she still smiling?

Nick turned her to face the young man in blue, who didn't meet her eyes. She blushed. 'I'm Lucy Palmer, the house-sitter. Yes. I heard glass breaking and there was a strange light moving in the lounge room.'

The young patrol man nodded. 'So you exited through the rear gate and rang Dr Kefes. Who rang us?'

'That's right. We...' She blushed again. 'We haven't seen anyone leave this way.'

The policeman glanced at her this time with a

slight smile. He raised his eyebrows but refrained from comment.

Nick stepped forward and pointed to the gate.

'This path also leads to the beach. It goes past the house, behind the pool and onto the beach.'

Still stunned by her response, Lucy let Nick take control because she was still a foot or two off the ground. At this moment he could run the show for all she cared. They'd stopped talking and it seemed like they were waiting for her to do something. Both of them looked at her hand holding the keys.

'Do you want me to open the gate?'

'If you give me the keys, we'll deal with this. I'm pretty sure they'll be gone now.'

Lucy handed over the bunch. 'The blue is for the gate, the red for the house, and the green for the gate to the beach,' she told the policeman.

'Would you both wait here for us?'

'We'll be here.' Nick pointed to his vehicle and the policeman nodded and motioned to his men to accompany him onto the property.

Nick and Lucy watched them go and the moment stretched to awkwardness as both tried to think of something, anything, that was not embarrassing to say.

Lucy was the first to give up on that unlikely occurrence. 'I thought I was seeing red lights because you were kissing me.'

Nick blinked and then smiled and soon they were grinning at each other. 'And I heard roaring in my ears, which was probably the patrol car trying to run us down.'

Lucy chewed her lip. 'At least no one from the hospital saw us.'

And then Nick said something she hadn't foreseen.

'Much more of that and we have the reality of finding you a new obstetrician.'

Lucy's stomach dropped and she thought, *No-o-o!* with an internal wail of distress. Nobody would be like Nick. She wanted Nick to look after her. Felt so safe under his care. Maybe it wasn't too late. They could pretend it had never happened. 'It was just the stress of the moment. What about if I promise never to kiss you again?'

Nick winced. She could promise that, could she? Maybe she hadn't felt what he'd felt. 'Actually, I kissed you.' *And I'm not promising anything of the sort.* He didn't know what had happened, but he didn't say it out loud.

So it seemed Lucy wasn't ready to hear anything like that and he wasn't going to rush her, or himself, but things had certainly changed.

Or had the possibility of change. And professionally his judgment could be clouded.

He wasn't ready to say just what it was between them but the chemistry was blatant. He wanted to enjoy more of her company, even if it had to be platonic, and he could not believe he was thinking this. That had to be a first.

But he could see she was upset. How to explain? 'It's becoming a little hard to manage your care with the dispassion that is required.' He winced. That sounded sensible but stuck up.

He took her shoulders and tried not to think about what he was feeling beneath his fingers. 'I'm already second-guessing myself, questioning decisions I don't question with other patients. That's not fair to you or to me.' And that was the truth. Apart from the fact his Hippocratic oath forbade him to have a relationship with a patient and he'd just kissed her. And wanted to do it again.

He dropped his hands. Definitely time to bail out.

Why did she have to look so crushed? But as he should have expected, she lifted her chin and accepted reality. It just took a few seconds, and he was reminded of the way she'd coped the first time he'd seen her in his rooms. No hysteria, no tantrums.

He heard her sigh. 'I think I understand, but I wish you didn't have to.'

He wanted to hug her again. More proof he was doing the right thing. 'I'm doing this because I still want to be here for you, Lucy. You're not losing me. You're just gaining an impartial second person.'

She nodded but he didn't think she was convinced. 'If you were impartial, you could keep looking after me.'

'Sorry. Not impartial.'

She smiled shyly and then chewed her lip. 'Do you want me to find the other doctor?'

No! Definitely not. What if she picked someone useless? Someone like Chloe had had? He'd be a mess. How could he say that diplomatically? 'Not unless you want me to. I have a very good friend, just moved back to Gold Coast City after his wife died, David Donaldson, whose care I think is excellent.'

He'd been Nick's mentor. David was old enough to be Lucy's father, and his own too, for that matter, but he was the best with twins, Nick reassured himself. 'I worked with him in IVF at another hospital and he's very experienced with twin pregnancies.'

'He sounds fine. Thank you.'

The conversation died when the police reappeared. They were carrying a plastic bag with a heavy metal bar in it. 'Seems they jimmied open the back door. You must have disturbed them because they left this behind.' He frowned at Lucy. 'Not sure you should stay the night here, miss, it's a bit of a mess in there, and you being pregnant and all.'

But where would she go? 'I'll be fine. I'll lock up and they wouldn't come back tonight.' She swallowed and stuck her chin out. 'Surely.'

She felt Nick bristle beside her and the officer sighed. 'It's up to you, miss.' But he looked at Nick. What was with that? It had nothing to do with Nick.

It was the other Nick who answered. The one from the hospital. Consultant Kefes. 'You're absolutely right, officer.' She could hear it in his voice. 'We'll arrange somewhere Lucy can stay tonight and sort it out in the morning.'

Lucy's mouth opened but Nick went on, 'Has there been a series of these break-ins?'

The officer nodded. 'Half a dozen over the last week, and some injuries to people who have disturbed them.'

Oh. Lucy's heart plunged. Okay. Not sensible to stay if she wanted to keep her babies safe. But a hotel room was going to hurt her budget severely. A wave of tiredness broke over her and she just wanted to go to bed. Somewhere safe.

Nick was shaking hands with the officers and distractedly Lucy thanked them as well.

The policeman shook his head. 'You did the right thing. Pregnant lady like yourself. You hear noises you don't understand and there's someone in the house, you get out, and ring us—any time.' He glanced at Nick. 'We'll respond as quickly as we can.'

'Thank you, officer. We appreciate that.'

Lucy was still trying to decide which hotel would be

the best at this time of night. That was one thing about the Gold Coast. Plenty of hotels. Or maybe she could find a free empty bed in the ward? The man nodded. 'Have a good night.'

They watched the police drive away but all Lucy could think about was how she wanted to sink into the ground. In fact, she wished Nick would go. She had a lot to think about.

Like where to sleep and…that kiss. And how she'd shown him just how much she was attracted to him and the fact that now he just wanted to get her off his books faster than a speeding bullet.

Cringe. Nick's voice broke into her swirling thoughts. 'Come to my flat.'

What? 'I can't do that.' As if.

He opened the passenger-side door of his car. 'Of course you can. It's just sleep. I've got a spare room.'

She couldn't go there. Maybe he could sleep at her place. But she knew he couldn't. Like he could sleep on her two-seater here or in her single bed.

But she couldn't go to his place. 'I can just imagine the gossip.'

'To hell with the gossip. I'm sure a single mother with twins created more gossip last week. And you survived. You can't stay here. It's crazy to pay two hundred dollars for a hotel when you're only going to use it for a few hours. Plus you shouldn't be alone after a scare like that.

'It's for one night.' He glanced at his watch. 'Actually, for about six hours. Are you working the morning shift or the evening?'

'Evening.' So she'd have to come home tomorrow night after work and do the whole thing again. Not an attractive thought.

'Again, problematic.' Nick looked at Lucy wilting under the streetlight. 'It's okay. Just be a little less independent for one night and get in the car.' He gestured to the open car door. 'We'll worry about it in the morning.'

He'd said 'independent' but by his tone he'd meant 'stubborn'. She wasn't being stubborn. Just realistic. It wasn't going to change anything for tomorrow, because this was still her home, but she had to admit it would be horrible to try to sleep at the flat tonight with the trashed house a few feet away.

But she needed to learn to cope with crises as they came along—because she was going to be doing this alone. Nick wouldn't always be there to rescue her.

Nick watched her struggle with the concept of accepting his offer. He wasn't sure either if this was the right thing to do or not, but she couldn't stay here.

She must have been too tired to argue because to his relief she moved past him and slid into the car.

He couldn't stop himself shutting the door quickly in case she changed her mind. He didn't have control issues but the idea of driving away from Lucy while he couldn't be sure she was safe just wasn't happening. He could hear his sister's voice, complaining, the word 'over-protective' ringing in his ears. But this was different.

Tomorrow he'd figure something out. He was good at that. He could fix this. Protect Lucy. Now that she was finally letting him do the work.

CHAPTER NINE

'WHAT FLOOR ARE you on?' Ten minutes later they were standing in the basement car park of Nick's units, waiting for the lift to arrive.

'Nine. It's got a great view.' Nick looked disgustedly relaxed about bringing back a strange woman to his flat after midnight. He probably did it all the time, Lucy thought tiredly.

It was like he hadn't even noticed the tension between them in the car, or the fact that she'd been almost glued against the door on her side, as if she could wipe away any thoughts he might have that she was attracted to him. Too late for that, though.

Lucy had her fingers crossed behind her back. Please don't let them meet anybody in the lift.

The place would be crawling with hospital staff on call for emergencies at all hours of the night and she did not need the stress of smiling and pretending everything was normal when her whole world had been rocked on its axis.

Or was she being a little prude to worry about taking just one night's shelter at a friend's house because her own had been compromised?

A friend she'd kissed, though.

She sighed and forced herself to relax a little. She really couldn't help it.

At that moment the lift doors opened and of all the people she didn't want to see was the glammed-up version of the night-duty midwife, Cass. Even more surprising, she was hanging on the arm of Dr Cade Coleman, and they were obviously on their way out somewhere for very late drinks.

Dr Coleman's eyebrows shot up but he didn't say anything except, 'Evening.'

Nick's sardonic 'Evening' back made Lucy wonder bitterly if this passing of ships in the night was a common occurrence in this building. Neither of the girls said anything, and Lucy's embarrassed smile was met by a disbelieving frown as she and Cass passed.

The lift doors shut and Lucy felt like stamping her foot in frustration. Of all people! Grrr. She looked at Nick, thinking *this was his fault*, and was even more incensed to see he had a slight smile on his lips. 'Well, I'm glad someone is amused.'

'Sarcasm, Lucy?' Nick said mildly, and then he draped his arm around her shoulder and hugged her once before he let her go. 'You're having a night from hell, aren't you?'

She was going to say yes, categorically, but then her sense of fair play, the reasonable side that allowed her to get over the disappointments she'd grown up with, remembered how Nick had come to her aid immediately, had worried about her safety and even provided an answer to her immediate dilemma.

She sighed out her frustration, tried another sigh, and felt better for it. Get over what you can't change. What did she care what Cass thought? But she'd tell the world, her inner caution wailed. Not a lot she could do about it now, though.

So it wasn't the worst night ever. Not quite. 'Not the best.' Though one particular part had been incredible, she wasn't going to think about that until she was safely back in her own house. 'But the night could have been a whole lot unhealthier if I hadn't had you to call on.'

The lift stopped and Nick waited for her to leave the lift in front of him. He lowered his voice. 'Number six. And you're welcome.'

Lucy followed the direction of the numbers until she came to the corner flat. Number six. Nick leant in front of her and opened the door with his key then held it to allow her through first.

Down a small hallway and across the huge living room, floor-to-ceiling windows held the eye, with sheer curtains and a narrow balcony that ran round the whole corner of the building and the view beyond. 'Wow.'

'Yep. It's nice. And there're two bedrooms, so you can have the guest room. You've got your own bathroom and there's towels and a robe hanging on the door if you feel like a shower before bed.'

Bed! It sounded divine. Night attire was a minor problem, but he'd said there was a robe. She looked down at her scrubs. She didn't want to sleep in them or she'd look a hundred times worse tomorrow morning when she met the next nemesis in the lift on her way out.

'I should have grabbed some clothes.'

He shrugged. 'I've got a heap of T-shirts. I'll try and find one that's not black.' He grinned at her. 'We'll sort all that out tomorrow'.

He went to his refrigerator and brought her an unopened bottle of spring water. 'Take that. You're dead on your feet.'

He scooped a folded T-shirt out of a laundry basket of clean clothes that was sitting on a chair, handed it to her and kissed the top of her head like she was a five-year-old he'd picked up from school. 'And I'll see you in the morning.' And then he left her.

Just walked into his room and shut the door.

Lucy blinked. Well, that had been easy. And bizarrely disappointing, which was ridiculous. But he was right about one thing. She *was* dead on her feet and she could worry about everything else in the morning.

Nick had to get out of the room. Or he would have drawn her into his arms again and who knew where that could have ended? Scary stuff.

He heard her bedroom door shut and a few minutes later the sound of the shower. He tried really hard not to think of Lucy naked, round and glistening, with the water running over the places he wanted to run his hands.

He decided a shower was a great idea because he was damn sure there wasn't much chance of sleep just yet.

The cold water helped and as he dried himself he knew he did need to hit the sack. He had a late start tomorrow but the day would be a long one. Especially if he hung around until Lucy finished work. There was plenty he could do in his office.

They had to sort somewhere safe for her to go. Or she could stay here.

He was getting way too involved in her life but she was like a freight train heading for disaster. Not that she'd see it that way.

After a brief, glorious shower, where she rinsed out her underwear, wrung them dry in a towel and hung them up for the morning, Lucy pulled the T-shirt over her head and tried to ignore the fact she was naked under something that had been against Nick's skin.

A slow heat started in her belly and she couldn't help thinking about Nick's arrival under the lamppost, and the kiss.

She was pretty sure he'd just meant to comfort her but she'd melted against him like a candle under a blow-torch. She would have been a puddle if he hadn't held her up.

She'd never been kissed like that. Nowhere near it. Had never lost herself until all she could feel was a need for more. Her face heated at the thought. And wanted more.

Maybe she'd just been scared? She'd been so glad to see him, and to be wrapped in his arms and protected by him had seemed the most natural thing in the world. Her babies shifted and wriggled and she patted them gently as her head hit the pillow. 'He's not your daddy. And he's not going to be. So get used to it.'

Suddenly there were tears on her pillow and her throat felt raw. She sniffed. 'Stop it.' She rolled over and after many determined breaths and tight closing of her eyes she did eventually fall asleep.

But her dreams were not so easily controlled. Someone was following her. Every time she stopped, they stopped.

When she turned round she couldn't see who they were but she knew they were there and she couldn't find the gate to get out of the house courtyard. Every path seemed to lead to a bare piece of fence with no opening and they were getting closer.

Suddenly she started to cry. She never cried. But the tears just fell more heavily.

A sob caught in her throat and she tried to hold back the flood because the stalker would hear her. Unconsciously she pulled her pillow over her face to muffle the sounds and cried as if her heart would break.

Across the lounge room Nick thought he heard something. Was that Lucy, talking to someone? He slipped from his bed and opened his door.

Nothing. No sounds. Then it came again. Very soft but audible out here. It was Lucy. Sobbing, and nothing could have stopped him knocking briefly and crossing the room to her.

'Shh.' He brushed the hair from her face but she just turned away. 'Lucy, wake up.' He shook her gently but she just became more agitated.

He couldn't stand it. He didn't know what to do except slip in beside her and pull her against his chest and cradle her in his arms. Nick wrapped himself around her until she buried her nose in his chest. He'd never let anything happen to Lucy.

Her hair was in his face. Her forehead in his chest. Babies up against his belly. Now, that was a new experience and he couldn't help a tiny smile.

'It's okay.' He stroked her back. 'My poor brave girl. Life just keeps throwing stuff at you.' He smoothed her hair. She mumbled something he couldn't make out. 'You're fine. You're safe.'

Slowly her breathing settled, and when Nick kissed the top of her head and then her cheek, still with her eyes shut she turned her damp face towards him.

He kissed her mouth gently and she smiled sleepily. 'Go to sleep. I've got you.'

She murmured something and rolled in his arms so she was facing the other way, spooned into him. Nick swallowed uncomfortably. Exquisite agony to lie there with her so trusting against him.

His hand rested as if it belonged in the gorgeous hollow between her breasts and the other splayed on top of her rounded tummy. She snuggled in even closer and he stifled a groan. If it had been anyone else but Lucy he'd have said they were deliberately teasing him.

He felt the first roll of her belly and then a clear kick from one of the little people inside, and he couldn't help but grin.

'Hello, there,' he whispered barely audibly, and the little foot or hand poked at him again.

Warm feelings expanded in his chest. Affection for these little scamps. These wriggling little babies who would have their mother's characteristics.

And their father's! They weren't his babies.

The thought crashed in on him and for the first time he felt the loss of not being a father. Not having the right to cradle a woman's belly and know that he had created a life—or two—within her. The loss stung unexpectedly. Especially with Lucy in his arms. And yet the man responsible wasn't here, and he was.

Nick wondered what sort of father he would have been. Would he have found it easy or hard to relate to his children? Maybe he would be no better than his own intolerant father, but even at this moment he knew that wasn't true. Especially if he had someone like Lucy to guide him.

The babies kicked again and Lucy murmured something. He smoothed the T-shirt-covered belly under his hand. 'Hey, don't wake your mother up.' And he knew he cared far too much about these tiny little girls or boys and had already invested in their future.

Was he just indulging the over-protective nurturing tendencies he'd carried since Chloe had been sixteen?

Tendencies that had been amplified by his profession? He'd always thought he had an inbuilt reservation about commitment. So where had that gone?

He was a fool. Had he invested his heart in Lucy?

Sure, she wanted him to look after her, but she also had no problem saying she'd never kiss him back again if he didn't pass her on to David. Not exactly the relationship he was looking for.

Unconsciously he tightened his hold and she murmured in protest. He loosened his hands and backed away. He needed to get a grip—and not on her. She seemed settled now and maybe it was time to go.

He slipped slowly backwards out of the bed and apart from a small disappointed noise she let him leave. An omen? He pushed his pillow into her back and tucked her in.

Definitely the most sensible thing to do anyway.

Lucy had the best dream.

When she woke up she was smiling despite the shaft of sunlight on her cheek and a baby playing trampoline on her bladder. And the smell of coffee.

Lucy stretched and admitted grudgingly to herself that it had been the best sleep she'd had for months. She slid out of bed and padded across to her bathroom.

After she'd indulged herself with another quick shower and climbed awkwardly into her now dry underwear, she looked at the scrubs and screwed up her nose.

Soon she would change back into a purple Teletubby but not yet. She lifted the thick white towelling robe from the hook on the door and slid her arms into the sleeves. She'd always wanted to walk around in one of these.

She grinned at herself in the mirror, surprised how light her spirits were considering everything that had happened the night before, but maybe that was because she couldn't do anything about all the disasters now anyway.

She tied the belt over her definitely growing belly, and opened the door.

Nick was in the kitchen, breaking eggs into a pan. He was wearing board shorts and a black singlet top.

She swallowed the 'Wow' that hovered in her throat and coughed. 'Morning.' Tore her gaze away and admired the way he added four little rashers of bacon to the pan.

He pointed to the coffee plunger on the bench. 'Good morning. Decaf, my lady?'

The heavenly scent. Oh, yes, please. She looked at him. There was something different about him this morning but she couldn't put her finger on what it was.

She poured herself a coffee and sipped the aromatic brew before she put the cup down and pointed her finger at him. 'You, Dr Kefes, are a prince.' She could squirm and beat herself up over being here or she could just enjoy this and to hell with the ramifications. No choice really.

'And I can even cook.' He smiled a long, slow smile that fitted right into the particularly gorgeous day outside and the incredible aromas inside. Life could not get any better at this moment.

'You look rested. And back to your incredibly serene self.'

She felt great. 'I am. This is a very nice hotel. Your bed is divine and comes with delicious dreams.' She could feel herself blush and went on hurriedly, 'Your shower is glorious.' She twirled and showed off her robe. 'And this is very trendy.'

He took his time admiring her robe. Or he might have been avoiding her eyes. She wasn't sure which.

'Sadly, they don't come in black, apparently.'

'Well, I'm not sad about that.' She picked up her cup and wandered over to the window with maybe a tiny hint of extra wiggle.

Nick must have pulled back the curtains when he'd got up because the unobstructed view of the ocean was breathtaking and there was even a cruise liner out on the horizon.

To the left the balcony looked over the Gold Coast city skyline. 'Wow.' She glanced back at him. 'It must be hard to leave this and go to work in the mornings.'

'Nope. Love my work.' He concentrated on turning the eggs without breaking them. 'Love my life.' The toast popped up and he tossed the slices onto the waiting plates with a whistle.

And let that be a warning to you, Lucy, she told herself sternly. He wasn't looking for a relationship any more than she was, let alone one that came with twin babies and commitments. And she had a very busy life to plan and some serious juggling to make ends meet. Hence the reason she was not moving out of the cabana.

But she wasn't going to let it spoil the short time she had before she dived back into reality.

'Good on you. I love my job, too.' She moved towards the long table set with two places. 'And where do I sit?'

He gestured vaguely. 'Either or. I don't eat here enough to have a favourite chair.'

'But you had bacon and eggs in the fridge in case?' Lucy raised her brows.

He shrugged. 'Mrs Jones does my shopping and laundry as well the flat. She keeps me stocked.'

Cleaning lady. Bliss. This was a five-star resort. 'Fine. I'll take the chair facing the view.'

So will I, Nick thought, and could barely take his eyes off her. Obviously she didn't remember the nightmare or the fact that he'd gone in to lie with her until she settled. In the harsh light of day that was a good thing.

He sat down at the table opposite Lucy and watched her tuck into her food, like she had that time they'd eaten together at the surf club, and it was surprising how much he'd enjoyed cooking for her. He enjoyed having her in his home.

And he wanted her in his bed. He'd lain awake for hours last night. Of course she'd had nightmares. It had been a shock and she could have easily been attacked. He'd spent a fair while beating himself up for not taking her all the way to her door or he would have been there when she'd been first frightened.

Which brought them to the next dilemma, but he let her finish her breakfast in peace before he brought that up. If he knew Lucy, it wouldn't take long for her to polish her food off.

Or disagree with his suggestion.

He could feel a smile tug at the corners of his mouth as she put her fork and knife together in the middle of her empty plate. 'Wow. That was good. Thank you.' Typically she followed that with, 'And I'm washing up.'

She just couldn't let him do anything for her without paying for it. Stubborn woman. He didn't know why that pushed his buttons but he almost ground his teeth in frustration. Maybe that was the reason he was less than diplomatic with his next wording.

'It's not safe to go back there after work tonight. You know that, don't you?'

He frowned at himself. But she was so darned independent she infuriated him. That wasn't to say after it came out of his mouth he didn't regret his bluntness.

She put her cup down and met his gaze steadily. Surprisingly even-tempered as she gently turned him down. Why did he feel like she was the grown-up here?

'I appreciate your concern, Nick, but I have to go back. It's my home. And my job to house-sit the big house.' She held his gaze. 'I need to save money for when I can't work, and it's rent-free.'

He would not lose this battle. 'And what if the burglars come back?' It seriously worried him and he couldn't believe it didn't worry her either.

Lucy sighed. 'The thought of getting home late at night and opening my door isn't a comfortable one, I admit, but I'll have a chat to Flora at work today and see if she can swap me to day shifts for a few weeks.'

He opened his mouth but she held up her hand. Bossy little thing. It had been years since someone had held up their hand to tell him to be quiet. He subsided reluctantly but stewed about it.

'I'll phone the owners this morning when I go home and see what the damage is. I'm sure they'll be happy to beef up the security and maybe even hire a firm to keep the place under surveillance. It's in their interests, too.'

He could see she was determined. But so was he. 'If you work this evening, before you can change to the day shift, I think you should spend one more night here.'

She opened her mouth and sardonically he held up his own hand.

She narrowed her eyes at him but he just smiled. 'My

turn. Another day or two will give the security firm time to make their adjustments as well.'

It was a sensible idea—and, though Lucy hated to admit it, it was an attractive one as well. And that was without the eye candy of a dreamy Greek doc cooking her breakfast. And in reality there was plenty of room here for the two of them.

It would only be for one more night. And the idea of not having to go back until the place was made more secure was very attractive. Maybe he'd let her pay…

'And if you offer to pay board I will stomp on your scrubs so that when you leave, everyone will think you slept in them.'

She widened her eyes at him. 'Ooh. Nasty.'

He wasn't fazed. 'I assure you. I can be.'

'Okay. Okay.' She had a sudden vision of Nick jumping up and down on her purple scrubs and bit her lip to stop an unseemly snort. But it seemed there was no stopping the eruption of giggles that escaped. She gave up and threw back her head and laughed at him.

'You crack me up.'

'Obviously.' He grinned at her. 'Now, that has to be good for you.' Nick was thinking that it was good for him, too. He loved the way she laughed. Loved a lot of things about Lucy because she continued to amaze him with her resilience.

'So you'll stay tonight?'

She nodded. 'Yes, please.'

'I'll walk you home. I've got a backlog of work so I'll meet you in the doctors' car park after eleven.'

'No.' She shook her head. 'It's two hundred yards across a road. Doesn't your sister walk home after an evening shift?'

Yes, she did, but this was a bit different. Or was it?

Was he going too far the other way? What was wrong with him?

Hmm. 'You're right.' He held up his hands. 'My brain's gone AWOL.' He stood up, walked over to an empty vase and tipped it up to retrieve a spare set of keys.

'The big one opens the door on the street to the foyer. The smaller one the front door to the flat.'

She looked at the keys in his hand and reluctance shone out of her worried eyes. 'I'll try and be quiet when I come in.'

'I sleep through anything,' he said to make her feel better, but he knew he wouldn't.

CHAPTER TEN

LUCY FELT THE change as soon as she walked into work.
The morning staff, normally chatty and warm, suddenly
stopped their conversations when she entered the tea
room, and even the friendliest midwives, while they
still smiled a greeting, didn't meet her eyes.

Lucy took one guess at what had happened. Cass.

She put her bag away and went back out to the ward
to wait for the clinical handover to start.

She'd thought she'd got over that insecurity thing
left over from her mother, that not-good-enough-to-be-
included cloud that had hung over her whole childhood.

So what if these people she'd hoped were her friends
thought that, because she was pregnant, she'd shacked
up with the nearest available rich guy and had just made
it easy for herself?

Now she wished she'd actually tried to seduce Nick
so at least she would have had the memory. And what
a memory that would have been…or would she have
been just like her mother? Looking for a quick fix to
her life's bigger problems?

Then they'd have the right to say she'd be a terrible
mother, too, but she knew in her heart that wasn't true.
She would love her babies with all her heart. Though

there would always be a part of her that belonged to Nick in her dreams.

Lucy lifted her chin. She'd always been a bit of a loner when the going got tough. Other people didn't need to know how she was feeling so she pinned a smile on her face and put her bag away.

But the unfairness burned a hole in her euphoric feeling of belonging here. How would they have liked a break-in? At eleven at night? When they were on their own?

All they saw was the pregnant little midwife who might be sleeping with the ward consultant. A man who wasn't even the father of her baby. Or maybe they thought Nick was.

Poor Nick. His only fault was that he'd helped her out. Well, blow the lot of them.

Flora appeared at her side. 'A moment, Palmer?'

Lucy felt her stomach plummet. She'd thought Flora would have given her the benefit of the doubt. 'Certainly, Sister.'

Flora steered her into her office and shut the door. Then, to Lucy's complete surprise, offered one of her jerky and uncomfortable hugs before she pulled back and stared into Lucy's face with concern. Not censure. 'Are you all right?'

Dear, dear, Flora May. Lucy stamped fiercely on the urge to cry. 'My landlord's house was broken into last night and I disturbed the robbers when I went home.'

Flora gasped.

It all tumbled out. 'Nick came and phoned the police and waited with me. He thought it wasn't safe to stay alone in the flat.'

'He's right.' Flora looked away and glared into the

distance. 'Stupid rumours. Stupid people.' Flora looked back at her.

Now seemed a good time to mention the roster change, Lucy thought. 'I was going to ask if you could change me to day shifts for a few weeks. I spoke to the owners today. A security firm has put the house under surveillance but I'd like to avoid going home at night for a little while.'

Flora nodded vehemently. 'Absolutely. Consider it done. You could have night shift if you wanted. Then you'd only be there in the daytime.'

But then she'd have to work with Cass and they just might come to blows if she still treated her birthing women like she'd treated young Sally. Or Lucy herself. 'Can I think about that?'

Flora nodded. 'No problem. Why don't you have split days off this week? Have tomorrow off and come in Friday and Saturday morning because I have a space on the roster then.'

Flora stepped back to the desk and checked her print-out. 'Yes. Then have Sunday off then do a week of mornings starting Monday?'

Sounded perfect. Lucy wondered if Nick still wanted to have breakfast together on Sunday—he might be sick of her by then after having her in his house for two days in a row—but either way she still wasn't working. Flora was a champion.

She did have friends. 'That sounds wonderful. Thank you.'

Flora glanced at her watch. 'Let me know if you want nights next week.' Then she looked back at Lucy's face. 'And where are you going tonight after work?'

'Um, Dr Kefes has offered his spare room for one more night.' Flora didn't look happy and Lucy went on,

'The new locks and cameras at my place will be installed tomorrow. So tomorrow night I'll go back there.'

'Fine. I'll have a word with a certain midwife.'

Lucy shrugged. 'It really doesn't matter. I should be used to it.'

Flora lifted her chin. 'You shouldn't have to be. But I will fix her little red wagon.' Goodness knew what that meant, Lucy thought, but she wouldn't like to be on the end of Flora's displeasure.

'Oh. And Dr Kefes said because it could be misconstrued, he's moved me on to a Dr David Donaldson. Do you know him?'

Lucy hadn't known that Flora could actually blush, though there was a definite heightened colour to her face.

The older woman seemed fixated on the ward clock now. 'Yes. I heard he was coming back.'

Lucy wasn't sure what the problem was, but she hoped it wasn't because Flora didn't agree he was the right doctor for her. 'Apparently his wife died.'

'Hmm.' Flora wasn't buying into the conversation. 'You don't see your mother much, do you? Did you ask her to come and stay with you?'

Lucy shrugged. Would her mother offer her help if she needed it? She really didn't want to find that out the hard way. 'She's got her own life. I respect that. And my flat's too small for two people.'

Flora nodded noncommittally. 'I have my own life, too, but I'd like to think that if you need a friend I am there for you, Lucy.' It seemed a strange thing to say and not related to anything.

Lucy mumbled, 'Thank you,' and the subject closed on that.

'Take birthing unit two,' Flora said. 'Judy is in there and will give you handover.'

Eight hours later, as the shift drew to a close, Lucy couldn't help the little release of excitement that had bubbled quietly all day because she'd be going back to Nick's flat again tonight. And everyone already thought they were having an affair.

But this was the last time she'd stay there. It had to be.

Tomorrow, a Thursday off for a change, she'd have all day to sort things out and be ready to sleep in her own bed tomorrow night. She needed to get back to running her own life.

A shame it had felt so safe at Nick's flat last night. As if the weight of the world had been lifted off her shoulders and this morning had been the perfect way to start the day. The picture of Nick, with his muscles, in the kitchen, cooking her breakfast, would be hard to beat.

As Lucy turned towards the consultants' flats she hoped she wouldn't meet anyone in Nick's lift this time but it probably didn't matter now. She was already the scarlet woman of the hospital, just like her mother, heading to sleep over at a man's flat.

Not such a good example to her children, and something she'd sworn when they were peanuts she wouldn't do, but this was different. How far she'd fallen since that first exciting day when she was going to be the best grad midwife GCCH had ever seen.

Lucy's hope that tonight's stay at Nick's would remain unnoticed shrivelled and died as the nurse walking ahead turned into the front entrance to Nick's lobby door.

Not much she could do about it unless she wanted to walk around the block in the dark, and that defeated the purpose of being safe, she thought grumpily. She rubbed the tender ache in her side where one of the babies had been poking her with an elbow or foot on and off throughout the day.

As she opened the foyer door a few seconds later with Nick's key she could see the other nurse was still waiting by the lifts so she'd even have to say hello.

She sighed and admired the thick loose twist of dark hair on the woman's head and even the escaping brown curls looked more artful than untidy. She'd always wanted to be able to do a bun.

Lucy brushed back the hair from her own eyes and felt hot and bothered and frumpy and fat. Where had all that excitement of five minutes ago gone?

Quite a few years older than Lucy, the other girl offered a friendly smile. 'Evening.' And Lucy wished for half her poise.

'Evening.' Lucy decided that must be what they all say around here and the conversation died because the lift doors opened.

'What floor?' the girl asked as she stood in front of the control panel.

'Nine.'

The girl's brow puckered a little and she glanced at Lucy more thoroughly as she pressed the button. 'I'm on nine, too. Haven't seen you before.'

Lucy studied the shiny white tiles of the lift floor. 'I'm just staying with a friend for tonight.'

'Oh.'

Lucy looked up at the change in tone. She saw the other girl digest her answer as she looked at Lucy's baggy scrubs and the unmistakable bulge of pregnancy at the front. Her eyes narrowed.

The tone wasn't unfriendly. 'I'm Chloe Kefes.'

Bingo. She had all the luck. 'Nick's sister.' Lucy tried to keep the resignation out of her voice.

'Yep.' Her gaze was drawn to Lucy's bulge. 'Would you be Lucy? His patient?' Chloe had a twinkle in her eyes that took the sting out of her next comment. 'The one the whole hospital is talking about with my brother?'

At least Nick's sister didn't seem to hate her. 'That would be me. And ex-patient. Actually, he's handed me over to Dr Donaldson.'

Chloe's eyes widened. 'I see. Good. I'd hate him to have to justify to people what he does naturally. He's the kindest man in the world and the best brother.' She raised her eyebrows at Lucy. 'Gets a bit over-protective at times.'

The lift arrived and Lucy had never been so glad to step out. 'I know. And I do understand. Nice meeting you, Chloe.'

'Interesting meeting you, too.' They walked down the corridor together and Lucy remembered Nick pointing out his sister's flat next to his. This just kept getting better and better.

Chloe's eyebrows rose when Lucy pulled the key to Nick's door out of her pocket but she didn't say anything. Before Lucy could turn the key Nick opened the door anyway.

'Hi, Lucy, Chloe.' He looked from one woman to the other. 'Did you guys walk home together? That's a good idea.'

Chloe looked like she might disagree but didn't comment. 'We met in the lifts. I'll see you in the morning, Nikolai. Bye, Lucy.'

Nick held the door for Lucy and she closed her eyes as she ducked under his arm. This was becoming more complicated by the second. She should have just gone back to her own home. She'd tidied up the big house before work today and maybe she would have been fine.

'I don't think your sister is happy I'm staying.'

'Tough.' He looked supremely uninterested. 'I'd be more unhappy if you didn't. Who matters most?'

She had to smile at that. 'I guess she's worried the gossip will taint you.'

He looked more closely at her. 'Have you had a bad day or was it just Chloe?'

She sighed and allowed herself to be steered into a chair. He handed her a soda water and she took a sip because she hated the way, even without intention, Chloe had made her feel. 'I'm a scarlet woman, having an affair with the consultant.'

He shrugged and then smiled crookedly at her. 'I hope I'm the consultant concerned?'

'Stop it.' But he did make her smile despite the gravity of the situation. Not that he seemed to think it grave.

He sat down opposite her. Caught and held her gaze. 'You're new here. You're not used to it. The place thrives on gossip. Next week it will be someone else.'

'I don't want to be this week's juicy titbit.'

Nick couldn't stand it. She looked so forlorn. Juicy titbit. She was that indeed, but at the moment she needed comfort, not his sexual frustration, and he'd promised himself he would not sleep with Lucy.

It wouldn't be fair. What single, pregnant young woman, after giving herself, wouldn't be hurt when he walked away?

And he wasn't capable of the emotional roller-coaster ride needed to stay. He owed it to her to be strong for both of them.

So gently, like a brother, he stood, reached down and

she put her hand in his without hesitating, and he held that thought as he stood her up. 'In that case, come here and get a sympathetic hug.'

Before she could pull away he'd folded her loosely in an embrace and just for a moment he felt her let the worries and stresses fall away. But only for a moment. Would she ever let him in? he thought ruefully, forgetting he'd agreed on keeping his distance, not thinking about his own walls that held them back.

A few more seconds and he'd have to let go. She felt too good, snuggled in against him, too rounded and lush and gorgeous. Maybe they should really give the gossipers something to moan about.

Lucy relaxed against Nick and tried to stop thinking. Just for a moment. Then she remembered the safe harbour last night, remembered the time he'd hugged her when she'd been frightened for her babies, remembered he'd kissed her once. She didn't want this for comfort, she wanted it because he desired her. Because all night while she'd waited for the clock to crawl around she'd hoped he'd do this, because she certainly desired him.

She just wanted him to sweep her up, show her the love she had no right to expect, because she had the horrible feeling she was reading too much into his kindness. Learning to rely on him too much. And he had a real life apart from being her shiny white knight in her fantasy.

She didn't kid herself he'd be dropping by with his paddleboard when she had two tiny babies to manage. What man would?

So she'd be the one doing the moaning if she let herself snuggle up to Nick for too long. She shouldn't have come here tonight feeling needy and emotional, and more than semi-sexually aroused at the thought of sleeping under Nick's roof again. She'd heard that the second half of pregnancy hormones could startle men. She smiled sadly to herself and prepared to ease back.

But she never got to take that step away because Nick lifted her chin with one long, caring finger, smiled into her eyes and kissed her. A soft and sweet and gentle kiss.

It was too much. Lucy despaired. The tragedy of this beautiful, too-perfect man, and the chance of him falling for her, nearly broke her heart. Something must have shown in her face because he gathered her even closer, whispered, 'Don't look like that, my gorgeous girl,' and kissed her again.

And then it was just like last night, under the street-light, a long star-studded, sensation-filled path to losing herself in a place where no rational thought was allowed.

'Hold me, Nick.' She didn't know where the voice had come from, or even if she'd said it out loud, but she felt the floor disappear from under her feet as he lifted her into his arms and carried her carefully into his moonlit room.

Nick put her down gently on her feet beside the bed, murmured, 'Far too many clothes,' and helped her pull off her purple scrubs so that she stood before him in her bra and panties. Then he pulled his T-shirt off and drew her back in against his chest. Skin to skin. Like a baby against its mother's breast. Her lace-covered breasts against Nick's chest.

She could stand like this for ever—his hot skin on hers, lean muscle against her soft curves. She pictured them in her mind's eye to save the memory, inhaled the scent of freshly showered man, leant into solid, muscular chest, lifted her hands to corded shoulders and slid her fingers along the rough growth of his un-shaven chin.

Every part of him felt as wonderful as she knew it would and her body began to dance to his music as his hands slid slowly from her shoulders to her hips.

He made her feel wanton, desirable, for a moment even beautiful, and she tilted her head as he dropped feather-light kisses along her jaw.

She'd dreamt of this but it had never felt as magical as this.

Emboldened, her hands began their own exploration, the play of muscle and sinew and raw strength under her fingers, the bulge of biceps, and with a woman's smile she felt his breath catch as her thumb slid across his taut belly.

The sliding doors to the veranda were open and the sound of the surf washed over them as he drew her down gently onto his bed and with her eyes shut by his kisses, the soothing sound of the waves and the salty freshness of the breeze surrounded her, along with Nick's arms as he lay down next to her—and pulled her more fully into his embrace.

When he kissed her again she sighed into him. This was where she wanted to be. She had been fighting against the dream, fighting against the taboos of falling for a man who wouldn't be there for her always, but it was too late. She loved him for what he'd done for her, loved him for looking after her babies, loved him even when he undermined her independence, even loved it that he was so confused about his own feelings for her—but that didn't mean he loved her.

I love you, she said silently to him, and hugged him tighter because she needed this one night before she returned to the real world tomorrow.

* * *

He hadn't meant to get to this point. he held Lucy in his arms and she felt so right, so perfect that it scared him. Terrified him that this woman—his hands slid with gentle reverence across her satin belly—and these babies—his breath caught—could be his responsibility.

But was he ready for this? Did she think he was? Was he open enough emotionally, worthy? Could he be trusted to never let them down, like his parents had let Chloe and himself down? He hoped so but hope wasn't good enough. In his heart he knew that 'not sure' was unacceptable.

But still he couldn't stop because she pulled his hand back when he tried to leave, answered when he kissed her mouth with a molten response that undid his intentions, pressed herself against him until his need for her outstripped his brain's refusal.

But this couldn't happen while he wasn't committed. He owed Lucy that.

So, after a timeless journey of sensation, intoxicating kisses and the tender wonder of this woman's beautiful body, Nick drew back. Shuddered the demons back into their boxes and stilled his hand.

Lucy sensed the change. In some pathetic part of her a tiny molecule was glad that one of them had stopped because this had no future and she would hate Nick to regret it.

It was fortunate indeed that Nick had more control than she did.

But, then, he didn't love her.

He probably cared for her and was happy to be there when she was having one of her many crises, but for now he soothed her disappointed murmurings with, 'It's okay. We'll talk in the morning. Sleep and I'll hold you.'

And she felt like weeping as he gently rolled her onto her side until they were spooned together, slid his arm beneath her pillow and then cradled her breast in one hand and her belly in the other. And she sighed away the longing, acknowledged in some recess of her brain this was how it would always have ended, and that when she woke tomorrow this book would close.

For ever. Because she couldn't open herself to this kind of pain again.

Lucy closed her staring eyes with the unpalatable insight that Nick was being kind and unintentionally she'd asked too much of him.

It took Nick hours to go to sleep. Apart from his screaming frustration as he held her gorgeous body against him, it was the generous innocence of her response that tore at him. The innocence testified to her pre-pregnancy inexperience and how low he'd been to even consider making love to this woman without a full commitment.

She was so different from the other women he'd been with. He hadn't understood, hadn't learnt what Lucy's kind of giving was about, so maybe he could cut himself some slack that he hadn't recognised what he was doing until almost too late.

But it had opened a deep well of wonder, and also great guilt.

He needed to rethink this whole Lucy world. Because that's what she was. A world. An amazing, generous, loving world that he wasn't sure he was ready for. Or deserved. He fell asleep wishing to hell he did.

When Nick finally fell asleep it was so deep he

didn't feel Lucy rise before the sun. Or hear the blinds being drawn across to darken the room from the pre-dawn light before she slipped away. Or the rustle as she dressed herself in the lounge room with the new clothes she'd picked up yesterday. Or the sound of his front door closing as she carried everything she'd brought with her back to her own house.

Lucy knew she needed to go. Preferably before Nick woke up because, unless she wanted to be the Nikolai Kefes groupie of the year, she had to get out.

She wasn't sure if this was a final stab at the inde-pendence she needed to survive or the ultimate in self-protection. All she knew was that her babies deserved more respect and she needed more self-respect than the morning after an almost-affair from a man who had only ever been kind to her.

And most terrifying of all, she needed to go before Nick trapped himself into something she refused to see him regret.

Even before Nick woke up his hand searched for the warmth of Lucy. His eyes opened but the dent in the pil-low beside his head only made him feel sad. He strained to hear the sound of movement in his flat but all he could hear was the relentless ocean, washing in and washing out across a deserted beach, and in his heart he knew she was gone.

He couldn't believe how empty, and deserted, his own life seemed, so different from yesterday when he'd bounded out of bed to make her a surprise breakfast. Today—it was just him. Like old times.

Times before Lucy. He couldn't believe how much he missed her.

Nick rolled out of bed, walked to the blinds and pulled them back. He wished he could share the sunrise with Lucy because she'd have enthused over it. He wished he could have seen her bathed by the golden light.

An ominous prickle under his skin asked the question. What if she never came back? If he never woke to Lucy beside him, ever?

He searched for a note but didn't find one. He resisted the urge to phone her. Had to give her space she'd silently asked for by leaving and take on board that it was time to sort out his own issues before he saw her again.

Tomorrow morning. At work. He could wait till then.

CHAPTER ELEVEN

LUCY TRIED SO hard not to think about Nick. About leaving his bed in the early hours like a thief.

But he was the thief. He'd stolen her heart and nobody was going to get it back for her so she needed to grow another one. And that wasn't going to happen unless she stayed away from Dr Kefes.

But it was so hard to pretend she didn't miss him. When she swept the path, she thought of Nick, and got hotter than she should. When she picked a frond out of the pool her stomach dropped as she thought of Nick. Opening her refrigerator even the water bottles reminded her of Nick.

But the worst, when she lay on her bed, she missed his warmth. His strength. His caring.

Could even hear him telling her to stay, the day he'd run all those errands for her, when she'd been scared she'd lose her babies. But she had to be strong.

For both of them. For all of them.

On Friday morning, Flora introduced Lucy to Dr Donaldson on his first day back at GCCH. He was a tall, smiling, stick figure of a man with very kind eyes, so it seemed strange, when Nick had endorsed the man to her, that Flora obviously wasn't comfortable with him.

Lucy's first antenatal visit with the new doctor was that afternoon after work. It had been arranged by Nick on Wednesday, with strict instructions not to miss it, and while she'd been steamrollered into changing doctors, it seemed now it was all for the best.

The shift was busy, but thankfully Flora was still allocating her non-Kefes patients. Lucy saw Nick twice in the distance, but ducked into a room each time before he saw her, and once she turned round when he'd started to walk towards her.

All painful, heart-wrenching choices she had to make, and at times she wasn't so sure she was doing the right thing. She had to face him some time but she was feeling too fragile yet.

Flora seemed preoccupied, and Lucy, hunting for distraction from thoughts of Nick, tried vainly for an opportunity to broach the subject of why she didn't like Dr Donaldson. If she wasn't having Nick, she wanted someone good.

Finally, at the end of the day as both were about to leave, Lucy caught up with the senior midwife. 'As far as Dr Donaldson is concerned, do you think he's a good obstetrician?'

'Of course.' Flora seemed a bit short, and Lucy still didn't feel any better.

I'm not reassured, Lucy thought, and tried again. 'Would you recommend anyone else?'

Flora stopped walking and sighed. She met Lucy's worried eyes with a strange expression on her face. 'David Donaldson is an excellent obstetrician. Very experienced with twin pregnancies and has a stellar reputation. You could do no better.'

Well, that was glowing, it just hadn't been said in an enthusiastic voice. But at least Flora wouldn't say something that wasn't true. And there was no doubt Flora would prefer it if Lucy dropped the subject.

So, reluctantly, she did. 'Thank you.'

Fifteen minutes later she was shown into the good doctor's new rooms and Lucy suspected that behind the twinkling grey eyes lay a very astute mind because he glossed over the point that Nick had handed her on for personal reasons and concentrated on her pregnancy.

After taking her blood pressure and weight, he helped her climb up onto the examination couch to feel her tummy. It just wasn't the same as doing this with Nick but she needed to stop thinking about that.

Dr Donaldson palpated the babies, and he must have been a little firmer with his hands than Nick because once or twice Lucy winced with discomfort.

He lifted his hands. 'Sorry. So you're twenty-four weeks, the babies are growing well, one is head first and the other breech today.'

She nodded. Wished she could tell Nick that one was breech at the moment.

The kind doctor smiled. 'You know they can swap and change for a few weeks yet?'

After he'd found and listened to their two different heartbeats he wiped off the gel and palpated one more time on the lower part of her abdomen.

Lucy winced again and he nodded to himself. 'I thought that was uncomfortable?'

She nodded and he quizzed her on her general condition. 'So you're well. No discomfort you didn't expect, babies moving as usual. Anything worrying you?'

Did he mean apart from tearing herself away from the man she wanted to spend the rest of her life with? She'd barely thought about her body—too obsessed with pining for Nick. 'Just a few aches and pains. But probably ligament discomfort or a mobile elbow.'

Dr Donaldson was more interested than she was. 'Show me where.'

Lucy pointed to the right side of her abdomen, the spot that he'd touched, and he nodded, and gently palpated the area again.

Lucy winced and his eyebrows drew together. 'Haven't had any temperatures? Sweats? Nausea?'

Well, actually… Hot and feeling sick? Lucy nodded reluctantly. 'Yes. I might have.'

He smiled kindly and helped her sit up. 'One or all three?'

To be honest? 'All three?'

He helped her down from the couch and directed her back to the chair beside his desk.

But she'd just thought the day was warmer than expected, the babies were growing and making themselves known, and the stress of moving back into her house, away from Nick, was making her feel a little rotten.

He sat back behind his desk and typed on the computer. 'I'd like you to go down to Pathology and have another blood test.'

Not again. But she wasn't having any unusual tightening of her belly. 'I've already been treated for a kidney infection.'

He smiled. 'I think it's more likely you have a grumbling appendicitis. Fairly unusual in pregnancy and quite complicated with twins on board, but we'll keep an eye on you.'

Lucy felt her mind go blank. Appendicitis? Where was Nick at this moment? What would he say about this? So it wasn't a baby elbow or knee. And it was still a bit achy from where he'd palpated. She couldn't afford a grumbling appendix. 'What happens if it gets worse?'

He smiled kindly. 'You have an appendectomy.'

Good grief. Why did this have to happen today? When she was being strong about not calling Nick? 'I didn't think I could have a general anaesthetic. What about the babies?'

Let alone the six weeks off work with no sick pay. And she wouldn't even have Nick to bring her healthy yoghurt and sympathise.

'Yes is the short answer. If necessary, your babies would be anesthetised as well, because the drugs do cross the placenta.'

Too scary to even think about.

'The babies would wake up when it wore off.'

This was a nightmare. And a hundred times worse because she couldn't share it with the one person she wanted to.

She needed him. But she couldn't have him. 'Don't tell Dr Kefes.' The words were wrenched out of her and were the direct opposite of what she really wanted. More than anything she wanted Nick with her. More than anything she knew she couldn't. This was the start of it. She had to push him out of her life.

This was her surviving the next crisis without Nick.

She'd already had two disasters he'd had to manage and she needed to sort this herself. The problem was, all she felt like doing was bursting into tears.

'You remind me of someone I used to know.' Dr Donaldson gave her a quizzical look. 'Determined to be independent. But I won't mention it if you wish. And your symptoms might go away. We can hope.'

He gave her his card and wrote his mobile phone number on the back of it. 'So take it gently. Phone me if there is a problem or the pain becomes severe. You must do that.'

She nodded, took the card and put it in her purse.

He opened his door for her and before she walked through he said gently, 'And don't forget to have that blood test done today.'

She stopped. Looked at him. He smiled blandly. Surely Nick hadn't told him she'd done that last time? She narrowed her eyes at him. She'd bet Nick had mentioned it. 'Thank you, Doctor.'

Nick found himself wondering how Lucy had gone with Dr Donaldson.

He'd woken so many times on Thursday night, wondering how she'd gone back to her house after the break-in. How she'd gone after leaving his bed. Was she thanking him for not seducing her or hating him? The jury was still out how he felt about that himself.

His eyes strayed to the clock again. She'd be in there now. He knew he'd miss Lucy but he hadn't realised how much he would miss his frequent interaction with Lucy's babies when he handed her on. And this was only the first visit. It was worrying how invested he'd become in her babies' well-being.

He'd been subtly trying to catch their mother's eye all day, without drawing the attention of the whole hospital, watching for developments, but it had been frustratingly difficult to even get close to speaking with Lucy.

He hated the distance he could feel between them and that was despite the fact he was ten rooms away. In the end he'd asked Flora how she'd gone at home, an innocent question, and had been told she was fine.

He'd have it out with her on Sunday, when they had breakfast, if she was still going to come with him. He didn't like to think how much he had riding on the assumption she would.

On Saturday morning Lucy felt well enough to work the early shift, despite the fact she'd been miserable all night, missing Nick, because the discomfort in her side remained constant but was no worse.

After work Flora was coming around late afternoon with some baby clothes and that was something she could look forward to. She needed more distraction like this if she was going to stay sane.

Baby clothes. She hadn't had a chance to do anything yet but her friends with their twins had promised to bring a load of things around next weekend. Lucy decided to ask Flora to come when they did and they could all have an afternoon together.

More distractions and moments to look forward to. Funny how her friends were all older now.

Her midwifery training friends were all far flung and busy partying. Finding herself pregnant on her first shift had made her less outgoing with her mind more on survival than on forming friendships.

Except with Nick. Always her thoughts came back to Nick.

He'd taken her under his wing from the first day. But you couldn't be a pseudo sister when you fancied the big brother so she was doing the right thing to get out of that situation as soon as possible. Before he did.

Everything else was fine. Truly.

She wouldn't be as lonely when she'd had the babies, went to play groups and met other mums. But for the moment it was brutally lonely and not just because she missed Nick. Mostly that, but not only that. She just needed to keep reminding herself.

By the time she finished work at three she didn't feel quite so well.

At four o'clock, when Flora arrived with her freshly baked scones, Lucy was feeling pretty darned miserable.

Flora took one look at her and made her sit down. 'What's happening here?'

Lucy felt like crying. Or being sick. Or both. 'Dr Donaldson thinks I might have a grumbling appendix.'

Flora felt her forehead. 'Hot! It looks to be more than grumbling. You need to go to Emergency, my girl.'

'Dr Donaldson gave me a number to ring him on if I got worse.' Lucy pointed to her handbag on the table. She didn't have the energy to get up and get it herself.

Flora picked up the handbag and brought it over. She dug out Lucy's purse and gave it to her. 'And you haven't?'

Another urge to weep. 'I didn't like to bother him on a Saturday.'

Flora patted Lucy's shoulder and stood up. 'I'll pack you an overnight bag. What about Dr Kefes? Nikolai? Have you told him you're unwell?'

Lucy felt so miserable. And hearing Flora say it only made it worse. 'I'm trying not to lean on Nick. He's treating me like his little sister. It's not fair on him and I have to learn to stand on my own feet...' She put her face in her hands and squeezed her eyes to hold back the tears. She was pathetic.

'Hmph,' Flora said as she stood up. 'I don't think it's a sister he wants.' Flora spoke more to herself than to Lucy as she bustled around. 'And you are a very capable young woman so stop beating yourself up. Shall I ring him?'

Nick would take control again. And she'd throw herself on his chest. She knew she would. She needed to learn to rely on herself. 'No. Don't bother him.'

Flora sighed as she busily rummaged through Lucy's drawers. She held up a soft nightgown. 'This one okay? These underclothes?'

Lucy sniffed and had to smile. 'Nobody has ever packed a bag for me before.'

Flora glanced at her. 'Maybe it's time you let them.'

'Let you?' Lucy would have liked to laugh but she didn't have one in her. 'Could I stop you?'

'I doubt it.' Flora came back to Lucy and leant down, all elbows and awkwardness, and hugged her. 'Stop worrying about putting other people out. They wouldn't help if they didn't want to. Now, do you have a small bathroom bag?'

The pain was getting worse. 'No. I've never needed one. But my toothbrush is there.'

'Never mind. I'll put it in a plastic bag and bring you one later.' She stopped for a moment and sighed again. 'Give me David's card and I'll ring him.'

It all happened very fast after that.

Flora drove her to the hospital, a scary trip in Flora's big off-road vehicle, and with Flora's attitude that everyone needed to get out of her way because she had a medical crisis.

Lucy wanted Nick. Needed Nick to hold her hand. Say her babies would be fine after the anaesthetic. But it was too late now.

The emergency staff knew she was coming, Dr Donaldson was waiting, and before she knew it she was repeating her name to the gowned theatre nurse as she was being wheeled into the operating theatre.

When she came round, it felt like she'd been stabbed.

Der, she had been, she thought groggily, and then she remembered her babies.

Her hand slid gingerly across her belly for reassurance and there they were. Probably asleep, like she wanted to be, and she glanced at the empty chair beside the bed and tried not to cry before she drifted off again.

Flora had arranged for Lucy to be cared for in the maternity section, and that meant she knew the people who cared for her. Except Nick didn't come.

In her groggy haze they all seemed genuinely concerned for her and maybe she wasn't quite as friendless as she'd assumed. Even Cass apologised for not knowing about the break-in, and her less-than-flattering comments that had caused the gossip storm.

Lucy brushed it away. She really didn't care any more but Cass apologised again when she brought Lucy jelly for breakfast before she went off. Lucy just wanted Nick but she knew she couldn't have him.

Down the road from the hospital Nick had gone round to Lucy's at eight o'clock as arranged for Sunday breakfast, but the gate had been locked and when he'd used the intercom she hadn't answered.

Late Saturday afternoon, when he'd got home from a function he'd promised Chloe he'd go to, he'd tried to confirm their date for today and just hear her say she was settled. But that hadn't happened.

He hadn't rung later, even though he'd wanted to, in case she was sleeping. He knew she was due to work yesterday to make up for the Thursday, that would be Thursday when she'd left his bed, but he pushed that thought away.

And he'd rung this morning but there had been no

answer and now she wasn't answering the intercom. He didn't like that one bit.

He'd told himself she was probably doing something industrious around the mansion but this time when he phoned and it again went through to the message bank his skin crawled at the thought of Lucy unconscious or, worse, attacked by criminals in her own home.

Why on earth had he agreed she should come back here when he knew it wasn't safe? Three nights she'd been here alone.

Nick strode the long way round and peered over the rear beach fence but again he couldn't see any movement. He called out but there was still no answer and now he was seriously concerned.

It wasn't easy but he managed to scale the gate without impaling himself on the protective spikes. He could just imagine the headlines in the Gold Coast newspaper if he did. *Well-known obstetrician impaled during break-in.* Lovely.

No doubt Lucy would have a giggle about that one. After he'd strangled her for scaring him.

And no doubt the security firm would be haring to the rescue by the time he got to Lucy's cabana. They'd better be, he thought grimly, or heads would roll.

When he reached Lucy's flat it was locked up. It seemed she wasn't lying on the floor unconscious from what he could see through the white curtains and the place didn't look as if it had been rifled.

He heard a car screech to a halt outside and the sound of the gate. At least that was slightly satisfying.

Maybe she'd just forgotten their meeting. Not good for his ego or his heart, but better than the alternative.

'Stop right there.' The burly security guard stood with his feet planted as soon as he got inside the gate.

Nick decided that attack was the best form of defence. 'Do you know where Miss Palmer is?'

Belligerent eyebrows shot up. 'And who might you be to her?'

Good question. What was he? He wasn't her doctor. He wasn't the father of her children. He certainly wasn't her brother or her father. 'I'm a concerned friend.' Certainly not her boyfriend—why was that? Because he didn't know his own mind!

It was becoming clearer by the second.

'Prove it.' The man's tone suggested he'd been lied to by experts in the past.

Nick didn't have time for this. He needed to find Lucy. 'I'm Dr Nikolai Kefes. I work at Gold Coast City Hospital.' He pulled his business card from his wallet. 'I want to know she's all right. I was here the other night when her house was broken into and she's supposed to meet me for breakfast today.'

The security guard took his card. Nodded. 'I can understand that, sir. But you will have to leave unless I get Miss Palmer's permission for you to stay.'

'As it seems neither of us knows the answer to her whereabouts I'll be leaving anyway.'

The man nodded. He stepped aside so that Nick had to leave first. At least the security seemed to be working, he thought.

The only other person who might know anything was Flora May. He'd try her first and then the police.

Flora answered on the first ring.

'Lucy is in hospital.'

Nick couldn't believe what he was hearing. 'She's where?'

'In Maternity, post-appendectomy.'

A sudden surge of anger took Nick by surprise and

he forced himself to hold back the explosion he would love to have unleashed. It wasn't Flora's fault. Or only a small part of it. She could have rung him. Finally he managed, 'The babies?'

'Seem fine. No sign of prem labour. Lucy is still very sore and a bit dopey from the pain relief but she's fine, too.'

He was still having problems comprehending that he'd been excluded. 'Why didn't someone phone me? Why didn't you? Or David? I can't believe this.' After all he'd done. All the other crises he'd helped with.

There was a pause. 'She asked us not to.'

Nick couldn't believe that Lucy had deliberately excluded him. Had his friendship to her not meant anything? 'She what?'

Flora paused again. Reluctant. 'I'm sorry, Nick. She said she didn't want to bother you.'

The words chilled him. Iced his veins in a way he hadn't expected. 'Bother me?' Her precious independence. It hurt so much that he wanted to smash something. He thought of the state-of-the-art twin stroller he'd been looking at. All the times he'd been there for her. God, he was such a fool.

'Fine. Thank you.'

'Nick.' Flora at her most urgent. 'Listen. She's young, doesn't want to lose her independence, is used to looking after herself. She's not good at taking.'

This was about that all right. 'I know all about her independence, Flora. She can have it.' He would have been there for her. All she'd had to do was ask. Or include him when she told the rest of the world.

'Nick?'

'Gotta go. See you Monday.' Not that he was looking

forward to that. Lucy would still be in hospital and he was hurting so much he didn't think he could talk to her.

Lucy didn't know what was wrong with her. Post-operative blues perhaps. She'd slept all night and through Sunday morning, her tummy was okay, the babies were waking up, and she had a beautiful vase of spring flowers from the staff. But she missed Nick.

She'd sort of thought he would have found out and visited by now. Maybe she should have asked Flora to ring him but it all seemed a bit needy now that everything was over.

Flora bustled in, on her day off, and brought a bottle of apple juice and a pretty glass instead of the usual foam cups to drink out of. 'My. Don't you look miserable.'

'Well, thanks for that.' Lucy stifled a weak laugh because even that hurt, and Flora looked contrite. 'No. You're right.' She guessed Flora knew that she and Nick were more than friends but less than anything else. You never knew what crossed the line with Flora.

'Um. Has anyone mentioned to Nick that I'm here?'

'He rang me this morning.'

Lucy had the feeling Flora was choosing her words carefully and her stomach sank. 'It would be fair to say he's upset we didn't inform him earlier.'

'Oh.'

Flora sat down and pulled her chair closer to the bed. 'I think you hurt him, Lucy. He was very—I was going to say upset, but I think angry and confused might be better words. And it's not something I've noticed before with our Dr Kefes.'

Lucy said, 'Oh,' again, in an even smaller voice, and wanted to hide under the pillow. 'I just didn't want to bother him.'

Flora sighed. 'So I told him. I think that upset him more.'

She pleaded with Flora but inside she knew really she was pleading to Nick. 'I don't want to be a nuisance. He's been so good to me. And I can't expect him to look after me.'

'Oh, don't I know that feeling,' Flora said softly, then she pointed her finger at Lucy. 'And why not? I got the impression he enjoyed looking after you.'

Lucy looked anywhere but at Flora. 'Because he has his own life. He won't want to be saddled with a silly young midwife who got herself pregnant with twins by another man.'

Flora snorted. She did it every well. 'You underestimate your attraction. Women do that. Why do you think he helped you? Allowed you to stay at his flat? Went to the trouble to hand you over as his patient?'

Lucy looked at Flora but maybe she had misread Nick's interest. 'Because he's kind? And I needed help?'

Flora shook her head. 'You have an inferiority complex. Not his problem if he didn't care. But he made it so.' She patted her hand. 'Do you remember me saying people wouldn't help if they didn't want to?'

Lucy nodded. Maybe she had been too prickly. Too determined she wouldn't be needy. Had too jealously guarded her independence and her ability to be hurt again by someone she loved.

'From what you told me, you did a lot for yourself growing up. I understand that. I'm not saying you should use people but you aren't very good at taking help from others. You might want to cultivate that skill.' She laughed. 'Especially with twins coming.'

Then Flora said something startling. 'Did I tell you I was an orphan?'

Lucy shook her head. Looked at this strong, powerful woman and tried to imagine her lost in a dormitory with motherless children. It was a heart-rending picture.

'Had to look after myself in the orphanage. I was the same as you. So when I grew up I found it very difficult to allow others to try to shoulder some responsibility for me. To the extent that eventually nobody tried any more.'

Flora chewed her lip. 'I lost a good man because I wouldn't let him in. He married someone else and I joined the army. Don't make the same mistakes I did.'

She squeezed Lucy's hand. 'Now I'll leave you to rest.'

Suddenly Lucy wondered, and maybe it was the loose-tongued side-effect of the pain relief or maybe her own emotional state but she blurted out the question before she put thought into it. 'Was it Dr Donaldson?'

Flora pursed her lips and didn't say anything for a moment. Then her eyes twinkled. 'Could have been. And I have learnt my lesson.'

She narrowed her eyes at Lucy. 'So you need to learn yours.' Then she stood up. 'Now, let's get you tidy and I'll fix your hair.'

When his sister knocked on his door after work on Sunday and Nick answered it, he saw her eyes widen at the sweat that poured off him, and he couldn't have cared less.

'I'm about to have a shower.'

'Good.'

Nick didn't need this. He'd run about twenty kilometres and he needed to sit down. 'Not in the mood, Chloe.

'So I see.' Chloe pushed a curl behind her ear. 'Just

thought you might want to know that your little friend had an emergency appendectomy last night.'

He grunted. 'I know.'

'Okay.' Chloe paused but Nick didn't offer anything else. She shrugged. 'Thought you might. Just checking.'

Nick wanted to shut the door but maybe he had been neglecting his sister lately for a certain someone who didn't want his attention. 'You okay?'

'Better than you, I think. Let me know if you want to talk, Nicky. It would be nice to be the one leant on for a change, instead of me relying on you.'

After his shower he felt better. And after fluids and food he felt almost normal. Much better for him than the bacon and eggs he would have had this morning. Which brought him back to this morning.

He'd really lost it when he'd realised he'd been excluded from Lucy's emergency.

He wanted to see Lucy. See for himself that she was okay. That her babies were okay. But now he didn't know if he could open himself up to offering her more support if she was going to turn him down.

He needed to re-evaluate his priorities. See his way to the woman he was beginning to think he needed more than he needed anything else in his life.

Should he talk to Chloe before he talked to Lucy? Because this was way outside his experience.

He didn't even know if he could do that. Be the one who needed help instead of the other way around.

Chloe opened her door and she shook her head. 'I don't believe it.'

'You said to come.' But now he wanted to leave. She

must have known because she put out her hand and took his wrist. Pulled it.

'Sorry. You took me by surprise. Come in.' And she drew him into her flat and sat him down.

Nick wondered what on earth he was doing here. His sister was looking at him like he had something terminal and he wasn't used to being on this side of the fence—not being the one who sorted out the chaos.

'Nicky, you're a mess.' She shook her head. 'It's about Lucy. Isn't it?'

He looked across the room at the sea outside the windows. 'I lost it this morning.'

'You never lose it.' He could hear the surprise in his sister's voice and there was a certain irony in that. There'd been times when he'd been close to losing it while he'd been trying to make ends meet as he'd waited for Chloe to grow up.

He shrugged. 'She told them not to ring me when she was sick. I would have been there for her. Why would she do that?'

He could read her sympathy. He didn't want pity. He wanted answers.

'I don't know.'

He knew it. Chloe had no more idea than he did.

When she said, 'Why do *you* think she did that?' he knew it was no good. He wasn't any good at asking for help.

He stood up and Chloe shook her head. 'I've never seen you like this, Nikolai.'

He hesitated and finally sat down again. Ran his hands through his hair. 'I've never felt like this before.'

'Lucky you,' his sister said dryly. 'And poor you.' Chloe chewed her lip. 'So you've slept with her.'

Nearly. 'I didn't sleep with her.' Well, he had but that was all. He didn't get the response he expected.

Chloe looked at him like she didn't know who he was. 'Why on earth not? I thought you fancied her. And I'm pretty sure she's in love with you.'

'Of course I fancy her but she's having twins, for goodness' sake. And I needed to get my head around where we were going.'

'You're allowed to have sex when you're pregnant, Nicky.' Chloe shook her head. 'You knocked her back and she left.' Chloe looked out the window herself and thought about it. 'I'd have slipped away while you were asleep.'

He blinked. 'She did.'

'After a knock back like that I wouldn't talk to you again.'

How did she know this stuff? 'She hasn't. She's moved back home. Avoided me.'

'She's decided to go noble.' She looked at him. 'Your Lucy is a good woman, Nicky. But I'm not surprised she told them not to ring you now she knows you don't love her. She doesn't want to trap you into something you don't want.'

What was Chloe talking about? 'But I do.'

'Do what? Give me specifics!' Chloe wasn't letting him off without him saying it.

'Love her. Want her.' He thought about that. Repeated the words in his mind. Of course he knew that. What the hell was wrong with him? 'But she's so darned independent.'

Chloe laughed. 'But isn't that what draws you to her? You can't control her. Isn't that one of the things you secretly love about her? Why she's worth fighting for?'

He stood up. Hell. Of course it was. And of course

he'd never said he loved her. He needed to do that. 'Wish me luck.'

Chloe hugged him. 'Of course I do.'

CHAPTER TWELVE

When Nikolai arrived at the hospital he didn't go straight to see Lucy. Running on instinct, he saw Flora May leave Lucy's room and followed her back to the lifts.

Flora turned when she heard him behind her. She smiled. 'So you came anyway.'

Nick shrugged and smiled ruefully. 'Wasn't going to.'

Flora sighed. 'It can be an awkward and difficult game.'

Nick knew what she was talking about. He wondered how long she'd known he was smitten. 'What game would that be?'

'Don't play with me, Nikolai. She's miserable. She's in love with you. Has no idea you're thinking long term.' She tilted her angular face at him and pinned him with a direct look.

'That is what you're thinking, isn't it?' Flora huffed. 'Because if you're not…'

Nick grinned. He liked this woman more and more, and Lucy could do worse when she looked for champions.

'Yes.' He held up his hands in smiling defence. 'I want to be there for Lucy. And for her babies. For ever.' He shrugged and the liberation of just saying that out loud, hearing those words leave his mouth, filled him with a feeling of marvellous resolution. This truly was where he was meant to be.

'She makes me smile just watching her. I love everything about her, maybe even her independent streak, which, I guess, I'll just have to get used to it.'

Flora laughed. 'Afraid so.'

'I love her you know.' He shook his head. 'Besotted and I didn't realise it.'

Flora said again, 'It's not always a smooth journey.'

Nick straightened. 'Now all I need is someone to ask for her hand.'

Flora's face softened and she patted his shoulder. 'Have my blessing. You're a good man. And a lucky man. And Lucy is the one you need to ask. I just don't know if our Lucy has even allowed herself to dream there could be a happily ever after.'

She stepped back and pushed the lift button. 'She's just had more pain relief. You should go and fix that misconception before she falls asleep.'

When Nick entered Lucy's room she had her eyes closed and her red hair was plaited neatly at the side of her face. He remembered Lucy saying she couldn't do a good plait, had never been taught, and he bet Flora May had done that before she'd left.

He put the single red rose down beside her bed on the chest of drawers and sat down. He'd watched her sleeping before.

She was frowning in her sleep and he worried, with a pang, if she had pain. He hadn't been here and she must have been scared when they'd told her she needed to have the operation.

'I should have called you,' she whispered, and he saw that she was awake.

He leant over and kissed her forehead. 'Yes. You should have.'

'I missed you. I'm sorry I didn't call you.' Her eyes glittered with unshed tears and his heart squeezed because she was upset.

'I'll let you off with it this time but don't do it again.'

She smiled sleepily. 'I only have one appendix.'

He smiled. She was so cute. 'I'm sure you'll find a new ailment some time in the next four months. And if you don't, there's always labour.'

Her eyes clouded. 'But you're not my doctor. You won't be there with me in labour now.'

He took her hand and held it between his. 'I'd very much like to be there with you if you'll have me. And I was thinking of a more legally binding arrangement than being your obstetrician.'

She frowned and he could see the drug was starting to work well.

'I'd like to be with you whenever I can.' He leant over and kissed her on the lips this time. Very gently. 'Go to sleep. I'll sit here and we'll talk about that when you wake up.'

When Lucy woke up Nikolai was still there. It hadn't been a dream. And as for the things he'd said before she'd gone to sleep, she hoped she hadn't dreamed that. He was playing with a single red rose, spinning it in his hand, and she drank in the sight of him until he noticed she'd woken up.

He smiled and the whole room brightened. She loved his smile. 'Hello, sleepyhead.'

Suddenly she felt very shy. Surely this tall and gor-

geous man hadn't said what she'd thought he'd said.
'Hello, there.'

He was still smiling. 'How are you feeling?'

Nervous. 'Better.'

'Good.' He nodded and there was that little catch
of accent she almost missed now because she was so
used to him. Maybe he was nervous, too. The thought
brought a little calmness.

He went on. 'And you are properly awake?'

She nodded and moistened her dry lips with her
tongue. Nick's eyes darkened and he leaned backwards
and picked up her glass of water and a straw from the
pile Flora had brought. 'Would you like a sip of water?'

Well, she would, but the suspense was killing her.
'Only if you're quick.'

He passed the water and she took a fast sip before
he put it back. He frowned over her words and then got
it. Laughed out loud. 'Am I being too slow for you?'

'Maybe a little.'

'Lucy Palmer, I should have told you earlier.'

'Yes.' Lucy wanted to cross her fingers he wasn't
going to ask her to be his patient again.

'I love you. With all my heart.' Words she'd never
hoped to hear.

Her mouth refused to work. How did you answer
that?

His brow creased. 'Is that okay with you?'

More than okay, but she still couldn't speak, so she
nodded. 'I love you,' he said again, and she blew him
a kiss.

Nick must have seen that as a positive sign because
he took her hand and went down on one knee beside
her bed. Stared into her eyes with an expression she'd

thought she'd never see on his face. 'Lucy Palmer, will you marry me?'

Lucy felt the tears sting her eyes at her gorgeous man, down on one knee, looking into her eyes with the promise of loving her like she'd never been loved before. Fulfilling dreams she'd only dared to dream as she fell asleep in her lonely bed, and here he was, offering her the world. His world.

Waking up with Nick every morning. Sleeping in his arms every night. Her babies would be their babies and if they were blessed they would make more. A family with Nick. How had this happened to her?

Then she said something dumb. 'Are you sure?'

He shook his head. Pretended to frown at her. 'Flora May said you wouldn't believe me. You're supposed to say yes!'

Lucy blinked. 'You've already told Flora?'

'I had to ask someone for your hand.'

She smiled. Loved the idea of Nick asking Flora. Someone else who had really been there for her. Joy bubbled up with the sudden belief that this just might be true. Nick loved her. She loved him so much. Had loved him from the day he'd taken her to breakfast.

'Um, can you ask me, again? Please?'

Nick nodded, suddenly serious, and she loved that, too. Nick serious was Nick seriously sexy.

'Lucy Palmer, I love you. With all my heart. Will you marry me?'

This time she had the right answer. 'Yes. Yes, please.'

He leaned forward and helped her sit up. Then his arms were around her and she felt as if she'd finally come home. Nick's chin on her hair. His arms around her. Home.

She was home with Nick. She'd found her man,

who understood her, loved her and would be her family for ever.

And she would be the home he'd lost at too young an age, the love he could always be sure of. The life he could trust his heart to. She would always be there.

CHAPTER THIRTEEN

LUCY AND NIKOLAI's wedding took place at sunrise on the beach at Coolongatta an hour south of the Gold Coast, two months after Lucy and Nikolai's twins were born.

As the sun peaked over the ocean horizon the bride walked slowly down the long silver carpet to the edge of the sea where her groom waited with love in his eyes and a swelling so great in his heart he could barely breathe.

Gold and red lights shimmered through her hair as she was blessed by the first rays of the sun, just like their marriage would be, and the trailing wildflowers of her bouquet danced and swayed in her shaking fingers as she closed the gap between them.

He glanced at the assembled guests, seated on white chairs in the sand, more wildflowers edging the silver ribbon that led her to him. To his baby daughters, Phoebe and Rose, being nursed at the moment by Callie Richards for the service.

To the attendants: his best man, David Donaldson, Flora May's new husband; his bridesmaid sister, Chloe, smiling beside Flora May, the Matron of Honour looking tall and gangly with joyful affection in her eyes when she, too, looked back at his bride.

Then his eyes were drawn irresistibly to his beautiful Lucy—the woman who had resurrected his belief in family, given him such joy—and healed his heart. His bride.

Lucy wore a ring of flowers in her hair and her neck rose from the circular neckline of her dress like a swan, and at the hem, her coral-tipped toes peeked out as she walked towards him. He'd always loved her bare toes.

When she put her slender fingers into his he linked her to him and finally believed this dream was real. He'd found the woman he wanted to spend the rest of his life with and he could barely wait to pledge his love, for ever.

* * * * *